HEART OF SHADOWS

LISA EDMONDS

CITY OWL
PRESS

HEART OF SHADOWS
Alice Worth, Book 5

CITY OWL PRESS
www.cityowlpress.com

Cover Design by Mibl Art and Tina Moss. All stock photos licensed appropriately.

Edited by Heather McCorkle.

For information on subsidiary rights, please contact the publisher at info@cityowlpress.com.

Print Edition ISBN: 978-1-949090-77-2

Digital Edition ISBN: 978-1-949090-76-5

Printed in the United States of America

To Alexandria and Madden –
May all your wildest dreams come true.

THE ALICE WORTH SERIES

BY LISA EDMONDS

PROLOGUE

ALICE

PRESENT DAY

KEEP WALKING.

The highway stretched out in front of me in a seemingly endless track of asphalt lined with fence and trees. In the distance, the tall, dark shadows of mountains loomed on the horizon. The sun blazed overhead in a cloudless sky and the road shimmered in the heat.

My chest felt hollow, as if something had been ripped out by the roots, leaving an aching emptiness. My heartbeat echoed inside my ribcage like reverberations in a deep, dry well. I was incomplete, fractured, broken. I didn't know how I'd come to be this way or what was missing—only that I'd once been whole but now was not.

A handful of cars and trucks had passed me in the last hour or so. Other than those few signs of life, I might have been the only person in ten square miles. I hadn't seen any houses, gas stations, or other buildings since I started walking. The only sounds were wind in the grass, the far-off lowing of cattle, and my boots on the pavement.

My legs grew tired and my feet hurt with every step. I wiped my forehead with the back of my hand. My pace slowed.

Keep walking and don't look back.

The command drifted through my head. The voice was familiar, though I couldn't attach a face or a name to it.

I realized I was walking quickly again. My feet hurt as if my boots were full of razors. My socks squished wetly with every step. I wasn't sure why, since I hadn't walked through any high water...at least, not that I could remember. The fact I was completely dry otherwise supported that assumption, so my wet socks were a mystery.

As was the small object clutched in my left hand. I vaguely recalled grabbing it and hiding it from someone, but I wasn't sure when or why. Still, I couldn't bring myself to drop it beside the road. My hand wouldn't open and let it go. My fingers cramped from holding it so tightly.

I walked on.

Hours passed. The sun crossed overhead and descended, slipping behind the horizon to my left and plunging the distant mountain peaks in front of me into darkness. The moon was bright enough in the clear sky for me to easily see the road. The pain in my feet was white-hot now, but I couldn't stop. I dragged myself on, putting one foot in front of the other, with that strange voice replaying endlessly in my ears.

Keep walking and don't look back.

Behind me, a truck engine rumbled. The sound grew quickly, as if the vehicle was moving very fast. I quickened my pace.

Bright headlights illuminated the highway in front of me as the truck crested the hill I'd just walked over. Tires skidded and brakes screeched as the truck pulled to the side of the road behind me. I kept walking.

The truck's doors opened and someone shouted, "Alice!" The male voice was a strange combination of relief, fury, and worry.

Footsteps pounded on the asphalt behind me. Suddenly, two dark-haired, muscular men with glowing golden eyes appeared in front of me. They wore jeans, long-sleeved shirts, and hiking boots.

The larger of the two grabbed me. "Alice," he said again, his voice growly.

I stabbed him.

—Or at least I tried to. My fingertips rammed into his hard stomach and I felt a sharp pain.

I looked at my fingers in confusion. For some reason, I thought I should have been able to gut him that way, but all I'd done was reopen the torn flesh where my fingernails were broken and caked with dirt.

"Oh, hell." The other man's voice was also growly, but he seemed less threatening than his companion. "Sean, she's bleeding badly."

"I smell it." The larger man held me by my upper arms, his eyes searching my face. "Alice, how did you get here? We've been looking for you." He scanned our surroundings. "Where's Malcolm?"

I had no idea who that was, or what these men wanted with me. I tried to pull free and start walking again, but his grip was like iron.

"I don't think she knows who you are," the younger man said, his voice full of worry. "I'm not sure she even knows her own name or where she is."

The larger man cupped my face with his hand and stared into my eyes. A strange scent teased my nose. *Smells like a forest*, some part of my brain said.

"Alice," he said carefully, "do you know who I am?"

Keep walking and don't look back.

I struggled against his grip, my gaze fixed on the distant horizon past his shoulder. I needed to walk. I couldn't stop—not now, not ever.

He swung me up in his arms and headed toward a large, black truck. I fought him, beating him with my fists and even clawing at him, but nothing I did fazed him in the least. The other man had his phone out and was texting, his face grim.

The larger man carried me to the truck. The other man opened the back tailgate. The big man sat on it with me in his lap and wrapped his arms around me, holding me still. I'd scratched his face, neck, and arms bloody, but he didn't seem to notice.

"Did you let the others know we found her?" he asked his companion.

"I told Jack. He'll tell the rest of the pack." The younger man rubbed his face. "I wish Nan was here, or Casey. We need a nurse."

"Take off her boots," the big man said roughly. Strangely, he seemed to be nuzzling the back of my neck. He held me so tightly I couldn't even squirm, much less get away, but he was also gentle, as if he was afraid of hurting me.

The other man unzipped my right boot. When he started to remove it, the pain was so intense I screamed.

The man holding me kissed my temple. A strange comfort washed over me, as if I'd suddenly been wrapped in warm blankets.

The younger man carefully removed the boot and swore. "Her feet are a bloody mess." His voice sounded agonized, as if it were his pain instead of mine. "She must have walked for miles. These boots were *not* made for walking, Sean. Her feet...they're just mangled."

The larger man shook with what looked like fury and grief. "Take off her other boot and her socks. We need to see how bad it is."

"It's bad," the other man said grimly. He gently peeled away my wet sock, revealing my bloody foot, and swore again. "The bottoms of her feet are all cut up too and half the skin is missing. I don't even know how she was *standing*, much less walking."

The man holding me made a strangely inhuman sound that was almost an animal's snarl. "Because she was *spelled* to walk. She couldn't stop, no matter how much it hurt. She would have walked until she dropped dead if we hadn't found her."

Gingerly, the other man took off my other boot and sock. It hurt—a *lot*. I fought to get away, but they held me still with seemingly no effort at all. I didn't understand why they were so strong.

The younger man got a bottle of water from the truck and washed the blood away. "She needs medical attention for her feet and severe dehydration," he said when they'd gotten a good look at the condition of my feet. "I saw a twenty-four-hour urgent care center about thirty miles back."

"No doctors, no hospital," the man holding me stated. "We'll take care of her ourselves. Get the first aid kit out of the back seat."

While the younger man went to get the kit, the man holding me stroked my tangled hair. He pressed a kiss to my jaw, his stubble scratching my sunburned skin.

"I don't know what happened to you," he murmured. "I don't know how you got here, or who did this to you, but I swear I will find out and I will end them." He squeezed me gently. "Please say something, Alice. Tell me you know who I am."

I turned my head and looked over the top of the truck, toward the mountains. "Let me go," I said, my voice hoarse. "I have to keep walking."

His chest rumbled. "You're not walking anywhere. Your feet are sliced to the bone. Whatever this magic is, whatever's been done to you, we're going to fix it. But first, we're taking you somewhere safe." His voice caught. "I'm taking you home."

The younger man returned with a white case and another bottle of water. My eyes locked on the water.

"She needs liquids," the younger man said, opening the case and taking out a pill bottle. "If we can't get her to a hospital, we've got to rehydrate her some other way."

The man holding me nodded at the pills. "Give her half of one of those and some water."

The younger man shook a large white pill into his hand. He broke it in half and opened the bottle of water.

"Alice, here's some water," the man holding me said. "Drink."

The other man brought the water bottle to my lips and gave me a little to drink. My mouth and throat were so dry that the sensation of water was both wonderful and almost painful.

The younger man slipped the half-pill into my mouth and gave me more water. I swallowed. He took the water away. I made a little protesting sound.

"You'll get sick if we give you too much at once," he told me. "Let's wait a few minutes and make sure you can keep the water down."

I wanted—I *needed*—to keep walking, but exhaustion tugged at me. I rested my head against the larger man's chest. This was comfortable, as if I fit just right against his body like pieces of a puzzle. It was a strangely peaceful feeling.

The pain receded. I sensed the younger man doing things to my feet, but it all seemed distant. The command to walk was still there, but my arms and legs felt as if they were full of lead and I couldn't obey.

"How did she end up like this, walking down a deserted highway so far from home?" the younger man asked as he bandaged my foot. His voice sounded like it came from a long way away.

"I have no idea, Ben," the larger man said, cradling me.

I stopped fighting to get away. The warm comfort he'd wrapped around me and the effects of the pill they'd given me made it so I couldn't think, couldn't move, couldn't even care about needing to walk. I should have been terrified that I had no memory of who I was or where I came from, and that I'd fallen into the hands of two powerful strangers who seemed to know me, but I was so very, very tired. My eyes drifted closed.

Just before sleep stole me away, I heard the man holding me add, "But I'm sure as hell going to find out."

1

SEAN

PRESENT DAY

THE TRUCK FLEW DOWN THE HIGHWAY, HEADED FOR THE DISTANT lights of the small town of Landers. Ben Cooper drove silently, his eyes gold with anger.

Sean Maclin, alpha of the Tomb Mountain werewolf pack, sat in the passenger seat, consumed by fury and frustration. He cradled Alice carefully and slipped chips of ice between her dry, cracked lips. He was grateful for the extra-large soda Ben had brought—the ice remaining in the cup was the best way to rehydrate her for now.

Despite the werewolf-strength painkiller and sedative they'd given her, Alice's sleep was restless. Her hands clenched into fists and sometimes she clawed at him, making desperate sounds as if she was trying to get away and go back to walking along the highway. Seeing his proud, powerful Alice like this made him want to tear something or some*one* apart, slowly.

Other than her physical condition, he saw precious few clues as to where she'd been for the past several days. After she'd fallen asleep, he'd managed to pry her fingers open and found a pink cigarette lighter. At first he'd thought she'd picked it up from the roadside, but it was clean and undamaged. He'd secured it in a plastic bag as a potential clue.

The lighter was all Alice had other than the clothes on her back, which were the same clothes she'd been wearing the day she'd disappeared. Her hair was matted and dried mud streaked her sunburned face. Her fingernails were broken and caked with dirt and her palms and knees were scraped. It was apparent from her sunken eyes and cheeks she hadn't eaten or had anything to drink in days.

Her scent was strange; she smelled as if it had been days since she'd bathed, but she'd been in water recently—water that wasn't clean. He smelled old blood, unfamiliar herbs, and ash. These strong odors overpowered all other scents except her perspiration. He wondered if the strange bath had been intentional, designed to keep him from smelling anything that might hint at where she'd been.

Still, he nuzzled her neck. Beneath the odor of herbs and ash, his sensitive nose detected the wonderful and unmistakable scent of honey and vanilla that had come to mean home and happiness to him. She smelled of pain, anger, and fear, too, and his Alice almost never felt fear.

Before they got in the truck and headed for the closest town, he'd checked her over for other major injuries and found three deep cuts across her back that looked very much like lashes from a whip. The wounds were at least a few days old and had become infected. At the thought someone had whipped her, his rage had gone white-hot and nearly forced him to shift.

Ben had tended to her cuts and abrasions, using antibiotic ointment and bandages from the first aid kit, but Alice needed more than that to recover. She didn't have a werewolf's healing abilities. The wounds on her back and feet were particularly serious.

As if that wasn't bad enough, he sensed no magic from her. Earlier, she'd tried to stab him with a blood-magic blade and nothing had happened. At the time he'd thought it was a result of her confusion, but he'd soon realized the terrible truth: she was powerless.

Usually whenever he was close to her, he sensed her peaceful green earth magic, the effervescence of white air magic, and the painful searing sensation of powerful blood magic. More recently, he'd also detected the cool blue of the water magic she'd borrowed from her ghost, Malcolm, and the hot golden shifter magic she might have inherited from her mysterious biological father. Normally, her magic buzzed on his skin like he was standing near a high-voltage wire. Now, he sensed nothing at all—not even the slightest spark.

In his mind, Sean's wolf bared his teeth, his ears back against his head. He showed Sean an image of a wolf tearing into the flesh of a faceless man. *Kill enemy*, the wolf said.

"I'm going to kill whoever did this," Sean snarled aloud.

Ben nodded grimly. "I'll help. Hell, let's invite the whole pack out here and let everyone get a bite of 'em, especially Jack. I've seen what he can do when he's pissed." He glanced at Sean. "We're getting close to Landers. Where do you want to stop?"

Sean shook his head. "I want to get her home." The need to take her back to the security of his den—his home—was so powerful, he nearly vibrated with it.

"We're a good two hundred and fifty miles from home. That's at least three hours, even if I haul ass. I don't think we should wait to treat her injuries. Besides, we need to stick around and see if her trail beside the road can give us any clues as to where she's been and who had her." Ben's tone was carefully non-confrontational. His alpha's temper rested on a knife edge.

Sean growled, but he knew Ben was right. Damn it, it was so hard to *think* clearly with Alice in this condition, especially after she'd been missing so long. "I saw a roadside motel pretty close to the edge of town that'll work. It had exterior doors so we won't have to go in and out through the lobby." He gave Alice another small piece of ice.

Ben slowed as they entered the city limits. "I see it. Looks like a no-frills place." The older, one-story motel was ahead, on the right. A neon VACANCY sign glowed in the office window.

"We don't need frills," Sean said as Ben turned into the motel lot and parked. "Get us two connecting rooms away from the office if they have them. And find out if there are any convenience stores or pharmacies still open."

"In this one-horse town at midnight I doubt anything's still open, but I'll ask." Ben got out and headed for the motel office.

Sean smelled fresh blood. He wasn't sure if it was from Alice's feet, the wounds on her back, or some other injury he hadn't yet seen, but it was enough to wrench a growl from deep in his belly. His bones ached with the strain of holding back his rage and the urge to shift and hunt Alice's tormentors.

His phone buzzed with an incoming text message. *Vaughan: Do you have news?*

There were few people Sean wanted to speak to at the moment less than Charles Vaughan, but he needed to let him know he'd found Alice so the Vampire Court could switch its efforts from locating her to uncovering why she'd been taken, and by whom.

Instead of texting back, he grudgingly made a call.

Vaughan answered on the first ring. "Have you found her?"

Even the sound of Vaughan's voice was enough to elicit a low snarl from Sean. He had nothing against vampires in general; as long as you never forgot their ruthlessness and endless plotting, they were no more dangerous than humans or any other kind of supernatural being. But Vaughan had taken advantage of Alice on more than one occasion, going so far as to bite her without her knowledge or consent while she lay in a coma, and then essentially blackmailed her into agreeing to a second bite.

Despite all that, Alice seemed to have a soft spot for the fangy son of a bitch. Sean loved Alice for her kind heart, but he worried it was a vulnerability she could not afford with so many enemies circling around.

As he had to do so often, Sean put his hatred of Vaughan aside for Alice's sake. "We found her."

"I am much relieved to hear this news," Vaughan said. Something about the way he said it—as if he had just as much of a right to be concerned for Alice's well-being—made Sean snarl again quietly.

His wolf growled in agreement. *Ours*, the wolf said. The wolf hated and distrusted Vaughan even more than Sean did.

"You are in Landers. How did she come to be found so far from home?" Vaughan asked.

Damned Vampire Court; they'd tracked his phone to know his location. Sean had no desire to prolong this conversation, but if he hung up, Vaughan would simply call back—or, worse, join them at the motel. He didn't want Vaughan anywhere near Alice. His control was already at its limit.

"We don't know yet," he replied, his tone frosty. "She wasn't coherent when we found her. We had to give her a sedative and painkillers. She's asleep."

"What can you tell me of her physical condition, then?" Before Sean could snarl a response, Vaughan added, "Valas will ask."

Sean was reluctant to reveal too much over the phone, especially Alice's apparent amnesia. "She's covered with cuts and bruises and her feet are torn up from walking."

Vaughan hissed.

"The Court all but forced her to take this case," Sean ground out. "I will discuss that with Madame Valas. But whoever took her—they're *mine* to deal with. Are we clear?"

"Perfectly clear." Vaughan's voice was crisp. "You will bring her directly to Northbourne for care and protection."

"No, I will not. Once we attend to her injuries and we think she's ready to travel, I'm taking her home. When she's recovered enough for you to talk to her, she'll come see you, or the Court can send someone to my house and interview her there."

Vaughan made a low sound in his throat. "That is not acceptable. The Court can better protect her."

"She isn't yours to protect, vampire."

"Nor is she *yours*, wolf."

Alice made a sound in her sleep that sounded almost like a plea. Sean held her a little closer and lowered his voice. "On the contrary, she *is* mine, and I'm hers. That's what the term *consort* means, as you well know. By shifter law—which you and your Court must honor—her well-being is my responsibility as long as she's incapable of defending herself."

Ben exited the motel office and headed for the truck, a piece of paper and two old-fashioned door keys in his hand.

"I will speak with Madame Valas and we will contact you again shortly," Vaughan said coldly.

Sean ended the call without bothering to reply. He tossed his phone on the dashboard and kissed Alice's forehead. "I hate that vampire," he murmured to her.

Ben opened the door and got in. "What did you find out?" Sean asked.

Ben put the room keys in the cupholder and the motel registration under the seat. "There's a convenience store a couple of blocks away, but they don't have much more than beer, lottery tickets, and cigarettes, the night manager says. She told me there's a twenty-four-hour pharmacy the next town over. It's about a twenty-minute drive."

He parked near the end of the motel and they took Alice into room fourteen. The furniture looked old but well-cared for and the room was clean. Sean laid her carefully on one of the double beds. She moaned softly, her fingers curling to grab the comforter, but she didn't wake.

Ben brought Sean's bag in and set the cup of ice on the nightstand. "What can I do to help?"

Sean rubbed his face. "I need to see what other injuries she has."

Ben put his hand on Sean's shoulder, lending his alpha support. "I'll give you some privacy, then. Knock when you're ready to talk."

"Thanks."

Ben quietly closed the door to their room.

Sean took the empty plastic garbage bag from the bathroom trash can and started removing Alice's clothing. Her shirt and tank top were torn. He used a pair of scissors from the first aid kit to cut them off.

His nose catalogued a host of scents on her shirt and top. He ignored those belonging to Alice and focused on the ones that were unfamiliar. Among the natural scents of dirt and plants, he caught a whiff of a strange musty odor that smelled almost like a swamp or bog, with notes of burned paper and roadkill. It smelled vaguely familiar, though he wasn't sure when or where he'd encountered it.

The shirt and top went into the bag. Her chest was scratched and dirty and covered with bruises. A large, dark bruise on her ribs indicated someone had punched or kicked her there. His heart ached to see her so battered. He wanted to wash her and clean off all the dirt and blood, but that could wait until they were home.

She looked strange without the familiar wolf amulet she'd worn for the past several weeks. Its absence explained why he hadn't been able to locate her with his own amulet, which hung around his neck under his shirt. He hadn't taken it off since Alice gave it to him. The trace of her magic it held had been a source of comfort for both him and his wolf while she was missing.

He removed her dirty jeans very carefully with the scissors rather than take them off and risk waking her or disturbing the bandages on her feet. Like her shirt, her jeans smelled of earth, blood, and that odd musty scent. She was not wearing underwear. Sometimes she chose not to, but its absence worried him.

"Alice, forgive me for this," he murmured, running his fingertips over her cheek lightly. It felt wrong to touch her in this condition, though they'd been lovers for months and he knew her body almost as well as his own.

After twenty years as a prisoner in her grandfather's crime syndicate, with little control over her own body, Alice had made it clear her autonomy was something she would rather die than lose. That made her injuries, particularly one on her ankle that might have been made by a restraint, difficult for him to think about. Now she was naked on the bed and helpless, and he was fully dressed. He was sure under normal circumstances she wouldn't object to him touching her. Even so, he hated to do it, especially since she seemed to have no memory of who he was or their time together.

To his immense relief, he didn't think her captors had sexually assaulted her; at least, he didn't see or smell anything that would lead him to believe they'd harmed her in that way. A little of the tension in his body eased.

His stomach roiled as he checked her for injuries. Her legs were even more scratched than her torso. The scratches had been made by small branches or thick grass. At some point she'd been naked and perhaps running through trees or a field. How and why she'd gotten back into her clothes afterward was a mystery, but not the most pressing one at the moment.

He found a sizable lump and a cut on the back of her head where she might have been struck and knocked unconscious. Her arms and legs had abrasions indicating she'd been tied to something, maybe a chair. Telltale finger-shaped marks on her wrists told him someone had grabbed her tightly and for long enough to leave bruises. Her right ankle was rubbed raw, as if she'd been shackled. He snarled at the thought.

Once he was certain he'd learned all he could from the scents and marks on her body, he covered her with a sheet and blanket from the closet.

Sean needed to tell Ben what he'd found out, but there was something he needed to do even more. Very carefully, he climbed onto the bed and lay down, mindful of her injuries and trying not to wake her.

Four days had passed since he'd held her—a nightmarish four days of fury, fear, and desperate searching. The desire to curl around her and wrap her in his arms was strong, but he made do with lying beside her and entwining his fingers with hers. He brushed her hair aside so he could nuzzle her neck, where her scent was strongest. His wolf growled and Sean made the same low, angry sound.

He kissed her temple. "Where's Malcolm?" he asked her softly. "Who stole your magic? How the hell did you get here?"

She made a little sound in her sleep, her breathing deep and raspy.

He inhaled and let her honey-vanilla scent settle into his bones. His wolf stopped pacing and settled down, still on high alert and angry, but no longer pushing him to shift and hunt.

Protect mate, the wolf commanded. *Heal wounds, then hunt.*

I will, he promised. *For now...I need to hold her.*

The wolf curled up, his head on his paws. *Mate home*, he said.

Sean wasn't sure if the wolf meant Alice had been found, he should take Alice home, or if Alice *was* his home. In any case, his answer was the same.

Yes—mate home, he agreed.

A few minutes later, Sean reluctantly got up from the bed and knocked on the connecting door.

Ben opened it immediately. "What did you find?"

Sean described Alice's condition and let Ben smell her clothes so he'd know the strange musty scent.

As he retied the plastic bag, Ben said, "What's been bothering me—other than her physical condition, obviously—is if someone's had her this whole time, did she escape, or did they let her go? She'd been spelled to walk, which makes it seem like she was released. Why release her?"

"The only thing that makes sense, at least right now, is that they'd gotten everything from her they wanted and didn't need her anymore."

"So they took her magic, erased her memory somehow, and dropped her off on the side of the road? If that's the case, where's Malcolm?"

"I don't know." Sean growled. "We need more ice, bandages, and water, and something she can eat. I don't think she's had any food since she disappeared."

"What about clothes and toiletries?"

Sean gestured at his bag. "I brought some of her things with me."

"You know, if she's been spelled to walk, if she wakes up, it might kick in again," Ben pointed out. "She fought us earlier trying to get away. I'm not sure I want to gamble the sedative will keep her asleep for the drive home. If she wakes up en route, you'll have to physically restrain her, and I know that's not something you'd want to do."

"Not unless I had no other choice." Sean took a deep breath and let it out. "I'll call Carly and see if she can help us break the spell."

Witch Carly Reese had become Alice's good friend and ally after she'd removed a dangerous hex intended to break up Sean and Alice's relationship. Carly had helped them find Alice when all other methods failed. Her visions had led them to this area, and then it was a matter of driving along the highway she'd seen until they came upon Alice walking alone, just as Carly had described.

He needed to call Carly anyway—he'd texted her while they were driving to the motel to let her know Alice had been found and had said he'd call with more news when he got a chance.

"If she thinks she can help, Jack can bring her here," Ben said. "I'd suggest Nan come too, and Casey, if we need a nurse. You know, Alice saved my life. Casey and I are planning our wedding right now because of her. I owe her my life." He growled. "And I owe whoever hurt her some serious pain and a dirt nap."

Sean felt the corners of his mouth turn up. "Alice has been known to say things along those same lines."

"I know she has." Ben grinned. "There's a reason I like her so much."

Outside, two large pickups pulled into the motel's lot and parked. Doors opened and closed and several sets of footsteps headed in the direction of their room.

Quietly, Sean retrieved his gun from his bag. The visitors hadn't tried to hide their approach, but he wasn't going to take any chances—not with Alice so vulnerable. Ben, his eyes glowing, took up a position between the door and the bed.

Three sets of footsteps stopped outside the door. Someone knocked loudly.

Sean flicked the safety off his Smith & Wesson. Gun at his side, he turned the deadbolt and opened the door, using his body to block their view of the room.

Three familiar werewolves stood on the sidewalk: two men and a woman who were members of the Blue Valley Pack. "Howdy, Sean," the large blond man in the middle of the group said, taking in Sean's body language and the gun in a glance. "We apologize for disturbing you."

"Lucas." Sean put the safety on his gun and tucked it into his waistband at the small of his back. "It's good to see you again. How's Mariah?"

In a plaid work shirt, jeans, and boots, the pack's alpha, Lucas Stone, radiated authority and fatherly pride. "She's doing well. We're expecting another baby in a couple of months. That'll be three babies for our pack this year. We're damn proud."

Like their alpha, Mike Vickers and his mate Andrea wore casual work clothes. All three were muscular, as shifters tended to be, but leaner than the wolves in his own pack. Rural shifters often were, as their larger territories allowed for longer runs in wolf form and more hunting. Differences between rural and urban werewolf packs were both cultural and physiological. Lucas's appearance at their motel room demonstrated how quickly their pack responded to reports of interlopers.

Sean glanced at the motel office. "Word travels fast around here."

Lucas smiled briefly. "We like to know when visitors are in town.

Martha, the night manager, is a friend of our pack. She passed along your pack mate's name and information, along with the news you had someone with you who might be hurt. Does your companion need medical attention? Andrea is a nurse."

Sean shook his head. "Thank you for the offer, but we're fine."

Mike growled low. "How would you like it if we came into your territory and acted like we owned the place?"

Lucas raised his hand, signaling his beta to stand down. "They're a city pack, Mike. They see members of other packs all the time." He turned back to Sean. "Pack territories work a little differently out here. We're less used to shifters coming and going in the area without contacting us beforehand."

Damn it—Lucas is right, Sean thought. "I apologize for that. I was focused on finding a missing person and didn't think to contact you."

Lucas nodded, accepting the apology. "We might be able to give you some assistance, if you'd be willing to tell us what brought you here and how your consort came to be injured."

No doubt the others had sensed Sean's fierce protectiveness and other telltale emotions and correctly interpreted them as concern for his consort. Alice's identity was no secret among the packs in the area, thanks to the controversy she'd caused on the Were Ruling Council, and her blood smelled distinctly human. It would be simple logic to deduce the identity of the injured woman sleeping in the bed behind him.

Andrea spoke. "Why don't you let me check on her? I know you feel very protective right now, but she smells like she's running a fever and I could at least clean her wounds. I have a first-aid kit with me. You can stand right next to me and the men will stay out here so we have privacy."

Sean sensed concern from Lucas and anger from Mike. To his surprise, Andrea put her hands on her hips and glared at them both. "This woman is hurt. If that's the only way he'll let me help her, then that's what we're going to do."

Sean felt a sharp pang in his chest. Andrea's defiance reminded him of Alice—*his* Alice, not the wounded, confused woman he'd found walking alone on the highway. Alice's feet and back *did* need care.

"Thank you," he said. "I appreciate your help."

Andrea hurried to one of the trucks, got a small duffel bag from the back seat, and went inside the room. Ben joined Lucas and Mike outside, leaving the door slightly ajar, as Sean followed Andrea to Alice's bedside.

Andrea folded back the sheet and blanket, revealing Alice's arm. She checked Alice's pulse, then checked her temperature with an ear thermometer. "She's got a temp of one hundred and one," she told Sean. "Why don't you give her more ice while I check her feet?"

Sean fed Alice ice chips while Andrea uncovered her bandaged feet. Blood had soaked through the wrappings. She very carefully unwrapped the bandages.

"You did a good job with these," Andrea said, discarding the bandages in the trash can. She slid her first aid kit closer and started tending to Alice's feet. Her demeanor was professional, but Sean saw sympathy in her eyes as she carefully cleaned the torn flesh and started re-bandaging. "It looks like she walked a very long way in shoes that weren't designed for that—and that was after her feet were already cut up from walking or running barefoot. I can't imagine how much that must have hurt." She glanced up at Sean before returning her attention to the bandages. Defiant or not, she couldn't hold eye contact with an alpha for long. "Your consort is one tough gal."

"Yes, she is," Sean agreed. The ice in the cup was almost gone. He'd have to send Ben to get more. He worried about Alice's fever. He hadn't noticed it so much before, since he was more concerned about her feet, but she felt warmer now than when they'd found her.

"Her feet are in bad shape, but that's not the source of the infection." Andrea rose. "Are there other wounds?"

He nodded. "On her back. Those looked like they were a couple of days old." Carefully, he rolled Alice onto her side, wrapping the sheet at her waist but allowing Andrea to see her back.

Andrea carefully removed the bloodstained bandages and winced. "These cuts are deep and badly infected. I'll clean the wounds and give her some antibiotics, but you should have a doctor check her over. If you're not sure who to trust in town, I can recommend Doc Verner. I work at her clinic. The clinic opens at eight, but she'd come here now if I called her."

He despised seeing Alice hurting but she'd told him long ago she had to avoid doctors and hospitals. Her blood might be used against her or reveal her real identity. Though Moses Murphy now knew who she was, no one else did. That meant doctors and hospitals were still out of the question.

"We'll take her to the hospital when we get back to the city," he lied. "Thanks for the offer. Please do what you can for now."

Andrea's mouth compressed into a grim line. She started to say something, then thought better of it and focused on cleaning the cuts on Alice's back.

Sean was sure she wanted to read him the riot act for letting Alice suffer. She wouldn't have been wrong to do so, but calling out an alpha from another pack was a prelude to a fight, so she'd bitten her tongue, if only barely.

Andrea finished replacing the bandages on Alice's back. Sean watched to make sure she put all of the soiled bandages and first-aid supplies in the trash can. He'd destroy them once she was gone.

"Thank you again," he said as she zipped her bag and headed for the door. "You're very kind to help us."

"You are very welcome." They stepped outside to rejoin the others. "Get her to a doctor as soon as you can. In the meantime, give her acetaminophen and keep cool cloths on her forehead and wrists to help bring her temperature down. Keep giving her ice chips while she's sleeping and then let her sip water when she wakes up—she needs liquids desperately."

"Is there anything else we can do to help?" Lucas asked.

Sean considered. "If it isn't too much of an imposition, I'd like to ask a favor."

"What can I do?"

"Would you be willing to go with Ben to see if you can follow Alice's scent along the highway? We'd like to find out how long she'd been walking, and the trail is going cold." Sean would have preferred to go himself, but he needed to stay with Alice. He trusted Ben to bring back whatever information could be gleaned from the scent trail.

Lucas held out his hand for Sean to shake. "Be happy to. We'll take my truck. Andrea, you should come too—we could use your nose. Come on when you're ready, Ben." He and Andrea headed for a gray pickup that read *Stone Construction* on the side. Andrea got in the back seat, leaving the passenger seat for Ben.

Mike headed across the lot. When he was inside his truck and the door was shut, Sean addressed Ben. "See if you can find any clues as to where she's been and where she walked from."

"I'll find out everything I can."

Mike backed out of his parking spot. To Sean's surprise, he re-parked near the motel office, facing their rooms.

"He's staying to keep an eye on us," Ben said, his displeasure evident.

Sean didn't like being under surveillance either, but he and Ben were the intruders here. "We're in their territory, so it's his right to do so. Rural shifters are more territorial. At least he's letting us know he's watching."

"If you need me, give me a call," Ben said. He lowered his voice. "Before the others get here, why don't you shift and lay down next to Alice? It will help calm both you and your wolf."

"I might do that after I make some calls. Text Jack and let him know I want him to come out here with Nan. They'll probably need to pick Carly up on the way. I'll confirm that as soon as I have a chance to call Carly."

"You got it." Ben clapped Sean on the shoulder, then headed for Lucas's truck and climbed in. They backed out and turned left on the highway, accelerating in the direction of where they'd found Alice walking.

Sean went back inside room fourteen. He turned off all the lights, put his gun on the table, and ran a couple of washcloths under cold water. He wrung them out and took them to where Alice lay sleeping. He sat carefully on the side of the bed and put one of the washcloths on her forehead. Her brow furrowed and she grabbed at the comforter again, but she didn't wake. He put the other washcloths on her wrists and gave her a few ice chips.

He took his phone to the adjoining room and sat where he could see her reflection in the mirror opposite her bed while he called Carly Reese.

Despite the late hour, she answered immediately and sounded fully awake. "How is she?" she asked, without bothering with a greeting.

He growled. "Not good." He described Alice's condition—her apparent lack of memory, the compulsion that had forced her to walk for miles on bloody feet, her missing magic, and her injuries. Carly reacted predictably, with a mix of anger and grief.

"I can't tell anything over the phone," she said when he finished. "I have some suspicions, but I need to read her aura."

"It's asking a lot of you, Carly, but—"

"I can come," she interrupted. "My assistant manager can open the shop for me. I need to pack some things, and then I'll be on my way."

"My beta Jack Hastings will pick you up. Nan Lowell is coming as well."

"Good." Her voice was brisk. "Miss Nan will be a big help. Text me their ETA, please. I'll need at least forty minutes to pack."

He exhaled. "Thank you. Do you have any way of finding out where Malcolm is? He's not with her."

"I can try. It'll be tricky since he's a spirit, but I'll give it my best shot. Let me get packed and we'll see you in a couple of hours."

They said their goodbyes and ended the call. Sean texted Carly's address to Jack and received a confirmation his beta was headed over to pick up Nan, and then they'd go get Carly.

Before he returned to the other room, Sean went to the sink, unwrapped a small bar of motel soap, and washed his face.

He and Ben had driven straight to the area when Carly had finally gotten a vision of where Alice was, or at least the general vicinity. He'd been up for more than twenty-four hours before that, furious, worried, and unable to sleep. Alice's absence had quickly become a source of physical discomfort and then, in the past day, actual pain.

It was Jack who'd explained how a mate bond—even a nascent bond—had physical aspects as well as emotional and metaphysical ones. Sean had experienced the positive effects of his and Alice's growing bond, but had never suffered the pain of separation before. Deeply content and complete at her side, he'd felt hollow and as if he'd lost a limb since she'd been missing. Those feelings weren't tied to proximity, since a bond was metaphysical. According to Jack, that had meant either Alice was dead or behind strong wards. No one, including Carly, was able to figure out where she was until just a few hours ago. Sean supposed that was when Alice had escaped, or her captors set her free.

Though most of his concern was for Alice, he also worried about Malcolm. During her absence, he'd taken hope and comfort from the thought that wherever she was Malcolm was probably with her. Now he wondered what had become of the ghost and whether Alice had faced her tormentors alone. Little could harm a ghost, but Malcolm was not invulnerable. Blood mages could discorporate him, sending him through the veil to whatever lay beyond. Doing so would cause great harm to Alice, perhaps even killing her, since they were bound.

He had the sudden terrible thought Alice's condition might be the result of Malcolm being discorporated. Alice had once said Malcolm being stolen from her could cause the equivalent of a lobotomy. He snarled.

They had entirely too many questions and not enough answers. For now, he'd focus on taking care of Alice. When the others arrived, they'd hunt down those responsible for her condition and get the answers, one way or another.

2

ALICE

ONE WEEK EARLIER

AGAINST MY BETTER JUDGMENT, I WENT TO A VAMPIRE BALL.

The grand ballroom at Northbourne Manor, headquarters of the Vampire Court of the Western United States, had transformed into the deck of an eighteenth-century galleon, complete with a plank floor, towering masts and sails, stacks of wooden crates and barrels, and a plank over a glass-enclosed tank of water in which two beautiful women swam, costumed as mermaids.

Valas, the ancient and powerful head of the Court, sat on a dais at the far end of the enormous ballroom. She was dressed as a queen in a deep red gown so beautiful and elaborate I couldn't even guess at its cost. She wore her long black hair piled high on her head and a beautiful ruby necklace, the signature red of her Court. Her tiara was also made of rubies.

Beside her on the dais were four members of the Court: Friedrich, David, Peter, and Marin. The others—Amira, Niara, Ossun, and Charles—circulated among the guests. All wore period-appropriate pirate attire.

I took a drink from my champagne. Sean grabbed me around the waist from behind. "Arrr," he growled in my ear. "Avast, me proud beauty, and let me plunder yer glorious booty."

I choked on my drink and started coughing. "How long have you been practicing that line?" I asked when I could talk.

He grinned. "Since we were fitted for our costumes."

His eyes glowed at the sight of my very low-cut blood-red gown, complete with layers of petticoats and a corset that tripled my normal cleavage and made deep breaths impossible. My wolf amulet rested on what I supposed I'd have to refer to as my bosom, given my attire. I wore ruby earrings, on loan from the Court. Everyone in the room wore either a red item of clothing or ruby jewelry, or both.

Sean was dressed as a gentleman pirate, in a jacket, trousers, three-cornered hat, and tall cuffed leather boots. A cutlass—a very real and very sharp one—hung from his belt. His unbuttoned shirt revealed the hard muscles of his chest, along with his matching wolf amulet and a borrowed ruby pendant. I'd tried to talk him into wearing an eyepatch to complete the look, but he was reluctant to impair his vision in a room full of potential attackers.

"You look like the cover of a swashbuckler romance novel," I told him, smiling.

He ran his nose along my hairline. "Does that mean I get to rip your bodice later?" he murmured, his breath tickling my neck. "Please say yes."

I shivered. "I'd love to, since there's nothing about the pirate fantasy I don't like, but I don't want to pay for this dress."

He nipped my earlobe with his teeth. "I'll happily pay for it. It would be worth every last doubloon, my lady." Suddenly, he tensed. I had an inkling what had caused him to abandon his flirtations.

Sure enough, Charles Vaughan approached, a glass of champagne in his hand. Unlike our drinks, his champagne was tinged pink with fresh blood. The dark-haired vampire was also dressed as a pirate, though his shirt was buttoned all the way to the ruffled collar. Like the other members of the Court, he wore a medallion on a red ribbon. His sword hung at his side. I wondered if he actually knew how to use it...and then realized a certain percentage of the guests at this event had witnessed the golden age of piracy firsthand.

Behind him was Bryan Smith, Charles's enormous head of security. Like most of the other enforcers at the gala, he was dressed as a queen's guard rather than in pirate attire. He gave me a nod.

To his credit, Charles's gaze stayed on my face and didn't stray to my bosom. "Good evening, Alice, Mr. Maclin. You are both resplendent, if I may say so."

"You look rather dashing yourself," I told him. "Why a pirate ship, Charles?"

I'd been curious about the chosen theme for the event since we'd seen our costumes. Vampires loved fancy-dress parties—the more opulent, the better—but when I'd accepted the invitation to tonight's gala I'd certainly never guessed we'd be wearing buccaneer couture.

Charles acknowledged a passing female vampire, who wore pirate garb rather than a dress, then turned back to us. "As you know, tonight's gala celebrates the visit by Elizabeth, head of the Chicago Court, and her entourage. Not long ago, rumor reached Valas that Elizabeth had once sailed on a pirate ship and had remarked that her memories of the voyage were pleasant."

I tried to imagine why a vampire would sail with pirates. "That's as good of a reason as any to dress up like the cast of *Pirates of the Caribbean*." I surveyed the room. "Speaking of Elizabeth, when will the guests of honor arrive?"

Charles pulled a gold watch from his jacket. "They are due to make their entrance in fifteen minutes, though I daresay Elizabeth will arrive when she pleases." He returned the watch to his pocket and gave me a bow. "While we wait, may I have the honor of a dance?"

I'd consented to dance with him at the gala in return for some information I needed. It appeared he was ready to cash in on that promise. Sean and I had agreed it seemed like a harmless request, but my wolfy pirate partner clearly didn't like it.

I glanced dubiously at the area in front of Valas's dais, where a dozen couples waltzed elegantly to music provided by a small orchestra. "I know I said I'd dance with you tonight, but I don't think I can waltz, especially in this dress."

He smiled. "The steps are simple. I am sure I can teach you."

"Well, if you insist." I handed Sean my champagne glass and kissed him lightly. "Be right back."

"Save the next dance for me," he told me, giving Charles a stare I couldn't quite read. Not a warning, because I didn't need him to warn Charles on my behalf, but something more like he thought Charles might have an ulterior motive for the dance. I'd bet my fancy slippers on it, since I'd rarely known Charles to do *anything* without an ulterior motive.

Charles drained the last of his champagne and handed the empty glass to a passing server. I took his hand and he led me through the crowd, moving with a dancer's grace. I found myself flowing along behind him, my skirts swishing past men and women in gowns, noblemen's garb, and pirate attire. Bryan followed us, never losing sight of his employer.

On our way to the dance floor, we passed a white-gloved attendant carrying a small crystal and gold decanter filled with blood. My blood magic tingled. The decanter was etched with spellwork that preserved the blood held inside. The blood would be added to the champagne consumed by the vamps at the gala.

Several guests eyeballed the decanter as the attendant passed, but everyone here was much too refined to vamp out or flash their fangs at the sight of blood.

Charles escorted me first to the dais where Valas sat. He bowed deeply to her. I started to follow suit, but the damn corset made it impossible, so I did the best version of a curtsey I could muster.

When I straightened, Valas was watching me, a slight smile on her lips. She inclined her head in acknowledgement. The smile could mean nothing...or everything. Figuring her out was a full-time job in itself.

Charles led me into the midst of the dancing couples. He placed my other hand on his shoulder and rested his hand on my waist. His dark eyes glowed softly, as if lit by moonlight from within. I shivered.

Recently, I'd nearly died after being attacked by a young werewolf from Sean's pack. Charles had healed me. The amount of his blood I'd ingested had a myriad of effects, even now. If Charles noticed my reaction to his touch, he didn't let on.

"Follow my lead," he said. "Step back with your right foot. Now left with your left. Close your right foot to your left. Step forward with your left foot, then right with your right. Close your left foot to your right."

He moved with me as I slowly learned the steps, keeping us from bumping into any of the other couples. We repeated the pattern in place several times.

"You are a natural," he said with a smile.

"I'm reciting the steps in my head," I admitted.

He chuckled. "Soon it will become like breathing. Keep your feet beneath you." And we were off, joining the others on the dance floor.

He didn't talk at first so I could focus on dancing. A few times I got tangled up in my own feet, but he led masterfully, disguising my missteps. Before long I was moving smoothly and no longer had to consciously repeat the steps in my head. I was no Ginger Rogers, but at least I wasn't embarrassing Charles too much in front of Valas and the rest of the Court. Yay, me.

"As I said, you are a natural," he said as we turned, my skirts swirling around us. "So light on your feet, you might be made of air."

"Oh, stop with the flattery," I said, somewhat crossly. "I'm stomping around with all the grace of a drunken rugby player and you know it. Sell that line to someone who'll buy it."

He laughed. The vampires around us glanced our way, startled by his sudden merriment. I didn't mind their curious glances. It had been a long time since I'd heard Charles laugh, or even seen him smile with anything like genuine amusement.

I'd recently involved him in the search for a spelled cup that allowed a vampire to walk in daylight for an hour. He'd used the cup, against the recommendations of those close to him, including me. He'd gotten a taste of what it felt like to be human again and when the hour was over, the reality of his undead existence had hit him hard.

He'd been morose ever since, to the point of desiring true death, or at least not fighting it when a vampire object of power nearly killed him. I'd saved him and he'd offered me a boon in return. It was a boon I might need soon. My grandfather Moses Murphy, the most powerful crime lord on the east coast, from whom I'd been hiding for five years, had found me a few days earlier. He'd threatened to kill everyone I cared about and take me back to Baltimore in chains.

As we turned, I glimpsed Sean standing near the dais, watching us. He caught my gaze and smiled. *Beautiful*, he mouthed. My cheeks grew warm, as did a few other parts of my body.

"Of course, this is all a fantasy," Charles said suddenly, drawing my attention away from Sean. "Cutthroats and buccaneers did not dance with lords and ladies, even if one were wealthy. We were not fit for halls like this one—which suited us perfectly well, as we quite preferred the raucous and lively inns and taverns along the waterfront."

I almost tripped—over his feet or my own, I wasn't sure. It was hard to tell since I couldn't see anything but my enormous skirt. "You were a *pirate?*"

"Unfortunately, no," he said with real regret. "The seafaring life was not for me. As you might imagine, a life at sea would be very perilous for one who cannot encounter the sun and is insensible during daytime. However, not long after I became a vampire, I invested my modest savings in a pirate venture. The captain was a man of adventure and his crew a fearless and opportunistic lot. They repaid my investment many times over and made me wealthy."

"You made your first fortune from piracy?"

"Indeed. I much preferred their company, if truth be told." He turned us with a flourish to avoid another couple. "For some years, I frequented their taverns dressed as a common workman and listened to their tales of adventure. As my business grew and required more of my time, I found myself in an office while others sailed on adventures I could not hope to join." His eyes darkened with remembered longing.

"I think almost everyone wanted to be a pirate at some point," I said, trying to distract him. "I can remember tying a scarf around my head, putting a stuffed animal on my shoulder like a parrot, and pretending I only had one leg. I had something I used as a sword, but I can't remember what it was."

My smile faded. I'd had so little time for play as a child. Between tutoring and practicing magic and doing what my grandfather wanted, I'd had to steal minutes when I could, often late at night. I'd played pirate by myself in my room in Moses's compound, staying quiet so my parents wouldn't hear.

I mustered a smile and put away those bittersweet memories. "Imagine you in threadbare clothes, swilling ale in a tavern and listening to tales of pirate adventure on the high seas. My image of you will never be the same."

The corners of his mouth turned up. "My heart still yearns for adventure, though you might not guess that of me."

"I do believe it, actually. Maybe that's why you chose to become a broker. Danger, secrets, money, schemes, treasures, and intrigue...it's not that different from pirate adventure, and you don't have to worry about seasickness or scurvy."

"It is certainly never boring," he agreed.

Dancing was a perfect opportunity to share thoughts, which we could do when in physical contact. I'd figured Charles would take this opportunity to speak to me privately, and I'd guessed correctly.

His hand tightened on mine and I heard his voice in my head. *I only learned Bell and Murphy were conspiring on the night of your raid on the bordello.*

Moses, my grandfather, had found me thanks to an elaborate trap laid by the late and unlamented Darius Bell, the former head of the local cabal. Bell had kidnapped a dozen mages and let it be known he intended to use them to break the wards on one of Moses's buildings, which would have killed them. One of the kidnapped mages was a twelve-year-old kid whose mother had hired me to find him.

To save them, I'd offered to break the wards myself in return for the mages' release, only to find once we'd gotten into the building that Bell and Moses had been in on it together all along and the kidnappings were designed to get me to reveal my identity.

Moses had killed Bell in a rage when the Vampire Court prevented him from taking me back to Baltimore. As it turned out, Valas had known about their plot and used our meeting to expose Bell's lies and betrayals. I'd wondered if Charles had known as well but not warned me.

I didn't have Charles's gift of sensing truth and deception, but my gut told me he was telling me the truth. *Valas plays her cards pretty close to the vest, I guess,* I told him.

I believe Valas did not reveal the truth to me until your operation was underway because she feared I would attempt to warn you.

Would you have warned me? I asked. *Even if she'd sworn you to secrecy?*

A long silence. *Yes.*

Charles would have disobeyed Valas and risked her ire to warn me. I didn't even know how to begin processing that.

He held my gaze with eyes that glowed. *I would give anything in my possession if you would look at me as you look at the wolf.*

I shook my head and started to move away, but he resisted and continued dancing. *I once thought to offer you wealth or treasures or even immortality, but I saw long ago none of these things would endear me to you. What you seek is something far more valuable: the heart of one who believes you to be an equal or better. I did not believe you could find such a partner in Sean Maclin, but I misjudged him—as I have misjudged you so many times. My miscalculation was my great misfortune, though I have not abandoned all hope.*

Of all the reasons I'd imagined for Charles to request this dance, unburdening his heart had not been one of them. *Why tell me this now?*

He squeezed my hand again. *So you may consider that I too could offer you happiness, fulfillment, and safety. We are more alike than not, Alice, and have more in common than you and the wolf. You have been drawn to me from the beginning, as I have been drawn to you. You cannot claim you do not know that in your heart.*

I couldn't deny it because he'd sense the lie, but I didn't like where this conversation was going. *Moths are drawn to a flame, but that doesn't mean the flame won't kill it.*

I do not wish to kill you, Alice. I wish to make you safe and happy.

I raised an eyebrow. *I didn't say you were the flame in this metaphor, Charles.*

He smiled. *Touché, my dear. Indeed, you burn very brightly.*

I shook my head. *I don't know if you do wish to make me happy. I think you want to win me. You want me in your arsenal and in your bed. If I'm happy being there that would be a nice bonus, maybe, but I'm quite sure that's far from your first priority.*

His expression darkened. *Why are you so certain? I am capable of putting your safety and happiness before my own. Is not Valas's decision to hide her plan from me proof of this? Never has she had cause to doubt me before this, before you.*

He guided me into a turn, spinning me slowly and meeting me at the end of the turn to grasp my free hand again. Instead of picking up where we'd left off in the waltz, he held me in place for a few beats, rocking us back and forth. The other couples moved around us in beautiful jewel-toned gowns, elegant evening wear, and pirate attire.

Despite my skepticism, I lost myself in the soft, sensual moonlight glow of his eyes. The music continued and the dancers danced, but they faded to the edge of my awareness and all I saw was Charles.

Finally, when we rejoined the waltz, I barely noticed my feet moving in time with his. His voice in my head was soft and almost dreamlike. *If you require further proof of my intent, I once had the means of your destruction in my hands and I chose to throw it into a fire.*

My blood ran cold, snapping me out of my near-trance like a bucket of ice dumped over my head. *What do you mean?*

His hand tightened on my waist. *Not long after I first made your acquaintance, a Vampire Court researcher looking into your background at my request uncovered an irregularity: a long-buried report from a police precinct in Chicago. A young man claimed he had witnessed the overdose and death of a woman named Alice Worth in the basement of an abandoned building.*

I shrugged, hoping he couldn't sense my shock. *Tweakers think they see all kinds of things: dragons, talking trees, dead people. Not the most reliable witnesses. I wouldn't put much stock in it.*

Despite my outward calm, my mind raced. *Double shit.* I'd always assumed the real Alice had overdosed and died in that basement alone. I'd certainly never heard of a police report that mentioned a witness to her death.

Charles continued, *Fearing he would be arrested, the witness ran away, but he later directed police to the location. They found no body and no sign of her. The police dismissed it as a drug-induced hallucination and it was forgotten, especially when Alice herself turned up some weeks later, alive and well.*

Of course it was a hallucination, I told him, my heart racing. *I was a drug addict back then and I hung out with a lot of addicts. And I'm clearly not dead, so he was obviously mistaken.*

I do not think so, he said, his voice in my head gentle but firm. *I believe Alice Worth died in the basement of an abandoned building in Chicago. Another young woman, desperate to avoid those who meant her harm, found a way to steal her identity and her appearance. Given recent events, I am now certain I know who that desperate young woman was.*

You're wrong, I told him. *I think we're done dancing, Charles.* Again, I tried to step away and bumped into another couple. The male vampire hissed softly at me, then glided out of our path with his partner.

Charles's hand tightened on mine. *If I had intended to use this information against you, I could have done so at any time. Instead, I kept your secret.*

I had no desire to make a scene on the dance floor, so I started waltzing again, but I was no longer mesmerized by the music and the soft glow of his eyes. *Even if all that were true, which it isn't, you can't tell me you never planned to blackmail me*, I accused him. *I know you better than that. Information is a valuable commodity—you've told me that a hundred times. When you found out by biting me that I wasn't the mid-level mage I claimed to be, you tried to blackmail me into working for the Court. I haven't forgotten that, Charles —or forgiven you for it.*

Information is *valuable*, he told me, *but some things are worth far more. When I first obtained the information, I did* intend *to use it to my advantage—I will admit that. As time passed, I realized by doing so I would never have the real you, the woman made of fire, and anything less would be meaningless. I could have blackmailed you, but I did not.*

I scowled. *Do you want a prize for not blackmailing me?*

He leaned close, his fangs inches from my throat. *No—I want* you.

Despite my anger and distrust of him, something surged inside me. Maybe it was his blood still running through my veins; maybe it was something else. I shivered.

His eyes silvered in response. *The day you came to my home to remove the stone that was poisoning me, I lay in my bed believing I might not wake at sunset. I sensed my true death approaching. I thought of many things—moments of pleasure, moments of regret—but uppermost in my mind were thoughts of you. Those might have been my last thoughts in this, my second and final life. That is how I know if I do not take this chance now by revealing all this to you, I shall regret it.*

Charles's words were an eerie echo of Sean's on the day we'd put in an offer on a farmhouse that would be our home together and a den of sorts for his pack. Sean had told me that after everything we'd been through, if we wanted happiness, we had to grab onto it when we had the chance. I was suddenly certain Charles knew about the house, and that was why he was saying this to me now.

I was startled out of my thoughts when Charles brought our movement to a sudden halt. It took me a moment to realize the music had stopped and the guests were moving to form a clear, wide path from the main doors across the length of the ballroom to the dais where Valas and the others sat. It would appear Elizabeth and her entourage were about to make their entrance.

Charles leaned close to my ear. "I must join the others," he murmured. "Please consider what I have said. We shall speak again." He disappeared in the direction of the dais.

Sean took his place at my side, entwining our fingers. His face was hard, his eyes glowing. He'd probably caught echoes of my emotions as I'd talked with Charles, enough to know our conversation had been very serious.

He bent his head so his lips were against my ear. "Are you all right?"

"Fine," I said, not quite convincingly.

"I take it Vaughan had a lot to talk about." His voice was more growly than usual.

I wasn't going to tell him what Charles had said about the police report from Chicago with so many sharp ears around us. As for the rest—I'd have to think about that later, when I had time to process it.

I squeezed his hand to let him know there wasn't any immediate threat. "He did. I'll fill you in when we get home."

As Charles, Amira, Niara, and Ossun took their places on the dais, Valas and the others rose from their chairs. The guests in the ballroom quieted.

At the far end of the ballroom, Hanson, one of Valas's personal guards, stood in front of the main doors. He folded his hands behind his back. "Madame Valas, members of the Vampire Court of the Western United States, and honored guests, I present Madame Elizabeth, Mr. Declan O'Rourke, and Ms. Ana Cedillo of the Vampire Court of Chicago."

He stepped aside as two enforcers dressed as queen's guards opened the doors.

Elizabeth strode in, followed by two other vampires and a dozen humans and enforcers. They all wore Court medallions on emerald green ribbons. Given Valas's attire and Elizabeth's role as head of the Chicago Court, I'd expected her to also be costumed as a queen. Instead, Elizabeth was dressed as a pirate—and not the sexy Halloween version, either. The sword hanging from her belt looked very real—and used. I suddenly wondered if her voyage aboard a pirate ship had been as a passenger or a member of the ship's crew.

Unlike Valas, who had dark hair and eyes and an unmistakably Mediterranean complexion, Elizabeth was blonde and very fair. She was thin, like all older vamps, but she radiated power. She would forever appear to be in her mid-twenties, but the centuries had given her the same predatory eyes as Valas. She was not as old as Valas—that much was readily apparent—but she was older than almost anyone else here.

The male vampire behind her, who I took to be O'Rourke, was red-haired and dressed as a gentleman of the court rather than as a pirate. Ana Cedillo wore a black-and-white gown with an emerald necklace and earrings. Unlike O'Rourke, who seemed to be several hundred years old, Ana was young, maybe only a few decades post-Change. She was petite and dark-haired. Her sharp eyes swept the crowd.

Elizabeth's advisors and guards followed her across the ballroom, down the aisle formed by the gala's guests. Two of the guards carried a large, flat item draped with green velvet.

As they approached, Valas descended from the dais to greet her counterpart from Chicago. The rest of the Court followed suit, standing at her sides in the same order in which they sat during Court sessions, with the oldest members of the Court in the middle and the youngest on the ends.

"I welcome Madame Elizabeth and her companions to our Court," Valas said. Her heavily accented voice carried through the entire ballroom. "We are honored by your presence here and hope our hospitality meets with your approval."

"I bring greetings from the Court of Chicago." Elizabeth's accent was distinctly British. Most vampires who now lived in the United States but were more than two hundred years old came from other countries. They tended to deliberately retain their original accents, I suspected to set them apart from younger, American-born vampires in not-so-subtle elitism. "I am pleased with your hospitality, Madame Valas, and find this gala much to my liking."

Valas inclined her head. "I am quite gratified to hear this."

Elizabeth gestured to her entourage. The two guards who carried the velvet-draped item hurried forward. They set it down carefully in front of Valas.

"As is our custom among all Courts, I have brought a gift to our host to show our appreciation for her hospitality and generosity." Elizabeth pulled the velvet cover off. "Madame Valas, please accept this gift."

What do you buy for a thousand-year-old vampire who has everything? I wondered. Given its shape and size, I'd thought the gift was a portrait—maybe a painting of Valas herself.

When the velvet cover fell away, however, Elizabeth's gift turned out to be a huge ornate mirror in a heavy gilt frame. It looked very old. A quiet murmur swept through the guests. Mirrors were significant for vampires, an unintended consequence of the mistaken lore about them not having reflections. Centuries ago, they'd become a symbol of a vampire's existence. More recently, they'd come to represent vampire identity and how they no longer needed to hide from humans.

"It's beautiful," I said softly to Sean. "Seems like the sort of thing she'd like."

Valas studied the mirror. At first I thought she was looking at her own reflection, but instead she seemed to be examining the mirror itself, perhaps trying to estimate its origin and age.

As I watched, the mirror rippled ever so slightly, like the surface of a crystal-clear lake in a light breeze.

"Did you see that?" I asked Sean in an undertone.

He frowned. "See what?"

Suddenly, the image in the glass seemed to be a mile deep instead of a flat reflection. Vertigo made me stagger slightly and sway as if a chasm had opened in front of me. I took a step forward before I realized what I was doing.

Sean's arm wrapped around my middle. His lips pressed to my ear. "What's wrong?"

I pushed the dizziness aside and met Valas's eyes in the mirror. Her black eyes glowed from within. Though I was only fifteen feet away, I had the disconcerting sensation as I stared at Valas's reflection that I was looking through time and across what felt like a terrifyingly vast distance.

The Valas in the mirror smiled at me. The Valas in the ballroom did not.

Realization dawned: Elizabeth's gift wasn't a mirror—it was a door.

"Alice?" Sean prodded. His tension prickled on my skin.

"I'm okay," I murmured, only half-aware of his arm holding me back. The mirror-door tugged on my blood magic. More than that, it seemed to pull at my blood *itself*. A door *and* a well-used blood magic artifact of immense power. I needed to keep my distance.

Before I could make sense of my reaction to the mirror-door, a commotion broke out on the other side of the ballroom. I heard shouts and what sounded like fighting. I barely had time to pull my gaze away from the mirror and try to see what was going on before dark magic surged from the direction of the shouting. Glass broke and several people screamed.

Pandemonium erupted.

All around us, vampires went for the throats of any humans they could see, throwing other vamps out of the way in their bloodlust. The couple I'd bumped into on the dance floor tore into the throat of a human server standing to our left. Warm blood sprayed across my face.

In a matter of seconds, the formal gala dissolved into total chaos. I lost sight of Valas, Elizabeth, and Charles in the sea of fighting.

Several vamps came at Sean and me. Sean intercepted two of them, moving so quickly he was almost a blur. I flicked my hand as if I were tossing a pair of dice. A four-foot whip made of bright green cold fire spiraled out of my hand. I lashed an attacking vamp and knocked him back, leaving a deep bloody gash across his chest. Two more rushed at me, only to be thrown back by my whip.

A cold hand closed on my upper arm. Sean punched the vamp who'd grabbed me. She went flying back, knocking down two other vampires. That punch would have killed a human outright. The vamp was dazed, but she wouldn't be down for long.

"Head for the door!" Sean shouted, drawing his cutlass and nearly taking the head off another would-be attacker. I didn't think he had much experience wielding any kind of sword, but he seemed to get the hang of it pretty quickly.

A female vamp dressed as a pirate—the one Charles had nodded to earlier—got her teeth into Sean's shoulder. I lashed her across her face and chest with my whip. She screamed and stumbled back. Two vampires jumped on top of her, attempting to restrain her. Whatever madness had taken over, it seemed to be affecting only some of the guests. The others were trying to either subdue the berserk vamps or protect the humans in the crowd, or both.

Two vamps grabbed Sean. Snarling, his eyes bright gold, he fought them, tearing free of one as the other sank his teeth into his arm.

Fangs tore into my left shoulder from behind. I cried out and tried to get myself free, but the vamp's teeth were locked in my flesh and she was out of reach of my whip. I staggered as she gnawed on my shoulder, sucking at the wound and trying to drag me to the floor. A second vampire sank his fangs into my right arm.

"Alice!" Sean struggled to free himself from the two vampires who were hanging onto him, trying to keep them from biting into his throat.

My blood magic, already seething in response to the bloodbath around us, blazed in response to my attackers' fangs piercing my flesh. Not counting Charles's bite while I was in a coma, I'd only been bitten by a vampire against my will twice before: once at my grandfather's compound, and once investigating a case a few years ago. Neither of those vamps had lived long enough to regret their mistake.

Given these vampires weren't in control of their actions, I chose, like Sean, not to kill my assailants. I had to disable them, however, and ensure none of my blood remained in their bodies, where it might be used against me.

As a blood mage, I sensed my blood as it passed from my veins through the fangs of my attackers. When they'd consumed just enough to make my counter-offensive effective, I pushed air magic through the flow. Both vampires twitched, aware on some level of my magic invading their bodies, but too consumed by bloodlust to disengage.

"*Burn*," I gasped.

My air magic ignited my blood in the vamps. They screeched and released me, white fire pouring from their mouths as my air magic burned away my blood and boiled their insides in the process. Faces and bodies contorted in agony, they collapsed.

Sean tore free of the vamp who'd latched onto his arm and punched him in the throat. The vamp fell, gurgling, as two more vampires subdued his other attacker.

His clothing torn, Charles appeared out of the melee, bloodied sword in hand. I supposed that answered my question about whether he knew how to use the blade. He skewered a young vamp who'd charged straight at us with fangs bared. The much-younger vampire staggered and fell, his hands on the wound in his abdomen.

Sean apparently decided the way Charles wielded the sword meant he could defend us. He returned his cutlass to his belt, ripped off his jacket, and pressed it to the wound on my shoulder as I held my bloody right arm against my body.

"Get us to the closest exit," Sean told Charles.

Before Charles could answer, I sensed a surge of familiar dark power. This magic carried an ancient scent I recognized.

Valas.

The power rushed over us like a rolling bank of fog. With it came a wordless command. My knees gave out and I collapsed. Sean tried to catch me, but he staggered and fell as well. Charles took two steps and went down next to us.

All around us, vampires, humans, and shifters dropped where they stood—even the members of the Chicago Court and our own Court.

Valas stood in the midst of the sprawled, torn, and bloody bodies. Dark power radiated from her in nearly visible waves. Her eyes glowed brightly with magic and rage.

The strange dark magic surged again, battering Valas's power. She staggered, almost falling against a nearby table—one of the few items of furniture still standing. Almost everything else in the room, from the oak barrels to the faux ship's masts to the stacks of crates, had been completely destroyed. Blood and torn bodies were everywhere. Two human servers lay to my right. They were dead, their throats torn out. One of the mermaids floated face down in the tank, the water around her still and red.

As the last of the combatants collapsed, the fighting ceased and the ballroom fell eerily silent. Beside me, Sean snarled and went still. I fought to stay awake, unwilling to surrender to the compulsion to close my eyes.

A familiar cold voice touched my mind. *Sleep now,* Valas commanded.

The words barely registered before I lost consciousness.

3

_____

"Well, that's one way to put an end to a blood frenzy: knock everyone out and sort it out later," Sean said, drying his face with a towel. His anger sizzled on my skin. He'd woken up furious and his anger hadn't abated, even after we'd showered.

"It worked," I pointed out, grimacing as I stepped into a blue short-sleeved sheath dress and my shoulder protested. "It was complete chaos in there. I honestly don't know what else she could have done. There were too many blood-crazed vamps. It was almost a massacre. The consequences—not to mention the death toll—would have been terrible."

We'd awoken in one of the private apartments at Northbourne, laid out next to each other on a king-sized bed. The bedside clock indicated it had been about two hours since Valas put us all to sleep. It was now a little after two in the morning.

Neither of us liked that we'd been manhandled in our sleep, though Sean had recognized the scents of who'd carried us upstairs: Bryan Smith and his sister Adri. While I slept, Adri had removed my blood-splattered dress and corset, leaving me in the long white shift I'd worn under the dress. Bryan had cleaned and dressed my wounds. The bite on my forearm was little more than two ragged punctures, but my left shoulder looked like a lion had gnawed on me. Sean's arm had already healed, leaving a faint scar where the vamp had torn his flesh. Bryan had left Sean in his bloodied pirate attire, minus his boots, belt, and cutlass. I appreciated that Bryan and Adri had seen to our comfort rather than enforcers we didn't know.

I couldn't help but think some of Sean's anger resulted from being denied the opportunity to rip my bodice. I decided I'd find a way to make it up to him.

Sean kissed me. "How are your wounds?"

"They hurt," I admitted. "Both bites were deep. I'll be able to fix them with a healing spell when I get home."

He growled and reached for the clothes someone had left hanging neatly on the back of the bathroom door: a dress shirt, slacks, and tie. "I'd like to know what the hell happened."

While we finished getting dressed, I told him about the strange surge of dark magic I'd sensed just before all hell broke loose. "It seemed to originate on the far side of the ballroom from where we were standing, but I don't know what caused it," I added. "Maybe the vamps know something."

Someone knocked on the door of our suite. Sean went to answer it as I stepped into the heels that had been left for me. I would have preferred jeans and boots, but I had to make do with what the vamps provided. At least the dress was business casual and not an evening gown. I tried to braid my hair, but my injured shoulder made that impossible, so I left it loose.

I emerged from the bedroom to find Sean talking to Bryan at the door. Bryan was out of his costume and back in his familiar all-black Court enforcer garb. "Hey, Bryan."

"Miss Alice," he rumbled. "How are your shoulder and arm?"

I made a wry face. "I'll live. Thanks for patching me up—again. Did you guys figure out what caused all those vamps to go nuts?"

"We believe so." Bryan gestured toward the corridor. "Would you follow me? Madame Valas would like a word."

I would have given almost anything to be home in bed, but we needed to know what the hell had happened. "Sure. Lead the way."

We followed Bryan down several hallways until we reached the wide second-floor gallery of Northbourne's enormous five-story lobby. A half-dozen black-clad Court enforcers waited there, on high alert. Sean's eyes shone gold, a reflection of his own tension and that of the guards.

Bryan led us down the grand staircase to a hallway I'd been down once before, when I'd come to ask for Valas's help to save Sean's life. At the end of the hall, two guards stood at attention outside a set of double doors leading to Valas's audience chamber.

Bryan paused outside the doors. "Madame Valas wishes to speak to Miss Alice privately," he told Sean. "You can wait here, back in your room, or in the library."

Sean and I exchanged a glance. Given the outburst of deadly violence at the gala, I would have preferred to stay together, at least until we knew what had happened.

Bryan read my expression and gave me a nod. "We understand your reluctance. Valas gives you her word—no harm will come to either of you."

A muscle moved in Sean's jaw. "I'll wait here," he said. He stationed himself along the wall next to the guards, radiating displeasure.

The guard on the right opened the door. Bryan ushered me into the chamber. The enormous room was lit by a chandelier high above our heads. When I'd met Valas here before, we'd sat in two chairs by the fireplace, but no chairs waited there now—just a large, open space, and no fire.

My attention went to the massive conference table that took up almost half of the remaining area. Valas rose from the head of the table as we entered and the others followed suit. She wore a long, dark red dress, her waist-length black hair loose. To her right sat Charles, in a suit.

Elizabeth stood to Valas's left, across from Charles, in slim black slacks and a white blouse.

"Madame Valas, Madame Elizabeth, may I present Miss Alice Worth?" Bryan said formally, escorting me to the table.

"Welcome, Miss Worth," Valas said, gesturing to the seat at the opposite end of the table from her own. "Please, join us."

Bryan held my chair as I sat. The others returned to their seats. I glanced at Charles. Like the others, his expression was inscrutable, but I knew him well enough to see concern in his dark eyes.

"Mr. Smith attended to your injuries?" Valas asked as I settled in. Bryan took a position to my right.

"Yes, thank you." I folded my hands on the table. "Do we have a body count from the blood frenzy?"

Elizabeth's brow furrowed. "You are impolite."

"What Miss Worth lacks in courtly manners, she makes up for in ability," Valas said.

I blinked. Did Valas just compliment me in a back-handed vampire sort of way?

Elizabeth raised an elegant eyebrow. "So you have told us, but I sense no magic in her."

"Nor will you," Valas said. If she was irritated by Elizabeth's interruptions, she didn't show it. "More than two dozen humans were severely injured. Regrettably, though aid was rendered quickly, five of the victims were beyond our help."

That number was both much lower than I'd feared and much higher than I'd hoped. "What about the vamps who attacked me?"

"They will recover." She inclined her head. "We extend our thanks to you and Mr. Maclin for your judicious use of non-lethal means of defending yourselves. Please accept my sincere apologies for our failure to protect you while you were here as our honored guests. I will, of course, extend my apology to Mr. Maclin as well, through official channels."

"On behalf of myself, then, apology accepted."

Valas gestured to one of her guards, who brought a tray with a crystal decanter. I recognized it as the vessel I'd seen filled with blood at the gala. It was nearly empty now.

Valas rested her forearms on the arms of her chair. "Miss Worth, I remind you everything discussed and seen in this room is confidential."

"I remember." I leaned forward to study the decanter. "Is this what caused the frenzy at the gala?"

Elizabeth's frown deepened at my blunt question, but Valas nodded. "We believe so. Our investigation indicates the vampires who succumbed to bloodlust imbibed champagne enhanced with blood from that decanter. Vampires who drank blood from other vessels did not exhibit violent behavior."

"Are the affected vamps still violent?" I asked.

Valas hissed. "Yes, though the effects are slowly waning. Those affected are isolated in holding cells and will remain so until we are certain they are no longer a danger to others."

I noticed a slight tightening of her eyes, almost a flinch. Valas was in pain. I'd seen her stagger when she was putting us all to sleep. The amount of power it must have taken to knock out hundreds of vamps, humans, and shifters... I couldn't even really wrap my brain around it. The older and more powerful the vamp, the more difficult it would be to force them into sleep, and a significant percentage of the vamps at the gala were at least several hundred years old—some even older.

"How can I help?" I asked.

"We wish to know the cause of the bloodlust," Valas said. "After examining the donors, I am satisfied it was not the blood itself that triggered violence, so the source must be the decanter. You must determine how this vessel caused such violence. Naturally, you will be compensated for your insight."

I'd long since become accustomed to her demands, so her imperious tone didn't bother me as much as it might someone else. What *did* bother me was that she was plainly worried, and with good reason. The attack was a shot across the bow of Valas's Court. The frenzy could have easily resulted in Sean's death or mine. For those reasons alone, I wanted to know who or what was behind it, so they could be held responsible for the deaths they'd caused.

I pondered the decanter. "I can't do it here, and I'm sure as hell not taking that thing or its magic home with me. I need a mage's work space, where I can contain the magic in the spellwork. Anyone who has shared blood with a vampire needs to be at least a couple of rooms away—and obviously no vamps in the vicinity, in case the magic gets loose. Can I use one of the work areas downstairs?"

Valas nodded. "Of course. You will have whatever you require."

"Where did this decanter come from?"

"We have others investigating the vessel's origin. We require your expertise in regard to the magic." Valas gestured at the guard, who picked up the tray. "Mr. Smith will escort you to the mage work area and see you have all the materials you require. I will take your report when you are finished."

As I stood, Elizabeth spoke. "You are a native of Chicago, are you not, Miss Worth?"

I paused. "I did live there, years ago, yes."

Alice Worth, the young woman whose identity I'd stolen after I'd escaped from my grandfather, was born and raised in Chicago. I'd lived there only a few months—just long enough to change my appearance and become Alice—but long enough to make the statement true. Other vamps had Charles's gift of sensing deception, so I always phrased my answers carefully, just in case.

"How is it you did not register as a mage until your move to this city?" Elizabeth asked, her tone icy. "If your skills are as Madame Valas describes, I should have preferred to have you in *my* Court. Why do you choose to serve here and not in your place of birth?"

I didn't *serve* anyone anywhere, but this wasn't the time or place to argue that point. "I made mistakes in Chicago, Madame Elizabeth. The name Alice Worth was infamous there for a while. I wanted—I *needed*—a fresh start." All true, as far as it went. The real Alice had made headlines for her hard-partying ways in the wake of her parents' deaths. People generally found it understandable that she'd wanted to get away from all that notoriety.

"Mid-level mages like yourself are common, and yet here you are treated most uncommonly." Elizabeth tilted her head. "It is perplexing."

I was a high-level mage, not the mid-level mage my mandatory federal registration indicated, but few people knew that. I suspected Valas was aware, but clearly she hadn't revealed that information to Elizabeth.

"Madame Elizabeth, perhaps this conversation is better saved for after Miss Worth has explained the magic used on the decanter," Valas interjected.

"Of course." Elizabeth's smile was downright chilling. "Do carry on, Miss Worth. We shall talk once this unpleasantness is concluded."

"I look forward to it," I told her. I hoped she couldn't sense that lie.

I started toward the door, but Valas raised her hand. "Please, use my private stairs," she said, gesturing toward the back of the room. "A much faster route to the lower level."

I didn't like leaving Sean out of this, but we were playing in the Court's sandbox, as my late mentor Mark Dunlap used to say, and they made the rules. I generally made it a policy to pick my battles with them. "Fine. Let Sean know where I've gone, if you will."

Valas nodded. "As you wish." Her eyes went to the decanter. "Have care, Miss Worth. We await your findings."

"As soon as I have some answers, you'll be the first to know." I glanced down at my knee-length dress. "One other thing: can I borrow some pants?"

———

Twenty minutes later, wearing a borrowed black T-shirt and pants, I stood barefoot in one of Northbourne's many mage work areas, hands on my hips as I studied the decanter sitting on the concrete floor in front of me.

"I'm sensing some seriously bad juju from that bottle," said the ghost to my right. As usual, Malcolm appeared to be wearing a long-sleeved button-up shirt, jeans, and wire-rimmed glasses. "I know you prefer to handle dangerous magic by yourself, but I'm glad you summoned me to help you with this, just in case. We don't need a repeat of the Dracula Incident."

I rolled my eyes at his verbal capitalization of the phrase *Dracula Incident*. "It wasn't an *incident*, Malcolm. It probably wasn't even Dracula who threatened me."

He scoffed. "A crazy-powerful vampire who speaks Romanian tried to throttle you with his magic for destroying a vamp object of power once owned by Vlad Tepes, aka Dracula. That's got to be Drac himself who said you should fear him. I'd say that qualifies as an *incident*."

"Even if it was, I'm sure he's got much bigger fish to fry than little ol' me." I waved a piece of chalk. "I'm going to start drawing a circle and some heavy-duty wards. Whatever magic is in that decanter, I don't want it going anywhere. You feeling up to charging the wards and holding them while I focus on the decanter's spellwork?"

"I was born ready," Malcolm said with far too much cheer. "You do the spells, I'll power them. Let's get this show on the road."

I crouched and started to draw. "What's the rush? You got a date tonight?" When he didn't answer, I glanced up. He flitted, clearly embarrassed. "You *do* have a date!" I crowed. "Mal-colm and Li-am sitting in a tree—"

"Alice, I will zap you if you finish that sentence," he warned me.

I went back to drawing runes, but I wasn't about to let it go. "That's two dates in two days."

"It's not a date. I'm just going out to the bordello and he's going to show me around."

Malcolm had met Liam when we'd attacked a very haunted former brothel belonging to my grandfather. Like Malcolm, Liam was a ghost. A former employee of the brothel who'd died a century ago, Liam had helped Malcolm rally the rest of the ghosts to help with our attack. They'd hit it off and had been spending a lot of time in each other's company since.

"A romantic moonlight walk—er, moonlight float—around the grounds of a haunted Victorian mansion. Sounds like a date to me." I finished one set of wards and started work on the next.

"You should probably just focus on what you're doing, Nosy Nellie." Malcolm hovered nearby, his arms crossed.

"I can draw these wards in my sleep." Still, he had a point. I stopped teasing him and focused on drawing spellwork.

By the time I finished, my fingers were cramping, my shoulder was killing me, and my legs hurt from crouching. I grimaced as I stood and studied the spellwork on the floor. "I think that ought to do it. Nothing's getting through those wards. You see any chinks in the armor?"

He shook his head. "Nope. Let's get in there and figure out what made those vamps go crazy."

I left the chalk on the work table and picked up a black crystal and a small knife from the assortment of supplies the vamps had provided. Crystal and blade in hand, I went into the circle and sat cross-legged on the floor in front of the decanter. I channeled power into the crystal so it would act as a beacon, drawing in any magic that got loose.

I closed my eyes and breathed deeply several times, inhaling through my nose and exhaling out my mouth, to clear my mind and focus. "Ready when you are," I murmured.

The circle flared around me as Malcolm funneled energy into it. The wards ignited, forming a barrier around me and a second smaller circle around the decanter.

Normally, I would have simply invoked one of the protection spells held in the crystals on my bracelet, but against unknown magic I needed stronger safeguards.

Using the small ritual knife, I cut two runes into the inside of my left forearm. I'd done this so often and the blade was so sharp that I barely flinched as I made the shallow cuts. I set the knife down and invoked the blood magic protection spell. My body tingled, a familiar sensation.

I closed my eyes, lowered my shields, and explored the spellwork on the decanter.

The spells had faded, but I immediately recognized the same dark magic I'd sensed just before the vamps went berserk. That confirmed, at least in my opinion, that the decanter *was* the source of the blood frenzy. Since the vessel was almost empty, they'd served almost all of the blood before the spell kicked in. Whoever had spelled the decanter had designed it so the frenzy affected the most vamps possible.

I delved deeper into the spellwork. Though it was fading fast, I saw the runes that formed the spells and sensed the magic of the person who'd created them. I recognized runes for *hunger* and *feed*, along with a few others that must have been the triggers for the spell. The runes were familiar, but the magic was twisted somehow. The gray vamp magic had black threads, but not the same color as black wards made with natural magic like mine. This black was like a void rather than a color, and it wove through the vamp magic like a barbed-wire fence.

I wanted to know more about that magic, but even with the protection spell playing around with unfamiliar magic was a quick way to get dead— or worse. Malcolm would probably be able to interact with it safely, since most spellwork had little effect on spirits unless specifically designed to do so.

I opened my eyes. Malcolm read my expression and frowned. "What's wrong?"

"The magic in the spellwork on the decanter has something in it I've never seen before."

"Well, that's not good. I can't imagine there's much of anything magic-related you haven't seen. What color is it?"

I described the odd void-black color the best I could.

"I don't think I've ever seen that either," Malcolm admitted. "And I don't like it one bit, so don't mess with it. We can do some research and I—"

Dark magic erupted from the decanter as a decaying spell fractured and broke. I caught a whiff of a strange musty odor in the half-second before Malcolm reacted and strengthened the circle around the decanter. I scrambled back from the inner circle as the magic battered the barrier, trying to escape.

A tendril of black-and-gray magic got through the inner circle, swirled in the air, then zipped straight toward me at lightning speed, completely ignoring the pulsing energy in the black crystal. The wisp went through my blood-magic protection spell as if it didn't exist—which shouldn't have been possible—and hit me square in my chest. The magic plunged through my breastbone like a blade or a barb made of ice and stuck there.

"Alice!" Malcolm shouted.

Icy tendrils of unknown void-black magic snaked out of the magical barb stuck in my chest, moving under my skin like tentacles. My investigation of the decanter's spellwork had just gone south in a big way.

I tried to unleash my blood magic on the invading magic, but for some reason, my blood magic couldn't burn the void-black tentacles. That had never happened to me, as far as I could recall. My blood magic had burned away everything from the werewolf virus to a meth-like drug called Black Fire and the vamp magic in the Tepes stone. It could even burn out sedatives and other drugs I'd been injected with at my grandfather's compound in his never-ending attempts to make me compliant. Whatever this magic was spreading through my body, I had no way to counter it.

One icy tendril snaked toward my pounding heart. I had no doubt what would happen if the void-black magic touched my heart.

"Malcolm, I can't stop it," I gasped, clutching my chest.

The outer circle and wards around me dropped instantly. Malcolm appeared above me, his expression grim. He plunged his cold hand into my chest and ripped the void-black magic tendrils out. The agonizing sucking sensation was like someone pulling a live and very angry octopus out of my chest. My heart stuttered. I screamed and fell backward, smacking the back of my head on the floor.

Malcolm vanished, taking the black magic with him. I sensed a familiar tingle of magic that told me he'd jumped to one of the spell crystals in my basement at home.

The remaining magic inside the inner circle dissipated as the last of the decanter's spellwork broke and faded. My chest still tingled like something cold was stuck in it. I couldn't sense the strange magic anymore, so the feeling might just be an echo or a fading trace. I rolled to my side and curled into a ball, instinctively trying to protect my chest, though the damage had already been done.

The door to the hallway was ripped off its hinges and tossed aside with a crash. Sean rushed in, his eyes bright gold. "Alice!" He stopped outside the wards I'd drawn, growling audibly. He knew not to touch me if I was using magic, but that didn't mean it was easy for him to stay back.

When I didn't immediately reassure him, he snarled. "Talk to me."

I started to tell him I was all right, but that wasn't true. I'd made a promise not to tell him I was okay if I wasn't. Instead, I reached out so he knew it was all right to come to my side.

In a blink, he knelt beside me and pulled me into his arms. "What the hell happened?" he demanded. "Are you hurt?"

"Seriously bad magic on that decanter." I let out a shaky breath. "Whatever it is, neither I or Malcolm have ever seen it before. It broke loose and some of it got into me. Malcolm tore it out and jumped back to my house."

He growled. "Are. You. Hurt?" he repeated.

I didn't want the vamps to know about the icy splinter in my chest, and I had to assume they were listening. "I don't think so." I glanced around the room. "They have cameras in here, don't they? You were watching."

He glanced up and to the right, toward tall shelves full of books and binders. I couldn't see the camera, but I'd figured someone was watching. I was a little surprised they'd let Sean observe, however.

"I told them I wanted to watch over you," he said in answer to my unspoken question. "Valas agreed it was a reasonable request. Is it safe for Court personnel to come in here?"

"It's clear. The magic dissipated quickly after the spellwork fractured. It was probably designed to do so. Makes it harder to track its source."

His chest rumbled. "Your shoulder's bleeding again. Let's get this wrapped up and go home so you can heal that wound and check on Malcolm. Can you stand?"

"Yes." I sounded more certain than I felt.

He rose and set me on my feet. The little icy splinter of magic in my chest twinged.

Bryan came in, followed by Charles. The vampire approached us, his brow furrowed. "Alice, are you well?"

"I'm fine," I assured him. He'd sense the lie but I hoped he wouldn't call me on it, not when others were watching and listening. "Should I give my report to you or directly to Valas?"

He studied me, probably trying to figure out what was wrong. "Madame Valas awaits your findings," he said finally. "May we escort you to her audience chamber?"

I wondered if it would just be Valas waiting for me or if Elizabeth would be there too. "Sure."

He glanced at Sean. "It will be necessary for you to wait again in the hall, as Alice's report is on a confidential matter related to Court security."

"Fine," Sean said. His voice made it clear the situation was anything but.

From her throne-like chair at the head of the conference table, Valas listened to my report on the decanter's magic without expression.

My other listeners, Elizabeth and Charles, were equally inscrutable—until I described the unfamiliar void-black magic and the way it erupted when the spellwork broke. Elizabeth's head tilted slightly and Charles's brow furrowed. Clearly, both were alarmed by this new threat.

When I finished, Valas asked, "You say you have not encountered this form of magic before. Speculate on its origin and purpose."

"I can tell you it's not a form of natural magic like I have or any form of vampire, demon, or shifter magic I've ever come across."

"Is the magic perhaps fae in origin?" Elizabeth asked.

I shook my head slowly. "I don't think so, though I have only limited experience with fae magic. All types of fae magic I've encountered were shades of violet, and this magic, as I said, is a deep black. I can't say for certain, but it didn't...*feel* fae."

"What are the possibilities, given what you know?" Charles asked.

I considered. "There are other esoteric forms of magic out there, almost too many to count. There's witch magic, I suppose, or various forms of occult magic. It didn't feel witchy, but that's doesn't mean it wasn't. If it's occult, there are nearly infinite forms of that kind of magic from around the world, and that's outside my area of expertise." I drummed my fingers on the arm of my chair. "Whatever it was, it felt...twisted."

"What does that indicate, precisely?" Elizabeth asked.

"When I say magic seems twisted, I mean someone has corrupted the original forms of the spellwork through curses or evil intent, for lack of a better word. The spell was designed to ignite the frenzy only after a lot of vamps had consumed the spelled blood. That tells me your event was targeted by someone with a lot of power and skill, who hoped for a bloodbath. They probably didn't realize you could put us all down and stop the carnage before it spun completely out of control. You said you had someone looking into how that decanter ended up being used at the gala. Any leads so far?"

"None," Valas said, and she looked distinctly displeased about it. "No one can recall how the decanter came to be in use or where it was stored prior to tonight's event."

"Well, at least this was an isolated incident." When no one replied, I added, "It *was* an isolated incident, right?"

"Not precisely." She tapped one slender finger on the arm of her chair, as if debating whether to tell me more. "Similar items have surfaced elsewhere, including a bowl that appeared mysteriously at the Chicago Court and a statue in the gardens of the Court of New Orleans."

The shape of Elizabeth's eyes changed. She wasn't happy Valas had revealed that information to me.

An attack on a Court or its people was a sign of weakness. Tonight's bloodbath would significantly damage Valas's reputation and undermine her leadership, especially since it had occurred during a state visit by another Court. I was still much more concerned by the loss of human life, but the cost to her authority couldn't be discounted.

"Those Courts are understandably reluctant to reveal details of the effects of those objects," Valas continued without looking at Elizabeth. "However, I have it on good authority blood was shed in both cases—both human *and* vampire. Rumor indicates other objects have caused deaths at other Courts around the country."

"And no one has any idea where these things came from?"

"None that any of my agents have uncovered." Valas rose. Elizabeth and Charles followed suit. "The Court is grateful for your insight into the vessel's magic. If you have nothing further to add, I am sure you would like to return home and attend to your injuries."

"Valas, I can help—"

The shadows gathered around Valas. Her dark magic prickled on my skin. "Mr. Smith, please escort Miss Worth and her companion to their vehicle and see they depart safely."

If we'd been alone, or if it had only been Valas and Charles in the room, I might have pushed the issue, but Elizabeth's presence complicated matters. The head of the Chicago Court was already much too interested in me; I didn't need to attract more of her attention than I already had by arguing with one of the most powerful vampires in this hemisphere.

I wanted to know where that damned decanter had come from, who'd spelled it, and why, but for some reason Valas didn't want me to get involved. I was sure she had a reason for excluding me. I was equally sure when I found out what it was, I wouldn't like it.

Bryan escorted Sean and me out of Northbourne. When we stepped outside, we found a familiar man leaning against a Maclin Security SUV parked in front of the wide front steps.

"Ben!" I said with a smile. "I didn't know you were our chauffeur tonight."

Ben Cooper grinned and met us at the bottom of the steps. Sean must have asked him to come pick us up. He was third in the pack hierarchy behind Sean and beta Jack Hastings. I was glad to see he appeared fully healed after nearly being killed during our attack on my grandfather's haunted mansion. Even with a shifter's healing abilities, three silver bullets and a fall from a helicopter had almost proved fatal.

"Hey, Alice," he said, reaching to open the front passenger door for me. "Hop in."

I climbed into the SUV and settled in my seat with a sigh. The dashboard clock said it was almost four in the morning. I was anxious to get home to check on Malcolm.

Sean got into the driver's seat as Ben took the seat behind me. He'd barely shut his door before Sean took off, driving around the circular parking area in front of Northbourne and accelerating down the quarter-mile-long driveway leading to the gate.

Sean put his hand on my leg and squeezed. "Now that we're alone, I want to know if you're all right."

As always, I hated giving Sean any reason to worry. "I don't know," I admitted, rubbing my chest. "Something feels weird, right here where the magic hit me."

"Weird how?"

"It's like a little icicle or a cold pin is stuck in my skin." I grimaced. "It doesn't hurt; it's just uncomfortable."

His hand tightened on my leg. "This isn't good, is it?"

"No, it's not. The good news is I don't sense any of that strange void-black magic. It might just be a trace or an echo left over from the initial hit. If so, it should fade fairly quickly."

A shadow moved behind his eyes, as if his wolf was pacing in agitation. "And if it doesn't fade?"

"Then I'll have to figure out how to remove it." *Easier said than done*, I thought wryly.

Ahead of us, Northbourne's imposing new gate rolled open and the retractable barricade slid down into the ground. Sean drove through the gate and turned onto the main road.

"How are you feeling, Ben?" I started to turn to talk to him and winced at a stab of pain in my shoulder. "Ow. Damn it."

Ben leaned forward so I could see him without turning around. "Take it easy. I'm good, thanks to you. What happened at the gala?"

Sean filled Ben in on the blood frenzy during the drive to my house. My eagle-eyed werewolf had seen enough of the carnage in the ballroom to give Ben a thorough report on what went down between the flare of dark magic and when Valas knocked us out. Ben didn't like that Valas had put us to sleep any more than Sean did.

As Sean drove and talked, I tried poking at the little cold splinter in my chest in every way I could think of using my air and earth magic, blood magic, and even the traces of golden shifter magic in my blood. Nothing seemed able to affect it. All forms of my magic slid past the splinter like it wasn't there.

By the time Sean turned into my driveway and parked behind my car, I was tired, frustrated, and increasingly worried about Malcolm. I'd expected him to jump to me at some point during our journey to let me know he was all right, but he hadn't.

My house was a modest two-story Victorian. I'd bought it a few months after moving to the city five years ago. I gave a little wave to the Vamp Court SUV parked in front, though the windows were so darkly tinted I couldn't see who was inside. In response to the threat my grandfather posed, the Court had provided twenty-four-hour security for my home. They would have preferred for me to live at Northbourne, or at least for me to have Court bodyguards, but I'd refused. It was bad enough they were watching my house; I wasn't going to have vamps or their employees breathing down my neck everywhere I went.

As Sean unlocked my front door, the familiar sensation of my house wards eased a little of my tension. "Home sweet home," I sighed.

We went inside, passing through the wards, which had been keyed to let us through but would prevent anyone else from entering my home.

Sean locked the door behind us and kissed me on the forehead. "Heal your shoulder."

I kicked off my shoes and headed for the basement door. "I'm going to check on Malcolm first. I'll let you know what I find out. Ben, are you heading out?"

"Not yet," he told me. "Casey's working night shifts at the hospital this week, so I might as well hang out and go over next week's installation schedule." He was the installation manager for Maclin Security.

I had a feeling they had more to talk about than security systems. Whatever it was, I was sure Sean would benefit from being with a member of his pack. "I'll leave you to it, then."

Sean's worry prickled on my skin. "Let me know if you need help."

"I will," I promised.

I went downstairs, passing through the heavy-duty wards that protected my basement. I'd divided my basement into two main areas: a library, with tall bookcases and a reading table, and an open work area with warded cabinets, a work table, and three concentric circles inscribed in the floor. Papers, books, little tubes of henna, pieces of chalk, half-made crystal jewelry, and assorted crystals in a variety of colors littered the work table.

The item I was most interested in was a medium-sized blue crystal I usually left in the middle of the table—the crystal Malcolm went to whenever he jumped to the basement. When I spotted the crystal, I stopped dead in my tracks, my heart in my throat.

At first, I thought the crystal had cracked. When I moved closer, I realized what I saw weren't cracks—they were thin void-black lines in the quartz.

"Oh, no," I breathed.

The deadly magic from the decanter had followed us home.

4

SEAN STUDIED THE BLACKENED CRYSTAL, HIS BROW FURROWED. "WHAT does it mean?"

I rubbed my face. "A couple of things. First, the magic from the decanter attached itself to Malcolm when he ripped it out of me. Second, that magic is capable of passing through my wards."

He growled. "I didn't think anything could get through your house wards, much less your basement wards."

"I didn't either." I leaned against the work table, sick with worry. "To my knowledge, nothing ever has, until now. I thought when Malcolm pulled the magic out of me and jumped here, it would burn away when he passed through my wards. I bet that's what he thought too. That might be why he didn't jump out of the crystal like he normally does—he knows he brought the magic with him and he doesn't want to risk releasing it."

"Can it get out of the crystal?"

I started to shake my head, then reconsidered. "I don't know," I said instead. "Ordinarily I would say no, but this magic isn't playing by the rules. It went through my blood magic protection spell back at Northbourne, then passed through both sets of my home wards. Just because it hasn't gotten loose yet doesn't mean it won't."

"So why hasn't it escaped yet?"

"That's a damn good question." I thought about it. "That crystal has a heavy-duty containment spell Malcolm cooked up. He powered my circles at Northbourne and the magic couldn't escape them. He was able to grab the magic that was in me when I couldn't, pulled it out of me, and brought it back here. Maybe my magic can't do much against it, but for some reason, *his* can." I thumped my forehead with my fist as I tried to make sense of this.

"Is it because he's a ghost, or for some other reason?" Sean asked.

"My best guess is because he's a ghost. He's a mage, so his magic is natural like mine, but it's affected by the fact he's a spirit. It's a different...flavor, I guess you could say. Something about that difference makes it at least somewhat effective against this magic." I rubbed my temples. "I have to get Malcolm out of there, and I need a ghost's energy to create a circle capable of containing the magic if it escapes the crystal."

"Where are you going to find a ghost who's willing to help you out?"

I pulled out my phone and scrolled through my contacts. "I have an idea."

His mouth quirked. "You have a ghost on speed-dial?"

Despite my worry about Malcolm and the strange magic, I smiled. "No, but I know someone who can help find a ghost who'll probably be able and willing to assist."

The phone rang a few times and then Cait Morse, my friend and an ace freelance researcher, answered. As I'd hoped, she sounded wide awake. Cait was even more of a night owl than I was. "Hi, Alice! How are you?"

"Having kind of a bad day, Cait. Sorry to get right to the point, but I need some info fast."

"I'm on it," she said briskly. "What are you looking for?"

"I need the full name of a man named Liam who worked and died at that old bordello out on Pierce Road. I don't have the exact year of his death, but it would have been around 1910."

Computer keys clicked rapidly in the background. "Your projects are always the best. You know, other people ask me to dig up boring stuff like secret former spouses, financial records, and so forth. You want me to find a man named Liam who worked at a brothel and died in 1910." A pause. "Bingo. Henry Liam Ashe, spelled A-S-H-E. Born October eighteenth, 1890, in Shreveport, Louisiana, and died April twenty-third, 1911. Cause of death listed as influenza."

"Only twenty years old," I mused. "Malcolm, you cradle-robber."

"What was that?"

"Nothing. How the heck did you find that so fast?"

"Hey, you're good at your thing, I'm good at mine. What else do you need? A copy of the death certificate?"

"Nope, just the name. Thank you, Cait. How much do I owe you?"

"For this? A cup of coffee sometime."

I smiled. "I just discovered a new place called Brew a Cup Tea and Coffee House. I'd love to take you there for coffee and scones. Later in the week, maybe?"

"Have your people call my people. Take care, Alice."

"You too, Cait. And thanks again."

We disconnected. I exhaled and looked at Sean. "Well, I guess it's high time we met Malcolm's maybe-boyfriend."

He squeezed my hand. "Never a dull moment around here."

I finished drawing the runes in the smallest of the three concentric circles inscribed into my basement floor and stood with a wince.

Sean, who was leaning against my work table with his arms crossed, frowned. "You should heal your shoulder. I smell fresh blood—you're bleeding through the bandage."

"I know." I set my chalk on the table and rested my forehead against his chest. "I've got to help Malcolm first."

He kissed the top of my head and held me by my upper arms. "You're exhausted and you're hurt. I'm worried about him too, but you can't always put everyone else ahead of yourself." His eyes shone softly. "Let's get this done so you can heal your wounds. What else do you need to summon Liam?"

I picked up a small ritual knife. "Just some blood and magic. You won't be able to see or hear him, so don't freak out when I start talking to thin air."

He smiled. "You talking to an invisible ghost is not even in the top five weirdest things I've seen or heard today."

I went to the runes I'd drawn on the floor, crouched, and cut the pad of my index finger. I traced two of the runes I'd already drawn with my bloody finger and magic rose.

I closed my eyes, spooled earth magic, and invoked the spellwork on the floor. It flared in a burst of bright green I saw with my mind rather than my eyes. "*Henry Liam Ashe,*" I said. The last part of the spell ignited in a puff of earth magic.

My wards tingled. A shout of alarm startled me. I opened my eyes to find a wide-eyed young man with red hair, wearing a shirt, vest, trousers, and cap, floating above me, looking equal parts confused and terrified. Malcolm was right—he *was* cute.

"Liam?" I asked, scrambling to my feet. "I'm Alice, Malcolm's friend. Do you remember me from the other night out at the mansion?"

He floated back and forth in consternation. "I...yes. Yes, I remember you, ma'am." He had a hint of a Louisiana accent. "I remember him too," he added, indicating Sean. "I'm sorry, I'm a bit out of sorts. Where am I?"

"My house," I told him. "I apologize for summoning you like this, but I need your help. Malcolm's in trouble."

He flitted in place the way ghosts did when they were very angry or afraid. "Where is he?"

I gestured at the blue crystal on the table. "In there." I explained briefly that Malcolm and I had encountered unfamiliar magic and he'd become trapped in the crystal with it.

Liam stared at the crystal. "I don't know much about your kind of magic. I want to help, though. Tell me what I need to do."

"There's something about a ghost's power that can affect the magic and contain it, so I'd like to use some of your energy to power a containment spell around the crystal."

"That's fine, ma'am," he said.

"Alice," I corrected him. "I'm sorry we had to meet like this. Malcolm's told me so much about you."

"And I've heard quite a lot about you." He glanced back at Malcolm's crystal, clearly worried. "What should I do?"

"You don't need to do anything—just let me channel your energy into this circle. I won't drain you, I promise. Will you be able to find your way back to the house, even if you're diminished?"

He nodded. "I'm...tethered, Malcolm calls it. I'll be all right. The house has a lot of power and I'll regenerate fairly quickly once I'm back home."

I reached for the crystal on the table. Sean blocked my hand. "Let me move it."

I blinked at him, taken aback. I couldn't remember a single time he'd physically intervened to stop me from doing something magic-related. "Sean, I've got this."

A muscle moved in his jaw. "That magic has already tried to kill you once."

Irritated, I nudged his hand aside and picked up the crystal. "Thanks for offering, but as long as the magic is in the crystal, there's little danger."

Sean's anger sizzled on my skin as I took the crystal to the smallest circle and placed it in the center. I used a piece of chalk to draw containment wards in the circle.

As I worked, Liam drifted over to me. "Is Malcolm all right?"

I hesitated. "Honestly, I don't know." I hated saying it out loud, but Liam deserved the truth. "There's not much that can harm a ghost, as you know, but that magic is like nothing I've ever encountered before. If you're ready, let's get him out of there."

"I'm ready."

I rose and wrapped my fingers carefully around his arm. He felt like cold, thick fog. "When I start to draw energy from you, don't resist," I told him. "You might instinctively try to block me, but try not to fight it. I promise I won't harm you."

"All right." He braced himself.

Gently, so I didn't startle him, I drew Liam's power into myself and channeled it directly into the wards I'd drawn in the circle. After an initial flinch, he didn't resist, so I slowly increased the flow of energy. He was surprisingly strong for a ghost who'd been around for more than a century, probably thanks to the energy in the bordello. I wished I could visit the house again and learn more about it, but since it belonged to my grandfather, I doubted I'd ever go back there for any reason. I didn't really like Malcolm going there, but I couldn't ask him not to see Liam, and as long as he stayed away from Moses, he was probably safe...or as safe as any of us could be, I supposed.

The wards hummed and glowed softly with bluish-silver spirit energy. I closed the connection between us and let go.

He drifted away from me, his eyes closed. He was almost transparent.

"Liam? Are you all right?" I asked.

He opened his eyes. "Yes," he said, uncertain and a little unsettled. "I've never had anyone drain me before. It didn't feel very pleasant."

"I know. I'm sorry. I wouldn't have asked you to do it if I had any other choice."

I crouched and studied the crystal. Normally, I had to touch it to release Malcolm, but I didn't dare, in case the magic escaped the crystal with him. I'd have to get him out another way, from the safety of outside the circle.

"I'm going to pull Malcolm out," I said, glancing back at Sean.

"Getting him out will probably leave me dazed for a minute, but I'll be all right."

"Thank you for warning me." He was still furious, but I didn't have time to worry about that right now, not until I knew whether Malcolm was all right.

I took a deep breath, exhaled, and closed my eyes. I reached for the cool blue-green trace of magic in my mind that was my connection to Malcolm, grabbed it, and pulled. The containment spell on the crystal resisted. I cleared my mind, breathed deeply, focused completely on the trace, and yanked hard.

Everything went black.

I wasn't out very long—maybe ten seconds at most. When I opened my eyes, I was staring directly up into a familiar pair of angry golden eyes.

I blinked to bring Sean's face into focus. His hands were under my head. He'd managed to catch me before I'd smacked my head, which I appreciated, since it was still sore from hitting the floor in the mage workshop at Northbourne.

His expression was grim. "You passed out. Are you all right?"

"I'm fine." I sat up, ignoring Sean's angry growl, and found the ghostly form floating silently inside the circle in front of me. "Malcolm?"

"Hey, Alice." His voice was quiet. Much too quiet. Fear wrapped icy fingers around my heart.

I staggered to my feet with Sean's help. He held onto my arm as I swayed. Malcolm's form appeared slightly out of focus. He wasn't nearly as solid as he should be.

I pulled out of Sean's grip and moved closer to the barrier of the circle. "What's wrong?"

"I damn near didn't make it—that's what's wrong." Malcolm drifted back and forth slowly, his form shifting around like sand in a glass. "That's some bad, bad magic. Whatever it is, we need to stay the hell away from it."

I glanced down at the crystal. The black lines were still visible. "Can you sense any of the magic in you, or did it stay in the crystal?"

"I think it's stuck in the crystal. When you pulled me out, it felt like you forced me through a sieve. All the bad magic was stripped out, and it's just me left...or what's left of me." His voice was hollow.

"I'm so sorry."

"It was the only way to save me without letting the magic out. You did what you had to do."

It didn't escape my notice that he didn't say it was okay, or reassure me he would be okay. I had the sudden, terrible feeling Malcolm was putting up a front and he was in worse shape than he appeared to be.

Malcolm turned his attention to Liam. "Hey, Liam."

"Hello, Malcolm." Liam floated over to the circle, careful not to get too close to the barrier. "I'm real glad to see you."

"You too." Malcolm mustered a brief smile. "I'm sorry you got pulled into our circus."

"She asked for my help. She didn't demand it," Liam said. "I was glad to do what I could."

"What should we do with that crystal?" I asked Malcolm. "I don't want to destroy it; that might let the magic out."

He thought about it. "You still have that warded box you used to contain the cursed pocket watch that belonged to Hilda Yates?"

"Who's Hilda Yates?" Sean asked.

I sighed. "She was a client from a couple of months ago, when you and I weren't together. The damn pocket watch destroyed half of her house and a couple of trees. Some family heirloom. Anyway, yes, I still have the box," I told Malcolm. Realization dawned. "You did the containment spellwork on it. It would be perfect for keeping the crystal contained. Good thinking."

He didn't smile. "I have my moments."

I broke the containment circle. Malcolm drifted toward Liam. Despite the strain on both their faces, they were an almost unbearably cute couple.

"If you don't mind, I'd like to go back to the bordello with Liam," Malcolm told me. "I'll recharge faster there because of the nexus, without having to draw energy from you."

I sensed there was more to his desire to leave than wanting to reap the benefits of the nexus. Whether he wanted some distance from me, the crystal, the weird magic, or all three, he needed space. I understood that need all too well.

"Go ahead. I'll get the crystal stashed away in the meantime." I took a step toward him. "Thanks for saving me at Northbourne. That magic could have killed you, but you didn't even hesitate to grab it."

"You would have done the same if the situation were reversed." He gave me a brief smile that had a little of the Malcolm I was used to seeing in it. "Get some rest. I'll see you tomorrow."

"Be careful."

"Always." He glanced at Liam. "Ready to go?"

"Yes. I'll see you again soon, Alice," Liam added. They vanished.

I rubbed my face. My shoulder throbbed and my head hurt. "Come to the Vampire Court gala, they said. It'll be fun, they said." I tried for a light tone, but it didn't quite work.

Sean moved in front of me, his expression stony. "Where's the box?"

"In one of the cabinets."

He headed for the back wall, where four large cabinets were lined up side by side. "Which one? The standard spelled ones, or one with black wards?"

I followed him. "One of the black-warded cabinets. I'll get it, Sean. What's this sudden overprotectiveness about? Since when do you insist on doing things for me?"

Silently, he stood aside as I traced four runes on the door of the second cabinet. The deadly black wards that safeguarded its contents shimmered. I opened the cabinet.

"Where is it?" he asked.

I pointed. "Second shelf."

"Can I pick it up?"

"Yes. It's not dangerous. The wards are designed to contain what's in it, not to harm anyone. I just put it in this cabinet as an additional safeguard against anyone who tried to track Malcolm's magic."

He picked it up carefully, two-handed, and turned around. His eyes glowed bright gold. "Let's get the crystal stashed before that magic can do any more damage."

Gingerly, I picked up the crystal and carried it like a live grenade. I set it carefully in the box and closed the lid. I traced two runes on the lid and a little frisson of magic indicated the containment wards were active.

"What now?" Sean asked.

I took the box from him and put it in the cabinet. "Now, you're going to answer my question about you being overprotective."

A pause. "Alice, I'm struggling."

"Struggling with what?" I asked, worried.

He ran his hands through his hair. "From the moment we met, you made it clear you weren't looking for a protector or someone to fight your battles for you. I love your strength and determination and fearlessness— you know I do. But damn it, I could do *nothing* to help you when Valas put us all down. I could do *nothing* when that magic broke loose and almost killed you. I can't make you heal your shoulder, which I can smell bleeding as we stand here."

He flexed his hands, a sign of how tense he was. "Our bond is growing stronger, and it's getting harder and harder for me to stand by while you risk your life. It doesn't just make me angry when you're injured and I feel helpless, Alice—it *hurts* me."

Stunned, I asked, "How long has this been going on?"

"The past few weeks, I've noticed it more. It's gotten noticeably more severe since the night Caleb tried to kill you."

"When I saw my wolf for the first time and felt shifter magic inside me."

"Whether that's the cause or it's just that our feelings for each other have gotten stronger recently, I don't know. What I *do* know is I'm not some possessive alpha male asshole, but I want to protect you and I don't want you to be hurting."

"I want to protect you and I don't want *you* to be hurting," I told him. "And I'm not an asshole either."

I'd hoped that would lighten the mood, but he shook his head. "You don't need a protector, Alice—I know that. You can protect yourself. You don't like me or anyone else to do things for you, or risk themselves on your behalf. I know that too."

He cupped my face in his hands. I leaned into the warmth of his touch. "I'm struggling because some part of me—maybe the wolf, maybe the man—wants to protect you and take some of the risks you're used to taking, like picking up dangerous crystals, but you're too stubborn and proud to let me. And damn it, I want you to stop putting me off and heal your shoulder *now*, not an hour from now or two hours from now or sometime later today after you've done everything you can for everyone else."

I bristled.

He kissed my forehead. "I'm not going to pretend anymore that it's not gotten more difficult to watch you risk your life. Even while I'm in human form, I'm hard-wired to want to keep you safe. I'm not going to apologize for that, or for loving you as much as I do."

In my bare feet, I was too short to kiss him without his cooperation. "Lean down," I ordered him.

He bent his head and I kissed him thoroughly. My shoulder hurt too much for me to put my arms around his neck, so I wrapped them around his waist and rested my forehead on his chest. He smelled so good, like a forest in spring.

"You don't have to apologize for wanting to keep me safe," I said into his chest. "But I'm not going to apologize for wanting to keep *you* safe, because I love you too." It still felt weird to say it, but not in a bad way.

He growled quietly. "You should've let me pick up the crystal and move it to the circle."

"Look what that magic did to me and Malcolm. There's no way to know what it might do to a shifter. What if that magic had hurt you?"

"What if that magic had hurt you, *again?*" he countered. "And there was no Malcolm to rip it out of you this time. That's all I could think about, watching you pick that damn thing up. You have to let me take some risks sometimes, Alice. We've had this conversation—I get to decide when and where I fight. Sometimes that fight is with a demon, and sometimes it's with dangerous magic."

He tipped my chin up with his fingers and kissed me again lightly. "This is what it means to be partners. Sometimes you do the heavy lifting. Sometimes I do. That doesn't mean either of us is weak. It means we are stronger when we share the load."

"I can't very well argue with that, can I?" I asked dryly.

He smiled. "No, you really can't."

I started to close the cabinet doors. My gaze fell on a small book on the middle shelf. All the books in the cabinet were illegally printed texts on blood magic theory and practice. Information about other forms of natural magic was easily shared online, so I rarely used my books on those topics anymore. Since blood magic was illegal, however, it was difficult to find information about its use online without risking arrest by the feds— hence the books.

I took the book from the shelf. "Can I borrow your pocketknife?"

Sean handed it over. I took the book to my work table and opened it to the back page. I slid the point of the knife under the endpaper—the page glued to the inside back cover of the book—and slit it very slowly around the edge. Sean watched as I separated the page carefully from the cover.

When I moved the page aside, it revealed a four-by-six photo lying face down. Two of the edges were singed and faint creases marked where the photo had been damaged.

I handed Sean his pocketknife. "When I escaped from Moses's compound in Baltimore, I couldn't take anything with me because I was afraid he would suspect I'd engineered the explosion to get away. I had only the half-burned clothes I was wearing...and this in my pocket." I turned the photo over and held it out.

Sean took the photo carefully, handling it by its edges where it hadn't been singed, and studied it. I hadn't seen it since I'd hidden it in the book almost five years ago. I'd considered destroying it a hundred times and talked myself out of doing so each time, despite the danger of keeping it. It was perhaps the only tangible evidence linking me to Ava Selene Murphy, Moses's supposedly deceased granddaughter.

"How old are you in this photo?" Sean asked quietly.

"I'd just turned eight." I swallowed around the lump in my throat. "By then, it was rare for me to get to spend much time with both of my parents, and even more rare for Moses to let us take a picture together. Maybe he felt something close to human that day. He let us spend the afternoon together and even let me go outside with them to play. We had guards with us, of course. One of the guards took this picture. My parents —Moira and John—walked with me between them. We held hands and even played tag for a while." I tried to smile, but it didn't work.

"They look like kind people," he told me.

"They were." I leaned against the table, suddenly so tired I could barely stand. "Two months later, they were dead. Moses found out they planned to take me and flee the country. He burned them alive in their house and then took me to see their ashes so I'd know what happened to people who crossed him."

Sean growled. "Even knowing what I know about Moses, it's difficult for me to imagine someone being that cruel to a child. Did you know about their plan to run?"

I took a shaky breath. "I had no idea; neither of them ever let on. Maybe that's the only reason Moses didn't kill me too, or maybe it was because he figured there would be no one else to help me once they were gone, so he thought I'd give up fighting him."

"There's no *give up* in you," Sean stated. "When I look at you then and now, I see determination. I always have, since the first night I met you. I can't believe he ever thought he would break you, the selfish, cruel bastard. He should have known by looking in your eyes it would never happen."

"I guess I should be grateful he never came to that conclusion, or I probably wouldn't be standing here."

I took the photo from him. In it, I wore a sundress my mother had bought me and a hat to shield me from the summer sun. My mother had on a sundress too, with sandals, her long hair braided the way I liked to wear mine now. As usual, my father wore jeans and a gray T-shirt, his brown hair a little long around his ears. We'd all smiled for the picture, but anyone looking at the photo could tell this was no happy family outing—even without noticing the high wall in the background.

"Should I burn it?" I startled myself by asking the question out loud.

Sean tucked the photo back into the book and closed it. "If you have to ask, I don't think you should. If it's ever the right time to get rid of the picture, you'll know. Until then, keep it safe."

I took the book to the cabinet and slid it into the gap on the shelf where I'd found it. I closed the cabinet doors and reactivated the black wards. They hummed on my skin, a familiar sensation.

Sean wrapped his arms around me from behind and kissed the top of my head. "Thank you for sharing that with me, Alice. It means a lot."

I crossed my arms over his and squeezed. We stood like that for a long moment. Finally he released me. "Now, if we're done down here, please go upstairs and heal your shoulder so we can get to bed. You've got a lunch date with Arkady, I have to be in the office by eleven for a staff meeting, and it's already almost dawn."

I yawned hugely. "You present a compelling argument."

He took my hand. "Come on, sleepyhead. Let's get some shut-eye."

As we climbed the stairs, I glanced back at the cabinet where I'd stashed the spelled box containing Malcolm's crystal. Despite the danger, I needed to know more about the strange void-black magic—particularly how to protect myself and others from it. I had a feeling we hadn't seen the last of it. I'd be damned if I was going to let someone's twisted magic hurt people I cared about or cause another massacre.

For now, however, I let Sean usher me upstairs. I turned off the basement light and closed the door.

5

AFTER MY LUNCH WITH MY FRIEND, COURT INVESTIGATOR ARKADY Woodall, I spent most of the afternoon at my house doing laundry and some long-overdue housecleaning. Malcolm worked on spellwork in the basement, trying to come up with a way to contain the void-black magic if we encountered it again.

He'd returned from the bordello this morning as Sean and I were getting ready to leave. My ghost had some of his old cheer back and recharging at the nexus near the house had significantly improved his condition. He assured me his brush with the void-black magic didn't seem to be affecting him nearly as much today. Still, I fretted.

Meanwhile, the icy splinter remained stuck in my chest. I'd expected to find it faded or gone when I woke and was surprised and concerned to find it felt no different this morning than last night. Sean had been reluctant to go to work because of the splinter, but I'd told him it didn't feel like active magic—just an echo. Once I'd promised to let him know if anything changed, he left, angry and worried.

Around three, the wards around my yard tingled, indicating I had a visitor. I peeked out the window as a delivery truck parked in the driveway. A young man in a uniform emerged from the vehicle with a small overnight box and headed up the sidewalk toward my front steps.

I opened the door as he reached the porch. "Hello," he said cheerfully and held out the box.

I stepped out through my wards to take it and glanced at the label. I'd ordered a pair of pants from an online retailer a day or two ago, though I'd thought I'd requested standard ground shipping, not the much more expensive overnight option.

The driver returned to his truck as I closed my front door and locked it. I tore the strip off the box and opened the flap, expecting to see a folded pair of pants.

Instead, I saw...bubble wrap. Huh.

I pulled out the box's contents. It looked like a prepaid phone, the kind I used to make calls or send messages to people when I didn't want their contact information or a record of those contacts on my primary phone.

I unwrapped the phone and found a small folded paper with it. When I saw it, my heart thudded in my ears. The outside flap had a drawing I recognized instantly: a small bottle with a skull and crossbones on the label and next to it, a rose.

A bottle of poison and a rose was the signature of a black-hat hacker I knew named Cyanide Rose, or Cyro. She'd helped Sean and me on several cases, communicating only through burner phones and encrypted e-mails, but we'd known nothing about her—or even that she was a she. Then, a little over a month ago, while Sean and I were on vacation in the Bahamas, I'd run into an African American woman who called herself Ree. We'd chatted at a bar on the beach before she'd vanished, leaving behind a note much like the one I held in my hand. In it, she'd warned me my aunt Catherine, who I'd severely injured with a bolt of lightning, had woken, and said if I needed help to let her know. She'd addressed the note to my real name, Ava.

The revelation that Cyro knew my true identity had left me shaken and fearful—as had her subsequent disappearance. I'd heard nothing from her since and the only number I'd had for her no longer worked. Her warning had indicated she might be on my side or willing to help if Moses came after me, but then she'd vanished for close to six weeks without a word.

I opened the note.

Take this phone to Fields Park. Go alone. Sit on the white bench near the pavilion. Don't take your own phone with you or turn this phone on until you reach the bench. Wait for my call.

Beneath that message, she'd written the words *Rum punch* and the initial *C*.

We'd enjoyed rum punches together in the Bahamas. I supposed it was her way to prove the message came from her, if the little drawing and her handwriting weren't enough.

"Malcolm," I called.

The ghost came up through the floor from the basement. "What's up?" he asked.

"Do you have time to go with me to the park?"

He looked surprised. "To play on the swings, or what?"

"Someone sent me a burner phone and told me to go to the park so they can call me. I need backup just in case this is not what it seems."

He immediately became serious. "Yeah, of course I'll go. What about Sean?"

"I'll message him. My instructions were to leave my own phone here."

He frowned. "Who's supposed to be calling you?"

"Cyro."

He blinked. "You're kidding. Do you think it's him?"

We'd all assumed Cyro was male because her electronically altered voice was male. I'd save explaining that for when we were in the car. "I think so, but I'm not taking any chances. That's why I'm bringing you."

"Sean's not going to be happy about this."

"I know, but I need to talk to Cyro. I have to take the chance."

I sent a text. *Me: Going to Fields Park to get a phone call from our black-hat friend. Instructed to leave my own phone at home and come alone. Taking M with me. Will call you within 1 hour or send M if meeting goes south.*

The response was almost immediate. *Wolf: I'll meet you at the park.*

I remembered my conversation with Sean last night, how it had gotten progressively more difficult for him to stand by while I risked my safety. His concern meant a lot to me, but I didn't want to lose this chance to talk to Cyro.

Me: I know what I'm asking is hard for you to do, but please stay a few blocks away. I need to take this call.

A pause. Finally, my phone buzzed. *Wolf: All right. Be safe. I love you.*

Me: Love you too. Yep, still felt weird.

I put the phone on the kitchen counter and headed for the door. "Let's go, Malcolm. I'll fill you in on the way."

I drove through the main gate of Fields Park and turned right, heading for the music pavilion on the park's east side.

"So Cyro knows who you are," Malcolm said as we arrived at the parking lot near the pavilion. "That must have really freaked you out."

"It did, big time." I parked in the mostly empty lot and spotted a small white bench near some trees. "Especially since I haven't heard from her in damn near two months. I had no way of knowing what she was going to do with that information."

"Well, let's find out, I guess."

I got out of the car and headed for the bench with Malcolm floating along beside me.

I sat on the bench and glanced around. Fields Park was enormous. This area was mainly used for outdoor concerts and stage plays and was deserted at the moment. In the distance, children yelled at the playground. A few runners went by on the path, but if someone was watching me, I couldn't see them.

I took a deep breath and turned the phone on.

A minute went by. Two. My palms grew damp.

The phone buzzed in my hand. The screen read *Incoming Call—Number Unavailable*. I took a deep breath and answered. "This is Alice."

"Hello, Alice. This is Cyro." The electronic voice was different than the one she'd used before, but something about the cadence indicated they were the same person.

Still, I needed to be sure. "What item of clothing of mine did you compliment when we were at the beach?" I asked.

I heard an odd sound. It was a laugh, filtered through the program she used to alter her voice. "Your shell bracelet," she said.

I exhaled. "Where have you been? Are you all right?"

"I'm fine for the moment," Cyro said. "I have to keep this call brief, but the short version is that two days after I saw you, the feds kicked down my door less than three hours after I vacated the premises. I had to go deep underground and stay on the move. I kept an eye on your situation as best I could, but I couldn't risk contacting you until I was relatively sure I could do so without putting either of us in jeopardy. Then you led an attack on your grandfather's haunted bordello the other night, and now I'm calling to check in."

I had a lot of questions—how she'd found out who I was, why she hadn't sold me out to Moses, why she'd warned me about Catherine—but I didn't want to waste time if she was going to end the call soon.

"I need to find someone," I said instead. "I don't know how much it will cost, but I think you might be the only person I can ask."

"Who are you looking for?"

When I hesitated, she added, "I'm sure you've realized based on our previous interactions that I don't like people who prey on others. That includes cabal leaders like Moses Murphy. You have no reason to trust me, I suppose, but you came to the park and followed my instructions, so you must be willing to take a chance."

"I'm looking for a man named Daniel," I said quickly, before I could change my mind. "He would have been associated with the Murphy cabal about thirty-one years ago, but left, possibly headed for California. He may be a shifter—specifically, a werewolf. That's all I know, or think I know. It's not much to go on."

"No, it's not, but I've found people with less information than that. If I locate this person, what kind of information do you need? Just a location, or a full background?"

"Full background," I told her. "The cost will depend on how long it takes you to find him, am I right?"

"Yes, or how long I look until I determine he can't be located based on the information you provided. How urgent is this?"

I swallowed hard. I'd just put something into motion I almost wished I could take back, but I also knew I needed this answer, and soon. My grandfather might go looking for Daniel too, and I wanted to find him first.

"Very urgent," I said finally. "Daniel's life may depend on finding him quickly. You might be racing someone else—someone who probably wants him dead, or wants to use him to get to me."

"I'll bump this to top priority," Cyro said briskly. "I'll be in touch, but not on this phone. Destroy it."

"Wait, tell me one thing: why are you helping me?"

A pause. "I told you I don't like people who victimize others. The details aren't important, but a year or so ago I ran across a couple of videos on the dark net of torture sessions at the Murphy compound. The recordings were about ten years old. The face of the girl being tortured was obscured, but you can guess who's in the videos."

My blood turned to ice.

"They apparently kept records of torture sessions. Who leaked them, I don't know. I couldn't find the source, and believe me, I tried. I scrubbed every copy I could find on the dark web. I inserted code into others that either bricked the device that downloaded them or included a tracer I could use to find them and turn them in to the feds."

I struggled to get a breath. My chest hurt like someone was standing on it.

"I sure as hell never thought I'd meet that woman in the videos or talk to her," Cyro added. "If nothing else, I figured no one had ever lifted a finger to help her back then, so the least I could do was do something for her now."

"Thank you," I managed to say.

"You're welcome. I have to end this call. I'll be in touch. Remember to destroy this phone."

"I will," I promised. "Be careful and watch your back."

"You too." The call ended.

Malcolm floated back. We stared at each other.

"Alice, I am so sorry," he said finally.

"Me too." I turned off the phone, opened the back, and took out the sim card. I got up and headed for my car. "Jump to Sean and tell him I'm fine."

"Okay, but before I go, who's Daniel?" Malcolm asked, floating along beside me.

"Sean can fill you in." I shook my head. "I don't want to talk right now. Tell Sean I'll see him later tonight for dinner. I need some time to think."

Malcolm hesitated.

"Go, please." I put the phone and sim card on the pavement behind the front driver's side wheel of my car. "I need some space. See you back at the house later."

"Okay, Alice. Summon me if you need me." He vanished.

I backed over the phone twice, then picked up the pieces and tossed them into a nearby garbage bin. When I drove out of the park, I didn't head home or toward Sean's house or anywhere in particular. I just drove.

I was relieved to hear Cyro was all right and not in the hands of the feds or anyone else. That relief was eclipsed by anxiety about the search for Daniel and the horrible sick feeling about the recordings of me being tortured at Moses's compound. The recordings were on the web. Cyro had seen them. Who else had watched me scream and cry and bleed? What sick, twisted people had gotten pleasure from my pain? I felt violated and angry and I had no one to take that anger out on.

I was doing better these days about talking things through with Sean and Malcolm, but sometimes I still needed to withdraw, especially when I felt vulnerable. Part of me hated that Malcolm knew about the videos and he'd probably told Sean, though I was really trying not to keep secrets from either of them anymore. Next to forgiving myself for the terrible things I'd done on my grandfather's orders, being honest was the most difficult challenge I'd faced since escaping his cabal five years ago.

I made a sound that was halfway between a sob and a growl.

Familiar pressure built in my chest and shifter magic surged. I shoved it down. During my confrontation with Moses, he'd mentioned my mother. In my anger, I'd gone a little bit wolfy—complete with bright gold rings in my eyes. It was the first time that had happened to me. In the days since, I'd sensed something coiled in my chest that hadn't been there before, as if I'd unlocked or unleashed some part of myself that had stayed dormant until now.

My reaction had tipped Moses off that I might be part shifter and the man I'd believed was my father, John Briggs, who'd raised me as his own, might not be my biological father. A magic mirror had recently shown me a forgotten memory of a conversation I'd overheard as a child between my parents. My mother had said if Moses knew who my real father was, he would have killed all three of us. His reaction to the sight of my golden eyes had confirmed he was angry about the possibility I might be part shifter. Why, I didn't know.

Sean had seen my eyes go wolfy, but we hadn't talked about it. He was waiting for me to process it. I didn't know how to go about making sense of this new, strange part of myself, or what power might have been unleashed within me—either by the werewolf attack I'd survived, my growing bond with Sean, or by some other factor I didn't yet understand.

Eventually, I headed north, toward my new favorite coffee shop: Brew a Cup Tea and Coffee House. I wasn't sure what I needed right now, but there was a good chance Brew a Cup's witch owner, Carly Reese, would know how to help.

6

FIFTEEN MINUTES LATER, I ARRIVED AT BREW A CUP. CARLY STOOD
behind the counter when I walked in. She wore an apron embroidered
with the shop's name over a button-up shirt, jeans, and ankle boots. Her
dark hair hung loose around her shoulders. Just the sight of her and the
smell of fresh coffee took a little of the tension out of my shoulders. I was
also relieved to see her assistant behind the counter was a blonde girl I
didn't recognize and not Katy, the pink-haired witch who'd helped hex me.

Carly looked up and smiled as I approached. "Alice, hi!" Her smile
faded. "Oh, dear. You're having a bad day. Trust me to make you a cup of
tea?"

I really wanted coffee, but I'd come here for help and that meant
taking her advice. "Sure, okay. And one of those blueberry scones, please."
I handed over my card.

"You got it." She ran the card and handed it back, then slid two mugs
across the counter. "Back booth. I'll meet you there."

I dropped a five in the tip jar and took the mugs to the back corner
booth. The table had a little placard that said RESERVED. I slid into the
booth, sensing the familiar parchment-scented magic of Carly's *Hush* and
Look Away spells that made conversations in the booth inaudible to others
in the shop and gently encouraged them to ignore us.

Carly joined me a few minutes later, a pot of tea in one hand and a
plate in the other. She set the pot on a mat on the table, handed me my

scone, and sat down across from me. "You want to tell me what's going on, or is it something you'd rather not share?"

I broke the corner off my scone and ate it while I thought about how to answer. Heavenly. I didn't know if Carly somehow baked magic into her scones, but it wouldn't surprise me in the least to find out she did. I took a moment to savor the deliciousness.

"Couple of things," I said finally. "I found out a while back there's a chance my dad wasn't my biological father. Today I started the process of trying to find the man who might be."

"Wow. That's a huge step. I can't imagine how exciting and scary that would be." She lifted the lid off the teapot and took out the infuser. The wonderful aroma of the tea wafted across the table. She poured tea into my mug. "What else?"

"Just some...unsettling news that's left me feeling really angry and violated." I blew on the hot tea and inhaled its scent. "I want to get back at the people behind it, but I can't. I needed some alone time, so I took off and ended up over here."

"Ah—that would explain this." She took her phone out of her apron pocket and waved it. "Sean sent a text a minute ago asking if you happened to be here. He says you don't have your phone with you."

I sighed. "I don't."

"Can I tell him you're here and we're chatting and you'll see him later?"

"Yes, please."

She sent the message. The phone buzzed. She smiled. "He says you're in good hands and he'll have dinner ready at six thirty."

"Tell him thank you." I sipped my tea. I couldn't tell what was in the blend, other than definitely chamomile and something lemony. We sat quietly and drank tea for a few minutes.

She refilled our mugs and set the pot back on the mat. "Have you heard anything back on your offer on the new house?"

"Monday morning, Sean got a call that the house is ours...if we want it."

She tilted her head. "You're not sure if you do?"

I toyed with my mug. "I think I am, but every time I picture actually signing on the dotted line and moving into the house, I get sick to my stomach."

"Well, I'd say that's completely normal. Buying a house is a big commitment. It's not that aspect of the decision that's scaring you."

"It's moving in with Sean," I admitted. "Seems silly, given I've accepted that I'm his consort and I have a role in his pack, but—"

"Have you really accepted that status?" she interrupted. "Your voice changes when you say the word *consort*, and you always refer to the pack as *his* pack, not *our* pack. You say you have a role *in* the pack, but that's not the same as being *part of* the pack."

"I'm not part of the pack," I argued. "I'm not a shifter, and I don't have a mate bond with Sean or share bonds with the rest of the pack."

"You're avoiding the question. When I first met Ben Cooper at my house, he referred to you as *our Alice*. You told me he said you were pack after you were attacked by Caleb. Your pack has accepted you as one of their own. Now you need to decide whether or not to acknowledge it."

I started to argue, then closed my mouth. Damn it. "It's really annoying that you always see things so clearly," I said instead.

She shook her head. "I don't always see things clearly. Your hesitation is pretty obvious; it doesn't take an empath or a witch to see it. The last time you were here, I told you that you need to work on forgiving yourself and accepting your past. Until you do that, you're going to struggle to accept Sean's love and your place in your pack, not to mention figure out who you really are under all those layers you've made around yourself. Worse, you'll sabotage your own happiness and hurt those who care about you, and they don't deserve that."

"You never pull any punches, do you?" I asked wryly.

She smiled. "I can be gentle when the situation calls for it, but with you I think a tougher approach is needed. You're not fragile; you can take it. I'm not telling you anything you don't already know, if you're being honest with yourself." Her smile faded. "We all need tough love sometimes. I'd rather tell you the truth now and risk ruffling your feathers than not say it and wish later I had."

Sounded like she'd learned that lesson the hard way. "Thanks, Carly. I'm working on it, I promise. I told Sean something on Monday I've never told anyone else. It was a really difficult story to tell about something I did a long time ago. He listened, and then he told me he didn't think I did anything wrong but he understood why I feel I did. He accepted it, just like he seems to accept pretty much everything else about me."

I'd told Sean how I'd become Alice Worth after finding the real Alice dead from a drug overdose in the basement of an abandoned building in Chicago. Not only had I stolen her identity, but I'd disposed of her remains and buried her ashes in a park. My guilt over that had gnawed at me for the past five years.

I finished my tea. "I also found out he knows a hell of a lot more about me than I thought he did, and he doesn't think I'm a monster."

"That's got to help with the whole forgiving-yourself thing. A big reason you can't forgive yourself is you don't think anyone else forgives you, but that's not the case, is it? Sean forgives you. Malcolm does too, I bet." She smiled. "Maybe you're not the irredeemable wretch you thought you were."

I smiled back. "Maybe not."

"I think you're hanging onto something, something beyond your memories and guilt." She tilted her head. "Maybe it's some*one*, not some*thing*, that's holding you back from committing to Sean and his pack. Is that possible?"

I started to say no, then thought of Charles and the way I felt when he touched me. The way my blood surged when he was near, and not just after he'd healed me—from almost the moment we'd met, five years ago. And try as I might, I couldn't pretend it wasn't true.

"Maybe," I confessed. "It's complicated."

"Of course it is. Matters of the heart always are." She reached into her pocket and took out a small, purple velvet bag. She slid it over the table to me. "I made this on the full moon so it's got some extra kick."

I opened the bag and found an oval-shaped amethyst about the size of my thumbnail, wrapped in gold wire and designed to be used as jewelry. "What's this?"

"A charm I've spelled to help you find some peace on days when the darkness in your head gets to be too much. It will need recharging from time to time, so when you feel it losing power, let me know."

"Thank you, Carly." I left the charmed stone in the bag and tucked it into my pocket. "I'll put it on my bracelet when I get home."

Her phone buzzed. She glanced at the screen and her expression darkened. "Goddess, not again," she murmured.

"Go ahead and take care of that if you need to," I told her.

With obvious reluctance, she read the text message. Her shoulders sagged. She put the phone face down on the table and reached for the teapot.

"Trouble?" I asked.

"A mountain of trouble." She refilled her cup and mine and set the pot back on the mat.

My mouth quirked. "So, you want to tell me what's going on, or is it something you'd rather not share?" I asked, echoing her words to me from earlier.

She smiled, but it was brief. Her unease worried me. "It's a rather long story, I'm afraid."

Despite her reluctance, I sensed she wanted to tell me, or at least tell me part of it. I also thought she might need help. "I'd like to hear it, if you'd like to share."

Instead of talking, she took a minute to think and drink her tea. I waited, blowing on my own tea and nibbling on the crumbs from my scone.

Finally, she folded her hands around her mug. "Trouble's name is Morgan. We've known each other our whole lives. Our parents were in the same coven, and we grew up like sisters." She glanced at me. "Do you have any siblings?"

"Not that I'm aware of," I said, trying not to let on how much that question hurt. My mother had told me not long before she died that she'd wanted at least two or three children, but after my grandfather took me away, she'd never had any more, unable to bear the pain of losing another to him.

Carly touched my hand. "You have Malcolm," she reminded me. "A brother in spirit, so to speak. No one loves you like a sister or brother, and no one can hurt you like one, either." She fell silent again.

Telling this story seemed difficult for her. I knew what it was like to tell a difficult story, so I waited quietly while she gathered her thoughts and her courage to tell it.

"There's something you need to know about me to understand the current trouble," Carly said, sipping her tea as if drawing strength from the hot liquid. "The coven Morgan and I grew up in—the one our parents were in, and the one her mother is still the High Priestess of—practices black magic."

I couldn't help it; at Carly's words, I recoiled slightly. She flinched at my reaction.

"I'm sorry," I said immediately. "I've no right to—"

"It's all right," she interrupted me. "You have every right to react that way. I feel the same way when I think of some of the magic we used and spells we cast. Our Rede says *And it harm none, do as you will*, but there are a surprising number of ways to define *harm*, and an equally surprising number of ways to justify actions many would consider harmful. That's if you care about following the Rede at all—which black magic practitioners don't." Her mouth twisted. "They weren't always a black magic coven, though. When I was young, before Morgan's mother Bridget became the High Priestess, our coven, like most, practiced gray magic."

I frowned. "I've heard that phrase. What exactly does that mean, *gray magic*?"

"Gray magic, as you probably would think, is part white magic and part black. For example, if I do a spell or ritual to help someone without them knowing, that's gray magic, since you should never do magic on someone, or on behalf of someone, without their permission, even if it's to help them. The spelled sand I made for you to help break house wards was gray magic, since that sand had the potential to cause harm if you'd hit someone with it instead of the house. If I cast a spell on my threshold so those who come into my house can't lie, I'm stealing their free will, so it's gray magic. Does that make sense?"

Hmm...I wondered if Carly really did have a spell on her threshold that made it impossible to lie. I'd have to remember that for the next time I visited her home. "It does. I can see why most witches would fall into that gray category. In my experience, life is mostly gray areas."

"That's been my experience too," Carly said. "Under our former High Priestess, while Morgan and I were growing up and until we were in high school, the coven was a wonderful place to be: a sisterhood, a brotherhood, a place of peace and strength."

Unlike witches, mages were usually solitary practitioners. Harnads were an exception—groups of blood mages working together to create powerful magic that often took the form of destructive energy or curses. Many mages formed communities for sharing knowledge and support. I'd had no such friends growing up as a prisoner of my grandfather, and until Malcolm, I'd never worked closely with any mage. I found myself more than a little jealous of Carly's childhood coven and the comfort she'd found there.

"So, how did it all go wrong?" I asked.

"Our High Priestess passed away. Morgan's mother Bridget took over, as we'd all expected her to. What we *didn't* expect was the direction she took our coven. The changes happened gradually—a darker spell here, a change to a ritual there—but within a year, some of us realized Bridget had a very different vision for our coven—one that took us farther from white magic. I didn't like it, but everyone told me not to worry so much because she would never lead us astray. I felt the Goddess's light grow dimmer in my heart every day, but everyone said..." Her voice drifted off.

She sighed. "It's hard enough to be a sixteen-year-old girl. Try being sixteen *and* a witch *and* the only dissenting voice in a coven slipping farther out of the light and into darkness. The pressure from everyone, including my parents, was too much for me to fight. Eventually I lost my way, and I stayed lost for several years. I did spells I didn't want to do and participated in rituals I wanted no part of."

Hearing Carly's story brought back a lot of my own memories from my years as a prisoner of my grandfather's cabal. I'd never gone to the Dark Side, not really, but I had done bad things and harmed a lot of people. Usually I'd had no choice. Sometimes, however, I'd simply done as I was told, too weary, too beaten, too tired of fighting to say no—and those were the memories that haunted me most.

To distract myself, I asked, "How did you find your way back?"

She refilled our mugs with tea. "The details aren't important, but during our sophomore year in college, Morgan tricked me into helping her with a curse that hurt several people. I let her use some of my blood to invoke the spells she used. The blood of two strong witches whose families have practiced the Craft for a dozen generations is a nuke."

I could only imagine. "So what did you do?"

"I was horrified. I confronted Morgan. She denied she'd deliberately misled me, or that she'd intended the curse to have such a terrible effect, but I knew she was lying. I couldn't tell the police Morgan was behind what happened—they'd think I was nuts. So I told my parents Morgan had tricked me into letting her use my blood. I figured if the police couldn't hold her accountable, our coven would. There's no twisting the Rede to justify what she did."

"Let me guess: the coven closed ranks around her."

"Yup, every one of them. Even my parents." For the first time since I'd met her, I saw fury in Carly's eyes. "And Bridget and the others helped. They advised her on the spellwork and covered for her afterward. Three weeks later, I left the coven. I haven't spoken to my parents or anyone else from it since."

"And they just let you leave?"

"Not at all. They threatened, begged, threatened some more. I transferred to Tulane for my final two years of college and studied with a hoodoo witch in New Orleans. Her protection spells are terrifyingly powerful. I made it clear if anyone from the coven tries to hurt or kill me, they'll die bleeding from their eyeballs." She studied me. "I suppose now you think *I'm* a monster."

"Far from it." I topped off my mug and frowned at the teapot. "Not to change the topic, but we've had a half-dozen cups of tea. How is this teapot still full?"

She smiled. "I'm not a witch for nothing, Alice. You've probably also noticed the tea stays hot in your mug."

I pondered my mug, belatedly noticing the runes etched on the bottom. "I could use that spell to keep my coffee warm," I mused. I glanced at her phone. "So, is that Morgan texting you?"

She nodded. "My parents and the others stopped trying to talk to me about ten years ago, but I hear from Morgan every once in a while." She pinched the bridge of her nose. "You might as well know—Morgan's daughter works here. You've met her."

Realization dawned. "You're kidding me. Pink-haired Katy? The witch who hexed me and tried to break up my relationship with Sean is Morgan's *daughter?* Why in the name of Aleister Crowley would you have Morgan's daughter here working for you?"

She sighed. "Katy ran away from Morgan and the rest of the coven a year ago. She wants no part of black magic anymore. Something happened to her. I don't know what; she'll tell me when she's ready. She knew who I was—the white sheep of the family, I guess you could say—and ended up on my doorstep, desperate and homeless. I helped her get an apartment, gave her a job, and let her join my coven. She needs guidance, counseling, and protection." She touched my hand. "Remember, Lily Anderson lied to Katy about why she wanted you hexed. Katy honestly didn't think she was doing anything wrong by making that poppet and hexing you. It's no excuse, but compared to the things she was used to doing as part of the coven, that hex was pretty mild."

I scowled. "It didn't feel very mild to me. It damn near killed me."

"Because Lily didn't follow Katy's instructions for invoking the hex." Carly shook her head. "As I said, I'm not making excuses. What Katy did was wrong and she knows that now. She grew up in black magic, Alice. She's learning a new way, but it's going to take her some time. Think how much her world has changed, and is still changing. I'm not saying she deserves your pity or forgiveness, but given your own past, maybe you can understand her better than the average person."

I leaned back in the booth, arms crossed. "I'll grudgingly concede your point. So why is Morgan texting you now?"

"Because she says her life is in danger and she needs my help."

"Why can't she just ask someone from her coven for help?"

"Because Morgan's really stepped in it this time. She's apparently been sleeping with the husband of one of her coven sisters and tried to spell him into leaving his wife. The spell didn't work and now she's worried when his wife finds out, she'll end up vomiting snakes."

"Is that a real thing?" I asked, horrified.

"There's some very dark magic in this world," Carly said heavily. "This is why it's a bad idea to sleep with anyone associated with the coven unless it's part of ritual magic. In any case, Morgan's begging for my help. She wants to know how to make some of the heavy-duty hoodoo protection spells I have—and how to use hoodoo magic against the man's wife. I told her I want nothing to do with her or her mess. I don't use hoodoo or *any* magic to harm, not anymore. She made her bed and now she gets to lie in it."

I read her expression. "It's not that simple, though, is it? You still worry about her, despite everything."

"No, I don't," she said automatically. At my skeptical look, she sighed. "Maybe. I know I shouldn't care, but damn it, I do. We may be estranged, but I still feel like she's my sister. I don't want her to end up dead—or vomiting snakes."

I tried not to think too much about the snake thing. I had enough nightmares rattling around in my head. "What can I do to help?"

"Nothing I can think of. This doesn't seem like the sort of problem anyone else can help me with."

"A lot of problems do seem that way, but I've come to realize there aren't many problems anyone really has to face alone. Sometimes it's a matter of talking it out with someone who understands where you're coming from."

Carly thought about that. "And if I did ask for your advice, what would you say?"

I mulled it over. "My gut tells me you should stay away," I told her finally. "I understand how you feel about her—believe me, I do. I'm not saying this lightly. If she's lying to you, this could be a way of dragging you back into the life you've worked so hard to leave behind. It's not just you and your soul at stake—it's Katy's too, and the rest of your coven. That kind of magic is insidious poison. It never just affects one person."

When she said nothing, I went on. "But let's say she's telling you the truth about her situation. The same concern applies. You've seen it happen before. It starts with one spell here, another there. The next thing you know, you're caught in that web again. It might be even harder to get out the second time."

I met her troubled eyes. "Is it going to hurt like hell if something does happen to her? Yes, it will. You'll feel guilty and it'll gnaw on you for a long time. Sometimes you can't save people from themselves, no matter how much you want to or how hard you try. Morgan has made a long list of bad decisions and has hurt a lot of people along the way. The decision to shack up with another witch's husband is just the latest bad choice. Maybe it's time for her to face the consequences."

"Some might say it's the Threefold Law coming back to bite her," Carly said quietly. "Thanks, Alice. I'll think it over."

"Isn't that usually my line?" I asked with a smile.

She chuckled. "Usually, yes. Thank you for listening. It means a lot."

"Thanks for trusting me with your story. I know it was a difficult one to tell."

She gathered up the mugs. I picked up the teapot and my plate and we took the dishes to the counter. "Would you like a couple of scones to go?" she asked. "It's on the house for listening to my tale of woe."

I accepted a couple to take home. "Thanks, Carly. If you need anything —or if Morgan won't back off—call me, okay? And thanks for the tea as well."

She smiled and hugged me. "I'll make a tea-drinker of you yet. Say hi to Sean for me, please. And whatever's holding you back from saying yes to buying that house, you owe it to him *and* yourself to let it go."

"I will do my best," I promised, though I knew that would be easier said than done.

7

Sean had to work late to deal with a personnel issue, so he ordered Chinese food for us and picked it up on the way to my house.

We ate sitting on my couch with takeout containers spread out on the coffee table. My dog, Rogue, sprawled on the floor under the table, hoping one of us would drop a piece of chicken. Malcolm had gone out, probably to meet Liam and give us time to talk.

I picked at my food, half-heartedly eating some fried rice and a few pieces of sweet-and-sour chicken before leaving my chopsticks in one of the containers and curling up next to Sean, my head on his shoulder. He ate with typical gusto, fueling his werewolf metabolism, but I could tell he was worried and not happy about my lack of appetite. An alpha's instinct was to make sure his mate was well-fed as well as safe. Given our conversation last night, I wanted to do what I could to reduce his reasons for worrying, but I just couldn't force myself to eat more.

Sooner than I expected, he stopped eating and left a half-finished container of stir-fry on the table. He finished his beer, wiped his fingers on a napkin, and folded both of my hands in his much larger ones. He kissed the top of my head and waited.

I stayed quiet and simply drew on his alpha magic to ease my hurt. He let me wrap myself in its warmth and comfort.

Finally, I took a deep breath and let it out. "So, what did Malcolm tell you?"

His answer surprised me. "That you spoke to Cyro and got some upsetting news and needed some time to process it. He said it was up to you to tell me the rest because it wasn't his story to tell. I'm ready to hear about it, if you want to tell me." He rubbed his chin on the top of my head, a very wolfy attempt to comfort me.

I closed my eyes, trying to hide my reaction. Malcolm hadn't told Sean what Cyro said, though I hadn't asked him not to. Despite his instincts, Sean had let me go to the park by myself and wasn't pushing me to tell him what I'd found out. They cared about me so much that sometimes my heart ached.

A little voice in my head told me I didn't deserve their love. I tried to silence the voice, but the nagging doubt remained. No matter what Carly or Malcolm or Sean or anyone else said, it was difficult to see myself as worthy of their love and support.

To distract myself from those thoughts, I revealed to Sean how Cyro had warned me about Catherine in the Bahamas and revealed she knew who I was. I also told him I'd asked for her help today to find Daniel and about the videos she'd found on the dark web.

When I finished, his hands tightened around mine. "I wish you'd been able to tell me in the Bahamas that Cyro knew your real identity," he said. "I'm sorry you had to bear that burden alone for so long. I knew you were worried about her being missing and wondered if there was more to it, but I didn't imagine she knew who you were—or that *he* was a *she*. I remember seeing a woman sitting next to you at the bar on the beach, but I didn't get a good look at her and didn't think anything more of it. I was too busy admiring you in that bikini to notice much else."

That made me smile, despite the pain in my heart.

"As for the videos..." He growled. "I can't even begin to tell you how angry and sorry I am those videos exist and anyone has seen them. I'm grateful to Cyro for doing what she can to help us."

"It hurts to know those videos are out there," I said, my voice quiet. "It hurts *so much*, Sean. The torture was bad enough, but I can't stand the thought someone wanted to record my pain and people want to watch such things. Even if they thought they were fake, what kind of person likes to see someone else suffer?"

"We've both known people like that," Sean reminded me. His warm golden magic surged and comforted me. "There are some sick people out there. I would do anything to make those videos go away."

"I know you would." I swallowed hard. "I'll come to terms with it, eventually. It's just going to take some time."

"I'll help you in any way I can, even if it's by just listening."

"Speaking of listening..." I rubbed my forehead. "I guess since we're talking, I might as well tell you what Charles told me while we were dancing. In all the chaos, I almost forgot."

"Did he tell you why he helped lead you into Murphy's trap by feeding us that fake intel about a weapons deal?"

Startled, I frowned. "He didn't know it was fake. Valas didn't tell him because she thought he might warn me."

"Or so he says." Sean's anger prickled on my skin. "I don't believe he didn't know. There never was a weapons dealer—just Bell in disguise at the mansion. Vaughan's too smart and too experienced at this game to fall for fabricated intel, much less pass it on to you. He would have double or triple-checked his sources and figured out what was going on if he truly wasn't in on it."

"He seemed truthful," I said, wondering if I sounded defensive and why I was so quick to take Charles's side. "The reasoning made sense for why Valas supposedly didn't tell him ahead of time."

"What, that she thought he might warn you even if she ordered him not to? Alice, I don't buy it." Sean rubbed his chin on my head again. "Even if he does truly care about you and your safety, I can't see him going against Valas and the Court, not even for you. Not after more than a century of allegiance. Not when Valas has both the disposition and the authority to make sure he suffered for betraying her."

I fell silent. Last night, I'd been so sure Charles had told me the truth when he claimed he hadn't known about Moses's plan to capture me, but now I was rethinking the whole scenario. What Sean said made a hell of a lot of sense. I couldn't argue Charles wouldn't lie to me about this or anything else, since he *had* lied to me on numerous occasions.

Once that seed of doubt was planted, everything else he'd told me while we danced—all the flowery words about how much he cared about me and wanted to keep me safe and happy—rang hollow. I didn't doubt Charles wanted me, but I knew he wanted my power, my body, and my allegiance to himself and the Court. He didn't love me and never would. I'd known from the night we met I was a prize, an asset, a mystery he wanted to solve, and a potential bedmate, and that was all. When had I forgotten that?

"Maybe you're right," I said finally. I was suddenly tired of vampires and their games, of never knowing where I stood or what the truth was. With Valas, with Charles, with all of them, it was always plots within plots, danger, lies, and betrayals. I knew better than to just believe anything Charles told me. "He tells me just enough truth that sometimes I believe him when he lies."

I'd really been talking more to myself, but Sean nodded. "That's how I see it. He very deliberately told you the truth about a couple of key things, like how he bit you while you were in a coma and how he got turned, and now it's harder for you to see when he's lying." He hesitated. "You've drunk from him a half-dozen times when you needed healing, and he's bitten you twice. I can't help but think that's making it more difficult to see his motives as clearly as you used to. Valas severed your telepathic bond, but there's still a connection of some kind between you and Vaughan." His hands tightened on mine. "Don't believe him, Alice. He's manipulative. His loyalty is to himself and the Court, not to you."

"I used to know that. Thank you for reminding me." I took a deep breath and let it out slowly. "There's something else."

I told him about the police report Charles said his researcher had uncovered five years ago, and how he'd supposedly kept that information to himself—maybe to protect me, maybe for some other reason.

Sean was quiet for a long time. Finally, he said, "I hate to say it, but my gut feeling is he's telling the truth about the report."

I exhaled. "Same. What can I do about it?"

"Other than simply being aware of its existence, I don't know that there's anything we can or should do at this point. Checking to see if it actually exists only calls attention to it. I think we're better off letting it stay buried and forgotten, unless you want to ask Cyro to hack into the Chicago PD computer system and delete the report from their records. Then all that's left is a paper file gathering dust in a box in a warehouse."

"That's a thought." I gave him a wan smile. "In the meantime, thanks for listening."

He kissed me. "Thanks for talking. I know that's still difficult for you to do."

"I'm getting better at it, though."

He wrapped his arm around me. "Yes, you are. That makes me happier than you can possibly imagine."

"Finish eating," I admonished him. "I know you're still hungry and the only reason you stopped was because of me. I had a scone at Carly's coffee shop and that kinda filled me up."

"*How* many scones did you eat at the shop?"

"One!" I said defensively.

I sensed him smiling. "And after you got home?"

I huffed. "Only one more. I left two for you."

He laughed and nuzzled the side of my neck. "I *am* hungry," he murmured, his lips against my ear. "Hungry for a beautiful mage." His teeth grazed my earlobe.

I swung my leg over his and straddled his lap. He rested his hands on my hips. "I wouldn't mind being eaten by a werewolf, now that I think about it," I said.

"I was hoping you'd say that." He licked his lips. "Mage is delicious."

"Of course, werewolves are quite tasty too."

"Maybe if we think about it, there's a way we can both get what we want." He held me with his hands under my butt and stood. I wrapped my legs around his hips and kissed him again as he headed for the stairs. "Where's Malcolm?" he asked.

I shrugged. "Out. Probably spending time with Liam, if I had to guess."

"Good." He started up the steps. "Then I can make you scream as much as I want."

And he did.

8

SEAN

PRESENT DAY

SEAN SPENT THE NINETY MINUTES BETWEEN HIS CALL TO CARLY AND Ben's return to the motel in wolf form, curled up on the bed.

The wolf rested, content to be at Alice's side. He didn't sleep, though he dozed for a few minutes at a time. Despite its location next to the highway, little traffic went past this late at night. The silence made it easy to listen for anyone approaching their room.

When Lucas Stone's truck turned into the motel's parking lot, the wolf rose from the bed and carefully stepped down to the floor before shifting back to human form.

Sean dressed quickly as the truck's engine shut off and its passengers got out. He put fresh cold washcloths on Alice's wrists and forehead, then slipped outside to meet Ben and Lucas. Andrea waved and got into her husband's truck next to the motel office.

From their expressions, he knew they had some information, but not the answers he'd hoped for. He and Lucas exchanged nods. "What did you find?" he asked.

Ben's anger seared him through their pack bond. "Alice's scent trail went for almost twenty miles. Her boot prints were easy to see in the wet gravel. They got rain here last night, Lucas says."

"Alice didn't get rained on," Sean said. He would have smelled it on her clothes if she had. "So she started walking after the rain ended."

Ben nodded. "Probably sometime this morning."

"Where did she walk from? Could you tell, or did you lose her trail?"

"She was dropped on the side of the road by an SUV or large truck," Lucas told him. "Her trail began at a set of tire tracks where someone pulled to the side of the road. Judging by the traces of blood on the pavement and the tire tracks, they pushed or dragged her out, made a U-turn, and headed north. From the amount of scent we found in the ditch, I think she was either unconscious for a while or waited until they were gone to start walking."

Sean snarled. "So that's a dead end."

"Looks like it." Lucas kept his distance so he didn't crowd Sean while the other alpha was on edge. "I made some calls, but no one saw the vehicle. I'll keep asking around. We'll keep an eye out for any vehicles or people we don't know. I'll forward you any information that might be helpful."

"Thank you. Anyone around here you can think of we should look at more closely? Anyone using magic you're not familiar with, or has a history of causing problems?"

Lucas shook his head. "I've been thinking about that and nothing comes to mind. I'd certainly tell you if there was. I'm sure you've already considered there's a good chance whoever took your consort deliberately dropped her off far from wherever they kept her."

"That's certainly my thought. I don't think we're going to find any answers here." Sean held out his hand. "Thanks for your help."

"Anytime, Sean." They shook hands. "You need anything else, you let me know."

"We've got a couple members of my pack on their way here to help us get Alice home," Sean told him. "They'll be arriving in about an hour. We'll be on our way not long after that, I hope."

"Take care of Alice. We aren't running you off." Lucas clapped him on the shoulder. "Mike's here to back you up if you need it. I'm taking Andrea home, unless you want her to check on Alice again."

"We're fine, thank you. Say hello to Mariah for me."

"Will do." Lucas made a hat-tipping gesture and returned to his truck.

As Lucas and Andrea drove away, Ben and Sean spoke outside before going into the motel room. "You shifted," Ben said quietly. "Did it help?"

"It did, but now I know we aren't going to find any answers here, I want to get Alice home." Sean rubbed his chin. "I'm tempted to tell Jack to turn around and meet us back at my house."

"We still have to deal with that walking spell," Ben reminded him. "They're less than an hour out. Let's go inside and check on Alice. You can shift back to your wolf until they get here."

Two large black SUVs with tinted windows turned into the motel parking lot. Sean immediately recognized both the lead vehicle and its driver. His wolf rose and walked stiff-legged to the front of his brain, showing his teeth. Sean echoed his wolf's growl. "Son of a bitch."

The Vampire Court vehicles parked beside Sean's truck. Bryan Smith emerged from the front passenger seat of the lead SUV and opened the rear passenger door for his employer.

Charles Vaughan stepped out, buttoning his suit jacket. The vehicle's driver, Adri Smith, stayed behind the wheel.

Ben snarled. There was no love lost between Vaughan and Sean's pack, thanks to the vampire's mistreatment of Alice.

Sean intercepted Vaughan halfway between the SUV and the motel room door. "Why are you here?"

Vaughan's expression was cold. "I have come at the request of Madame Valas. She wishes an update on Alice's condition and for me to ascertain what harm has befallen her."

"You are not going in that room," Sean informed him.

Vaughan raised an eyebrow. "Oh?"

"I told you earlier on the phone Alice is in no condition to be questioned and I'm responsible for her safety and care. That hasn't changed."

The vampire's eyes silvered. "Alice is an employee of the Court. Her injuries are evidence that must be examined as part of a case Madame Valas has deemed a matter of Court security. We recognize the situation has caused a great amount of strain for you and your pack; therefore, we have made allowances. However—"

"Vaughan, I won't accept any threats from you," Sean said icily. "*Therefore*, you can take your *allowances* and shove them up your ass."

"What would Alice say about this territorial behavior? I am sure she would not stand for it."

"If it were me in that room and her out here, she would say the same words to you." Sean met the vampire's silver eyes with his own golden ones. "We both know what Alice has done to protect the people she loves.

If you want to find out what I'm willing to do to protect her from harm, you can find out right now."

For a moment, Sean thought Vaughan would take a swing at him. As much as he would welcome the opportunity to put the vampire in his place, he very much doubted it would happen. Brawling in a motel parking lot was hardly becoming for a member of the Vampire Court.

Vaughan's expression became fixed. After a moment, he said, "Madame Valas would like to extend her condolences for the injuries to your consort." His voice was neutral. To Sean, it was clear Valas had been listening somehow and instructed him to defuse the situation. The vampires' ability to communicate telepathically with each other over such vast distances was disconcerting. "She respectfully requests you permit me to see Alice, so I may report on her injuries and offer my assistance to determine where she has been held. No harm will befall her, by my hand or any other, by order of Madame Valas."

"I guarantee you won't harm her," Sean stated. "This isn't about the chance of you harming Alice. You don't respect boundaries—physical, ethical, and otherwise—or my authority as the alpha of the Tomb Mountain Pack. You assumed you have the right to demand access to her and you do not. I said no and you refused to accept my decision. Madame Valas, at least, had the courtesy to ask."

Vaughan ignored the first part of his statement. "And what is your answer to Madame Valas?"

Sean was well aware if he refused to honor Valas's request, it might jeopardize the long-standing cooperation between the local shifters and the Court. Perhaps more importantly, Alice was still obligated to Valas for the latter's help in saving his life. Exactly what the terms of that agreement were, he wasn't sure, but he was reluctant to do anything that might cause Valas to put that contract up for sale. She'd hinted at that possibility before. As bad as it was for Alice to owe Valas a favor, there were others who would be worse.

Once again, despite serious misgivings, Sean made the choice that was best for Alice.

"You may come in," he said.

Vaughan stood beside the bed, his face expressionless as he studied Alice's sleeping form. Bryan Smith waited near the door, his eyes on Sean. Ben leaned against the wall next to the connecting door, arms crossed, watching Vaughan.

What the vampire was thinking, Sean wasn't certain, but both he and his wolf bristled at how possessively Vaughan looked at her. Since Vaughan's arrival, the wolf had been pacing in Sean's mind, angry and jealous. He showed Sean an image of his teeth in the vampire's throat. The urge to shift intensified.

Vaughan's eyes turned completely black in barely suppressed rage. Alice's condition clearly angered and distressed him, which indicated the vampire had not been involved in her disappearance—or, at least not in the abuse she'd suffered. "You say she has no memory of who she is, who *you* are, or where she has been?"

"That's correct." Sean's voice was more than half growl. "I can't tell much from her clothes or her injuries, other than I think she was kept underground. There's a strange scent on her clothes." He picked up the plastic bag containing Alice's shirt and jeans and handed it to Vaughan.

The vampire untied the bag and lifted out Alice's shirt. He inhaled carefully, parsing the different odors as Sean had done earlier. His brow furrowed. "How odd. I do not recognize this scent." He glanced at Sean. "I assume you also do not know it?"

"No."

Vaughan set the bag on the floor and reached for Alice.

In a flash, Sean had the vampire pinned against the wall. Behind him, Ben intercepted Bryan as Charles's head of security moved toward his employer.

"Don't touch her," Sean growled.

Moving vamp-fast, Vaughan knocked Sean's arm away. Sean held his ground and stood toe-to-toe with the vampire. "I mean it, Vaughan. You wouldn't dare put a hand on her without her permission if she were awake, so you sure as hell won't when she's unconscious."

Unperturbed by their brief scuffle, Vaughan said, "I must see her injuries. The longer we delay, the more these clues will degrade and diminish the likelihood of identifying her kidnappers."

Sean snarled. "You treat her respectfully, or you'll answer to me—and to her, when she wakes up. I'd be more afraid of the latter."

A muscle moved in Vaughan's jaw. "Stand aside, wolf. I will not ask again."

If Alice were awake and herself, Sean thought, she would say something sarcastic and tell them both to back down.

There were few things he wanted to do less at the moment than show any of Alice's body to Vaughan, but her wounds *were* evidence and she would have shown them to the vampire for that reason.

He gently moved the sheet and blanket and showed Vaughan the restraint marks on her wrists and ankles, her scratched arms and legs, and her bloody, bandaged feet. Other than taking occasional sniffs of her wounds, Vaughan was almost unnervingly silent and still.

When he told Vaughan of the three deep lashes on Alice's back, however, the vampire hissed, his eyes going black again. "Those bastards," Bryan Smith muttered.

Sean carefully tucked Alice back under the covers. Her brow furrowed and she whimpered in her sleep. The sound nearly broke his heart.

"The full wrath of the Court shall be visited upon whoever is responsible for these injuries," Vaughan pronounced.

Something about the phrasing and his tone made Sean think he was repeating Valas's words. Sean wondered if Valas had watched through Vaughan's eyes, or if he'd reported each detail back to the head of the Vampire Court telepathically.

"We will double our efforts to locate her abductors," Vaughan added. "In the meantime, we must wake Alice and discover what, if anything, she remembers."

Sean crossed his arms. "When we found her, she'd been spelled to walk. She'd been walking since early this morning. That spell is probably still in effect. I don't want to have to restrain her unless we have no other choice."

To the best of Sean's knowledge, Vaughan had no idea who Alice really was, or that she'd been held captive by Moses for twenty years. Sean couldn't imagine what it must have been like for her to be a captive again, chained in some underground prison for days. He'd be damned if he'd restrain her. Holding her as they sat on the back of his truck, while she'd fought to get away, had been bad enough.

"Someone put her in a shackle," he added. "Whoever did that is going to die, either by my hand or hers. I'm not going to compound their cruelty."

"What do you propose?" Vaughan asked. "We cannot keep her unconscious indefinitely. We must have answers."

"There's someone coming with my people who I think will be able to break the spell she's under."

Vaughan nodded. "Ah, yes—the witch, Carly Reese."

How Vaughan knew who Carly was and that she was on her way, Sean wasn't sure, but he was sure he didn't like it.

Vaughan checked the time. "They are perhaps thirty minutes away. While we wait, I will speak with my personnel privately in the next room, and then return to heal Alice's injuries."

If this presumptuous vampire didn't get the hell out of their room in the next ten seconds, Sean reflected grimly, he would likely run out of reasons not to put his fist in the middle of Vaughan's face. "No, you won't."

Vaughan hissed. "You are a selfish bastard if you would rather her suffer than allow me to assist."

"You're a pompous ass if you think you're the only person who can help her, or that I have any intention of letting her suffer. I let you see her injuries at Madame Valas's request. Now *get out,* so I can take care of Alice."

A pause. "Very well. At Madame Valas's request, I will excuse myself. For Alice's sake, I hope you reconsider and permit me to heal her." Vaughan gave them a stiff half-bow. He circled the bed and used the connecting door to go into the other room. Bryan followed him out and closed the door behind them.

"She probably needs those washcloths replaced," Ben said quietly. "Want me to do it?"

"I've got it." Sean took the washcloths to the sink and ran them under cold water. Keeping his hands busy helped calm both him and his wolf.

Once he carefully put the cloths back on Alice's forehead and wrists, he took a small black cloth bag from his suitcase. The bag contained three spell crystals: one green, one blue, and one purple. They pulsed with magic.

"Which one do you think you'll need?" Ben asked.

"The blue." Sean put the other two back in the little bag and set it on the nightstand. "It's a mid-range spell. That should be sufficient to heal her."

"When did you buy them?"

"After Caleb's attack. I decided I never wanted to be without a way to heal her if she was hurt." He growled. "As long as I can help it, she'll never have to drink vampire blood again, unless she chooses to do so."

Ben put his hand on Sean's shoulder. "Glad to hear it. Do you want me to step out?"

He shook his head. "Guard the connecting door, please. I don't want Vaughan back in here. I'll be occupied until the spell is done."

"You got it." Ben put his back to the door, crossed his arms, and waited.

Moving slowly so he didn't jostle her, Sean climbed onto the bed and settled in beside Alice. The healing spell buzzed reassuringly in his hand.

Since Alice's stockpile of healing spells could only be used by someone with natural magic, he'd had to buy these on the black market. Blood magic was illegal and very expensive—even blood magic healing spells— but he would have walked across broken glass to get them. Without this healing spell, tonight he would have been forced to choose between allowing Alice to suffer, or letting Vaughan feed her his blood *again*, without her permission, giving the vampire more influence over her than he already had.

Carefully, he laced his fingers through hers, the crystal pressed between their palms. Its magic surged, ready to be unleashed.

He took a deep breath, exhaled, and closed his eyes. "*Fè byen.*"

The healing spell erupted in a burst of red and black blood magic and swirls of golden shifter magic he saw with his mind rather than his eyes. The shifter magic was his own, an addition by the hoodoo mage who'd made the spells for him. It allowed him to take all the pain of the healing spell, while Alice would feel none. Had she been awake, she would have been furious.

Waves of intense pain left him breathless as the healing spell pulsed from the crystal through Alice's battered body. He opened his eyes and focused on her face and his memories of her until the pain became distant.

She moaned and rolled her head to the side, sending the washcloth sliding off onto the bed. He resisted the urge to squeeze her hand tighter and wrapped her in comfort instead. Slowly, the bruises, cuts, and other injuries healed.

Finally, the last of the spell gave out. He dropped the crystal on the bed and nestled his head next to hers. Pain had a distinct scent. She'd smelled strongly of it since the moment they'd found her. It was waning now, and that did as much to calm him as seeing her wounds fade.

"Do you want me to check her feet?" Ben asked quietly.

Sean's wolf growled. "I'll do it," Sean said, his tone harsher than he'd intended.

Fortunately, Ben understood his protective instincts and would be the last person to take offense. He stayed on guard at the door while Sean rose, checked to make sure all Alice's injuries had healed, and put the soiled bandages in a trash bag to be destroyed.

"It'll help a lot when the others get here—especially Nan," Ben said. "Let Jack and me keep watch out front while you and Nan help Carly with Alice. Once Alice is de-spelled and back on her feet, we'll see what she remembers, and go from there."

"I was thinking that." Sean frowned and touched Alice's forehead. "She's still too warm." He sat on the bed and resumed giving her chips of ice.

"Your wolf is pushing you hard to find the people who hurt her and kill them."

Sean brushed some hair back from Alice's face. "Yes."

"Does Alice know your wolf thinks she's your mate?"

"Yes...technically."

Ben's eyebrows went up. "What do you mean, technically?"

"I mean she knows the wolf thinks of her as his mate. I don't think she fully understands what that means—or has accepted it." It hurt to say the last part out loud, but Sean trusted Ben not to share that information with anyone else.

"That's making things even harder, isn't it?" Ben frowned. "I thought the fact you two haven't established a mate bond was making you and your wolf frustrated and restless."

"It's more than the lack of a bond. She's holding back, or backing off. I can tell, and so can my wolf." Sean gently rubbed Alice's arm. "When we put in the offer on the farmhouse, she was ready to sign on the dotted line and move in together. The day before she disappeared—the day we had dinner over at Karen and Cole's—she said she needed some time to think about it."

"Did she say why?"

"Moses Murphy is part of the problem. No matter what I say, she believes she's putting me and the rest of the pack at risk."

"But the risk to us is the same whether you two live together or in separate houses, right?" Ben read Sean's expression. "You think there's more to her hesitation, don't you?"

"There's something else," Sean admitted. His eyes went to the connecting door. "Maybe someone else."

Ben was silent. "I wish I could disagree with you, but even I noticed it on the night we met with Vaughan, Darius Bell, and the others at Luciano's," he said finally. "Your wolf knows it too. No wonder you both want to tear out Vaughan's throat. Is it because she's needed his blood for healing several times?"

Sean shook his head. "I think it predates all that. He's been after her for five years and he's a manipulative, lying son of a bitch. He's played a long game to get past her defenses and weasel his way into her head. I hate to say it—I hate to even *think* it—but I suspect he's succeeded, at least partially."

"She loves you," Ben pointed out. "I can sense it. We all can."

"She does." Sean covered Alice's hand with his own much larger one. "Or she did, before this. I'm not about to let him trick her into believing his lies."

"Do you think he's behind this?" Ben asked, giving voice to the suspicion several members of the pack had harbored since Alice's disappearance.

Sean shook his head again. "My instincts say no, not this time. I don't trust him, though, and I never will."

"What will you do?"

"Whatever I have to." Sean kissed Alice's forehead. "Because she'd do the same for me."

9

TEN MINUTES LATER, A FAMILIAR TRUCK TURNED INTO THE MOTEL'S parking lot as Sean put fresh cold cloths on Alice's forehead and wrists. Her fever still hadn't broken, despite her wounds being healed, and it worried him.

"It's Jack, Nan, and Carly," Ben confirmed from the window as vehicle doors opened and closed outside and voices drifted in from the lot.

"You and Jack keep watch outside and ask Nan and Carly to come in here," Sean told him.

"Sure." Ben slipped out and shut the door. Sean's sharp ears heard him talking to Jack and the others outside.

While he had a moment of privacy, he leaned down and pressed a gentle kiss to Alice's forehead. She whimpered again and her hands twisted in the comforter.

"Carly's here," he murmured. "Rest a little longer until we can figure out how to break this spell, all right?" He kissed her again and ran his nose along her hairline, breathing in her scent.

Someone tapped on the door. He rose from the bed and went to open it. Nan and Carly waited outside, weary but determined. Jack and Ben stood near the truck, talking in undertones. Jack gave him a grave nod.

Nan hugged Sean tightly. "We'll take care of her," she murmured.

As he'd hoped it would, Nan's touch eased some of his anger and frustration and cleared his brain enough to think more clearly. His wolf curled up in his mind and rested his head on his paws, watching quietly. The prickly feeling of fur pushing at his skin faded for the first time in days.

He released Nan and gave Carly a quick hug. "Thank you for dropping everything and coming to the rescue," he told her.

She squeezed him. "I'll do what I can. Let me see her."

He stepped aside so the women could enter. Carly took two steps into their room and spotted Alice lying on the bed. She gasped. "Oh, Goddess...her aura."

Sean closed the door. "Sharp ears in the next room. What's wrong with her aura?"

Carly lowered her voice. "Most of it has been scoured away. What's left is scorched and blackened."

"What can do something like that?" Nan sat beside Alice and put her hand gently on her arm. Alice murmured and exhaled, as if Nan's touch comforted her.

"Not many things," Carly said, setting her bag on the table. "It's dark magic, Sean. *Very* dark magic."

He growled. "How do we break the spell that forced her to walk?"

"Technically, it's a curse, not a spell. That shouldn't be too difficult. I brought what I thought I'd need." She unzipped her bag. "We'll need a warm bath, deep enough to submerge her entire body. The bathtub should work fine. Before we run the bath, however, I need to test a theory."

"Do you know what's happened to Alice's magic and her memories?" Sean asked.

Carly started to clear off the nightstand beside the bed. "I think I do, but I pray I'm wrong. In any case, we have to find out for sure."

She took out a folded black cloth with a pentagram on it and spread it over the top of the nightstand. She unwrapped several small objects and placed them at the points of the pentagram: a feather, a white candle, a stone, and a seashell. At the top of the pentagram, she put a ceramic angel. Finally, she took out a strip of white cloth and a pair of latex gloves.

"Come to the bed," she told him. "I need to cast a circle around us to contain anything that might be released by this spell."

He took Nan's place on the edge of the bed next to Alice. Nan sat at the small table by the window.

Carly took a small ritual knife from her bag. Alice had told him it was called an athame. She touched the tip of the athame to the middle of the bed's headboard and took several deep breaths. "I cast this circle three times three to protect those in the circle that no harm may come to them or those outside the circle."

She walked around the bed, then traced the tip of the knife gently across the headboard. She repeated the circle twice more, then placed the athame on the altar she'd made on the nightstand.

Next, she took out a small cast-iron cauldron and filled it halfway with water from a stoppered bottle. "Rain water," she told Sean. She added three drops from two different bottles. "White sage and pine essential oils."

He wondered if she was telling him what she was using to assuage his worry, or if it was force of habit since she was a teacher. In either case, he appreciated her thoughtfulness. He trusted Carly and her magic, but he had less tolerance for unknowns tonight than usual.

She stirred the mixture clockwise three times with the athame. "Great Mother," she murmured, "Tell us if Alice has been poisoned with black magic."

Sean stifled a growl. He didn't want to frighten or distract her in the middle of a spell, but the mention of black magic had his wolf pacing again.

Carly put on the latex gloves and carried the bowl to Alice's bedside. "I need a few drops of blood from her right hand," she told him. "Will you allow it?"

Grimly, he took the washcloth off Alice's right wrist. He laced his fingers through hers and presented her hand.

She used the tip of the athame to pierce the tip of Alice's right index finger. A bead of bright red blood welled up. Carefully, she held Alice's hand over the bowl and squeezed her fingertip. One by one, drops of blood landed in the spelled water.

When the third drop hit the water, the liquid turned pitch black. Sean's nose caught a hint of an unfamiliar scent—one that reminded him, inexplicably, of suffering and death, tinged with a hint of sulfur and that odd unpleasant odor he'd smelled on Alice's clothing. The water bubbled for a moment, then went still.

"Black magic—the blackest there is," Carly whispered. She set the bowl on the altar and wrapped the strip of white cloth around Alice's finger. "Thank you, Great Mother, for showing us the truth of what is wrong with Alice." She removed the latex gloves, her face pale.

Sean locked down his emotions so the other members of his pack couldn't feel his anger and fear. "A witch?" he asked, his voice even.

She shook her head. "Worse: a sorcerer. A practitioner of occult malevolent magic, one who is also a servant of a demon lord. Alice's blackened aura was a dead giveaway, but I had to make sure." She took a deep, shaky breath. "Let me break the circle. Then we'll talk."

Sean waited impatiently. Once she'd put the athame back on the altar, she turned to him. "This is beyond my abilities, Sean. I'm sorry. Even if—" She broke off mid-sentence and rubbed her face. "I'm sorry."

"Even if what?" he demanded. "There has to be something you can do."

She glared at him. "Even if I wanted to, I can't go down this road. You need a sorcerer or black witch to fight a sorcerer. Black magic to fight black magic. I'm no sorcerer or black-magic practitioner. Not...not anymore."

Despite his worry, he softened his tone. "I wouldn't ask you to do anything you don't want to, not even for Alice's sake. Do you know anyone who could help us?"

She closed her eyes and hung her head.

Nan went to Carly's side, putting her arm around the younger woman.

After a long moment, Carly raised her head. "I know someone, but I doubt she'll help you unless someone makes it worth her while. I don't want you tangled up with her, Sean. Not you, or Alice, or anyone you care about. She's poison."

"We might not have much of a choice," he said. "While we think this through, are you comfortable breaking the curse that forced Alice to walk?"

"Yes. I have what I need with me. But—"

He held up his hand. "Let me worry about your friend the sorcerer."

"Morgan's not my friend," Carly told him. "And she's not a sorcerer, though I suspect she dabbles in sorcery. She's a very powerful black witch."

"Powerful enough to undo what's been done to Alice?"

She nodded unhappily. "I think so. If not by herself, then with her mother's help."

"Then we'll figure out a way to make this work," he stated. "Nan will help you prepare the bath so we can break the walking curse. I need to go talk to someone while you get ready. I'll be back."

The thought of involving Vaughan and the Court left a bitter taste in his mouth, but for Alice's sake, against an unknown enemy, Sean had no alternative but to ally himself with the devil he knew.

Jack and Ben stood on either side of the door to room fourteen like sentries, their eyes bright gold.

Sean gave them a nod as he stepped outside. "I have to talk to Charles Vaughan. I need you to guard Alice's room while Nan and Carly are inside with Alice. No one goes in." The last was more than half growl—his wolf speaking with his human mouth.

Jack nodded. "I'll take care of it."

"Thank you."

With his guards in place, Sean went to the room next door and knocked.

Bryan opened the door and stepped aside for Sean to enter. Vaughan sat at the small table, reading something on a laptop. Two other enforcers —Bryan's sister Adri and a man named Kirwin—stood near the door that connected to Alice's room.

"I need to speak with you," Sean said to Vaughan. "Privately."

At Vaughan's nod, Adri and Kirwin went outside. Bryan stayed, standing at Vaughan's right.

Sean closed the door and turned to the vampire. "I have some information."

Vaughan listened silently as Sean revealed what Carly had determined about the black magic that had stolen Alice's memory and magic.

"Carly thinks she can break the curse that forced Alice to walk," he said. "She's working on that now. She also says she knows a powerful black witch who might be able to undo what the sorcerer did to Alice. She doesn't trust this witch, and she says the witch won't help unless we make it worth her while." He studied Vaughan. "Before we go that route, does the Court have a sorcerer or a black witch on its payroll?"

Vaughan's gaze became distant, as if he were speaking to someone in his head. *Probably Valas*, Sean thought.

Finally, the vampire shook his head. "Not at the moment, unfortunately. What is this black witch's name?"

"I haven't asked yet." Sean's eyes glowed. "Will the Court take responsibility for bringing this person in and keeping her on a leash in order to deal with this sorcerer?"

Another pause. This time, Vaughan appeared to be thinking. "You do not want Alice indebted to a black witch."

"I don't want Alice *anywhere near* a black witch, but the situation leaves us little choice. The best and safest option is for the Court to hire this witch to deal with the sorcerer. Madame Valas must see the sorcerer pays for what he's done, and the witch does no harm to any of us, especially Alice."

"Very well," Vaughan said briskly. "The Court will make the arrangements. Once Alice is free from the walking spell and we determine what, if anything, she remembers of her time in captivity, you will—" He paused. "*We ask* you to bring Alice to Northbourne, so the black witch can be consulted in an environment we control."

"Agreed, but I stay with Alice at all times." When Vaughan started to object, Sean shook his head. "Not negotiable."

After a moment, Vaughan nodded. "These terms are acceptable to Madame Valas. Please alert me when Alice wakes."

Sean turned on his heel and went outside. Adri and Kirwin returned to Vaughan's room and closed the door as Sean joined his pack mates outside room fourteen.

"No trouble," Jack told Sean. "Should we wait out here?"

He nodded. "Carly's helping Alice. Keep watch, please."

He tapped quietly on the door, knowing Nan would hear. She opened it for him and he slipped inside. Alice was still sleeping, but she'd rolled onto her side and curled up with the blanket pulled to her chin. Both he and his wolf longed to curl around her as they'd done so many times, but that was not an option. The wolf snarled, angry and unhappy.

"Carly's preparing a bath," Nan said, no doubt sensing his wolf's fury. "She discovered something on Alice you should know about."

Carly emerged from the bathroom, her sleeves rolled up to her elbows. "The bath is ready."

"What did you find on Alice?" he asked.

She indicated the mud on Alice's forehead. "I didn't notice it at first. When I touched her a few minutes ago, I sensed a trace of magic here. When I took a closer look, I realized this isn't just mud—it's the remains of a curse someone drew on her forehead in mud, ash, and blood."

"What kind of curse?"

"It's black witch magic. I recognize the spellwork. It's meant to hide someone or keep others from finding them. I think it's why I couldn't see her until this afternoon, and why no one stopped to offer her a ride, even though you said she was dropped off on the side of the road this morning and walked along the highway for twenty miles." She pointed to mud on the back of Alice's hand. "At some point, she wiped her forehead and smeared the spellwork, which broke the curse and allowed us to find her.

Whoever let her go, they wanted to be far away when we came looking for her."

"So we have both a black witch *and* a sorcerer working together?"

"Looks like it. The walking curse is probably black witch magic too. That's a bit of good news in a way, since that means the bath will almost certainly break the curse. If it was sorcery, we might have needed something more powerful to break it."

"What do I need to do?"

"She has to go entirely under the surface of the water, head to toes, for three times three seconds, or nine seconds. The curse should break and she'll wake up, probably confused and pissed off, but without an irresistible urge to walk." She hesitated, clearly unhappy. "I added something to help keep her calm. Normally I wouldn't do any kind of spell on someone without their consent, but if the walking curse doesn't break or she wakes up terrified, it will give you a chance to talk to her."

"Thank you." He touched Alice's hand. "What if the curse doesn't break?"

"Then we'll try something else." She squeezed his arm. "Have faith, Sean. There's no black magic spell or curse we can't undo, one way or another." She joined Nan by the small table. "We'll wait here."

Sean nodded at the outside door. "Give Ben the information about your black witch acquaintance so he can pass the information on to the Court. He's right outside."

"I will," she promised.

Sean scooped Alice up, still wrapped in the sheet and blanket. She nestled her head against his chest and murmured in her sleep. He carried her to the bathroom and closed the door with his foot.

With Alice on his lap, he sat on the edge of the tub. The water smelled of salt, rosemary, garlic, lavender, and a variety of other herbs and oils. He also detected the telltale parchment scent of Carly's magic. Whatever she'd put in the water, he hoped it would break the walking curse. Deep down he knew there was more wrong than that, but they had to solve one problem at a time.

He unwrapped the sheet and blanket and dropped them on the floor, then lowered Alice carefully into the warm water, his hand under her head. She made a little protesting sound in her sleep.

He was nearing the very limits of his patience and control. If this didn't work, he was likely to lose the battle with his need to shift and hunt those responsible for Alice's disappearance and condition, and his first stop would be the arrogant vampire in the next room.

Please remember, he thought, as if he could will Alice's memories back into her head.

Her eyelids fluttered. She was waking up.

Sean took a deep breath and pushed Alice's head under the water.

10

ALICE

FIVE DAYS EARLIER

THE MORNING AFTER CYRO'S CALL AND MY VISIT TO CARLY'S COFFEE shop, the director of the county historical museum contacted me about wards for a couple of valuable new artifacts. I jumped at the chance to distract myself from thinking about Daniel, the torture videos, and Moses.

Malcolm and I went to the museum at nine to meet with the director, who I'd worked for before. We spent the rest of the morning and early afternoon making the wards and adjusting them to the director's requirements. I could tell Malcolm still wasn't quite himself, but he didn't seem inclined to talk about it. I gave him space while we focused on the wards. He'd talk when he was ready.

We got back to my house a little before three. Malcolm went downstairs to work on spellwork and I curled up on the couch to rest. I hadn't gotten much sleep last night. Sean had kept me up late—which was fun for both of us—but then I'd tossed and turned for the rest of the night, which was less fun. On top of that, making wards took energy. Sean and I were scheduled to have dinner at the house of two pack members, Karen Williams and her human husband Cole, so I wanted to nap before he got home from work.

Around three thirty, just as I started to doze, my perimeter wards tingled, indicating I had a visitor. Vehicle doors slammed outside. I groaned.

Heavy footsteps crossed my front porch and someone knocked. I heaved myself off the couch, ran my fingers through my hair, and shuffled to the door.

I peered through the peephole and was surprised to find Bryan Smith on my doorstep. I opened the door. Two Vamp Court SUVs were parked in my driveway in addition to the one parked on the street in front of my house.

"Miss Alice," Bryan said without waiting for my greeting. "I apologize for disturbing you, but our security guards caught a man watching your house. We have him in custody."

Magic sparked on my fingers. Had Moses sent someone after me, or to spy on me? "Who is he? Who does he work for?" I demanded.

He handed me a battered leather wallet. "His name is Robert Hamlin. He claims he doesn't work for anyone. He also claims he knows you."

I opened the wallet and found about nineteen dollars in cash, a couple of cards, and a recently issued Illinois driver's license showing an unfamiliar blond man in his early thirties.

"I don't know him," I said, offering the wallet back to Bryan.

He didn't take it from me. "Check again behind the cash." I couldn't read his expression, but his tone had me worried.

Frowning, I reopened the wallet and found a small, faded photo of a couple. It took me several seconds to recognize the much younger and thinner man in the picture as the same man from the driver's license. He wore a Chicago Bears T-shirt and ripped jeans and had his arm around a young woman in a tank top and shorts. She stared at the camera, unsmiling, her face half-shadowed.

My blood went cold.

The woman in the photo was Alice Worth—the *real* Alice Worth. This Robert Hamlin had been a friend of hers back in Chicago. Judging by their appearances, they'd known each other during Alice's drug-fueled party days.

This was one of my worst nightmares come true: someone from the real Alice's past showing up on my doorstep. I didn't know what had caused him to look me up five years later, but he needed to be gone before he or anyone else started wondering too much about Alice or me or my time in Chicago.

"Are you sure you don't know him?" Bryan rumbled, his brow furrowed. "That looks like you in the picture."

Bryan knew about Alice's past problems with drugs and alcohol, so I shrugged with a nonchalance I didn't feel. "It was a long time ago, back when I wasn't sober most of the time." I tucked the photo back into the wallet and handed it back. "I didn't recognize his name or the driver's license picture right away. Where did you find him?"

"The guards out front saw him down the street, clearly watching your house. They asked him for I.D. and he threw some punches." He studied me. "He says you're old friends and he just wanted to talk to you. I want to take him back to Mr. Vaughan's residence and make sure he's not working for Moses Murphy—or someone else."

Damn it. "I'll talk to him, but not out here. Bring him inside."

Bryan shook his head. "That's not a good idea."

"Search him for weapons before you bring him in. I can protect myself, plus I've got backup. Malcolm's here. If I think there's any chance he's got an agenda beyond what he's told you, you can take him with you. I'm hoping once we talk, he'll just head back to Chicago."

"If I leave you alone with him and something happens, Mr. Vaughan will be very displeased with me."

I had no doubt that was true, but Charles's ire was the least of my concerns. I needed Robert Hamlin to go back to Chicago. As far as I could see, the best way to do that was to find out why he was here and then say whatever I needed to say to get him to leave and not come back. That meant talking to him face-to-face, and not in the Vamp Court SUV—which was probably bugged—and not in front of the enforcers, who would report every word back to Charles. I didn't want Robert in my house, but the situation left me very few options.

My expression hardened. "Bryan, let me talk to him and find out what he wants."

He turned on his heel and headed back to the SUV without a word.

I went back inside and closed the front door. "Malcolm?" I called.

He came up through the floor from the basement. "What's up?"

Quickly, I told him about my surprise visitor from the real Alice's past. Malcolm's expression was grim. "Crap. Okay, what do you want to do?"

"I'm going to invite him in for a chat. Hopefully whatever he wants, it will be a simple issue to resolve and then he'll be on his way back home."

"And if he's here to cause trouble?"

"Then I'll deal with it."

"Do you want me to go tell Sean about Robert?"

I shook my head. "I don't want to bother him at work if this turns out to be nothing. I just want you to hang out in here, in case Robert gets any funny ideas."

"You got it."

Bryan knocked on the door again. Malcolm went invisible. He was only visible to me, but I'd found him distracting if I was trying to talk to someone, so he'd developed the habit of going invisible whenever I had company.

I took a deep breath, touched the doorframe, lowered my house wards, and opened the door.

Robert Hamlin stood on my doorstep, flanked by Bryan and another enforcer I didn't recognize. Robert was tall and he'd added some muscle since he'd posed for the photo with Alice. He looked healthier too, though his eyes had a dark, haunted look.

"He's clean," Bryan rumbled. "No weapons."

"Thanks," I told him.

Robert looked me over, almost drinking in the sight of me. Part of me had worried the moment he saw me, he would point and shout, "Imposter!" He didn't, however. He simply stared.

Several emotions flashed in his eyes: anger, sadness, and hurt. I was suddenly sure he and Alice had been more than friends, and the situation became instantly much more complicated.

"Hello," I said finally, because one of us had to say something.

Robert cleared his throat. "Hey, Alice." He jerked his head at Bryan. "What's with the goon squad?"

"It's a long story. Come in."

Bryan took a half-step forward, partially blocking the doorway. "Bryan," I said sharply.

Unfazed, Robert met Bryan's glare. Despite my unease, I had to admire his moxie. "I won't lay a hand on her," he told Bryan. "I never would. I never have."

Clearly not mollified, Bryan moved aside.

Robert stepped into my foyer. I shut the door, leaving the enforcers on the porch. He and I stared at each other.

"Would you like something to drink?" I asked. "I have water, diet soda, and beer."

He didn't answer for a moment. "Water would be great. Thank you."

He followed me into the kitchen while I filled two cups with ice and water. I handed him one and led him into the living room. "Have a seat."

"Thanks." He perched on the edge of the sofa. I sat in the loveseat and set my cup on the side table. I sensed Malcolm near the couch, keeping a close watch on my visitor and radiating suspicion and unease.

"So, what brings you to California?" I asked.

His laugh was bitter. "Seriously, what brings me to California? Why don't you ask me about the weather? Maybe about how the Bears are doing? Jesus, Alice. Could you be any colder?"

I raised my hands. "What would you like me to say?"

He set his cup on the coffee table. "I don't know—maybe start with how the hell you're alive. Then explain why you moved out here and never once tried to contact me in the last five years."

"I'll do my best to explain, but tell me this: why are you only just now showing up? Like you said, it's been five years."

"What the hell kind of question is that?"

Clearly I was supposed to know why he hadn't tried to contact me, but I didn't.

At my blank look, he grew even angrier. "Are you serious? You *are* serious." He took several deep breaths, clearly trying to control his fury. "I was in jail. I served four years, ten months, and eleven days for possession. I got out three weeks ago."

"But if you're on parole—"

"Yeah, I'm violating my parole by leaving the state. They're going to send me back to jail if they find out." He shrugged. "I'll serve another year, maybe two, plus whatever they give me for the parole violation. But before I go back, I want some answers. I think I deserve at least that much."

Malcolm muttered an expletive. My sentiments exactly.

I thought about telling Robert he could have called or written me, but I kept my mouth shut because that wouldn't make the situation any better. He'd known he could have done that. Instead he'd made the choice to come to California to talk to me in person, no matter what it would cost him. My guilt over what I'd had to do to steal Alice's identity came roaring back, twice as bad as before.

Robert rested his forearms on his knees, his eyes haunted with memory. "I thought you were dead, Alice. You weren't breathing. You had no pulse. I panicked and ran and left you there. Damn it, I am so sorry."

I let out a breath. Now I knew the source of the police report Charles's researcher had found. Robert had been with Alice the day she'd died in that basement. He'd directed police to the site days later, but her body was nowhere to be found because by then I'd burned it and buried the ash in a park.

"I hated myself for leaving you like that," he said, his voice rough. "I rationalized it by telling myself there was nothing I could have done to help you and I didn't want to go to jail, but it chewed me up. I couldn't sleep. I couldn't eat. I tried to OD a couple of days later, but someone found me and called 911. Paramedics showed up and shot me full of naloxone. Cops threw my sorry ass in the back of a patrol car. I told them where to find your body, but when they went to the basement, there was nothing there. They thought I was making it up or too high to know what happened, but I *know* what I saw...or at least I thought I did. You're here, so obviously I was wrong."

He rubbed his face. "When Jenny told me you were back home a couple of weeks later, I thought she was making it up. She came to see me at the jail and she had a picture of you out in front your house. She said you weren't talking to any of your friends anymore and you were selling your house. I thought you'd come see me, or, shit, at least write me a letter, but you didn't. Not one word. I loved you, Alice—you know I did. You could have fucking said *something*." His pain and anger were so raw that I flinched.

Malcolm touched my shoulder. *This is not your fault,* he said emphatically in my head. *This is not your fault. Don't you dare blame yourself. He made his own choices. The other Alice made hers. None of that is on you.*

I shrugged my shoulder slightly and he moved his hand away. Intellectually, I knew damn well I wasn't at fault for the real Alice's death, but if I hadn't burned her body and stolen her identity, Robert would have gotten the closure he deserved. He could have grieved her death and moved on. Instead, he'd spent the last five years in prison thinking about Alice and wondering why she'd just left without a word.

The only way I could think to respond was to stick to my fabricated story and apologize. What else did I have to offer him?

"I'm sorry," I said finally. "When I woke up in the basement, I realized I'd just almost died, and if I didn't make a change, the next time I might not be so lucky. I checked into a cheap motel and detoxed. I was really sick. I was in no shape to talk to anyone for weeks."

He stared at me in disbelief. "You *detoxed* in a motel room by yourself with no meds? How the hell did you even survive that?"

I'd told these lies a dozen times, but for the first time, the words tasted rancid. I hated lying to him—hated it more and more with every word I said, though I wasn't exactly sure why. I didn't know this man at all, so why did his pain stab me right in my heart?

I couldn't let him figure out I wasn't the same Alice he'd known, so I had to lie. I had no choice. "I don't know," I said tonelessly. "I was too stubborn to die, I guess. When the worst of it was over, I wanted a fresh start somewhere far away from the mess I made. I sold everything and moved out here and trained to be a private investigator. I needed a new life, so I left the old one behind. I hurt some people to do that, but it was the only way I could survive."

"Well, good for you." He went to the window, his back to me. "Good for you, Alice. Some of us didn't get that lucky. Jenny died, you know, a couple months after you left. Dee and Ian too. I almost did. I felt like I didn't have anything to live for anymore. You don't know how many times I thought about hanging myself in my cell. I don't know why I didn't. Even after I kicked the heroin, which damn near killed me even with meds, I wanted to die."

Robert turned to face me, his eyes fiery. "The only thing that kept me going was the hope that someday I'd find you and you could explain what the hell happened and why you left. And now I've found you, it doesn't feel any better."

"I'm sorry," I said again, painfully aware of how hollow the words sounded. I wanted him to leave so I could be alone with my guilt and grief. "Is there anything else you want to know?" My tone was harsher than I'd intended.

"Yeah, there is." He approached, his expression and tone suddenly hard. I sensed Malcolm right next to me, ready in case Robert got violent. "I've got one more question for you, Alice, and it's really damn important. What happened to the baby?"

I was shocked speechless for several seconds. "I don't know what you're talking about."

"Of course you would say you don't know what I'm talking about." His mouth twisted. "Either you really *don't* know, or you're lying. I'm not sure which is worse, to be honest."

"I'm not lying," I insisted, though the sick feeling in my stomach intensified. "I really don't know what you're asking me."

"Well, maybe I can jog your memory, then." Robert crossed his arms. "The day you...the last day I saw you, you told me you thought you were pregnant. You were crying. We were both dope-sick so I wasn't thinking right, but I remember every word you said. You were worried you wouldn't be able to get clean. I told you we'd go to the clinic and find out and if you were pregnant, we'd both get clean for the baby's sake. You said we would go, and then...then you did the hit."

He swallowed hard. "For the longest time, I thought maybe you'd taken too much on purpose. I thought you'd tried to kill yourself and our baby. I hated you for it. I grieved. I'm *still* grieving—for you, for the baby, for everything. We didn't have much, Alice, but it sure as hell hurt to lose it all, just like that." He snapped his fingers. The sharp sound made me jump.

I sensed a tingle of magic. Malcolm had just jumped from the house to somewhere else. I had a feeling I knew where he'd gone.

"There was no baby," I told Robert emphatically. "I was wrong about being pregnant. I've never been pregnant, and that is the truth."

I had no idea if the real Alice had really been pregnant when she died, but I needed him to believe me and let that part of his grief and anger go. It was the least I could do.

"I would never have tried to kill myself like that," I added. "It was an accident—a dumb, stupid accident. I'm sorry for all the pain and grief and anger I've caused you. I'm sorry, Robert."

A long silence. I couldn't tell what he was thinking.

"Rob," he said quietly. "No one ever calls me Robert."

I exhaled. "Rob, yes. I know. I'm sorry. It's...it's been a long time. I forgot."

"That tells me a lot, actually."

Before I could ask what he meant, my phone rang. I picked it up and glanced at the screen. *Wolf Calling.* I sent him a brief text: *I'll call you back.*

I stuck the phone in my back pocket. "Sorry about that."

"Was that your boyfriend? The werewolf?"

"How—"

"The big guy from the Vampire Court told me about him. *Warned* me, really. Said you were tough and powerful enough to be the mate of an alpha werewolf, and I should think about what that meant before I did anything stupid. You're running in some very different circles these days. You used to be afraid of shifters and hated vampires, and now look at you."

I sensed Malcolm return. "I guess I've changed," I said.

"You sure as hell have." Robert took a step back. "You're not my Alice, that's for damn sure."

My stomach dropped.

"Not the Alice I knew," he continued. "The Alice I knew had her problems, but she was kind and loving. I didn't expect a happy reunion, but when you opened the door, you looked at me like you'd never seen me before in your life. You've got a werewolf boyfriend and Vampire Court bodyguards. Whoever you are now, I don't know you anymore. You're a different person. Your attitude, your friends....even your eyes are different. They're harder. Colder. Angry."

I couldn't think of anything to say, so I said nothing. He didn't suspect I wasn't the real Alice, but I didn't feel anything close to relieved about it. My heart and stomach hurt too much.

He backed toward the door. "We loved each other once. Maybe I still love you, despite everything, but you're cold. I thought prison made *me* hard, but you're much harder than me. I guess almost dying did that, or maybe you had to make yourself hard in order to leave us all behind and move out here. You feel nothing for me now but pity. I don't want your pity, Alice."

"I'm sorry," I said helplessly. "I truly am."

"I believe you." He turned away, maybe so I couldn't see his face. "It doesn't make me feel any better, but I do believe you're sorry."

I followed him to the door as Malcolm hovered somewhere close by. Robert paused with his hand on the doorknob. "Thanks for telling me the truth about the baby. At least I can try to let that go. I'll have to let you go too, somehow. Where I'm going, I guess I'll have time to figure it out."

He opened the door. Bryan and the other enforcer waited outside. Bryan's scowl was thunderous.

"Take care, Alice," Robert told me.

"You too, Rob," I said.

He turned to Bryan. "Want to give me a ride to the bus station?"

Bryan glanced at me. I shrugged. I was too emotionally drained to do more than that.

"Be glad to," Bryan told Robert. "Let's go."

They headed down the sidewalk. Bryan opened the back door of one of the SUVs and Robert got in. I closed my front door and raised my wards.

Malcolm went visible. "Alice—"

"I'm going upstairs," I told him, my voice strained. "I don't want to talk about it with you or Sean."

"I know. Sean's on his way, though. We'll just wait downstairs until you're ready to talk. I'm not sorry I went and told him what Robert said. I was worried about you."

I wanted to be angry at him, but I didn't have the energy. I just headed upstairs.

The tears started before I could even close my bedroom door.

About fifteen minutes later, my perimeter wards tingled. Sean's truck pulled into my driveway in a swoop of tires in gravel. The truck skidded to a stop and the door slammed. He must have broken every speed limit on his way here—the drive from his office to my house usually took nearly a half-hour.

Malcolm had said he and Sean would wait downstairs, but Sean wouldn't stay away. Part of me wanted to lock my bedroom door and keep him out. My hurt was too raw. I didn't want anyone to see me like this, not even Sean.

I turned my face into my pillow and tightened my grip on the little amethyst charm Carly had given me. Her parchment-scented magic offered some comfort, but not nearly enough. Cyro's news about the torture videos had cut me to the bone. Rob's visit had gutted me.

The front door slammed and footsteps rushed up the stairs without pausing. It sounded like Sean was taking them two at a time. If Malcolm had warned him I didn't want to talk, he hadn't listened. He had to be sensing my pain—he might have been feeling it since Robert walked through my front door. I didn't know how to block him from sharing my hurt. I'd asked him once how to do that, but he'd told me he didn't want me to shield him from my happiness or my pain.

My bedroom door opened and closed almost soundlessly. Sean toed off his shoes and curled around me, burying his face against the back of my neck. Warm comforting magic covered me. I tried to push it away, but he refused to let me.

"I'm sorry," he murmured, his lips against my skin. "Alice, I am so sorry." His arms tightened around me. I made a broken sound.

He held me while I wept, quietly nuzzling my neck as I cried myself out. In the warmth of his embrace and with the comforting scent of forest filling my nose, the pain slowly faded to tolerable levels. Eventually, I lay in his arms, too spent to move or talk. He knew without asking that I just wanted him to hold me while I struggled to process my hurt and guilt.

"I didn't know about him," I said when I could talk. "If I had, I would have sent him a letter. I would have let him call me so I could explain."

"I know you would have." He laced his fingers through mine. "This is not your fault, Alice. Not in any way."

"If I hadn't stolen—"

He squeezed me. "Robert Hamlin could have written you or called any time in the past five years to get the answers he wanted. I'm sure he wanted to ask you in person, but he didn't *have* to. He certainly didn't have to come here and hurt you like this." He growled. "I'm not unsympathetic, but this visit seems like it was more vindictive and intended to hurt you than as if he's really trying to find peace. Why else wait five years to ask those questions?"

I turned to face him. He brushed hair back from my face. "His appearance may call attention to that report Vaughan's researcher found," he added. "I hate that he's inadvertently put your security in jeopardy. Where was he headed when he left the house?"

"He asked Bryan for a ride to the bus station. I'm not sure if Bryan will take him straight there—he mentioned something about wanting to make sure Rob wasn't working for someone. They might take him back to Northbourne for a little Q-and-A before dropping him off at the station." I exhaled. "I hope Alice wasn't pregnant when she died. I think he believed me when I told him I wasn't. That's something, at least."

"Thank you for trying to ease his pain." He tilted my chin up so he could look into my eyes. "Now do the same for yourself and try to let this go. Alice's choices and Rob's actions are not burdens you should carry. Everything was over before you even found her in the basement. Don't stand in the middle of someone else's ruin and blame yourself for it."

"I'll try. It's going to take a while."

"I know." He kissed me. "I love you."

"I love you too." I kissed him back, my fingers in his hair.

He raised his head to smile down at me. "I know this is rotten timing, but maybe it will help distract you. The realtor called today asking if we were ready to move forward with the farmhouse. The sellers are getting antsy."

My stomach lurched. "What did you tell her?"

At my tone, his smile faded. "I said I thought we were ready to sign, but I'd talk to you and call back. What's wrong? Have you changed your mind?"

"Not...exactly."

He cupped my face with his hand. "Talk to me. Tell me what you need from me to be as happy about this today as you were the day we toured the house."

"A lot has happened since then. Caleb tried to kill me, my grandfather found me, Darius Bell died, Ben *almost* died, someone tried to kill everyone at the Vamp Court gala, Malcolm's still not recovered from whatever that weird magic did to him, and I've still got that splinter stuck in my chest." I rubbed the cold spot in the middle of my sternum where the magic from the decanter had hit me. "Now Cyro's looking for my biological father. And Rob..." I swallowed hard. "Rob just dropped a couple of bombshells. I just can't *do* this right now."

He pinched the bridge of his nose. "I'm not asking you to move in with me—I already asked you, and you said yes. I'm not asking if you want to buy the farmhouse—you already said yes to that too. The process is going to take a while. We won't be moving tomorrow, or next week, or even this month, but we need to get the ball rolling."

"I know that. I just need a little more time."

His expression darkened. "More time for what?"

"To be sure."

"What are you not sure of? That I love you? That you love me? That the farmhouse is perfect for us?"

I shook my head. "I'm sure of all those things."

"Then what aren't you sure of?"

How could I make him understand? "The problem is, those are the *only* things I'm sure of. Everything else—"

"Everything else is less important," he interrupted. "Those three things are by far the most important things in our lives right now, other than our pack and Malcolm. We will sort the rest of it out *together*. We can do that while they're working on the paperwork. I'm ready to move forward with our lives together. I thought you were too."

Carly's words echoed in my head: *Whatever's holding you back from saying yes to buying that house, you owe it to him and yourself to let it go.* But damn it, I was still clinging to something—my independence, my past, my fear, maybe even Charles, though it made no sense to do so. I wasn't ready to let go.

"Give me a couple of days," I begged. "I don't want to go into this feeling so tangled up. I'm sorry if that doesn't make any sense to you. I'm not changing my mind. I just...need more time," I repeated.

He was silent for a long time. I rested my head on his shoulder, sensing his anger and frustration. Guilt chewed at me because I'd caused it.

"I'll see how much time they're willing to give us," he said finally, resting his chin on top of my head. "I know it's hard for you to do, but talk it out with someone. If not me, then maybe Malcolm, Carly, or Arkady. I told you a long time ago that I want to make you happy, and I still do. Your happiness and security are essential for my own."

"Your happiness and security are essential for me too," I told him, squeezing his hand. "I wish I did a better job of making you happy and secure."

"Hey, you *do* make me happy, even when you're making me frustrated and a little crazy, which you've been doing since the night I met you." He nuzzled my hair. "I've gotten used to it, and I think I'd miss it if you stopped. As for security, that's going to be difficult without putting you in a cage, and that's something I'll never do. Whatever's got you all tangled up about the house, sort it out. In the meantime, do you still want to go to Karen and Cole's?"

I'd almost forgotten about our dinner plans. A few minutes ago, I'd wanted to lock myself in my room until my hurt went away. Now Sean's touch was healing my heart, and I knew being around other members of his pack would help too.

"Can you hold me a little longer before we go?" I asked.

He kissed the top of my head. "Of course."

1 1

THE MEAL AT KAREN AND COLE'S HOUSE WAS A SMALL GATHERING—JUST the hosts, Sean and me, Nan Lowell, and Sean's beta Jack Hastings and his wife Delia. Sean parked beside Nan's Toyota in the yard.

He came around to my side of the truck and took my hand. "Are you going to be all right talking to Jack and Delia?" he asked.

When I didn't reply immediately, he halted me with a hand on my arm. "Alice."

"It's all right," I told him, though it wasn't. Delia had instigated the hex that had nearly killed me and threatened me in wolf form the night of the full moon. While Jack had changed his mind about me being trouble for the pack and a poor choice for Sean's mate, Delia still strongly disliked me. She wanted Sean's mate to be a shifter, and preferably submissive. I was neither. Though she'd acknowledged I was more dominant, she was a long way from accepting me.

Still, Sean's motive for inviting them to dinner was obvious, and my strained relationship with Delia didn't outweigh their need. "They're hurting over Caleb's death," I murmured. Everyone was probably inside the house, but I didn't want to be overheard. "They need to be around the pack, especially you and Nan. I'm not sure me being here is going to help, but we all need to work on healing and it has to start somewhere."

He kissed my forehead. "Thank you."

"You owe me, though," I added.

"That sounds ominous. What do you have in mind?"

"I have a couple of thoughts," I told him with a faint smile.

He ran his nose along my hairline. "Strangely, your punishments always seem like the exact opposite of punishment."

"Maybe I'm misunderstanding the concept of punishment," I mused. "Because you *do* seem to really enjoy them."

He growled low, but not in anger. "I really do."

The front door opened, revealing Cole, Karen's husband. "Come on in," he said, stepping aside so we could enter the house. "We're eating out back since it's such a nice evening."

Karen appeared, carrying a covered dish from the kitchen to the open patio door. "Hi, you two!" she said cheerfully. "Help yourselves to whatever you'd like to drink and join us on the deck."

Sean and I grabbed beers from the fridge and followed Karen outside. The back of the house faced east and was shady and cool, a perfect setting for an evening meal.

Cole and Karen frequently hosted pack gatherings like this one, as did Jack and Delia. One of the reasons Sean wanted to buy a different house was so he—so *we*—could take over hosting duties. The farmhouse Sean and I had offered to buy had an even larger back deck, perfect for meals, parties, and other pack gatherings. I tried to imagine us living together in that house and having the whole pack over for such events. My stomach churned at the thought of so many people coming and going in our home.

Sean glanced at me, his brow furrowed. He'd clearly sensed my unease. I forced a tight smile.

"Alice!" Nan Lowell hurried over and gave me a hug. She shared Sean's ability to provide comfort to her pack mates and her touch eased the pain in my heart.

She held on for a few extra beats, as if sensing I was hurting, then stepped back. "Are you all right?" she asked in an undertone. The others would hear her, but I'd realized that shifters would pretend *not* to hear, giving the illusion of privacy.

"Tough day, but I'm better now." I smiled at her. "I'm glad you're here."

Jack and Delia had been standing by the railing, talking quietly when Sean and I arrived. They approached us. Sean's tall, blond beta looked weary. "Sean. Alice."

Sean shook Jack's hand. "It's good to see you both. How are you, Delia?" His voice was gentle.

Jack's much-shorter wife glanced at Sean, then returned her gaze to the deck. She didn't look at me. "We're getting by."

I'd been around Delia enough to know she wasn't a hugger, but the others—Sean, Nan, and Karen—gathered around her and Jack, offering comfort and support. Nan put her hand on Delia's arm. Delia flinched, but didn't move away.

Strangely, I felt compelled to join them, to offer whatever comfort I could. Delia's amber eyes flicked up to meet mine. Her expression made it clear I wasn't welcome. Then she looked down again, unable to hold my gaze for long.

Instead of backing away, I moved closer to Jack. He was hurting too— he was just hiding it better than Delia. That made me worry about him more, since I knew all too well that bottling up pain didn't make it go away.

"Thank you all for coming over," Karen said. Cole held her hand.

Everyone still hurt over Caleb's death—even me. My grandfather's threats and the bloodbath at the Vamp Court gala had distracted me from the guilt and pain, but I deeply regretted I'd had to kill Caleb. The fact it was in self-defense didn't do much to assuage my guilt, and the memory of his death haunted me.

"Let's eat before everything gets cold," Sean said finally.

We settled in around the table. I sat between Sean and Jack and across from Nan and Karen. I expected to feel less than comfortable next to Jack, but instead his presence reassured me. In fact, sitting in the midst of the pack helped ease my worry about my grandfather, and the attack at the gala, and pain over the news about the videos and Rob's surprise visit.

Dinner for the shifters was steak and chicken—served hot but not necessarily cooked—plus casseroles for carbohydrates. Cole and I, on the other hand, had smaller steaks cooked medium, salads, and helpings of the casseroles. We exchanged smiles as the shifters filled their plates and "wolfed" down their meals.

Eating with shifters led to overeating, since they put away a hell of a lot of food at one sitting, so I ignored how much they ate and focused on my own meal. I hadn't had much of an appetite lately, but I managed to eat enough that Sean didn't frown at me or my plate.

Gradually, as their stomachs filled and the pace of their eating slowed, the others started chatting. Unsurprisingly, the main topics of conversation were Karen's pregnancy and Ben's recent engagement.

I'd learned it was more difficult than average for a shifter female to get pregnant and not miscarry, whether the baby's father was shifter or human, so Karen's happiness had taken on additional meaning for me. While Delia remained lukewarm about the news, everyone else was thrilled to welcome the pack's first new baby since John and Brandon's third child was born via surrogate seven years ago.

"Can I ask a nosy question?" I said during a pause in the conversation.

Karen smiled. "What do you want to know?"

"If your baby is a shifter, does it shift in the womb just when you shift, or on its own?"

She laughed. "That's actually a good question. If the baby is a shifter, while it's inside me it will stay in human form and only shift when I shift. After it's born, it will shift only on the full moon until puberty. If it's a human baby, obviously, it will stay human."

"It's a relief to know the baby would only shift on the full moon," Cole said with a grin. "I'm excited about having a baby, whether it's human or shifter, but I have to admit the prospect of chasing a wolf pup around day and night wears me out just to think about it."

We laughed.

"What about you, Alice?" Delia asked, leaning forward so she could see around Jack. "Would you want your kids to be shifters, or human?"

The chuckles died away. Nan looked sharply at Delia. I sensed Sean's displeasure. Delia's tone and expression were innocent, but I doubted her question was as casual as she wanted to make it seem. Damn it, every time I tried to keep the peace with this woman, she went and did something like this.

Sean said nothing; he was letting me deal with Delia. I wanted to be considerate of her in the wake of Caleb's death, but her question was over the line. On top of that, I was still raw from Rob's visit and the revelation about the real Alice's possible pregnancy.

"My reproductive choices are really none of your business," I told her, my voice frosty.

"They most certainly aren't any of your business, as you very well know," Nan said with a frown. "And human or shifter, every child is very much welcome in this pack."

"I apologize, Alice," Delia said. To my surprise, she sounded sincere. "I didn't mean to start something."

After a beat, I said, "Apology accepted."

The others engaged in quiet conversation as I ate the last of the hash brown casserole on my plate and tried to figure out what to think about

Delia's apology. She could have been faking her apparent remorse, or she might have been truly chastised by Nan's rebuke. To my surprise, it was difficult for me to figure out which.

I used to think Delia was the highest-ranking woman in the pack in terms of dominance, but was beginning to realize I'd been wrong. Delia was more aggressive, for sure—there was no mistaking that. Nan's strength and will was greater, albeit quieter. I'd seen the others back down from her, even Ben and Jack, without her even raising her voice. Sean respected her as much or more than anyone else in the pack.

My phone buzzed. I glanced at the screen and saw it was Bryan Smith calling. I excused myself and took my phone into the house, closing the patio door behind me and moving into the kitchen so I couldn't be overheard. "Hi, Bryan."

"Miss Alice," he rumbled. I could tell by his tone there was a problem. "You're needed immediately, by request of Madame Valas."

I glanced out the window. The sun was still almost an hour from setting. The older the vamp, the earlier they woke. I wondered how long Valas had been awake—or if she slept at all. "What's going on? Has there been another attack?"

"Madame Valas prefers I not discuss the specifics over an unsecured line. There is a crime scene that requires your expertise. Should I send a car to your location?"

"Hang on." I muted the call and went to the patio door. I caught Sean's eye and motioned for him to come into the house.

When he was inside with the door closed, I said, "Valas has asked me to go look at a crime scene. Bryan says they can send a vehicle. I might as well get picked up and use a Court vehicle until I can get my own car." I hated using Court vehicles, since I knew they all had GPS trackers and were probably bugged. Even if I was working for the Court, I strongly disliked being spied on.

Sean's eyes turned golden. "I don't trust them—any of them."

"I don't trust them either, but I've solved cases for them for five years. Besides, just because I'm going to see what happened doesn't mean I have to take the case. I'm not employed by the Court; I'm an independent contractor. If I don't want to get involved, I'll tell them to give the job to someone else."

"Why are they asking you, instead of one of their full-time investigators?" he wanted to know.

"My guess is that it's something to do with what happened the other night at the gala."

When he didn't reply, I squeezed his hand. As much as this new protectiveness—or this newly overt protectiveness—grated on my nerves, I understood it came from his love for me and his desire to keep me safe, a desire that was both conscious and instinctual.

"I want to know what this magic is," I reminded him, tapping my chest where the little cold splinter still twinged. "I know you don't want me to be in danger, but I'm a mage private investigator. Danger comes with the territory. I'm not giving up my job." My voice was gentle but firm. "I know how to protect myself and I know how to call for help if I need it."

A muscle moved in his jaw as he struggled with his dislike and distrust of the Vampire Court. "Take Malcolm, please."

"I plan to." I unmuted the call. "Sorry to leave you holding, Bryan. Send a car." I gave him Karen's address.

"Adri is on her way," he said briskly. "She'll be there in fifteen minutes."

"I'll see her in a few, then." I ended the call and looked up at Sean. "I'm sorry to bail out on dinner."

"It's all right." His expression darkened. "Do you want me to say something to Delia?"

"Nope—it's my battle. Besides, she apologized, which was weird."

"That's Nan for you. No one defies Nan." He kissed my knuckles. "I love you."

I kissed him thoroughly. When we broke apart, I smiled. "I know."

I SAID GOODBYE TO THE OTHERS, THEN SUMMONED MALCOLM AND explained where we were going before stashing him in my bracelet for the trip to the crime scene.

Adri arrived in one of the Court's signature black SUVs exactly fifteen minutes after Bryan's call. I hurried outside as she parked in front of the house, glad I'd worn jeans and boots and not a sundress and sandals like I'd been tempted to do. My T-shirt was decidedly casual even by my standards if I had to go to Northbourne later, but I could do little about it short of going by my house or Sean's to change. Judging by Adri's grim expression, there wasn't time for that, so the vamps would just have to deal with my attire.

Adri barely waited for me to get my door closed before she headed back down the driveway toward the main road.

I buckled my seatbelt and dropped my bag on the floor at my feet. "On a scale of one to ten, what kind of crisis am I walking into?"

She shook her head. "I don't know any details. I'm just your driver."

"Fair enough." I paused. "So, has Elizabeth gone back, or are the Chicago vamps still here?"

Adri glanced at me. "They're still in town."

Drat. I was hoping they'd left. Elizabeth had asked me a lot of questions. With Robert Hamlin's sudden appearance, I was nervous that too many people were interested in the events surrounding Alice Worth's decision to move to California from Chicago.

Adri headed south instead of in the direction of Northbourne. We chatted on the way to our destination, taking the opportunity to catch up.

"I heard you put in an offer on a country farmhouse," Adri said as she wove through traffic. "I never pegged you as a country girl. You know they don't even get pizza delivery out there." Her tone implied living somewhere without pizza delivery was akin to living on the dark side of the moon.

"It's a beautiful house. We can make our own pizza." I pictured Sean in the kitchen, twirling pizza dough with flour on his nose, and smiled to myself.

She did raise an important point, though. How *did* people survive without food delivery options? Next time we talked about the new house, I'd have to ask Sean about that.

Adri turned onto a residential street in a quiet neighborhood and parked behind two black Court SUVs in front of a small blue house. The door of the house opened. Matthias, a Court enforcer, emerged, looking grim—well, more grim than usual. Matthias was not what I'd call a cheerful guy. Arkady had told me at lunch yesterday they were fighting about what had happened at my grandfather's mansion. I wondered if his mood was a result of their fight, the scene inside the house, or a combination of both.

"He's got you from here," Adri told me. "When you're done, Matthias will drive you wherever you need to go. I'm headed back to Mr. Vaughan's estate. If you need anything, tell Matthias."

"Yeah, I'm sure that won't be awkward," I muttered, grabbing my bag.

She made a face. "Considering you and Arkady are BFFs and they're currently fighting, I can imagine."

I sighed. "Is there anything going on with anyone associated with the Court that everyone doesn't know about?"

She thought for a moment. "I don't think anyone knows Valas's guard Hanson has been sleeping with Leah, Amira's head of security."

Despite my worry about what was in that house, I chuckled. "See you later."

I hopped out of the SUV, shut the door, and headed across the yard. As Adri departed, I paused to adjust my jean cuff over my boot and touched the green crystal on my bracelet. "*Release.*"

Malcolm appeared beside me. "Hey, Alice." He glanced around. "What are we dealing with?"

"Don't know yet," I murmured. I straightened, put my bag on my shoulder, and continued in Matthias's direction with Malcolm trailing along behind me.

Matthias gave me a brief nod as I approached. "Ms. Worth."

"Matthias." I joined him on the porch. "What have we got? Is it messy?"

He shook his head and opened the door. "Not messy."

Thank goodness for small favors. I went inside with Malcolm. Matthias followed us in and closed the door.

I glanced around the living room and kitchen. Bachelor pad, for sure, but reasonably tidy except for a pizza box containing a half-eaten pizza on the coffee table next to a couple of beer cans. A pair of running shoes waited near the door. A stack of mail was piled on the counter, and a laptop sat on the couch. I glanced at the receipt taped to the top of the pizza box to see when it had been ordered: just after eight o'clock last night.

"Down the hall. Third door on the left," Matthias told me.

I walked ahead of him, passing open doorways that led to a bathroom, spare bedroom used as a workout room, and laundry room. Malcolm followed.

The crime scene was at the end of the hall, in the larger of the two bedrooms. The dead man lay face down on the carpet near the foot of the bed, his head at an odd angle. He wore a black T-shirt and sweatpants, and his feet were bare. A beer can lay next to his body, its contents spilled into the carpet. Whatever had happened, it had happened fast and dropped him right where he stood.

"Has anyone been in here but you and me?" I asked Matthias as Malcolm floated near the body.

He shook his head. "I came here to check on the decedent and found him like this. I touched nothing."

"You came to check on him? Who is this?"

"Madame Valas would like to hear your unbiased assessment of the situation."

"Has anyone called the cops?"

He looked at me.

"Okay, no cops." I crouched next to the body. "He's probably been dead since last night, since that pizza was delivered around eight thirty or nine and he was holding one of the beers he drank with the pizza when something killed him." I prodded his shoulder with my fingertips. "He's stiff. Not a surprise, if he's been dead about twenty hours at room temperature." I studied him more closely. "Looks like his neck's broken. Can you roll him over?"

Matthias complied. The dead man wasn't large, but dead weight wasn't easy to move. As an enforcer, however, Matthias drank vampire blood regularly, which made him far stronger than a normal human. He turned the body over with minimal effort.

The blood had settled and the result was unpleasant. I forced myself to look at the man's discolored face. Despite the effects of lividity, he looked familiar, but I couldn't place him. I thought maybe I'd seen him at Northbourne recently. He wasn't built like an enforcer, however. Rigor had frozen him in the position he'd been in when he died, so even when Matthias rolled him over, his neck stayed at that unnatural angle.

"Maybe someone snuck up behind him and snapped his neck, but I don't see any bruising or other visible trauma," I noted. "There's something odd on the side of his neck, though—it looks like a little V-shaped mark." I pulled the collar of his shirt aside to get a better look.

Familiar magic snapped at my fingers like electricity arcing from a frayed wire. Malcolm cursed and flitted back. I scrambled away as a tendril of void-black magic lashed in my direction. The icy barb in my chest twisted painfully. I bit back a yelp and covered it with my hand.

Lightning fast, Matthias jumped in front of me, shielding me with his massive body from a threat he could neither see nor sense.

The flare was short-lived. The magic fizzled and dissipated with a little puff of that strange musty odor I recognized from the decanter.

"Damn it." I rubbed my chest.

"Are you injured?" Matthias glared at the body as if he thought the dead man might jump up and attack us.

I got to my feet. "I'm fine. That was the same weird magic that was on the decanter. I guess that confirms this is definitely connected to what happened at the gala." Something clicked in my head. I moved around Matthias to look at the dead man's face. "I *do* know this guy. He's the server I saw carrying the decanter on the night of the gala. Is that why you came here to talk to him?"

Matthias nodded, his eyes still on the body. "His name is Ted Watson. We questioned him on the night of the gala. He said he didn't know anything about the decanter's origin, only that he'd been asked by one of the staff to bring it out to the bar. The vampires determined he was truthful. When we spoke with the staff tasked with preparing the blood for consumption, we were unable to corroborate his account. I was sent to question him again this afternoon and found him dead."

I crouched to look at the mark on Watson's neck. It was a rune, or part of a rune. One side of the wide V was straight, the other curved slightly like a bird's wing.

Malcolm floated over and touched my shoulder. *Was that magic left as some kind of booby trap?* he asked in my head.

I don't think so, I told him. *It was a weak remnant of magic. Do you recognize this rune?*

No—it doesn't look familiar. He let go of my shoulder and drifted back.

I knelt to get a closer look at the mark. It hadn't been made by any ordinary blade, but with a spelled implement like one of the ritual daggers I used to cut runes into my skin. Unfortunately, that didn't help me narrow down what kind of magic this was, since that practice was common.

I took a picture of the rune with my phone, then checked Watson for other marks. There weren't any, at least that I could see. I also checked for more magic, but that one little zap seemed to be all that remained. Even the trace had dissipated, leaving nothing I could track. Damn it.

The little cold splinter in my chest buzzed slightly. Whatever the magic was, it had done something to the splinter. I rubbed my chest.

"Theories?" Matthias asked, startling me out of my thoughts.

I stood and stuck my phone in my back pocket. "I'm sure the Court will autopsy Mr. Watson to confirm this, but I'm thinking someone used that magic to snap his neck. They cut the rune into his skin sometime before last night, maybe for this purpose, or maybe for some other reason we don't know about yet."

Matthias made a sound like the beginning of an avalanche. "Could that person have controlled Watson through this rune? Used it to force him to smuggle the decanter into the gala and then serve blood from it to the guests?"

I thought about it. "That would take some *serious* power, but it's possible. That might be why he seemed truthful when the vamps asked him about the decanter—he could have been spelled *not* to remember, or to remember a different version of events."

Matthias regarded the dead man. "Everyone who worked at the gala passed through wards that were supposed to disrupt any spells."

"We're dealing with something new and it's a serious threat. This magic is capable of getting through the wards at Northbourne."

He was already texting before I finished speaking. The reply was instantaneous. "They're sending a crew," he said, glancing up. "Madame Valas requests you accompany the body to Northbourne and present your findings and theories in person."

This magic was dangerous and it had already left its mark on both Malcolm and me, but I wanted this barb out of my chest. I needed to fix Malcolm and destroy the magic still stuck in the crystal in the box in my basement. To do that, I had to know what it was and who was wielding it.

"Ms. Worth." Matthias's voice was impatient.

"Let's go to Northbourne." I sent Sean a text to tell him where I was headed. It was going to be another long night.

Valas listened to Matthias's report, then dismissed him. He departed silently, leaving me alone with the head of the Vampire Court.

I described what I'd seen and felt at Watson's home, then offered my theory about how he'd been spelled into bringing the decanter to the gala and killed when his usefulness was at an end.

My pronouncement that the unknown magic was capable of crossing the vampires' wards elicited exactly the response I'd anticipated: anger.

"You will alter our wards so this magic cannot enter Northbourne again," Valas stated. Her fangs were visible, but she was much too old to lisp around them. "Our people and property must be protected."

"I would if I could, but I can't."

She hissed. "That is not acceptable."

"This isn't my magic, or any kind of magic I've encountered before. I have no effect on it and without knowing more about it, no ward I can make will keep it out." Malcolm's might, but I didn't want her to know that. Her desire to protect the Court might cause her to demand Malcolm's services—or enlist them, at any cost.

"Then you will discover the magic's origin and determine how we can counter it."

Her imperious command grated on my already frayed nerves, but I resisted the urge to tell her to shove it. "The other night, you didn't want me involved in searching for the decanter's origin. Why the change of heart?"

"The situation demands I set aside my personal concerns for the good of my Court." Which was not really an answer to my question. "The Court authorizes premium compensation, plus a bonus of fifteen percent upon completion of the work."

"If I'm going to put myself and everyone around me in this kind of danger, I need more than that."

Her eyes narrowed. "I am curious as to what terms you wish to propose."

I'd been thinking about this since the night of the gala, when I'd suspected I'd end up looking for the source of the decanter. "I'll find out where the decanter came from and what kind of magic this is, and who is behind these attacks. In return, you'll pay me at premium rates *and* count this against the debt I owe you for your assistance in saving Sean's life."

Her all-black eyes glowed in anger. "I refuse."

"You need me to do this." I leaned forward. "You trust me to get the answers. If you thought you could use one of the Court mages, you'd have gone that route. You need me to find out who is responsible for the bloodbath at the gala and protect you and your people from this new threat. You also need me to make a certain journey on your behalf, as we've already discussed. And now I've seen the gift Elizabeth brought you, I know the time is coming for me to make that trip."

Irritation flashed in her dark eyes. She hadn't expected me to link the mirror-door to our deal, and she wasn't happy I'd figured out the mirror was intended for my use.

"I'll find the source of this new magic," I said. "Then I'll go on your little errand, and then we'll be square. Otherwise..." I shrugged. "Find someone else to figure out where this new magic came from and how to fight it."

She rose and placed her hands on the heavy wooden table. The table vibrated against the stone floor with a sound like distant thunder. "You threaten me?"

I stayed seated. "Not a threat—a proposal. You must have considered the possibility I would make this proposition." If she hadn't, I'd eat my boots. Valas was much too smart to have been truly surprised by my terms. Her overt show of anger was part of our negotiations.

Or so I thought, until the table split down the middle with a sharp *crack*. "You are in no position to renegotiate the terms of our agreement," Valas said, her voice so cold I half expected icicles to form in midair between us. "You overestimate your bargaining power and you try my patience. Neither is advisable, at this moment or any other."

I stood and slid my chair back from the table. "Then give this case to a different investigator. You'll have my report on everything I've done so far by the morning."

Her eyes flashed silver. Shadows gathered around her shoulders and dark power rolled over me like a bank of thick fog, bringing with it Valas's unique scent. The head of the Vampire Court was visibly angry and I was the cause.

I squashed a little spike of fear. This was my best and possibly only chance to improve the terms of my deal, and I was going to take it, even if it meant playing with fire.

Her dark power tightened around me. "You like dangerous games," Valas mused. "Perhaps I shall point out you are here now, rather than chained in Moses Murphy's compound in Baltimore, because I have deemed you a favorite of the Court—a designation I can rescind at any time."

"If I go to Baltimore, you don't have anyone to go through that mirror and fetch your doohickey."

"And once you have reclaimed my *doohickey* and you are no longer of use to me, how do you propose to stay free from Murphy?" Valas sounded genuinely curious. "You grievously injured his only surviving daughter. His desire for revenge is all-consuming. He will come for you."

She had no idea Moses was coming after me for a much more important reason than what I'd done to Catherine. "Maybe he will, and maybe he'll get a surprise when he does. That's my problem to deal with." I spread my hands. "For now, do we have a deal in regard to this case and our agreement?"

Silence.

"Seven days," she said.

I shook my head.

"Seven days," she repeated. "You will discover the source of the unknown magic, find a way to protect us from it, and bring me the person responsible for the attack on the gala."

"I don't work like that. I solve a case as quickly as I can, but I can't guarantee—"

Eyes flashing like a lightning storm in the desert, she flew directly at me, passing—impossibly—through the table as if her lower body had turned to smoke. Before I could react, she had me by the throat.

To my surprise, she didn't squeeze—just curved her fingers around my throat, the tips of her nails biting into my flesh. Her scent was nearly intoxicating.

"You work as I tell you to." She seemed to be completely solid again, standing toe-to-toe with me.

I pushed blood magic out through my fingertips, forming a blade. "Let go of me."

Her fingers tightened. "Do not attempt to cause me harm, Alice Worth, or you will be dead before you can draw your next breath."

"Let go," I repeated. "No one touches me without my permission, not even you."

She smiled slightly. Silver ringed her black eyes. I'd never seen a vampire with silver rings in their eyes. I resisted their mesmerizing glow.

"Ah, child, you are fierce," she murmured. She released my throat. Her fingertips trailed down my upper chest, leaving a trail of dark gray vamp magic. I stepped back before she touched the little cold splinter. "Like myself, you are many things masquerading as one. Perhaps that is why I find you so intriguing, and why I indulge your rudeness." The smile vanished. "You will bring me answers in no more than seven days."

"And if I'm not able to?"

She regarded me coldly. "Many on the Court do not understand why I permit you to continue to operate as an independent contractor, as you call yourself. Charles has successfully persuaded me in the past that your independence and apparent neutrality has value, especially when you must interact with human law enforcement on our behalf. In light of recent events, I have decided those benefits do not outweigh our need to formalize your relationship with us. The majority of the Court agrees."

"Valas—"

The silver rings in her eyes brightened. "Solve this mystery within seven days, and I will permit you to choose which member of the Court will hold your bond. Fail, and *I* will choose."

I shook my head. "No deal."

"There will be no argument on this matter," she snapped. "Elizabeth continues to show great interest in you. She may insist you pay an extended visit to the Chicago Court, and I have no recourse to stop her. You can no longer continue to reap the benefits of association with the Court without giving us something of equal or greater value in return. You cannot have your cake and eat it too, Ms. Worth. Your status—and

Charles's long indulgence of your whims—has caused dissension on the Court and among our employees, and both end *now*."

This was exactly what I'd long feared would happen if I came to the attention of too many powerful people: a fight over who owned me. Deep down, I'd never truly believed I could avoid this forever. I'd had five years of relative freedom after escaping Moses's cabal, but my power was bound to be noticed and my anonymity lost. That didn't make my impending loss of independence any easier to accept.

On the other hand, I wasn't bound to anyone on the Court yet. I had seven days to solve the mystery of the decanter and figure out a way to stay unbound. Other than the unwelcome news about Valas's intention to bind me to the Court, I'd mostly gotten what I sought from our negotiation. The deadline was not something I'd expected or wanted, but I'd probably be able to get to the bottom of this mess within a week.

Probably.

"Seven days," I said. My blood magic blade vanished. "What did you mean about me being many things? And how did you go through the table like that?"

"The first question is one you must answer yourself. And the second, I suggest you consider before you try my patience again. You may go. Matthias will drive you home."

I bowed. "Good night, Valas."

When I straightened, her eyes were thoughtful. "I expect a report waiting for me when I wake tomorrow evening. You are dismissed."

13

MATTHIAS DROPPED ME OFF AT SEAN'S HOUSE JUST BEFORE THREE IN THE morning. I unlocked the door, slipped inside, and locked it behind me. Malcolm was with Liam at my grandfather's mansion, still trying to regenerate and repair himself after his run-in with the unknown magic.

Rogue got up from his bed in the living room and met me in the entryway. "Hey, fur-face," I murmured, scratching him behind the ears as I put my bag on the floor next to the door and toed off my shoes. He followed me up the stairs and down the hall to Sean's room.

The room was dark, but Sean wasn't asleep. No matter how quietly I snuck into the house, his sharp ears would have heard my arrival.

"Hey," he said softly as Rogue settled into his bed by the window.

"Hey," I echoed. I went into the bathroom to wash my face, brush my teeth, and change into pajamas. When I emerged, the bedding rustled. In the faint light coming in through a gap in the curtains, I saw Sean raise the comforter for me to climb in next to him as I usually did.

Instead, I went around to the other side of the bed and crawled under the covers behind him. I curled up, fitting my body against his, and wrapped my arm around his stomach. I buried my face against his back and drank in the scent of forest.

"This is different," he murmured.

"Bad different or good different?" I asked, my voice muffled by his shirt.

I sensed him smiling. "Very good different." He raised my hand so he could kiss my knuckles, then tucked my arm under his. "I could get used to this." We lay quietly for a while.

"Are you all right?" he asked finally.

"I'm all right."

"But?" he prodded.

I sighed. "But that icy splinter in my chest is buzzing now. Malcolm and I still can't figure out what kind of magic this is."

His chest rumbled. "Something happened while you were out."

"I can't tell you the details," I reminded him. "Confidentiality agreement."

The rumble became a growl.

"I *can* tell you I wasn't hurt." I laced my fingers through his. "I did take the case, though. Solving it may help me figure out what this splinter is and get rid of it, and make sure no one else is in danger from the same threat. I also negotiated a much higher pay rate than usual, since this situation is outside the realm of what I usually do." Because my deal with Valas—and our negotiations tonight—were confidential, I couldn't reveal either, but when everything was said and done and I'd fulfilled my part of the bargain, I'd tell him everything.

"And more dangerous and unpredictable." He turned to face me. His eyes reflected the moonlight in a telltale golden sheen that told me his wolf was looking at me too. "I'm glad you have Malcolm as a partner on this."

"I am too." I smiled. "It's good to have someone watching my back."

"You used to think the only way to work was alone." He kissed my forehead. "I'm glad you changed your mind."

"I thought it made me safer to work alone." My smile faded. "I was so busy thinking about all the ways people could hurt and betray me that I forgot all the ways they could care about me. Thank you for reminding me."

"Having you here with me is the only thanks I need." He nestled me against his chest and rested his chin on top of my head.

Ever since we'd used them to save each other's lives, our matching wolf amulets hummed whenever they were together. The warm feeling of their magic drowned out the cold sensation of the splinter. Contented, I closed my eyes.

I expected Sean to fall back asleep immediately now I was home and in bed, but he didn't. As I drifted off, it occurred to me he never fell asleep before I did when we were together, as if he couldn't let go until he was sure I was sleeping. If I was upset or worried about something, he wanted to know. I hadn't noticed it until just now.

Despite the splinter and my worry about Malcolm and my new case, I fell asleep smiling.

Sean left for work early in the morning to meet with a client. I headed out before eight. Valas's seven-day deadline weighed on me like a clock ticking over my head. I intended to go to Northbourne to get another look at the decanter and do some research on the mark I'd found on Ted Watson's neck.

On my way to Brew a Cup for coffee and breakfast, I summoned Malcolm. He looked and felt stronger after spending time at the mansion, and more cheerful too. The former I attributed to the house's ambient power and the latter to Liam's company. My ghost was clearly smitten.

Even after his terrible death and everything he'd seen and been through since meeting me, Malcolm had never been morose or angry, but I didn't think he was ever truly happy either. He seemed that way now, however, and his happiness made my heart light, despite the pressure of Valas's deadline.

"You're in good spirits," I said as I parked in front of Brew a Cup.

He rolled his eyes. "A ghost joke? *Really*, Alice? I thought we were past that."

"It was the best I could do before coffee." I got out of the car. "Besides, ghost jokes never get old."

"Says you." Malcolm floated beside me. "You look tired."

"That's why we're here." I opened the front door of Carly's coffee shop, stepped inside, and inhaled. "Mmm."

"Alice." Malcolm's voice held a warning note. "Look."

I glanced at the back of the shop. Instead of working behind the counter, Carly stood near the window, talking in low, angry tones with a red-haired woman whose back was to me. Katy, the pink-haired young witch who'd helped hex me a little over a week ago, was making drinks behind the counter, but she glanced nervously at Carly and the other woman as she worked.

Katy caught my eye. Once before, when I'd come to the shop while she was working, she'd avoided me by going into the back room. This time, I got the distinct impression I was the least of her worries. She went back to her work, forcing a smile for the customer who'd asked for a different lid for his coffee.

Based on Carly's body language and Katy's worry, I put two and two together and came up with black witch. For confirmation, I touched Malcolm's arm. *You sense any dark magic on that redhead?*

Big time, he said. *Her aura looks like a layer of soot.* He went invisible and stayed near the door in case the witch could sense the presence of spirits.

I headed in Carly's direction. She was focused on the redhead and didn't see me approach until I was a few feet away. Dismay flashed in her eyes.

The redhead turned. I saw the resemblance to Katy immediately. This had to be Morgan, Carly's former friend. Morgan was an inch or two shorter than me, but she somehow managed to look down her nose at me.

Carly's expression was distinctly unfriendly. "Yes? Can I help you?"

I was taken aback until I realized she was pretending not to know me. As much as I didn't want a powerful black witch noticing me, I felt protective of Carly. I reminded myself she was a very powerful witch in her own right. Morgan was on her turf, and I'd be willing to bet if hex came to shove, Carly could defend herself.

Still, it took effort to play along and let Carly take care of her own business. "Sorry to interrupt," I said. "I just wanted to say how much I love your scones."

"Thank you. Katy can take your order." She turned her attention back to Morgan.

I went to the counter. Katy looked equal parts angry, worried, and scared. She swallowed hard and met my eyes. "What can I get you?" Her voice shook.

I was still a long way from forgiving her for her role in hexing me, but I understood all too well what unwanted family reunions felt like. "Large coffee and two blueberry scones, please."

"Would you like the scones warmed up?" she asked.

"One of them, yes." I intended to take the other scone to Sean at work if I had a chance. If not, it would make a good snack later.

She ran my card, then poured my coffee and slipped the cup into a sleeve. I took the cup to the table by the windows where the shop kept the various creamers and sweeteners. I added cream and a couple of packets of raw sugar and stirred it slowly, taking my time while Katy warmed my scone.

Carly and Morgan talked in undertones ten feet away. Try as I might, I couldn't hear anything other than a few words here and there. Morgan mentioned Katy's name more than once. Judging by Katy's hunched shoulders, she was aware she was a topic of conversation.

I took a small notebook from my bag and jotted a quick note. When my scones were ready, I returned to the counter.

Katy handed me two paper bags and gave me a small smile. "Thanks for coming in. Have a great day."

I slid a folded piece of paper across the counter. "I'll come back later if you think you'll have more scones."

She glanced at the message I'd written, then tucked the note into her apron pocket. "We might," she said without looking at Carly and Morgan. "I'll ask and let you know."

My phone rang. I didn't recognize the number, but it was local. "See you later," I told Katy. I stuck the scones in my bag and headed for the door as I answered the call. "Alice Worth."

"Ms. Worth, this is Hanson, calling on behalf of the Court."

I was mildly surprised to hear his voice. I wondered if a call from one of Valas's personal guards meant there had been a development. I pushed the door open with my shoulder. "Hi, Hanson. Any leads turn up on the decanter?"

"We may have a lead." His voice was characteristically brusque. "There's a paleography expert at the museum who may be able to decipher the meaning of the inscribed symbols on the decanter."

"A paleo what?" I set my coffee on top of my car so I could dig out my keys. I sensed Malcolm nearby, waiting.

"Paleography expert," Hanson repeated. "Dr. Cyril Blackstone. He studies ancient writing. I'm sending you an image of the inscriptions to show him."

I got into my car. "I thought the museum didn't open until ten."

"Dr. Blackstone will meet you at the rear door. May I tell him your ETA?"

I made a face at the phone. "I'll be there in about thirty minutes, depending on traffic. Send me the picture."

"Sending it now. Thank you, Ms. Worth." He disconnected.

Malcolm appeared in the passenger seat area. "What does Carly have to do with a black witch?"

I headed in the direction of the museum. Between gulps of coffee and bites of scone, I gave Malcolm an abbreviated version of the story Carly had told me about her former coven and her strained relationship with Morgan.

When I told him Morgan was Katy's mother, Malcolm cursed fluently and creatively. "How does Carly know Katy's not just spying on her?" he demanded.

"I had the same thought, but Katy seemed truly shaken by Morgan being at the shop today. I couldn't overhear what Carly and Morgan were talking about, but I heard them mention Katy a couple of times."

My phone rang. I glanced at the screen, then answered using my car's hands-free feature. "Carly, is everything okay?"

"Yeah, I'm fine." Carly sounded equal parts angry and frustrated. "Sorry about brushing you off. I didn't want Morgan thinking we were friends and trying to find out who you are."

"I figured as much." I stopped at a red light. "Did she leave?"

"Yes, a few minutes ago. I went out back to smoke and calm down before I called you."

I blinked. "I didn't know you smoked."

Her laugh was dry. "I don't anymore, but Morgan Clark showed up at my coffee shop demanding I help her, so I ended up bumming a smoke from one of the guys at the cell phone store next door."

"Was she asking about Katy too?"

"You heard us?"

"Only a few words." The light turned green and I hit the gas. "Katy looked pretty shaken."

"Morgan still can't accept Katy's decision to leave black magic behind. She accused me of stealing Katy from her and leading her away from her coven and family. Poor Katy. I offered to let her go home if I could find someone to cover her shift, but she doesn't want to be alone." Carly sighed. "Thanks for your note offering to help, by the way. I honestly don't think Morgan knows what to do when someone defies her. Some things never change, I guess."

"Is she still worried about that witch whose husband she's been sleeping with?"

She chuckled, but without humor. "Yes, and rightfully so. Dina is quite possibly the worst witch in the coven to cross. There's not much love between Dina and her husband, but she's possessive and vindictive."

"What's Morgan going to do?"

"She asked me for the name of the hoodoo witch who taught me, but I wouldn't tell her. I advised her to get out in front of this mess and deal with the situation. She wasn't interested in my advice. Eventually, she tossed out a couple of parting threats and left."

I made a sympathetic sound. "What a mess. I'm sorry, Carly."

"Me too." A long pause. "It gets worse. I think Morgan's been dabbling in sorcery."

My knowledge of witch magic was rather limited, but I understood the difference between Carly's magic and sorcery. Sorcery was occult black magic and the source of its power was demonic. I hadn't caught a whiff of sulfur off Morgan, but there must have been some clue that Carly had picked up on during their conversation.

"Shit," I said.

"Yep." Her voice was heavy. "I didn't let on that I suspected anything, but if I'm right, she might try to use sorcery to harm Dina. I can't help but wonder if Morgan's mother, Bridget, knows about the sorcery."

"Bridget's who led the coven into black magic, right? So she might be into it just as much or more than Morgan."

"I had the same thought. I don't think there's anything I can do to help either of them except pray, if that's the case. Thanks again for stopping by."

"Thank you for the coffee and yummy scones. I'll see you soon." We said our goodbyes and I ended the call.

"Sorcery, huh?" Malcolm said, shaking his head. "As if black magic wasn't bad enough. You remember when you went to so much trouble to avoid getting noticed by John West and his group of blood mages? Seems so quaint after the last few months. Now we're worried about your grandfather, black witches, and possibly sorcery."

"I still wouldn't want to have to face a group of blood mages, but point taken." I took a long drink of my coffee. "Who knew we'd look back on the West-Addison Harnad as the good old days, huh?"

***

Since museums tended to be heavily warded and full of magical objects that posed a variety of potential dangers, I stashed Malcolm in my bracelet for the meeting with Dr. Blackstone. I parked in the back of the museum, put my bag on my shoulder, and headed for the service door.

I'd received the photo of the inscriptions on the decanter while I was on the phone with Carly. The symbols meant nothing to me as either a language or as runes for spellwork. I hoped Blackstone would recognize the language and be able to point me in a useful direction.

The thick steel door opened, revealing a smiling older man wearing a sweater, glasses, and charmingly crooked bow tie. "Come in," he said cheerfully in a British accent. "You must be Miss Alice Worth."

"That's me." I stepped into a long, dimly lit service hallway lined with numbered doors. I held out my hand. "Thanks for meeting with me on such short notice."

He shook my hand. "My pleasure. Apologies for bringing you in through the service entrance. Won't you follow me to my temporary office?"

"Are you not an employee?" I fell into step beside him. He walked faster than I'd expected, given his age.

"Temporary employee," he informed me, somewhat primly. "I'm curator of a special exhibit on the history of Near East typography."

"Sounds fascinating."

He smiled. "To some it is."

We walked to the end of the hallway, where Blackstone used a key card to open a door marked SPECIAL EXHIBITS. I preceded him through the door and found myself in the museum proper, in a wide hallway lined with artifacts on the walls. "Is this your exhibit?" I asked.

He nodded. "The office they've given me to use is in the basement. It's quite a walk from here. Perhaps we don't need to go farther if I can give you an answer now. You brought something to show me?"

I dug out my phone, pulled up the photo Hanson had sent, and handed it to him. "I'd like to know if you recognize these symbols."

He squinted at the image and clumsily expanded the picture to get a closer look at the inscribed symbols. Muttering to himself, he held the phone closer, then farther away, and tilted it to look at the symbols from different orientations. I waited, trying not to seem impatient.

"Ah," he said finally. "I think I see. The symbol here." He stuck the phone under my nose. "It is quite Persian. Ottoman Empire, if I'm not mistaken. Follow me." He headed down the hall at a brisk walk.

I scurried to catch up. "Dr. Blackstone—"

"I have seen this symbol before, you see," he said, turning left to go into a smaller room. "Here, I will show you."

I followed him into the room. One wall displayed a very old tapestry. Another featured a beautiful mural. Across from it hung a large mirror with a mosaic frame. I eyed the mirror distrustfully.

Blackstone headed for the tapestry on the opposite wall, still muttering. "Yes, quite Persian," he said to himself. "Late ninth or tenth century, perhaps? Hmm."

"Dr. Blackstone," I tried again.

He gestured. "Come, see for yourself. It is the same symbols on this rug."

Okay—rug, not tapestry. "But what do the symbols mean?"

He was still focused on the image of the inscription and didn't appear to have heard me.

I sighed. The rug was about ten feet tall and eight feet wide and very faded except for the figure of a woman in the middle. She wore a brightly colored dress with wide sleeves and a bright green sash tied around her hair. She stood in a garden, her arms outstretched as if welcoming visitors. I looked closer and saw it wasn't a garden—it was a vineyard.

"The symbols are on her sash." Blackstone pointed. "Look closely."

Normally I wouldn't get close to a museum treasure, but the curator himself had instructed me to do so. I set my bag on the floor so it didn't accidentally brush against the priceless artifact and moved as close as I dared. I squinted, trying to make out the details of the symbols on her sash.

Behind me, Blackstone murmured something, his tone strangely like a command.

I frowned and straightened. "What did you—"

The woman in the rug moved like lightning. Her arms wrapped around me, pinning my arms to my sides in a vise-like grip. Her flesh wasn't flesh; it was the rough material of the rug, and it smelled distinctly of the same magic as the decanter. Did the rug belong to the person who'd sent the decanter to the gala?

I tried to twist out of her nightmarish embrace, but she held me in place. I reached for my magic, but couldn't summon up so much as a spark. Something in the material of the rug was dampening it. I attempted to pull Malcolm from the crystal on my bracelet, as I'd done the night of the gala, but that didn't work either.

"What the hell is going on?" I demanded.

Behind me, Blackstone tutted. "Sssh, don't struggle. It won't hurt if you don't struggle."

My grandfather's blood mage smiled at me and raised her hand. Blood magic blades appeared on her fingertips. "Don't struggle, Ava," she purred, slicing the skin on my back. "It just hurts more if you struggle."

I made a sound I'd never made before—part human shout, part wolf howl, it came from deep inside my chest. I fought to free myself, but the rug-woman's horrible scratchy arms didn't budge.

Hanson. Hanson had sent me here. Valas's personal guard had set me up, presumably on the orders of whoever sent that decanter to the gala. That son of a bitch was a dead man. He'd better hope Valas got to him before I did.

"I will kill you," I promised Blackstone.

"*Devam*," he said, his voice triumphant.

The rug-woman holding me turned in place as if on a rotating base. I struggled and yanked as hard as I could, but got nowhere. I caught a glimpse of Blackstone standing over my bag, my phone in his hand. It began to ring. He dropped it on the floor and stomped on it until the phone was in pieces.

I looked up into the face of the rug-woman. Her eerie smile remained warm and welcoming. She was still just the figure of a woman woven into an old rug, but her arms were wrapped around me and I couldn't escape. Nothing about what was happening was possible, but that didn't stop it from happening.

I reached for the trace of Sean's golden magic in my head and shoved the images of Blackstone and the rug at him as hard as I could. I doubted it would work—we had neither a pack bond nor a mate bond, and those bonds weren't telepathic anyway—but I couldn't think of anything else I could do to help him figure out what was happening to me. I tried to push my love through to him as well, but I was dizzy from trying to send him the images of the rug and Blackstone, so I didn't think it worked.

Then the rug-woman turned the rest of the way away from the room and toward where the wall should have been, but there was no wall—only a deep, dark fall into absolutely nothing at all, with those awful, coarse arms around me, holding tight.

14

SEAN

SEAN LOOKED UP FROM HIS LAPTOP WHEN HIS BUSINESS PARTNER RON Dormer tapped on his office doorway. "Sean? You about ready to go over the proposal for the bank security upgrade?" Ron glanced at his watch. "They just called to say they need to push the meeting to ten, so we've got a little time if you're in the middle of something."

"This is the second time they've pushed a meeting back a half hour." Irritated, Sean sent the proposal draft to the printer on the side table and rose. "I've got a meeting at ten forty-five with the dentist who wants new cameras at her office and I don't want to reschedule it again."

"I can finish up with the bank so you can keep your appointment with the dentist. I think she likes you better anyway." Ron grinned. "She seemed very interested in whether you had a significant other, as I recall from our first meeting. She tried very hard to get your cell number."

Sean sighed and took the pages from the printer tray. "Cass told me she called back and asked again later that day." Cass was their office manager. She'd found the dentist's determination quite humorous, as did Ron.

"You just seem to have that effect on some women." Ron took the proposal from Sean and leafed through it. "You should tell her what a crack shot Alice is. If she's smart, she'll take the hint."

"I'll just—" Sean began.

The surge of fury and fear that washed over him made him stagger. He recognized its source immediately. In his mind, his wolf howled in anger and alarm.

"What's going on?" Ron demanded as Sean grabbed his cell phone from the desk.

"Something's wrong with Alice." Sean called Alice's number. The phone rang five times, then went to voice mail. He called back and again she didn't answer.

Alice's fury intensified until it seared him. In the midst of the anger, something pushed at his mind, an unfamiliar and acutely uncomfortable sensation.

Hoping it was something Alice was doing, he lowered his shields. He caught fragments of two images: a smiling older man wearing glasses and a bow tie, and a strangely clothed woman in a garden. He didn't recognize either of them.

Alice, he tried to shout in his head.

Her anger faded. In its place, he sensed a weak surge of love tinged with desperation. It felt like a kiss, or a goodbye.

And then, abruptly, nothing.

Alice was gone.

"She's not dead," Sean stated.

"I believe you." Jack Hastings stood beside his alpha in the living room of Sean's house, radiating menace. "Pack bonds or no pack bonds, I think we would have sensed it if she'd died."

"She just disappeared, like she's behind a ward. Someone took her." Sean's fists clenched. He'd become accustomed to the faint but reassuring sensation of Alice's presence on the other end of their nascent bond. Now there was nothing but a terrible emptiness. The silence was worse than an itch. His wolf paced incessantly in his mind, ears back and teeth bared, pushing him to shift and hunt.

Jack looked grim. "Still no word from Malcolm?"

"Nothing. Not a damn thing." Sean had hoped the ghost would come tell him what had happened, but as time passed, he became increasingly convinced Malcolm had been taken along with Alice—or chosen to go with her. If so, at least Alice wasn't alone, wherever she was.

Nan sat on the sofa, her anger and worry evident. "No calls from the Vampire Court yet either."

Sean had immediately called Bryan Smith, Charles Vaughan's head of security, to ask if he or anyone else associated with the Court knew where Alice had gone. Bryan had reported no one did, as Alice hadn't spoken to anyone from Northbourne that morning. The Court had deployed its own people to search for Alice and her car, but Sean wasn't going to sit and wait.

In the next room, Ben was making phone calls, trying to get a lead on where Alice had gone after leaving the house. Sean had made a few calls of his own already, trying to track Alice's phone, but it wasn't active. A hacker friend who went by the name Toram was trying to get her cell records, which might give them a place to start.

He picked up his phone and called Carly's cell. She answered just before the call went to voice mail. "Sean? What's going on?"

The witch's sixth sense must have told her something was wrong. "Have you seen Alice today?"

"She was here about two hours ago getting coffee. I was talking to someone so I didn't get to chat with her until after she'd left." A pause. "She's missing, isn't she?"

He told her about the feelings of anger and fear and the images he'd received before Alice had vanished. "I don't know how she was able to send me those two images, but she did," he finished. "Do you know where she was headed when she left your shop?"

"She was driving when we spoke on the phone, but I don't know where. Hang on—let me ask Katy if she knows anything."

Muffled voices in the background. Sean waited impatiently. Finally, she returned. "Katy says Alice didn't say where she was headed, but she got a phone call as she was leaving. Katy doesn't know who it was."

Sean growled. They desperately needed Alice's phone records. "Do you have any idea who took Alice or why?"

"Not at the moment," she said, which was not the answer he wanted to hear. "I'll see if I can get a glimpse of something that might help. I may need to come by and get something of hers to use as a focus. Have you tried finding her using your amulet?"

"That was the first thing I did. It didn't work."

"So she's behind strong wards."

"Yes." He rubbed his face. "Let me know if you get anything that might help."

"I will," she promised. "Keep me posted."

As he ended the call, Ben appeared in the living room doorway, phone in hand. "Any news?" Sean asked.

"I don't know if this is in any way related to Alice's disappearance, but there was a strange death at the museum," Ben said. "I don't have much detail, but he was an expert on ancient writing."

An expert on ancient writing sounded exactly like someone Alice might consult on a case. "Do you have a name?" Sean asked.

Ben handed over his phone. "Dr. Cyril Blackstone." He'd pulled up the museum's website and found information about a special exhibit currently housed there.

Sean recognized the smiling man on the screen. "That's the man Alice tried to tell me about in the vision." He handed Ben's phone back and scrolled through his own, looking for Bryan Smith's number.

Bryan answered on the first ring. "Do you have news?"

"Call your people," Sean said. "We need access to a crime scene."

Dr. Cyril Blackstone lay at the bottom of the museum's basement stairs, feet from the door to his office. As in the image Alice had sent Sean, his bow tie was crooked.

So was his neck.

Detective Ernie Diaz of the Major Crimes division scowled at Sean. "We've got Blackstone's security pass being used to open the rear door on his arrival at seven thirty this morning. He used it again just after nine to open the door from the inside."

"Like he was letting someone in," Sean said.

"Yes," Diaz said curtly. He didn't like Sean or anyone from the Vampire Court at his crime scene, but someone had clearly given him orders to let them see Blackstone's body. "Who, we don't know. A dozen employees used that door to enter the building before someone found the body, so there are more fingerprints on the door than crayons in a box."

Sean glanced at the camera above their heads. "What about video?"

"The video system didn't record anything after nine o'clock. The backup didn't record either. The security guard says it was a glitch."

"They have glitches like that often?" Sean asked.

Diaz shook his head. "Guard says no. We've got a forensic computer tech coming down here to look at the system. If someone's messed with it, we'll find out."

Bryan and Matthias, wearing all-black Court security attire, studied Blackstone's body. "Broken neck," Bryan said, exchanging a glance with his colleague.

Matthias took a pair of latex gloves from his pocket and put them on. He squatted beside the body and pulled Blackstone's collar aside, running his fingers along the neck of the shirt until he found what he was apparently looking for: a small, wide *V* cut into the dead man's neck.

"What is that mark?" Diaz demanded.

Matthias took a photo of the mark with his phone. "It appears to be a rune of some kind," he said, rising.

"A rune? As in, a mage's rune?" Diaz made a note in his notebook and drew the rune. "What does it mean?"

Matthias shook his head. "We don't know."

"How did you know how to look for it?"

"We've seen a similar mark before." Matthias was exchanging texts with someone, presumably someone at Northbourne.

Diaz glared at the enforcers. "If you have information that has bearing on this case, you are required to share it with us."

"Our researchers are attempting to determine the rune's meaning," Bryan rumbled. "As soon as we have the information, we'll get it to you."

"I don't believe in coincidences." Diaz jabbed his pen into the spiral of his notebook. "We've got a death, a rune, a mysterious visitor coming in before museum hours, and erased security footage. And Court involvement. I want to know how this man ended up dead, Mr. Smith."

Bryan shook his head. "We know nothing more than you do about Dr. Blackstone's death."

"Bullshit." Diaz glowered at them. "I don't believe that for a damn minute. Which one of your people came up here this morning to visit him?"

"None of our people came here," Bryan stated. "If we find out who did, we'll let you know."

Diaz cursed again. He turned to Sean. "What's your interest in Blackstone, Mr. Maclin?"

Sean had no intention of telling Diaz that he suspected Blackstone's visitor had been Alice. Diaz knew her—they'd crossed paths on a number of cases. Diaz had grudging respect for her, but Sean didn't want the police involved in her disappearance, at least not yet.

He'd already checked both the museum's public and employee parking lots and found no sign of her car, but every instinct in his body told him Alice had been here. What involvement, if any, she'd had in Blackstone's death he wasn't sure, but the curator's death and Alice's disappearance had to be connected.

"I didn't know him," Sean replied. "I don't know anything yet that might help you, but I'll let you know if I get any leads."

Bryan put his phone in his pocket. "We'd like to talk to the guards who were on duty this morning, if you don't mind."

"Be my guest," Diaz said sourly. He gestured at one of the uniformed officers at the top of the stairs. "Hawkins, take these gentlemen to the museum security office, will you? One of their people can show you around. I've got work to do." He turned his attention to the body.

Sean, Bryan, and Matthias passed the medical examiner on the stairs. They followed Officer Hawkins to the museum's main security office. Diaz's partner, a dour-looking man named Ferguson, was interviewing two security guards.

"I want to see the service door," Sean told Bryan.

Bryan gave him a nod. "Let's go."

They left Matthias to talk with the security guards and followed a maze of hallways to the back of the museum. When they reached the service door, Sean inhaled deeply. He smelled a dozen unique scents, including Blackstone's distinctive cloying aftershave. Despite the host of competing odors, Alice's familiar honey-vanilla scent was unmistakable.

The wolf showed his teeth. *Hunt*, he urged.

"Alice was here," he told Bryan, his voice low so they couldn't be overheard.

"I smell her too," Bryan said. An enforcer's strength, eyesight, sense of smell, and hearing were enhanced by drinking vampire blood regularly. The practice turned Sean's stomach, though the benefits were obvious. "Let's see where she went," Bryan added, gesturing down the hall.

They followed Alice's scent to a door labeled SPECIAL EXHIBITS. Unlike the service door, which smelled of a dozen people, this door smelled strongly of Blackstone and only a few others—including Alice.

Bryan produced a key card and held it against the scanner beside the door. The door unlocked. He stuck the card back in his pocket and opened the door.

The door led to an exhibit hall containing artifacts in a half-dozen small rooms. The items ranged from paintings to sculptures, ceramic bowls and urns, and a handful of other items like mosaics and rugs.

Alice's scent led directly to the third room on the left. It contained a rug, a mirror, a mural, and a couple of paintings. Given Alice's strange reaction to the mirror Elizabeth had given Valas at the gala, Sean expected the mirror to be what had attracted Alice's attention. Instead her scent led to the opposite wall, where a large, very old rug hung next to a placard giving information about its creation and history.

The rug was faded by time and use, but Sean could make out the figure of a woman standing in what appeared to be a garden or vineyard, her back to the viewer.

Startled, Sean realized the woman's clothes resembled those of the woman in his vision. The vineyard looked very much like the garden he'd seen, but in the vision her clothes had been brightly colored and the woman had been facing Alice with her arms outstretched. This woman had her back to them and her clothes were as faded as the rest of the rug. Alice's scent was on the rug, though he couldn't imagine why she'd touched it.

He caught a hint of an strange musty smell, like a bog or wet roadside ditch. The odor seemed to come from the rug. Odd, but probably a result of the rug's age.

Alice must have come into this room, then gone to another where she'd seen a similar rug featuring the same woman from a different angle. He wanted to find the other rug.

Something cracked under his shoe. He crouched and found a small broken piece of black plastic and two shards of glass.

"Looks like part of a cell phone," Bryan said.

"Could be Alice's." If it was, there went any chance of tracing her phone. Sean pocketed the pieces and headed for the door. "I want to find the rug that matches this one."

Bryan followed him. To Sean's surprise, Alice's scent did not continue down the hall to any of the other rooms. He searched the rest of the exhibit but found no other rugs resembling the one Alice had looked at, and no other trace of her scent. It was as if she'd walked into that room and never come out. He even searched for hidden doors and found nothing but solid walls.

Finally, angry and frustrated, he stood in front of the rug again, trying to figure out why the image Alice had sent him had shown the woman facing her with arms outstretched.

He lifted the rug away from the wall to look at its back. He'd hoped to find some hint as to how it related to Alice's disappearance, but the back was just as he'd expected: the reverse of the rug's front, not meant to be seen. He smelled Alice's scent on the back and another whiff of that unpleasant musty odor, but what that meant he had no idea.

Damn it, Alice, I'm here, he thought. *What were you trying to tell me?*

His phone rang. He glanced at the screen and answered. "What do you have?"

"I've got one incoming call to Alice's phone from a burner phone at eight thirty-two." Toram's voice was brisk. "Lasted forty-eight seconds. The same caller sent a picture a few minutes later. I'm forwarding it to you along with the number, but the phone is not currently trackable. The caller probably destroyed it as soon as they sent the photo."

Sean swore, though the news was not surprising. Someone had sent Alice to the museum, presumably to meet Blackstone, then snatched her somehow and killed Blackstone. He wondered if Blackstone had been an accomplice or merely in the wrong place at the wrong time.

"Let me know if you get anything else that might help us," Sean told Toram. "Thanks."

"Will do." The call ended.

The photo Alice had received from the burner phone was a close-up of the bottom of a round glass decanter or pitcher, showing an inscription in the glass. He couldn't be certain, but it looked like the decanter that had caused the blood frenzy at the gala.

Sean showed the photo to Bryan. "Someone sent Alice here to ask Blackstone about this inscription and then grabbed her. Someone with access to the decanter set her up."

"One moment." Bryan sent a text. "It's possible the photo was taken before the decanter was brought to Northbourne," he pointed out, his eyes on his phone. "The person who set her up might not be affiliated with the Court."

"Or maybe you've got a traitor in your midst."

A muscle moved in Bryan's jaw. "We're looking into it."

Sean put his phone in his pocket. "I want to know what that mark was on Blackstone's neck and how you knew to look for it. No more bullshit. Alice is my heart and my life. Whatever case she's working on for you, it brought her here. I think one of your people is working for whoever engineered the blood frenzy at the gala and set her up to be taken. So I want some answers and I want them *now*."

Their phones buzzed simultaneously. Sean took his phone out and read the text from Ben as Bryan read the message he'd just received. Sean's wolf threw his head back and howled in rage.

Bryan's expression was grim. "Let's go. We'll take the Court SUV and I'll fill you in on the way."

15

HIKERS HAD FOUND ALICE'S CAR ON A DEAD-END GRAVEL ROAD ABOUT fifteen miles from the museum. When the fire department got there, nothing remained of the vehicle but its shell.

By the time Sean, Matthias, and Bryan reached the scene, they knew the police hadn't found a body in or near the car. Until he got that confirmation, Sean's fury and fear were so intense the enforcers were uneasy, aware his rage might push him to shift.

Once they knew Alice hadn't been found in the car and Sean could think more clearly, Bryan had told him she'd been hired to find out who'd sent the decanter to the gala. Matthias described Ted Watson's strange murder and the presence of the rune on his neck, and Alice's theory it had been used to control and then kill him.

"Blackstone had the same rune?" Sean asked.

"Yes," Matthias said from the back seat. "His neck was broken, just like Watson's. We can't be sure if they tried to make it look like an accident by killing him on the stairs, or if the timing was a coincidence."

"Blackstone might have been spelled to follow commands, like Watson," Sean said. "And just like Watson, he was expendable the moment his usefulness ran out. I assume you're searching everyone at Northbourne for a mark?"

"Yes." Bryan turned onto the gravel road where Alice's car had been found.

Ahead, the road was blocked by two squad cars with lights flashing. Twenty yards past the police cars, Sean saw a fire truck, two more police vehicles, a half-dozen firefighters, and the burned shell of Alice's car. He snarled.

Bryan parked well away from the police barricade. Matthias had expressed concern their presence would cause Diaz to connect Alice's burned car to Blackstone's death, but Sean had made it clear he was headed to the scene with or without them.

As they approached the barricade, a man wearing coveralls emblazoned with the fire department's logo intercepted them. "I'm Cabe Jackson with the fire marshal's office. You from the Vampire Court?"

Bryan nodded. "I'm Bryan Smith. This is Matthias Albrecht."

The fire investigator turned to Sean. "And you are?"

"Sean Maclin of Maclin Security and alpha of the Tomb Mountain Pack." He nodded at the burned car. "That vehicle belongs to my partner, Alice Worth." They'd find out the connection sooner or later, so Sean figured he might as well be up front with the information.

Jackson studied him. "Is that so? Where is Ms. Worth?"

Bryan spoke. "On assignment for the Court and not currently available. Her vehicle was stolen this morning."

Jackson glanced at Bryan, then back at Sean. "Mr. Maclin?"

"The car was stolen," Sean confirmed. "Any clue who torched it?"

The fire investigator said nothing for a few moments. "My instructions were to share information with the Court investigators," he said finally. "Which I don't like one damn bit. You people ask us what we know and never give us anything in return. I can't investigate this case with one hand tied behind my back."

Bryan's phone buzzed. He read the incoming text message. "I have good news for you, then. You should be getting a notice from Captain Benitez soon letting you know Court investigators will be taking over the investigation."

Jackson's face reddened. "Since when does the Court have the authority to do that?"

"Ms. Worth is an employee of the Court." Bryan stuck his phone back in his pocket. "This incident is directly related to the case she's working on, which makes her vehicle and this scene subject to the Court's jurisdiction. Your captain agreed your time is better spent elsewhere, since we have both the experts and resources to make this investigation our focus. The Court will reimburse the city for resources already spent here at the scene."

Jackson swore. "Listen—" His phone rang. He glanced at the screen, glared at Bryan, and answered the call. "Captain." He walked away from Sean and the others, heading for his truck, parked behind the fire engine. The back of his neck turned red. Jackson was not shy about expressing his displeasure.

"I don't think we're making any friends today," Sean said.

"I'm more concerned about Miss Alice than a fire investigator's feelings." Bryan headed for the remains of Alice's car, his eyes on the ground. "Careful of the tire tracks." He pointed. "The fire truck and Jackson drove around to the side and the patrol cars went to the left, so these might have been from the vehicle that followed Miss Alice's car and left after it was torched."

Sean crouched and took photos of the tracks. "Big tires, like an SUV or a large truck."

"Probably not a big help to us, but we'll have someone take pictures and do plaster casts," Bryan said, sending another text.

Bryan and Sean went over to the car. Matthias stayed behind to keep anyone from destroying the tire tracks while the fire department and police left the scene.

Alice's car was completely gutted. The fire had burned hot enough to destroy everything that wasn't metal, and some of the metal had buckled. Sean's nose immediately alerted him to the reason for the fire's intensity. "Gasoline," he said.

Bryan nodded. "They rolled the windows down so there was plenty of oxygen for the fire to burn. Not amateurs." He looked down. "Footprints here, filled with water. Men's athletic shoes, size ten or eleven, not firemen's boots. Probably the prints of whoever torched the car."

"Moving the vehicle from the museum makes sense," Sean noted. "They probably didn't want us to know where she was taken from. If it weren't for the visions, we'd have no idea she was even there, or that Blackstone's death was connected. Unless you have someone in the ME's office who would have told you about the rune," he added, glancing at Bryan.

The enforcer's expression was neutral. "We might have found out about it that way," he said, studying the remains of Alice's car. "So why burn the car? It attracts law enforcement attention and would alert us that something had happened to Miss Alice."

"Misdirection," Sean said. "Distraction."

Bryan raised an eyebrow. "The case isn't about what happened to Miss Alice's car."

"It's about how someone got Alice out of that museum without leaving a trace, and who killed Blackstone and Watson with magic." Sean crossed his arms. "The car, those tire prints, and the footprints are red herrings."

"We go back to the beginning—to the decanter and the attack at the gala," Bryan said. "We have Miss Alice's reports on the magic she sensed at the gala and what she found on the decanter. Do you know anything that wasn't in her reports?"

Sean hesitated. Alice hadn't wanted the vamps to know about the magic splinter in her chest or how the strange unknown magic had been able to get through her wards, but she'd been taken and that magic might be a clue to who was behind it.

He jerked his head at the SUV. "Let's get out of here. I'll tell you in the SUV."

Matthias fell into step beside them as they headed back to the Court vehicle.

"Solve it already?" Cabe Jackson asked snidely as they passed.

"We'll send you our report when it's done," Bryan said. "A crew is on its way to pick up the car."

Jackson cursed at them as they got into the Court SUV.

Bryan turned the key in the ignition. "Okay, Maclin, tell us what you know about Alice's case," he said.

———

That night, just before midnight, Sean sat on the back patio of his house, an untouched glass of bourbon in his hands. His elbows rested on his knees. He stared into his backyard, where Rogue chased insects, as his wolf paced in his mind with teeth bared.

The entire pack had come to his house earlier in the evening, but most had gone home. Nan, Jack, and Ben stayed and joined him out back for a much-needed drink. Even the proximity of the strongest members of his pack wasn't enough to lessen his anger, frustration, and fear.

"I have nowhere to look," Sean told them. "We have nothing but dead ends. We don't know who spelled Ted Watson, gave him the decanter, or killed him. We don't know who sent Alice to the museum, how they got her out, or what role Blackstone played before he died. The vamps don't know anything about the strange magic on the decanter. They've looked over their people and didn't find anyone else with the rune. There's no footage from the museum, no trace of Alice's phone, and nothing from Malcolm."

"What about Carly?" Ben asked. He'd already finished his first glass of bourbon and held a second one. Other than Sean, Ben was taking Alice's disappearance—and their lack of leads—the hardest.

Sean shook his head. "She came by and took a couple of Alice's things to help her see where Alice is or who might have taken her, but she's had no luck so far. It's like Alice just fell off the face of the earth."

Nan put her hand on his arm. "Alice is strong," she reminded him. "Maybe stronger than you or I. Whoever has her, they'll find that out soon enough. She'll come back to us, Sean—I promise you that." Her eyes glowed and she growled. "When she does, we'll find the people who took her and demonstrate why werewolves and the mages they love aren't to be targeted by *anyone*."

Abandoning his game of chasing bugs, Rogue returned to the patio. He leaned against Sean's leg and rested his head on his knee, apparently not bothered by the presence of four angry werewolves.

Sean scratched Rogue's ears and left his hand on the dog's head. Alice had adopted Rogue after his former owner, a homeless man, had died at the hands of the West-Addison blood mages. She lovingly called the dog "fur-face" and let him sleep on the bed when Sean wasn't with her. He pretended not to notice the dog hair on the bed because having Rogue nearby made Alice happy, and her happiness meant everything to him.

He dumped the bourbon into the grass and went inside to pour himself two fingers of Dalwhinnie, Alice's favorite brand of Scotch whisky. He returned to the porch and sat down.

He wanted to tear the world apart until he found her. He couldn't remember ever feeling such boundless rage—or such terrible helplessness.

"We will find her." Ben drained the rest of his bourbon. "Alice will come home."

Sean closed his eyes and pictured his Alice: her smirk, her kind heart, her magic. The beautiful golden rings in her eyes that proved she was part wolf shifter. He focused on that image and pushed a thought at Alice, wherever she was. *I love you*, he told her. *We will find you, I promise.*

Silence.

He raised the glass of whisky, inhaled its familiar scent—a scent he would always identify with Alice—and drank.

16

ALICE

PRESENT DAY

I CAME AWAKE SPUTTERING AND COUGHING, WITH STRANGE-SMELLING water filling my nose and mouth and burning my eyes.

Someone was holding me under the water by my upper arms. I couldn't see who it was—only a large, dark shape looming over me. Whoever he was, his hands were gentle but incredibly strong.

As I struggled to free myself, my feet and elbows hit the sides of what felt like a bathtub. I had a strong feeling of déjà vu, as if something like this had happened to me quite recently, but the sensation was eclipsed by the thought I was being drowned. I kicked frantically, sending water sloshing over the side of the tub. I grabbed his arms and tried to pull myself up, desperate for air, but he held me down.

Abruptly, he lifted me so my head and torso were out of the water and released my arms. I sat up and leaned over the side of the tub to cough and gasp. My body tried simultaneously to clear the water from my lungs and get air in, and neither process was working particularly well at the moment.

Finally, I could breathe raggedly. My chest felt odd—not pain, but a strange empty feeling. My eyes burned and watered uncontrollably from whatever the hell was in the water.

"Here—let me help." The man tipped my chin up and poured clean water over my face, then handed me a towel.

I wiped my eyes and face and blinked rapidly so I could focus. He looked familiar, though I didn't have a name or any details about him. He was very good-looking, but that hardly seemed the most important detail right now. I judged him to be in his mid-thirties. He wore a long-sleeved shirt and jeans, soaked with the strange bathwater I sat in. He had several days' worth of beard and looked haggard, as if he hadn't slept in a while.

His dark brown eyes glowed softly gold as he crouched beside the tub. "Alice?"

He said the name as if he thought it was mine, but it didn't register with me like it was. It did, however, bring back a fuzzy recollection of two men calling me Alice and confronting me while I was walking along a highway. Why or where I'd been walking, I couldn't remember—only that it was very important I keep walking and not look back. That didn't make much sense, but maybe this man could explain it to me.

I remembered he'd held me in his arms in the back of a truck, while a second man tended to my feet. I glanced at my feet and was surprised to find they were no longer injured and bloody. I was also surprised to discover that other than a variety of tattoos, I was naked. The man didn't seem to notice or care about my nudity. His eyes were focused on my face rather than my body.

He'd already seen pretty much all of me there was to see, but I covered myself with the towel anyway and pushed wet hair back from my face. "Who are you?"

He jerked like he'd been slapped. "My name is Sean," he said, his voice gruff. He watched me closely, as if hoping for a reaction.

I did remember the second man saying that name on the side of the road, but other than that hazy memory, it meant nothing to me. "I'm sorry, but I don't remember who you are."

His look of hurt deepened, but I was more concerned by why he'd been holding me underwater than his feelings at the moment. "Why were you trying to drown me?" I demanded.

"I wasn't," he said instantly. At my incredulous expression, he shook his head. "It's a long story. I will explain everything to you, but I promise I wasn't trying to drown you."

He seemed sincere, so I asked the next most obvious question. "Where are we?"

He rubbed his face. "We're at a motel in Landers, California, about two hundred and fifty miles from where we live. Your name is..." He hesitated. "Your name is Alice Worth. You're a private investigator. You've been missing for four days. We finally found you tonight walking beside the highway."

"I've been missing? And you came looking for me?"

"You don't remember me," he said, as if he had trouble accepting it. I had no memory from before I'd been walking along the highway, and no memory of him, but clearly he knew me well. Knew me...and cared about me.

"I'm sorry, but I don't." I rubbed my chest.

"Does your chest hurt?" he asked, his brow furrowed.

"It doesn't hurt. It feels...hollow, like something's missing." I frowned. "It's weird. I keep trying to reach for something that's not there, but I don't know what it is."

"Do you remember anything at all from before you were walking?"

I thought hard. "Little bits and pieces. Being in a car, I think, and a bathtub like this one, with water that smelled really bad. Nothing from before."

Silence. "Nothing at all?" he asked finally.

I shook my head.

I thought he would ask more questions. Instead, he said, "I'm sure you don't want to sit in that water any longer than you have to. Why don't you get cleaned up? We can continue this conversation in the other room. I brought some clothes for you. I'll leave them on the counter." He paused. "Do you remember how to shower?"

"Yes." I remembered how to talk, how to move, how to do things like shower and get dressed. Everything else—all of my memories of who I was and where I'd been and how I'd ended up here—were gone. My name was Alice and I was a private investigator who'd been missing for days, and that was literally all I knew.

I was suddenly short of breath. The calm I'd felt since waking was rapidly wearing off. I made a small, choked sound.

Sean reached out to cup my face with his hand. I recoiled from the intimate touch.

Pain flashed in his eyes at my reaction. He put his hand gently on mine, where I had a white-knuckled grip on the side of the tub. His skin was very warm.

"We will find out what happened and undo this if it's at all possible," he promised me. A shadow lurked in his eyes. I had the sudden strange thought something else was looking at me through his golden gaze. "You are not alone, Alice. You have a whole pack who love you and are here for you." The warm comforting sensation I'd felt on the roadside wrapped around me again, taking away much of my fear.

The word *pack* was a strange way to describe a group of friends and loved ones. For some reason it made me feel better to think of a pack, or maybe that was just the warm sensation wrapped around me. I had precious few sources of comfort at the moment.

"Are you doing that?" I asked. "Making me feel safe and less afraid?"

He nodded. "I have some special abilities to take care of those I love when they're hurting."

He *did* love me; I saw it as plainly as I'd seen his hurt and worry and anger. I searched for something similar in my own heart and found nothing. He was a stranger to me. A kind stranger, but still a stranger.

"Did I love you back?" I wasn't sure why I'd asked, but I felt like the answer mattered.

He lifted my hand and pressed a kiss to my knuckles. "Yes, you did." He squeezed my hand. "We're going to find out who did this and get your memory back, Alice, no matter what it takes."

I blinked. "What do you mean? Do you think someone wiped my memory on purpose?"

"I do."

Someone had stolen my life from me and left me on the side of the road to wander alone. Anger surged, pushing my fear aside.

To my surprise, Sean smiled. "There's my Alice."

My Alice. What a strange way to refer to me. I wondered if I'd thought of him as *my Sean*. The idea wasn't unpleasant.

He let go of my hand and stood. "Shower, get dressed, and come out when you're ready, and we'll find out what the hell is going on."

Sounded like a plan to me.

***

Showering took a long time—not because I was indulgent or because I didn't know how to clean myself, but because my hair was horribly matted and I had to wash myself with soap several times to get the smell of the strange bathwater off my skin and out of my hair.

When I finally pulled back the shower curtain, I found a stack of clothing and some toiletries beside the sink. I combed my hair and braided it, then dressed in a T-shirt, jeans, and socks. I ached all over and I had a strange metallic taste in my mouth, even after I brushed my teeth. I sniffed myself and couldn't smell garlic anymore, so I supposed that was something.

Low voices murmured outside the bathroom door. I found myself listening for Sean's now-familiar voice. I was relieved to hear him talking to what sounded like two women and a man I recognized as Sean's companion when they'd found me walking beside the road. Sean had called him Ben. He'd been kind to me. He'd given me water and bandaged my feet.

Silence in the next room. They must have heard me go quiet. I fidgeted with my hair, suddenly nervous. The people on the other side of that door knew me, but I didn't know them. I didn't even know myself. The longer I stood here, however, the more likely they were to think I was afraid. For some reason, I very much did not want them to think I was afraid.

I raised my chin a little, turned the doorknob, and stepped out of the bathroom.

A woman with graying brown hair, who looked to be in her late forties or early fifties, stood beside Sean a few feet from the bathroom door. A second woman, a petite brunette wearing jeans and an oversized button-up shirt with its sleeves rolled up, waited next to some kind of altar on the nightstand. Ben stood in front of the door as if guarding it. Though Sean had changed out of his wet clothes, Ben still wore the same clothes he'd had on when they found me walking, so I must not have slept for very long.

Oddly, Sean's knuckles looked battered, though I was sure they hadn't been when he was in the bathroom with me. Had he been punching something, or some*one,* while I was in the shower? I noticed two wooden chairs by the window, but no table—at least, not anymore.

"How do you feel?" Sean asked before I could inquire about his hands.

"Glad to be clean. Thanks for the clothes."

A strange emotion crossed his face. "You're welcome."

The woman standing next to him spoke. "I'm so relieved to see you, Alice. I'm Nan Lowell. May I give you a hug?"

I hesitated. "Sure."

She hugged me and didn't let go right away. I sensed another wash of comfort, similar to Sean's. Whatever odd gift he had, apparently she had it too. I gave her a little squeeze. She responded by squishing me tightly enough to make my ribs sore. When she stepped back, I noticed a faint glow in her eyes.

I wiped my forehead with the back of my hand. "It's warm in here. Aren't you all too hot?"

The others exchanged glances. "You're running a fever," Nan told me. "Do you feel ill?"

I shook my head. "I just feel really hot."

Frowning, Sean went to the window A/C and turned it up. Nan brought me a cup of ice water. I took a long drink. "Thank you," I said. I glanced at Ben. "And thanks for helping with my feet."

"It's the least I could do," he said, puzzling me. I supposed I might have done something to help him before, but I had no idea what that might have been. "I'm glad to see you on your feet and not trying to walk to Oregon anymore."

I frowned and drank more of the cold water. I was desperately thirsty, as though I hadn't had anything to drink in days. "Was I trying to walk to Oregon?"

"We're not sure where you were headed," Sean said. "You were just walking northeast. Do you remember why?"

"Someone told me I needed to walk and not look back." I thought hard, then shook my head. "It's a woman's voice, but I don't recall her face, or why I was supposed to walk." I turned my attention to the brunette who'd watched me silently. "I'm sorry—do I know you?"

"My name is Carly Reese." When I didn't react, she added, "We haven't known each other as long as you've known Sean and the others, but we're friends. I helped them find you and made the bath for you so you aren't compelled to walk anymore."

"Thank you." I took a closer look at the altar on the nightstand. "Are you a witch?"

"Does that bother you?"

I thought about it. "No," I decided. I glanced around at the others. My eyes fell on Sean's hands. A few minutes ago, his knuckles were cut and bloody. The blood was still there, but the cuts were gone. "What about the rest of you? What are you?"

Sean didn't hesitate. "We're werewolves."

Ooooookay. "Well, that explains a bunch of things, like why you used the word *pack* earlier and the glowing eyes," I said finally. "Am I werewolf too?"

He shook his head. "You're a human mage."

"What does that mean?"

Before he could answer, someone knocked on the connecting door. A cultured voice with a faint, almost British, accent spoke through the door. "May I enter?"

All three werewolves growled. Whoever was at the door, they didn't like him. Beside me, Sean swore under his breath and exchanged a look with Nan. She moved to my other side.

"Come in," Sean said, his voice cold.

The door swung open, revealing a dark-haired man in a suit. He was very pale and thin, to the point I thought he might be ill. He entered our room and studied me in a way I immediately resented.

Behind him was another man, wearing all black. The second man was so large, his head and shoulders brushed the doorframe.

"Alice," the man in the suit said, his voice strangely intimate. "Are you well?"

"As well as can be expected," I told him. "Who are you?"

My question startled him. "You do not remember," he murmured. "You recall nothing of your past?"

"Not yet. We're working on it." My instincts told me to be cautious around this man. "You haven't told me your name," I reminded him.

A hint of smile turned up the corners of his mouth. "No memory, and yet so very recognizably Alice." He approached and held out his hand. "I am Charles Vaughan of the Vampire Court."

I'd felt no fear or revulsion at the revelations Carly was a witch or the others were werewolves. The fact Vaughan was a vampire didn't frighten me either, though maybe it explained my instinctual wariness. Why I wasn't afraid of these people, I wasn't sure.

A witch, a pack of werewolves, and now a vampire. I certainly had an eclectic circle of acquaintances.

I took his hand. To my surprise, he bowed and kissed my hand, his lips as cool as his flesh. "I am quite relieved you are with us once again," he said, his fingers sliding through mine as he released my hand. "I give you my word the Court will do everything in its power to see your memories and abilities restored."

"Thank you." I wasn't sure what my supposed abilities were, but something told me I would rather ask Sean about that than Vaughan.

"To that end, I invite you to accompany me to Northbourne Manor, headquarters of the Vampire Court of the Western United States, to consult with experts in magic who may be able to assist you in restoring your memory." He gestured at the room's exterior door. "If you will?"

I'd taken two or three steps toward the door before I realized what I was doing. I stopped in my tracks, suddenly certain I hadn't moved of my own accord. "Did you do that?" I demanded. "Make me walk?"

"My apologies," Vaughan said smoothly. "It was not intentional. Some vampires can deliberately compel a human to act or think a certain way. Sometimes when we are careless, we do so inadvertently."

Someone had stolen my memories and whatever abilities I had and dumped me on the side of the road. All I had left were the people in this room, my free will, and my determination to fix myself. Even if only for a few moments, this man had stolen my will—and not by accident.

My anger rose. Again, I felt as if whatever had once been housed in that hollow place in my chest would have risen along with my ire, but nothing happened.

For a moment I felt powerless, but I pushed the feeling aside. As long as I was on my feet and in control of my own mind, I wasn't powerless.

"Don't ever do that again," I warned the vampire. "Not on accident, not on purpose."

He inclined his head. "Again, my most sincere apologies. I give you my word I will not compel you again."

I didn't believe him, but I nodded as if I did. "Apology accepted, then." I glanced at Sean, who'd watched my interaction with Vaughan with a stony expression. "Sean, would you be willing to escort me to Northbourne?"

I caught a flash of displeasure in Vaughan's dark eyes.

For some reason, the vampire's anger seemed to please Sean. "It would be my privilege. We can be on the road in ten minutes." He glanced at Vaughan. "If you'll excuse us, we'll get packed and meet you outside. We'll follow you to Northbourne."

Vaughan gave him a curt nod. "Very well. Please excuse me, Alice," he added with a slight bow. He returned to the connecting room. The big man closed the door behind them.

"Why do they want to help me?" I asked Sean as the others packed their things.

"There's a lot of history between you and the Court. Their motives are complicated. I'll tell you everything on the way to Northbourne." He picked up two plastic trash bags from the corner by the bathroom door. He put the larger one on the bed and brought the other to me. He untied it and held it out. "Before we go, take a look at this and tell me what you remember."

Inside the bag, I found a pink cigarette lighter. At first I didn't recognize it at all, but then a fragment of memory surfaced. "I grabbed it," I recalled.

"Grabbed it from where?" he prompted, his voice gentle.

"From the SUV I was in." I tried to remember. Everything was so blurry. "I couldn't see anything—I think there was a bag on my head. A woman dragged me out of the car. I grabbed this and hid it from her. It was the only thing I could reach. I remember thinking if someone found my body, it would be a clue."

Sean closed his eyes. When they opened again, they glowed brightly, like suns. "It *is* a clue, Alice. Thank you."

He retied the bag and handed it to Carly. "Please see if this gets you anywhere." He indicated the other bag on the bed. "Those are the clothes she was wearing when we found her. It's all we've got."

Carly took the bags and set them next to her duffel. "One more thing, before you take off." She approached me with a smile. "You have a tattoo on your stomach of a wolf. It contains a spell designed to summon a ghost named Malcolm. I would like your permission to touch it."

A strange pain twisted in my heart. "Malcolm?" I asked.

Sean moved closer to us. "Do you know that name?"

I didn't know it any more than I'd known Sean's name, or Ben's, or Vaughan's, but unlike theirs, the name *Malcolm* elicited a definite feeling of grief and pain. "I lost him," I said, more to myself than them.

Sean's expression darkened. "What do you mean?"

"I don't know," I confessed. I was suddenly tired and my heart hurt, for reasons that weren't quite clear. "It's just a feeling I have, that I lost him. And I don't even know who he is." My eyes filled with angry tears.

Nan squeezed my hand, offering warm comfort. "We'll solve this," she promised. "One step at a time."

I squeezed back, then lifted my shirt to bare my abdomen. "Do what you need to do," I told Carly.

Gently, she touched the wolf tattoo, her fingers tracing a pattern in the lines. "There's none of his trace here," she told Sean regretfully. "It's been purged."

I didn't know what that meant, but Sean was clearly disappointed by the news. "We have objects he's used at Alice's house," he said. "In the basement, in her workshop. I'll get them for you once we're done at Northbourne. They'll have strong trace."

"I have other ways of trying to track Malcolm in the meantime," Carly said. "For now, I'll focus on the lighter and the clothes." She put the plastic bags in her duffel.

While we'd been talking, Nan and Ben had packed up what little they'd brought with them to the motel. Sean washed the blood off his hands and went to the motel office to check us out. The others took their things outside. I refilled my cup with ice and water for the drive. Sean came back to get his bag.

I started to open the door, but his voice stopped me. "Alice."

I turned around. "Yes?"

He joined me at the door and lowered his head so he could speak very softly into my ear. "What do you think of Vaughan?"

"I don't trust him," I murmured. "He compelled me on purpose, and he lied when he said he wouldn't do it again."

Sean stared at me. "How do you know?" He didn't seem to be arguing —only curious. And angry.

I shrugged. "I just know." I didn't want to ask this question, but I thought I needed to. "Have he and I ever...been lovers?"

I'd hoped for an immediate answer of no. Instead, Sean seemed to consider his response. "Not to my knowledge," he said finally. "Not for lack of trying on his part."

"Good. I'd like to think I have better taste than that."

His cough sounded suspiciously like a truncated laugh. "I think you do."

"Can other vampires do what he did?"

His expression lost all hint of mirth. "The older ones can. It's against the law, and it's wrong, but it happens. Before this, you had a way of protecting yourself from their compulsions, but you may have lost that ability along with your memory."

I hesitated, then asked, "Can you help me make sure he doesn't do it again, or that anyone else does while we're at Northbourne?"

He appeared surprised by my request, but pleasantly so, as if helping me was something he wanted and liked to do. "Of course."

"Thank you. I'm sorry I tried to stab you on the side of the road earlier."

"You remember that?"

I nodded. "You grabbed me and I didn't know who you were. I'm glad I didn't actually hurt you."

"I'm sorry I grabbed you."

"You had no way of knowing I didn't know who you were."

"I shouldn't have grabbed you in any case." He started to lean down to kiss my forehead. He stopped himself and instead brushed my fingers with his own. He certainly liked to touch me whenever he got the chance. I thought of Nan's desire to hug me and wondered if lots of touching was a werewolf thing.

"I have a lot to tell you," he said. "We've got a three-hour drive ahead of us. I want Nan to ride with us, if that's all right with you. Some of what I have to tell you won't be easy for you to hear. I'm sorry I have to tell you everything at once, but the more you know, the better prepared you'll be to face what's ahead. Nan's presence will be comforting for you, I hope."

Sean's presence was comforting by itself, though I didn't say so. A wonderful scent filled my nose when he was near. I recognized it from our meeting on the side of the highway. I remembered thinking it reminded me of a forest, though I wasn't sure why, or how it eased my worry.

He'd told me he loved me and I'd loved him back. I supposed some part of me still remembered that, even if my brain didn't. I appreciated his kindness and that he respected my boundaries—and that at no time, even when I was naked in the tub, had he looked at me with even a fraction of the intimate possessiveness Vaughan had when he walked into our motel room.

I still had so much to understand and learn about my life and the people in it. One thing was already crystal clear: I needed to know everything about my past—the good, the bad, and the ugly—and if that meant I was about to get a three-hour crash course on my own life, so be it.

"Let's go," I said and opened the door.

17

THE GOOD, THE BAD, AND THE UGLY WAS RIGHT.

For well over two hours, Sean drove and talked while I ate peanut butter crackers and other snack foods someone had bought for me from a vending machine at the motel. Sean told me he thought I hadn't had anything to eat or drink in days. Judging by my sunken eyes, lethargy, thirst, and hunger, that might have been true.

Nan listened quietly from the back seat. She placed her hand on my shoulder during the worst parts. I asked a few questions, but mostly just ate and listened as Sean told me what he knew about my background before and after I'd come to California.

He made it clear he didn't know everything about my past because I hadn't shared everything with him, but what he *did* know was more than enough to leave me angry, sad, and horrified in turns. And very, very frustrated, because I didn't remember a damn bit of anything he said. I might as well have been listening to the life story of a complete stranger— the kind of life story that could have made a good movie or TV series, if anyone would have thought such a story was even believable.

I might not have believed it myself except for Sean's raw honesty. That honesty continued into the portion of the story that involved him, from our first night together—a one-night stand, which embarrassed me a little, though neither he nor Nan seemed the least ruffled by it—through my disappearance four days ago. We'd had our ups and downs, but we'd planned to buy a house together.

"Missing one of our own is like missing a limb," Nan said, squeezing my shoulder. "When the alpha's partner is gone, it's even worse. We were missing our heart."

My emotions were all over the place from everything I'd been told, but I liked the sound of the word *partner*. I thought of how Sean had stood beside me as I faced Charles Vaughan, showing his support but letting me deal with the vampire. He didn't stand in front of me or tell me what I should or shouldn't do, and I appreciated that. Something told me a werewolf's instinct was to take control and protect. While I was sure Sean would protect me if push came to shove, he didn't try to take control over the situation, despite my loss of memory.

The hardest news to absorb was about Malcolm and my stolen magic. Malcolm's absence and the empty feeling in my chest, where my magic had once been, were the only losses I truly felt. Even the report of my parents' murders and the death of my mentor Mark Dunlap only registered as additional items in the long list of bad things that had happened to me. I was saddened by their deaths in the way you grieved for the losses of a friend's loved ones.

Malcolm's name hurt my heart. I was afraid of what that might mean. Was he truly dead? If I was free from my captors, why wasn't he with me? And why did I keep thinking that I'd lost him, when I had no other memory of anything else before I was dumped on the side of the road?

As for my magic, it sounded both wondrous and like a kind of curse. My grandfather Moses Murphy had kept me prisoner for twenty years so he could control it, and had threatened to kill everyone I cared about unless I went back to Baltimore with him.

I didn't say it out loud, but the thought occurred to me Moses wouldn't want me now if I had no magic. Hard on the heels of that thought came another: if I was no longer of any use to him, he might just kill me outright in retaliation for my escape and the injuries I'd inflicted on his daughter, my aunt Catherine. And then he might go after everyone who'd known me, including Sean and his pack, and I wouldn't be there to help protect them. So I needed my magic back pronto, before word got out about my condition.

When Sean finished explaining how they'd found me on the side of the road and what had taken place at the motel before I woke, I went quiet for a long time. It was a hell of a lot to process. I would need more than tonight to sort it all out and figure out where to go from here, but I understood why Sean had wanted me to hear it before I got to Northbourne. Forewarned was forearmed, or at least I hoped so.

We were the second vehicle in a four-vehicle caravan. Ahead of us was the SUV carrying Charles Vaughan and his two security escorts. The big man was named Bryan and the driver of the SUV was his sister Adri, who was half her brother's size but no less intimidating. Behind us, Jack, Sean's beta, followed in his truck with Ben riding shotgun and Carly in the back seat. The second Vampire Court SUV brought up the rear. It was quite the entourage. And we drove *fast*—well over the speed limit. We passed several speed traps on the way, but no one tried to pull the caravan over. I supposed that was because of our Vampire Court escort.

I found another package of cookies in the snack bag and tore it open.

Sean grimaced. "We'll get you some real food soon, I promise. That was the best we could do in the middle of the night."

"These aren't that bad." I ate a cookie and washed it down with more water. "Can you turn the A/C up?"

Sean did as I asked and tilted one of his vents so it blew cold air at me. He was plainly worried about my temperature. I felt fine otherwise and in the scheme of things, a fever seemed like the least of my problems. I ate my cookies and stared absently out the window for the rest of the journey to Northbourne.

When our caravan exited the highway and turned onto a country road, Sean glanced at me. "We're about five minutes from Vamp HQ. I made it clear to Vaughan I was not going to leave your side for any reason tonight." His grip tightened on the steering wheel. "If you'd prefer I not go in with you, tell me now so I can argue with you before we get there."

I thought about it, but not for long. All my instincts told me I could trust Sean and I couldn't trust Vaughan—and based on Carly's warnings regarding her black witch acquaintances, I doubted I could trust them either. I needed allies I could count on when the chips were down.

"Come with me," I said. "How many escorts am I permitted to have?"

He frowned. "Who else do you want with us?"

"Nan, if that's all right with both of you."

"Of course it's all right," Nan said. "Why me and not Jack or Ben, though?"

I tried to figure out how to explain my feelings. "Because I think you're as powerful as Jack, but they'll underestimate you. They'll be more suspicious of him and we might need the element of surprise."

Silence. I couldn't tell if I'd said something wrong. Sean kept driving and Nan didn't say anything.

"You said Jack's got a temper and Ben almost died because members of the Court didn't intervene when my grandfather put him aboard his helicopter," I added when no one spoke. "So maybe taking either of them into Vamp HQ tonight isn't the best idea."

Sean picked up his phone and made a call. When someone answered, he said, "Nan's coming into Northbourne with us. I want you and Jack to take Carly home, then come back to Northbourne and escort us home when we're done." He must be talking to Ben. "I don't know how long we'll be, but I'll keep you posted."

After Ben acknowledged Sean's instructions, Jack's truck slowed and turned left, heading for the lights of the city. Sean put his phone back in the cupholder and looked at me. "Don't tell anyone else what you just told us about Nan, please, Alice." To my relief, he didn't seem angry, just very serious.

"I hadn't planned to," I assured him.

He glanced in the rearview mirror. "Nan, everything you've heard in this vehicle tonight about Alice goes no farther than the three of us."

"Of course," she said. She rested her hand on my shoulder again.

We'd been driving along a high brick wall for quite a while. When our caravan slowed, I spotted a large gate ahead with five motorized barriers in front. As we approached, the barriers retracted into the ground and the gate rolled aside.

We followed Vaughan's SUV down a long and winding private road that ended at a circular drive with a fountain in the center and a truly enormous mansion the size of a museum. Sean said it was part government building, part courthouse, part residence, part magic workshop, and part prison.

I'd hoped when I saw Northbourne I would feel some sense of recognition, but it was every bit as strange and unfamiliar to me as everyone and everything else since I woke. I stifled a sigh.

Our caravan parked in front of the wide steps. Bryan got out and opened Vaughan's door as black-clad security people emerged from the building and hurried to our vehicles.

Sean looked at me. "Ready?"

"Ready as I'll ever be." I opened my own door and hopped out of the truck without waiting for one of the guards to open it for me. Nan and Sean did the same.

Charles Vaughan met us at the foot of the steps. "Alice, if you are weary from our journey, I would be pleased to provide you with a room where you can refresh yourself and rest."

"I could use a bathroom," I told him. We'd made no stops between the motel and Vamp HQ. "I don't need to lay down. I want to talk to these witches and find out how we're going to get my memories and magic back."

"As forthright and impatient as ever." He smiled at me. "How delightful it is to speak to you again, though I certainly would not wish it to be under these circumstances."

Why did everything this man said sound like a lie, even the things I thought were true?

I'd learned from Sean that Vaughan had bitten me twice: once with my consent, in exchange for a magic relic I needed to save Sean's life, and once while I lay in a coma. I had no memory of either, but it might explain why I'd distrusted him from the moment he walked into the room. Maybe much like how my body seemed to remember Sean's presence was comforting, it also remembered Vaughan's violations, even if my brain didn't.

"Nan is coming with me too," I informed Vaughan. "I hope that's not a problem."

"Not at all," Vaughan told us, though I got the distinct impression he wasn't happy about it.

Sean addressed Vaughan. "Before we go any farther, I need your word that Alice, Nan, and I will be permitted to leave Northbourne when we wish, and no one will make any attempt to compel or force us to remain."

The vampire inclined his head. "On behalf of myself and Madame Valas, you have our word. If you will please follow me?"

Charles and Bryan led us into Northbourne with Adri at our rear. Sean and Nan scanned our surroundings, seemingly disinterested in the grandeur of the mansion. I found myself admiring the enormous lobby, with its five-story rotunda, sweeping grand staircase, and wide second-floor gallery.

Our group made a brief stop at an elegant bathroom just off the main lobby. Nan waited in the small lounge while I used the toilet and washed my hands.

Vaughan met me at the door when we emerged. "Are you well enough to take the stairs to the lower level?" he asked me in an undertone. "If not, an elevator is available."

"I'm perfectly fine," I told him, though it wasn't quite true. My legs ached mercilessly, but I wasn't about to admit any kind of weakness to Vaughan. Sean had told me I'd walked twenty miles in boots and I definitely felt every mile now. I had my pride, however, and I didn't want anyone, least of all a vampire, to think I was weak.

If Vaughan could tell I was fibbing, he didn't call me on it. Sean had warned me Vaughan could sense deception, so I had to be careful how I phrased things, especially anything related to my past.

Vaughan and Bryan led us down a wide hall to a set of doors leading to a beautiful stairwell. Sean and Nan remained stoic, but I suspected they disliked going underground. I didn't care for it myself, actually.

My trepidation increased when we reached a set of secure doors with a biometric lock. As Bryan placed his palm on the scanner, Sean touched my hand and comfort washed over me again. I almost laced my fingers through his, but didn't. Instead, I gave him a brief smile of thanks.

The locks disengaged and we entered a very different area of the mansion. Instead of the luxurious carpets, murals, and elegant light fixtures I'd seen on the way here, the hallway was bare concrete, with recessed lights and what appeared to be emergency lighting.

"This area is dedicated to workshops and apartments for mages and witchcraft," Vaughan said in answer to my puzzlement. "Magic is quite volatile. Simple surroundings are most prudent."

Our group headed down the hall. We stopped at the fourth door on the right. The room wasn't numbered, but I spotted a circle with an inverted pentagram beside the door. Bryan knocked on the door, then opened it.

Vaughan gestured grandly. "After you, Alice."

I went in without hesitating, to show him I wasn't afraid. Like the hallway, the room I entered was mostly bare concrete and stone. One area contained bookshelves, a large wooden table with a variety of knives, stones, and other strange implements laid out, and several closed cabinets.

The other half of the room was empty except for a large inverted pentagram inlaid in a circle on the floor. Near the circle, a small table was draped with a red cloth and set up as an altar. It resembled the one Carly had made in the motel room, but the pentagram was upside down. Black candles in black quartz candle holders marked each point of the star. A silver tray filled with bottles, jars, and other items waited in the center of the altar.

Two women in hooded cloaks rose from the large table when we walked in. Vaughan exchanged a nod with the blond male security escort who stood against the wall near the women. "Hanson, thank you for waiting. You are free to return to your duties upstairs."

Hanson's eyes went from Vaughan to me and back again. "Yes, sir," he said after a beat. He didn't seem very happy to see me, or maybe I was imagining it.

Hanson departed without looking at me. I turned my attention to the mother and daughter black witches the Court had retained on Carly's reluctant recommendation.

Vaughan cleared his throat. "Alice, may I present Morgan Clark and her mother, High Priestess Bridget Clark, of the Silver Thorn Coven."

The women pulled back their hoods just enough for me to see their faces. Neither woman offered me their hand, so I kept mine at my side. "Nice to meet you," I said.

"Likewise," Bridget said, not bothering to disguise her lack of enthusiasm.

Both were tall and slim, with green eyes and fair skin. Bridget appeared to be in her early sixties, Morgan in her late thirties. Morgan had long, bright red hair, while Bridget's was mostly gray and cut shorter, just above her shoulders. Under their cloaks, both wore dark slacks. The younger woman wore an emerald blouse. Her mother wore a gray sweater.

Morgan studied me with her brow furrowed, as if she thought she might know me and was trying to figure out how. Bridget watched me too, with a mildly disdainful expression.

"We understand you believe you've been the victim of sorcery." Bridget's tone was amused. "What makes you think so?"

Resentment swelled. I saw nothing remotely humorous about my situation. "A witch told me so." I held up my bandaged right index finger. "She did a test with a bowl of rain water and three drops of my blood, and the water turned black. And if you can see my aura, you can see what's left of it is scorched black."

Bridget sniffed. "Many things can damage an aura. Who is this witch who thinks she knows so much about sorcery?"

I felt protective of Carly, so I shook my head. "It doesn't matter. If it's true, I need to know how a sorcerer suppressed my memories and my magic, and how to get them back."

"That is the reason you are here," Vaughan interjected, leveling a cold stare at the witches. "You are to be well compensated for your time, but the Court's favor hinges on your success. I suggest you focus on ascertaining the cause of Alice's memory loss."

"Of course, Mr. Vaughan." Bridget turned back to me. "True sorcery is rare." Her tone was that of a teacher explaining something for the third time. "I doubt the witch you spoke to has any experience with it. Before we pursue that avenue, I want to see for myself whether it's sorcery we're dealing with. Come to the circle. Morgan, bring our things from the altar."

"Yes, Mother." Morgan's tone was perfectly neutral, but I caught a flash of resentment as she went to the altar.

I didn't much care for being ordered around either, but I followed Bridget to the inverted pentagram on the floor.

"Stand here," she told me. I moved to the center where she'd indicated. With a sigh, she nudged each of my feet a few inches this way and that until I stood precisely where she wanted me to be.

I already missed Carly a great deal. She'd seemed so kind and caring, and Bridget seemed...well, like something that rhymed with *witch*.

Sean and the others waited by the table as Morgan joined us in the circle, carrying the silver tray. In addition to bottles and jars, it held a small cast-iron bowl, and—most distressingly—a long silver needle.

Bridget picked up a dagger with a bone handle and went to the edge of the circle. She pointed the tip of the blade at the floor and walked counterclockwise around us. "I call upon Minerva and Ahriman as I cast this circle three times three to keep the energy raised to help us determine the type of magic in use on this human."

She walked around the circle three times, then returned the dagger to the tray and picked up a different one with an ebony handle and a much sharper blade. "Hold out your right arm."

If she expected me to be afraid, I had no intention of giving her the satisfaction. I stuck my arm out and didn't flinch when she held the bowl under my forearm and drew the razor-sharp tip of the knife across my skin. The cut wasn't superficial. Blood ran into the bowl in a steady stream.

Another surge of prickliness from Sean and Nan. If Bridget noticed or cared about their reaction, she didn't let on. I watched my blood run into the bowl.

When the blood was about an inch deep and the flow from the cut began to slow, Bridget dipped a finger into one of the jars and smeared a dollop of a strange-smelling greenish-gray goop across the cut on my arm. The sting made my eyes water, but the cut stopped bleeding almost immediately. She handed me a long strip of white linen from the tray. I wrapped it around the cut and tucked the end under to hold it in place.

"What's that you put on Alice's arm?" Sean asked.

Bridget didn't look up. "An ointment to seal the wound and prevent infection." She added a few drops from a couple of the bottles and a sprinkle of a black powdery substance that smelled like roadkill to the bowl.

She set the bowl on the floor at our feet and closed her eyes. "Minerva, show us the truth of whether Alice Worth has been touched by sorcery or black magic." She struck a match and dropped it into the bowl. With a quiet *whoosh*, the contents of the bowl ignited. Black flames shot up at least a foot.

The witches stared at the fire. Morgan gasped. "So much power," she said, sounding envious.

Bridget shot her a quelling look. "Thank you, Minerva, for your revelation." She pondered the black flames. "So, it is sorcery after all. How unexpected."

"It can't have been *that* unexpected," I pointed out. "We did tell you it was."

Her eyes narrowed. "This is not good news for you. A witch's curse is far more easily removed than a sorcerer's spell—if indeed this *is* a spell."

"What else would it be?" I asked. "I have no memories. I can't access my magic. All I've got left is this weird hollow feeling in my chest."

Bridget and Morgan exchanged a look. "What?" I asked.

Bridget reached out. Sean and Nan moved closer to the circle, their eyes bright gold. I held my ground as Bridget touched two fingers to my sternum. "Here?" she asked.

I nodded. "It feels like something was pulled out, as strange as that sounds."

"It doesn't sound strange to us." She picked up the long silver needle. Up close, I saw it had symbols etched along its length. "Lie down," she ordered me.

I shook my head. "I'll stand." Even with Sean and Nan in the room, the mental image of her looming over me with that needle was enough to keep me on my feet.

"If you move or faint, you'll cause great damage to yourself and the spell won't work. So *lie down*."

"I won't faint." I planted my feet. "Do it."

"Prideful and stubborn." Bridget shook her head, disgusted. "Let it be on your head."

I didn't look back at the others as she anointed the needle with dabs of oils and powders from the tray. She murmured as she did so. The words sounded like Latin.

"What are you using for the spell?" I asked.

She glared at me. "This isn't witch school. These are all necessary ingredients, and that's all you need to know." She aimed the tip of the needle at my sternum. I gave her a nod and braced myself.

She touched the needle to my flesh and applied increasing pressure until it punctured my skin. I didn't jerk away, but I couldn't stop the agonized cry that escaped my clenched jaw as the needle dug into my breastbone.

"Minerva, please show me what is here," Bridget commanded.

An inky black substance oozed from my chest and slithered up the needle, coiling around it like a snake. It smelled like a combination of dead animal, burned paper, and rotten eggs. I stared at it in horror, struggling not to scream or pull away. The hollow feeling in my chest intensified sharply. "I can't breathe," I gasped.

Bridget yanked the needle out of my chest. Morgan tossed a pinch of the roadkill-smelling powder onto the needle. The black goo hardened instantly.

I stumbled back. My heart thundered in my ears, and for the first time since I'd woken up in the tub, I felt like I might pass out. I made a choked sound and sat on the floor, fighting nausea.

I pulled the collar of my T-shirt down to see an angry red mark and some blood where the needle had stuck me, but no inky goo on my skin or shirt.

"Alice, are you all right?" Sean asked.

"Do I look all right?" I rubbed my chest and glared up at Bridget. "What the hell was that?"

She studied the needle critically and didn't bother looking at me. "The needle's results are clear. This is no sorcerer's spell. What has been done to you cannot be undone."

Shock left me speechless for several moments. "What do you mean, it can't be undone? There has to be a way to reverse this curse or whatever it is and unlock my magic and my memories."

"You're not listening," she snapped. "This is neither a spell nor a curse.

Your magic and your memories aren't suppressed—they're *gone*. This sorcerer has ripped them from your body for his or her own use."

"What do you mean, for their own use?" Sean demanded.

"Power, obviously. How do you suppose this sorcerer became so formidable? Sorcerers steal power."

"Why her memories, though?"

"Memories have as much power as magic—sometimes more." She regarded me appraisingly. I didn't like the way she seemed to be assessing me as something that might be useful to her. "Painful and traumatic memories are a potent ingredient for sorcery. If Ms. Worth had such memories, the sorcerer took them for that reason."

Sean had told me in the truck that I'd had plenty such memories—far more than he knew about. Someone had stolen them as a power source for sorcery, intending to benefit from my pain and suffering. For some reason, that was worse than believing my memories were just wiped to prevent me from remembering what had happened to me.

"Alice has been nulled before," Sean said, his voice a low growl. "She can regenerate her magic."

Bridget made a frustrated sound. "This is not nulling. Ms. Worth's magic and memories were pulled out *by the roots*, as one would pull a weed or uproot a tree. The wound they left behind is very, very deep, hence her hollow feeling. There will be no regeneration because there is nothing to regenerate *from*. Do you understand?"

I scrambled to my feet and found my voice. "Magic can always be undone. What's been stolen can be recovered."

"You know this based on your own vast experience with such magic?" Her smile was cruel. "I would help you remedy your situation if it was possible. The Court has offered me an enormous incentive to do so. Regrettably, it is *not* possible."

Vaughan joined Sean and Nan at the edge of the circle. "You will not leave this room until you have devised a way to restore Alice's memories and magic."

She glared at him. "You can't hold us prisoner here."

He smiled, showing his fangs. "I assure you we can."

"There's no point," she raged, throwing the needle back on Morgan's tray with a heavy clatter. "There's no way to undo what's been done to her."

"What has been torn out can be replanted." Vaughan paced around the perimeter of the circle. "The Vampire Court has access to more than six thousand years of lore from around the world. With the help of our best researchers and other experts in black magic, you will consult our library and find a way to undo what this sorcerer has done."

Bridget crossed her arms. "I refuse."

"Choose to do this of your own accord, or we will compel you," he told her. "You *will* do this."

"Stop," I said.

At the sound of my voice, Vaughan and the others turned. I'd taken refuge on the far side of the circle, away from all of them, but I advanced on Vaughan. "Stop threatening her," I told him. "I want my magic and my memories back more than anyone here, but you're not going to enslave someone or steal their mind to do it."

Vaughan's expression darkened. "You are not yourself."

"Maybe I'm not the Alice you knew before, but I sure as hell am myself." I knew that, even if I didn't know anything else. "Look me in the eye and tell me you can envision any version of me that would sanction what you're threatening them with. Besides, do you think I'd trust any magic she'd use on me if you forced her to do this? Would *you* trust that kind of magic?"

He had nothing to say to that.

I turned to Bridget. "I believe you when you say my memories and magic were stolen. I feel the emptiness where they were. But I also believe there is a way to fix it. In all of magic, there has to be a way." I had a hunch she'd respond better to flattery than threats, so I added, "And I also believe *you* may be the only person capable of finding it."

Her eyes narrowed. "It would take time and a great deal of power."

I shrugged. "We don't have a hell of a lot of time, but power we can get."

She slid a glance at Vaughan. "And certainly just compensation would be in order, for such a remarkable and unprecedented feat that is clearly of great importance to the Court."

"We will discuss terms privately," he said coldly.

"Give me your word no one from the Court will compel them or imprison them here," I said to Vaughan.

I really didn't have much leverage to make that kind of demand, but after a moment, he inclined his head. "Very well."

I had no doubt the witches were in this for the money. Bridget and Morgan had made it abundantly clear the reward was far more important to them than anything else. We'd have to make sure they understood they'd only benefit if they fixed me, and I was worth more to them alive and well.

Vaughan's expression was completely devoid of emotion. No doubt he'd figured that out too. "Results yield compensation. Accurate and true results are the only kind that interest us."

I glanced at the bowl at our feet. "Do you have any need for that anymore?"

Bridget shook her head. "There's nothing there but ash."

"Still, I want what's left in the bowl destroyed and my blood cleaned off that knife." I might not know much of anything about magic now, but was fairly certain I couldn't leave my blood lying around—especially not in the possession of a couple of black witches.

Bridget opened the circle around us while Morgan cleaned the knife with a piece of linen. I pocketed the cloth and inspected the knife. Then I followed her to a small bathroom and watched as she cleaned the bowl and disposed of the ashes by flushing them down the toilet.

"Mr. Vaughan shouldn't have threatened my mother and me," Morgan told me in an undertone as she wiped the bowl clean.

If she was trying to get me on her side, she was barking up the wrong tree. "Your mother got what she wanted by acting like she couldn't fix me," I said. "More money and acknowledgment of her abilities."

Morgan glared at me. "That was no act," she hissed. "We truly know of no way to undo what the sorcerer did."

"You'll figure it out. You have all the resources you could want at your fingertips and the vamps will pay you well, but only if you're successful. Having the Court's favor won't hurt either."

She set the bowl on the counter. "I know who told you about us. I remember you from the other day at Carly's coffee shop. She pretended not to know you, but I had a feeling you were someone I needed to pay attention to—especially when she was rude to you. Carly's many things, but rude to a customer isn't one of them." She smiled in a way I didn't like. "Sweet Carly, always so helpful, and so full of judgment and smug superiority. I guess she wanted no part of sorcery and black magic, so she told the vamps to call my mother and me. And now here we are, in the basement at Northbourne, about to make a fortune by helping you. I wonder how best to thank her."

"Leave Carly alone."

"Or what?" she scoffed. "What will you do, Little Miss No-Magic?"

"Do you think all I had was my magic before this?" I asked her. "Do you think I'm weak now, just because I don't have magic? I am so much more than that, Morgan. You saw how Vaughan backed down from me. Think about that before you make threats."

We stared at each other. I supposed her glare was intended to be withering, but I wasn't afraid of Morgan Clark any more than I feared werewolves or vampires.

"Alice?" Sean called from the other room. "Are we ready to go?"

"We're ready," I said, knowing he'd hear me without me having to shout. I returned to the main room.

Nan and Sean waited near the door. Morgan joined Bridget at their altar. I wondered what they would have to say once we were out of the room. I hoped the vamps would be listening.

"Please excuse us," Vaughan said to the witches. He and Bryan led Sean, Nan, and me out into the hallway. Adri went inside to keep an eye on Morgan and Bridget, and Bryan closed the door.

Vaughan turned to me. "Madame Valas and I request you reside here at Northbourne until this matter is resolved. An apartment has been prepared for you. Mr. Maclin may stay as well, if you wish," he added, with obvious reluctance.

I shook my head. "I want Sean to take me home." I had no idea what my home was like or even where it was, but even so, it sounded a million times better than staying at Vamp HQ—no matter how fancy their apartment was.

"You have no magic with which to protect yourself." Vaughan's eyes glowed silver. "There are those who would take advantage of your vulnerability. We will protect you."

"I'm not yours to protect," I said automatically.

He stared at me, clearly startled. "You have said that to me before."

"Then I shouldn't have had to say it this time." I was so tired I wanted to lean against the wall, but I didn't. "I'll be fine. I've got a werewolf pack backing me up."

"A werewolf pack may not be sufficient if a powerful enemy comes to your door," he said ominously.

Sean growled.

"If someone does come knocking, I guess we'll find out," I said. "Good night, Mr. Vaughan."

He studied me. "You have not called me that in a very long time. You may address me by my first name."

I had no intention of doing so, but I didn't argue. I didn't want to make an enemy of him, or of anyone, until I knew more about my situation. I needed allies, even if I didn't trust them.

Something in Vaughan's eyes told me he was angry at my refusal to stay —maybe at me in general. "Good night, Alice. We will contact you the moment we have news. Adri will escort you to your vehicle."

I didn't like the way he said my name, savoring the syllables like a lover, but I simply nodded. "Thank you."

Vaughan and Bryan went back into the room to talk to Bridget and Morgan Clark. As we followed Adri down the hall, Sean asked me, "How are your arm and chest?"

"Sore. I guess we might have to swing by a pharmacy on the way for first-aid stuff, unless you've got some in your truck."

He paused. "I do have a first-aid kit. I'm used to you telling me you'll go home and fix your injuries with healing spells. I guess that's not an option tonight."

"I guess not." I thought about it. "Healing spells, huh? That sounds handy. Did I use those a lot?"

He started to laugh and tried to disguise it as a cough. When I glanced up, he smiled wryly. "Yes, pretty frequently."

And that was when the lights went out.

18

THE DARKNESS WAS ABSOLUTE.

Something very cold wrapped around me, freezing me in place. I had the sudden feeling the darkness was in my own head, which was far more terrifying than if the hallway had gone dark. I fought a sudden surge of panic.

Alice.

The voice in my head was unfamiliar and heavily accented. Something about the accent made my stomach churn and my heart race, though I wasn't sure why. Having someone talk in my head was definitely the weirdest thing that had happened to me since I'd woken up, but my adrenaline and nausea were from something more—a fear rooted deep in my brain.

My name is Valas, the voice said.

So this was the head of the Vampire Court talking in my mind. I immediately disliked the intrusiveness of telepathy.

You have no memory of me. It was a statement rather than a question.

I focused hard and tried to think back at the voice. *Sean told me you hired me to find out where the decanter came from.*

It would seem you found the answer and paid dearly for it. There was no sympathy or anger in her voice—no emotion at all, actually.

Her coldness made me angry. *Someone stole my life because of this case.*

Someone stole your memories and your magic; they did not steal your life, she corrected me. *While you live, there is hope what you have lost can be restored.*

Sean told me you're powerful. Can you...fix me? The witches don't seem to think it's possible.

Possible and impossible are not useful concepts when magic is involved. Perhaps I can restore your powers and your past if we find this sorcerer and reclaim them before it is too late.

What do you mean, before it's too late? I demanded.

The cold sensation intensified. I got the impression my tone had not been received well. *If the sorcerer intends to use your magic and memories for power, they may be consumed. If nothing remains when we find the sorcerer, nothing can be restored.*

What about my magic? I hated that my voice in my head had a hint of desperation, but if ever a situation called for desperation, this might be it. *Even if my memories are gone, can you at least give me some magic, or find someone who can? I can't rely on others to protect me forever from those who want to hurt me.*

I may be able to do so, Valas said, her tone thoughtful. *Perhaps an arrangement can be made.*

Warning bells went off in my head. Valas wouldn't help me without getting something in return and I was already indebted to her. Sean had told me that I'd made a deal with Valas to help save his life. He didn't know the terms of the agreement, but Valas was deadly serious about me fulfilling my end of the deal.

If I am able to give you some form of magic, we will discuss terms, Valas said. I wasn't sure if she'd heard my thoughts, or if her own thoughts had simply mirrored mine. *Until then, you must allow the Court to protect you.*

Sean will protect me.

You bring danger to his pack, she said. *There are children in the pack and humans who cannot defend themselves against your enemies. If you do not stay here, you endanger their lives.*

I'd be willing to bet she didn't care about the lives of Sean's pack—she wanted me here at Northbourne and away from Sean's protection. Even so, the thought I was endangering children made my stomach hurt.

I'll stay with Sean, I repeated, though my voice lacked the confidence and defiance it had only seconds before.

As you wish. Her tone made it clear she wasn't pleased. The cold feeling vanished and the darkness released me before I had a chance to respond.

Suddenly, I was back in the hallway. Disoriented and momentarily unsure of where I was, I stumbled.

Sean caught me by the arm and set me back on my feet. "Are you all right?"

I blinked up at him, surprised he was so calm. "How long was I gone?"

All three of them stared at me. "You've been walking beside me since we left the witches' room," Sean said carefully, his brow furrowed. "Where do you think you've been?"

I leaned against the wall. "Oh," I said, because I couldn't think of anything else to say.

"Alice." Sean moved into my line of sight. "Talk to me."

"I'm sorry—I'm just tired." I didn't want to tell him what had happened until we were alone. "Let's get out of here."

He didn't push the issue. "Okay, let's get you home."

We followed Adri upstairs, through the enormous lobby, and out the front doors. I took a deep breath and let it out. I didn't realize how tense I'd been in Northbourne until we were outside.

Despite Vaughan's promise we would be allowed to leave, I wouldn't have been the least surprised if they'd insisted I stay. Luckily, it seemed they'd opted to allow me to leave with Sean and the others.

Of course, we weren't through the gate yet.

Sean signaled to Jack and Ben, who waited in Jack's truck beside Sean's. Sean opened the passenger door for me to get into his truck, then spoke to Nan briefly before she went to get in with Jack and Ben.

"Jack and the others are going to follow us to your house," he told me as he got in. "We'll have members of the pack staying with us until we get all this sorted out."

When I didn't respond immediately, he touched my knee. "I know you're worried about putting us in danger. I won't tell you not to worry, because it wouldn't do any good, and because there is good reason for us to worry about who might be coming after you. But we are *not* afraid to face them, and we are proud to stand with you."

Stand *with* me. There it was again—that feeling of strength and support. And belonging.

"All right," I said.

"You're not going to argue with me about being protected?"

"No. Would I have argued with you about it...before?"

"Yes, very strenuously."

"Why?"

"Because you're strong and proud and independent and you don't like putting others in danger on your behalf."

I smiled wryly. "I'm still all of those things, I guess. I definitely do *not* like putting others in danger—especially the members of the pack who can't defend themselves as well as you, Jack, Ben, and Nan can. But I know I need help and you're willing to help me and I think I can trust you."

After a hesitation, he touched my face with his fingertips. This time, I didn't flinch away from the warmth of his hand. "You are so much like my Alice—the Alice I've known—but different is so many unexpected ways. Everything you went through made you suspicious of everyone, especially people who want to help you. You spent so long only being able to rely on yourself that it's been a long, hard road to get to the point where you're willing to rely on anyone else."

I didn't know what to say to that. The fact he'd been willing—and happy—to stick with me through everything we'd faced, including this, meant more to me in that moment than I could have put into words.

"As for trust," he added, "you've put almost as much trust in me today as you did the day you disappeared, and you distrust Vaughan and his people as much as I thought you would if you ever had the chance to see them for who they are." He smiled, and I decided I liked the way the corners of his eyes crinkled when he smiled. "The world's gone topsy-turvy."

"I'm sorry I've turned your world upside down."

"You've been turning my world upside down since the moment I met you," he said, surprising me. "Obviously I like it that way because I'm still here. I'm sorry *your* world is upside down. We'll figure out how to set it right, Alice. There has to be a way."

I thought about telling him what Valas had said about restoring my memories and magic, but I didn't. No sense getting his hopes up until I knew if there was really a chance Valas would be successful and what her price would be.

I settled into my seat and buckled in. "Let's go home."

———————

I breathed more easily once we were through the gate and on our way to my house. I found another package of crackers in the bag of snacks Ben had bought and ate them while I told Sean what Morgan had said to me while we were in the bathroom.

I wasn't kidding when I'd told Sean I was tired. I fell asleep on the way to my house right in the middle of a sentence. One moment I was telling him how I suspected Bridget knew a way to restore my magic and memories and had just been angling for a bigger payday—

—And the next I was startled awake by Sean's hand on my arm. "We're here," he said.

I looked out the truck's windshield and saw a beautiful little two-story Victorian-style house with a carport on the side and a backyard with a tall wooden fence.

"I live here?" I asked, surprised. "It looks like a fairy tale house."

He chuckled and unfastened his seatbelt. "In a way, it is—your happily-ever-after once you got away from your grandfather. You know, the night we met, this exact same thing happened," he added. "You fell asleep on the way home from the bar where we met and I had to wake you up when we got here."

"This must be kind of eerie for you," I said as we got out. "For me, everything is brand new and unfamiliar, while you must feel like you're starting over."

"Yes and no." He came around the front of the truck to join me. "I did get a strong feeling of déjà vu when you fell asleep, but nothing about tonight is anything like what we've been through before."

Jack's truck turned into the driveway and parked. When they didn't get out, I said, "Aren't they coming inside?"

"They're waiting to see if we go in. I told them I'm not sure we'll be able to get inside."

I blinked, confused. "Do you not have a key?"

"I *do* have a key." He held it up. "Let me rephrase what I said. I'm not sure *you're* going to be able to get inside. Your house has extremely powerful wards. They're keyed to let me in and out, and to you, obviously —but the *you* with magic. I don't know if they'll recognize you without it."

"I guess there's only one way to find out."

We went up the front steps to the porch. A cute porch swing hung to the left of the door. No décor I could see, except a plain gray throw pillow on the swing. My tastes must run toward the utilitarian.

The moment I got close to the door, I got a strong urge to back away. "I feel the wards. They don't feel very welcoming."

"Before, you told me they feel good to you, like coming home," he said.

"So they feel like this to everyone else? Even you?"

"I've gotten used to it, but...yes."

It made me sad to think my house didn't feel welcoming to anyone, even my lover. Tentatively, I touched the front door. *Zap.* Magic bit my fingers. I yelped and jumped back. I stared at the door, more deeply hurt than I could even describe. My own house didn't know me.

Sean touched my lower back. "Why don't you sit here while I go inside to get the items Carly needs to look for Malcolm?" he suggested, his voice gentle. "I'll just be a minute."

"All right." I went to the swing and sat down. Sean let himself into the house and closed the door quietly.

I swung back and forth with my feet, mindful of Ben, Jack, and Nan in the truck watching me. My chest hurt, and it had nothing to do with sorcery or a black witch's giant needle. I couldn't go home. I had no way to defend myself if Moses came looking for me, so I had to rely on a werewolf pack I barely knew to keep me alive. Malcolm was gone—lost, somehow, and I couldn't shake the feeling it was my fault. Valas had told me the sorcerer hadn't stolen my life, but it sure as hell felt that way.

True to his word, Sean was back in less than five minutes, carrying a small duffel bag. He locked the door, then sat beside me, the bag at his feet. "This is not the first time I've consoled you on this swing," he said, his tone light, though I saw grief in his eyes. My rejection by the house had hurt him too. "It's seen more than its fair share of dramatic moments."

I stared straight ahead so I didn't see his sympathy. "Before I knew I had a house, I didn't miss it. Now, I can't think of anything I want more than to go inside, except getting my magic and my memories back."

"I know. I'm sorry." He put his hand beside mine on the swing. "You can stay with me, of course. I haven't gotten a new bed in the guest room since you set it on fire, but the mattress is flipped so you should still be able to get a good night's sleep."

I turned to stare at him. "I set your guest bed on fire? *On purpose?*"

He chuckled. I liked that sound even more than I liked the way his eyes crinkled. "Not on purpose," he assured me. "Accidents happen, even to the best of mages."

I was fairly certain he'd brought up the burned mattress to distract me from my sadness, but I couldn't bring myself to mind.

I covered my mouth and yawned. "A good night's sleep sounds really fantastic, to be honest, though at this point it'll be a good day's sleep. It'll be dawn soon."

He patted my hand and we rose. "Then let's go back to my house and get settled in. Jack and the others will stay with us. Before we leave, let's go see your backyard. I can't wait to show you your man-eating garden."

I stopped dead in my tracks halfway to the porch steps. "Show me my *what?*"

We didn't talk much on the way from my house to Sean's. Despite my wonder at my backyard garden full of giant carnivorous plants, I was quiet and morose. He didn't force me to chat, though I was sure he would have preferred to distract me from my unhappiness.

I was relieved when he turned into the driveway of a two-story brick home and the garage door opened. Sean's house was larger than mine, and in a much fancier area. It didn't have the charm of my little Victorian, though, and I preferred my tree-lined street to his much more modern-looking neighborhood.

He parked in the garage. One bay was empty and the third held a pair of jet skis on a trailer. I was almost too tired to imagine what he might look like riding a jet ski. *Almost* too tired, but not quite.

Jack parked out front as Sean closed the garage door. He led me into the house, then went to the front door to unlock it for the others.

I looked around the living room and spotted a dog bed by the patio door. "Do you have a dog?" For some reason, it hadn't occurred to me a werewolf would have a dog, though that seemed silly now that I thought about it.

"*We* have a dog," he told me. "His name is Rogue."

The fact we had a dog stirred something in my heart. Yes, he'd told me we'd had the beginnings of a mate bond and we'd discussed buying a house together, but having a *dog* meant something very special, though I couldn't quite figure out how to phrase it.

"It's like we had a little pack or something," I said without thinking.

He paused halfway to the kitchen. "What makes you say that?" His tone was strange.

"You, me, Rogue. A little pack within the bigger pack." I shook my head. "I'm sorry—that made no sense, I'm sure. I'm tired."

"Alice, we are exactly a little pack within the bigger pack." Sean rejoined me in the living room. It didn't escape my notice that he'd used present tense to describe our relationship.

"That's how shifter families feel, even shifter-human families," he added. "You might not have shifter magic at the moment, but you're still part shifter—or at least we think you are. You've always had strong instincts—human instincts *and* I suspect shifter instincts. I said earlier you've shown a lot of trust in me and my pack today, and a lot of distrust of people associated with the Court. I'm pretty sure without memories you're relying on your instincts, and they're telling you who you can turn to now, and who you need to be wary of."

Someone cleared their throat loudly outside the front door. After a moment, it opened and Jack, Ben, and Nan came in. I was fairly certain it had been Ben who'd alerted us they were within earshot.

"Where is Rogue?" I asked.

"My daughter Felicia is dog-sitting," Nan told me with a smile. "We weren't sure how long we'd be gone, so she took him back to her place. She'll bring him over on her way to work in a little while, though."

I rubbed my face. "That'll be nice."

"Let's get you up to bed," Nan said. "I'll help you get settled into the guest room."

"I'll be up soon to check on you." Sean touched my hand. "Your clothes are in the dresser in our bedroom and your toiletries are in the master bathroom."

"Thanks. Good night," I said.

Jack and Ben wished me good night. I followed Nan up the stairs, moving slowly because of my sore legs. She led me to the master bedroom so I could change and continued down the hall to the guest room.

Sean's bedroom—*our* bedroom—didn't look any more familiar than his house, my house, or Northbourne. I stood just inside the room, looking at the king-sized bed. We'd shared that bed, apparently. Slept in it...and had sex on it. I didn't have to wonder if the sex had been good—for some reason, I was sure it was. He seemed like the type who made sure both parties enjoyed themselves thoroughly.

Before I got too caught up in those thoughts, I went to the smaller of the two dressers and found pajamas. I took them into the bathroom, changed, and figured out which toothbrush was mine. I washed my face, brushed my hair, and tended to my cut arm and the puncture in my chest with first aid supplies I found in a drawer.

When I emerged from the bathroom, my eyes fell a photo on the wall above the nightstand closer to the window. It was a framed photo of Sean and me lying in a hammock. His arms were around me and we were both smiling. It was me in the photo, and still somehow not me. I imagined that before my memories were stolen, I must have smiled every time I saw that photo. It was tangible proof we'd been happy.

Reluctantly, I left the master bedroom and shuffled barefoot down the hall to the guest room. Nan had turned down the bedding, closed the curtains, and switched on the bedside lamp.

"You look ready to fall asleep on your feet," she said.

"I am. That bed looks very inviting. Thank you."

She held up the covers. "Get in."

I crawled into bed like a kid and let her tuck me in. She sat on the edge of the bed. "Strength comes in many forms. For people like Jack, it's overt physical strength. Sean is physically strong too, obviously, but his real strength is in his heart. That's what makes him a truly great alpha, one we're happy to love and follow and trust. Some alphas have all the physical strength, but little heart. They rule by fear." Something told me Nan knew that from her own experience.

She tucked some hair behind my ear. "Sean is fearsome—all alphas are. You haven't seen that side of him since you woke up because he's hiding it from you. That man downstairs is playing a role because he thinks that's the best thing he can do for you right now, and he believes what's best for you is what's best for him."

"Why is he hiding who he really is?"

"He doesn't want you to be afraid of him. An alpha's strongest instinct is to protect his mate, and he couldn't protect you from being kidnapped, tortured, and abused. What's happened to you has broken his heart—and made both him and his wolf more furious than you can imagine."

Everything she'd said rang true, even the part about Sean not being himself because he feared he'd scare me. A lump formed in my throat. "What should I do?"

"Just be yourself. He knows your soul, and you know his, even if you don't remember. Our memories go deeper than neurons. You heal him just being at his side, and vice versa." She rubbed my arm through the covers.

My heart ached from all the hits I'd taken today, but Nan hadn't said these things to hurt me. She'd said them out of love—love for Sean, and for me.

While I absorbed it all, Nan continued, "Our pack recognized early on you are a source of strength, not just for Sean, but for all of us."

I flinched. "And I came back without my magic. I'm a liability now."

"No, you aren't," she said sharply. "You came back, and that sense of strength is back. If your strength was just from your magic, we would have noticed the difference. We can tell you don't have your magic, but you're still strong. Think about Jack and Ben's body language around you and tell me you think they don't still think you're strong."

I blinked at her. I hadn't even thought about it, but she was right. Ben and Jack had deferred to me, and not just because I was Sean's partner.

"Sometimes strength is easy to see, and sometimes not." She patted my arm and rose. "And sometimes it works very much to our advantage for others to not be able to see our strength until we want them to."

"Is that why you keep yours under the radar?"

She smiled briefly. "Why I do what I do is a long story. I'll share it with you another day. But the short answer to your question is yes." She touched my forehead with the back of her hand and frowned. "You're still running a fever. If it hasn't broken by tomorrow, take acetaminophen. And remember: lots of water."

"Okay." I snuggled deeper under the covers. "Good night, Nan. Thank you for talking to me."

"Good night, Alice." She turned off the lamp and left, closing the door quietly. I listened to her steps going down the hall.

My eyes felt dry and scratchy from exhaustion, but what Nan had said about Sean wouldn't stop rattling around in my head. I tossed and turned for a while, but sleep wouldn't come.

I threw the covers back and crept to the door, listening. Silence. I opened the door and tiptoed down the hall. I couldn't hear anything from downstairs. Maybe they were talking outside.

I went to the master bedroom and around to the side of the bed with the photo of Sean and me on the wall. On the nightstand was a jewelry box filled with earrings and little odds and ends. Next to the box were a couple of pens, a notepad, and a battered paperback biography of Steve McQueen.

I slipped under the covers. They smelled strongly of Sean. Part of me felt like I was trespassing in someone else's bed, but that feeling faded quickly as the forest scent filled my nose. I curled up under the covers. Weird how being in this bed felt like being home.

In moments, I was sound asleep.

19

I WOKE NOT LONG AFTER AND FOUND MYSELF IN BED NEXT TO AN enormous black and silver wolf.

The wolf raised his head and looked at me with bright golden eyes. I wondered if he'd been asleep and woken when I did, or if he'd watched over me while I slept.

"Hey, Sean," I whispered.

The wolf nuzzled my hand, then did the same with my throat. I held still as the wolf's nose brushed against my skin. I probably should have been scared to have a wolf's teeth that close to my jugular, but I wasn't. I knew I had nothing to fear from Sean, either in human or wolf form.

I noticed a chain around the wolf's neck. From it dangled a small stone carved in the shape of a wolf's head. I held the stone in my hand. It was warm and somehow comforting.

Something moved at the foot of the bed. A large black-and-white Husky mix dog repositioned himself against my feet. "Hi, Rogue," I said with a smile.

He made a quiet chuffing sound and wiggled until his back was against my shins, clearly happy to be near me. He was asleep again almost instantly.

I looked back at the wolf. For some reason, I thought he seemed concerned. "I'm all right," I told the wolf, my voice soft. "Go to sleep."

He laid his head down, but he didn't close his eyes. *You first*, his expression said.

It was very warm under the covers, with a wolf beside me and a large dog curled up against my legs. I stuck one of my feet out from under the bedding so I'd be a little cooler, settled in, and closed my eyes.

I ran like a pack of hellhounds were on my heels.

The labyrinth was endless. The walls were made of razor wire that cut my flesh if I got too close. The blades of grass were actual blades and they sliced the bottoms of my feet. I was naked and bloody from head to foot, but I ran faster.

I tripped and fell. Behind me, someone laughed and clapped. "Run, little wolf," a man said, his heavily accented voice full of merriment. "Run, run, run! All paths lead back to me."

I scrambled to my feet and found myself at the end of the labyrinth and the edge of a vast field. In the distance, I saw a fence and a huge, gnarled old tree. Beyond it stretched a road that gleamed like pure silver. I had to make it to that road.

I ran on and on, but the field grew before my eyes and the tree kept getting farther away. Desperate, I tried to fly, but I fell again and again, rolling and bouncing along the ground as the sharp grass cut me to the bone.

The man's laugh hurt my ears. He was singing to me now, his voice in my ear as if he was beside me. "Run, run, run, little wolf. Keep running and you'll run back to me."

I found a little stick on the ground and got back to my feet, brandishing my makeshift weapon. He was right behind me—a figure wearing all black, his eyes glowing red. "Little wolf, little wolf," he sang.

I jabbed at him with my stick, but he tore it from my grip. "Alice!" he said, his voice a growl. "Alice, wake up."

I scrambled away from him and suddenly there was nothing under me. I fell off the bed and landed on the floor.

Breathing hard, I looked up and found Sean standing beside the bed, wearing pajama pants and the stone wolf pendant around his neck on a long chain. His eyes glowed golden. "Alice?"

He held a pen in his hand—one of the pens I'd seen on the nightstand before I went to sleep. Realization dawned. Horrified, I stood and backed away. "Did I almost stab you?"

He stuck the pen in his pocket, hiding it from my sight. "You were having a nightmare."

The blood drained from my face. "I tried to stab you. Oh, God."

Sean approached. I retreated until my back hit the wall, raising my hands to keep him back. He stopped in his tracks, his face like granite. "Are you afraid of me?"

I remembered what Nan had said last night about Sean worrying I would fear him. "No, not at all," I told him. "You should be afraid of *me*. I just tried to stab you, *again*."

"You didn't try to stab me." He stayed where he was, his expression hard. "You tried to stab the person who hurt you."

"And I almost injured *you* in the process." My chest hurt. "I shouldn't be here. I'm a danger to you and everyone else if I can't tell the difference between what's real and what's not. I should get as far away from you and the rest of the pack as I can."

"Don't you dare tell me the best way to protect me is to break my heart, Alice Worth," he snapped.

I stared at him, open-mouthed.

He advanced on me, his eyes blazing gold. "Ever since I figured out who you really were, I worried you would run away to protect me and my pack from your grandfather. I told you repeatedly not to run because it's my choice whether I fight beside you or not. Nothing has changed for me; I still choose to stay by your side."

"But—"

He cut me off. "When you vanished four days ago, I damn near went crazy. I had no leads, no way to track you, no clue where you'd gone or who took you. Every way I turned, I hit a brick wall. I couldn't eat, couldn't sleep, couldn't even *think* until I found you last night walking along the highway. I just got you back, so I am not going to let you walk out that door because you think I'd be better off, or because it would make you feel better if you thought I was in less danger."

Sean cupped my face with his hand. He felt so wonderful and warm. I leaned against him. He was angry, but he was holding so much more anger in.

"I'm not afraid of you," I told him, looking up into his eyes. "I don't know much, but I know I could *never* be afraid of you. Don't hold back from me, Sean. I want you to be real with me because I need to know what's real right now. Don't hide your anger like you did when you smashed the table at the motel while I was in the shower and got rid of the evidence before I came out of the bathroom."

"You should fear me," he said, his voice a low growl. "I turn into a wolf when I get angry enough to lose control. Even when I'm human, I can be violent."

"Are you trying to scare me off? Because I don't scare easily. You'll have to be scarier than that if you want me to be afraid of you." I covered his hand with mine. "You're furious because you want to keep me safe, but I got kidnapped and someone stole my memories and magic. Let all that anger out before it gets to be too much and you explode like a volcano."

He leaned down and ran his nose along my hairline, making me shiver. It was such a wolf-like thing to do. He kept his face close to mine, breathing in my scent. I shivered again, but this time it wasn't because his breath tickled my skin.

He inhaled deeply. "Think about cold showers," he told me roughly. "Stop thinking about whatever you're thinking about, because damn it, you smell so good."

"You smell good to me too." And that bare chest inches from my eyes and nose pushed thoughts of cold showers far from my brain. I echoed his movement from a few moments before and ran my nose over his hot skin. "I guess there are fun ways to blow off steam."

He made a sound somewhere between a growl and a groan and pulled away. "It wouldn't be right," he said, his voice strained.

I frowned. "Why not? We're consenting adults. You said our first night together was the first time we met. This isn't even a one-night stand, because you know me very well, and I know you well enough to know what I want." I studied him. "Unless you think my judgment is impaired. I don't think it is, but then again, if it was, maybe I wouldn't know."

A long silence. "I'm not sure if your judgment is impaired," he said finally. "You haven't done anything that would make me think it is."

"Then what's your hesitation?" I glanced below his waistline. "Because I think you want me, and I want you."

"I do want you. I always have. Part of me wants you more than anything in the world. Not just *that* part," he added, with a brief, rueful smile. He tucked some hair behind my ear. "You're not yourself, Alice, as much as you say and think you are. Unless I'm sure you know what you want and you're thinking clearly, I'm not going to risk hurting you in a way I could never take back, or deserve forgiveness for."

My shoulders sagged. I sat on the edge of the bed. "First my house rejects me, now you."

He sat down beside me. "This is not a rejection. I am not turning you down because I'm a heartless bastard or because I don't want you. I want you like I want air to breathe." He covered my hand with his much larger one. "You know how you instinctively trusted me and others in the pack, and instinctively distrusted Vaughan?"

I nodded.

"My instincts tell me I'd be taking advantage of you if we had sex right now. I've over-ridden my instincts when it came to you before; I told you that last night. And we both suffered when I did." He raised my hand and kissed it. "So I'm going to listen to my instincts this time, even if it's killing me to do so, because doing anything that would hurt you is the absolute last thing I'd ever want to do."

"That makes sense, in a very logical and sensible sort of way." I sighed. "But you still need to stop suppressing all your anger. I meant it when I said I don't want you to hold back or pretend you're fine because you're worried about scaring me off. I've got a lot of things to be scared of right now, but you're not one of them. What do you normally do to vent your anger?"

"Since you and I have been together, I'm rarely angry enough to need to vent, but sometimes I go to a gym and punch a heavy bag for a while— one made to withstand punches from a shifter. Other times, I shift to my wolf and go running and hunting on our pack's land outside the city."

"Which would you rather go do?"

"To be honest, what I want to do is be by your side while we get the answers we need about your disappearance and figure out how to get your magic back."

"Does me being with you help?"

He squeezed my hand. "Very much so."

"Okay, then I'll stay by your side." I tapped the stone wolf around his neck. "What's the significance of your wolf necklace?"

"It's an amulet." He held it closer so I could see it. "Carly gave us each one. You hung mine around my neck a couple of weeks ago and I haven't taken it off since. We've used them in the past to find each other, but it didn't work this time. The wards hiding you from us were too strong."

I liked that we'd had matching amulets. "Mine looks the same?"

"Yes, in reverse, with my name on the back." He showed me the back of his. The name *Alice* was inscribed across it. "The amulet was one stone, carved into two wolves facing each other. We broke it in half."

"I didn't have mine when you found me."

"No." His voice was growly.

"I want it back from whoever took it." I rested my head on his bare shoulder and breathed in his scent.

"You're wearing my favorite pajamas," he told me.

They'd seemed surprisingly whimsical to me, which might have been why I'd chosen to wear them. My heart had been heavy last night. "Why are these your favorite?"

"Wolves like sheep." He kissed the top of my head. "You still feel too warm."

"I know. I don't know what me being warm means."

"We'll figure it out." He lifted my hand to his mouth and kissed it. "We're going to figure all of this out, together."

"So what's our first step?"

"I'm going to make us breakfast and coffee, then we're going to go talk to Carly."

I thought about it. "I think I would love some coffee."

He smiled. "Still my Alice."

20

We arrived at Carly's little blue bungalow just after three o'clock. Sean parked out front and a Maclin Security SUV pulled up behind us. Ben had gone to work and Nan was home resting, but Jack stayed on guard duty, accompanied by pack member and fellow Maclin Security employee Karen Williams. She'd greeted me with a warm hug when I came downstairs at Sean's house.

Jack and Karen stayed outside on watch while Sean and I went to Carly's door. She opened it as we were climbing the porch steps, wearing a T-shirt that said WITCH PLEASE and yoga pants. "Hello, you two," she said, stepping aside to let us in. She waved at Jack and Karen, then closed the door behind us.

"I love your house," I told her. Everywhere I looked, I saw crystals, plants, bookcases, and cozy little nooks. Various herbs hung drying in the kitchen and dining area. The house smelled wonderful.

"Thank you. I'm sorry you're seeing it again for the first time." Carly studied me. "Your aura looks a little better today. Yours too, Sean. Never underestimate the healing power of love. Why don't you come into the kitchen while I make us tea?"

Sean had told me on the way over that he'd called Carly last night to tell her what had happened at Northbourne with Morgan and Bridget. He'd also warned her Morgan had recognized me and deduced Carly had given their names to the Court.

"I'm sorry Morgan and Bridget know you're involved in this," I told Carly as she selected a jar of loose tea from a cabinet.

"Don't apologize. I knew there was a good chance they'd figure it out." She measured the tea with a spoon and poured it into an infuser. "I'm not afraid of them, which vexes them to no end. I'm more afraid *for* them, truth be told."

"Because they use black magic?" I asked.

"That, and because I think Morgan's been dabbling in sorcery." She lowered the infuser into a teapot, poured in hot water from a kettle, and put the lid on the teapot. She leaned against the counter and crossed her arms. "I can't imagine Morgan doing so without her mother's permission, so maybe Bridget has been dabbling too. That might help them figure out how to undo what this sorcerer has done to you, but I still hate to see either of them going down that road."

She put the teapot on a tray with three mugs and headed for the living room. We followed her and sat on the couch. She set the tray on the coffee table, poured us mugs of tea, dropped a cube of sugar into each, and handed them to us. She took her own mug to a large, comfortable-looking armchair and curled up in the seat with her legs tucked under her.

My tea smelled wonderful, like lavender and lemon. I expected it to be too hot to drink, but it was perfect. I sipped and looked around the living room.

"Did you have any dreams?" Carly asked me.

I glanced at Sean. He touched my hand. "She'll understand," he murmured.

Hesitantly, I described my dream: the strange labyrinth made of wire, the sharp grass, the field and tree, and the figure in black with red eyes who mocked me as I ran. I also admitted I'd almost accidentally stabbed Sean when he tried to wake me.

"Sean's right: you aren't to blame for that," Carly told me. "I believe your dream is a fragment of a real memory, something that happened after your memories were stolen. You tried to escape but were caught. We might find some clues in the dream. The voice you heard was male?"

I nodded slowly. "Yes, he was definitely male."

"What else can you remember about him? Don't strain to remember; just let the impressions come to you."

I closed my eyes and thought about the dream. "Tall and slim," I said finally. "In the dream, he was wearing all black, but that might have just been the dream. It would be very cliché for a sorcerer to wear all black in real life, wouldn't it?"

She smiled. "Terribly cliché. Describe his voice. What did he sound like?"

Run, run, run, little wolf. All paths lead back to me.

I shivered. "An accent. Middle Eastern, maybe, but not strong, like he's been in the U.S. for a while."

"This is good." Carly set her mug on the table beside her. "And the labyrinth you ran through? Your description of it is strange."

"I know." I opened my eyes and sighed. "They weren't solid walls—just tall fences, almost, but strung with big loops of razor wire. It cut me when I ran past it. I guess that's where all the cuts on my arms, legs, and feet came from."

"Sorcerers can transform things, if they're powerful enough," Carly said. "He could have turned the fence into razor wire and the grass into blades."

"Well, that's terrifying. Any luck with the lighter or my clothes?"

She shook her head. "Vague impressions only from the clothes and nothing yet from the lighter. I tried a tracking spell with the clothes and got nothing but glimpses of the highway where you walked, probably because the place you were held has extremely powerful wards and the sorcerer himself is shielded with occult spells."

"What impressions did you get from the clothes?" I asked.

"Nothing about the sorcerer, but I caught glimpses of a blonde woman who I think is a witch. She might be the witch who cursed you to walk."

"Do you think that's her lighter? I grabbed it from the car—or at least, I'm pretty sure I did." The few memories I had were all so jumbled and fuzzy.

"It's possible. I haven't given up. I also want to try to locate Malcolm."

Sean indicated the small duffel bag he'd brought with us. "I have a few of the items from Alice's house that Malcolm used: spell crystals and the tube of henna Alice used to write spells on her skin that protected Malcolm."

Carly smiled. "That's great. I'll try a strong tracking spell later. It will take time for me to set everything up for that. In the meantime, while you're here, I'd like Alice's help."

"What can I do?" I asked.

"I've already tried to locate him using a pendulum and map and got nothing—again, probably because of how well he's hidden." She picked up something wrapped in black silk from the table beside her and rose. "Join me at the coffee table?"

"Yes, of course," I said.

She tossed a couple of cushions on the floor and moved the tea tray aside. We sat cross-legged on our cushions on opposite sides of the table. She placed the silk-wrapped object on the table between us.

"Before we start, I need you to clear your mind of everything you brought with you today." She rested her hands palm-up on her knees. I mirrored her pose. "Close your eyes," she instructed me. I obeyed. "Now breathe deeply: in through your nose…and out through your mouth." I inhaled slowly, then exhaled. "Again," she said. "Imagine everything that's worrying you floating away as you exhale. Let everything go."

We focused on breathing and clearing our minds. The room around me faded away. My shoulders went down and tension I didn't know I was carrying eased from my neck and back.

"Think of Malcolm," Carly told me. "I know you don't remember him, but that's all right. You don't have to picture him to think about him."

I thought about what I knew about Malcolm. He and I were like brother and sister. He'd been sent to be my companion and protector, possibly by angels. I missed him, though I couldn't remember anything about him, or even what he looked like.

"Goddess, I ask you to help us find Malcolm, who is lost to us," Carly said quietly. "If his location cannot be revealed, please grant us knowledge of whether he has passed through the veil, or remains here."

I opened my eyes. Carly unwrapped a stack of handmade tarot cards and spread the black silk out on the table. The backs of the cards bore a beautiful compass rose, surrounded by flowering vines that matched the vines tattooed on Carly's right forearm. She must have made the cards herself.

"Keep our request in your mind, along with your thoughts about Malcolm," Carly instructed me. "Pick up the cards and shuffle them however you like."

Carefully, I did as she'd instructed. I set them back on the silk when I finished.

She picked up the cards, took the top card, and placed it face up and horizontal near the top of the silk. The card showed a gray horizontal line. Below the line was a wispy figure of a person, painted with watercolors. In the upper left corner, I saw a small arrow pointing up.

On top of it, she placed the second card, also face up but vertical. This card showed a closed door, upside down. Below those two cards, she placed a third card, also vertical. This card had a drawing of a figure with enormous wings that were folded in front of their body. The figure held a sword in both hands, its point aimed at the ground. Together, the three cards formed a cross.

She set the deck to the right and studied the cards. "Malcolm has not crossed the veil," she told us. "He remains on this plane."

I let out a breath. "He's not gone." I realized Carly still looked grim. "But...?" I prompted.

"He's imprisoned." She indicated the card with the upside-down door. "Trapped in a place we can't get to him, and he can't get out."

"How do we free Malcolm from this prison?" My throat felt tight.

Carly indicated the third card. "An archangel will show us the way when the time comes."

My eyes widened. "There are *archangels?* And how the heck do we know one?"

She smiled, but it was brief, with a hint of sadness. "Your reaction the first time I mentioned archangels was much more subdued, but then again, you were very tired that day. Yes, there are archangels. I am relieved to know one will assist us."

I rubbed my face wearily. I still struggled to make sense of my own nightmarish past. Now, in addition to that tangled mess and the werewolves and vampires in my life, I had archangels with swords to think about. Best to put that aside until we solved more immediate concerns, I supposed. "But we still don't know where Malcolm is, or who this damn sorcerer is."

"How is a sorcerer able to use magic that's so different and powerful?" Sean asked.

Carly propped her elbow on the table and rested her chin on her hand. "A witch or wizard can use black magic and sorcery as part of their occult practice. To become a true sorcerer, a practitioner has to die in an occult ritual and be reborn. His soul becomes the property of the demon lord he serves. There's a lot of debate in the Craft over whether a sorcerer is living or undead, or even some kind of revenant, since his soul no longer inhabits his body and he has become essentially animated flesh."

I gaped at her. "Like a vampire?"

"Similar, though vampires retain their souls and don't serve anyone except their makers or Courts—and it's not the same kind of servitude." She folded her hands on the table. "It's possible the lack of soul enables a sorcerer to commit evil without remorse, or makes him utterly amoral. There aren't many true sorcerers around anymore, as far as anyone knows. Few people are as willing these days to make a deal with a demon lord, even for the promise of near immortality and enormous power. Long ago and in other parts of the world, it was far more common."

She wrapped the tarot cards and put them aside. She brought out a second, larger deck wrapped in purple silk and set it on the table. "I'd like to do a second reading—this time, for you."

Startled, I asked, "Why for me?"

"You're standing at a crossroads and you're going to have to make some difficult decisions about how to move forward."

She wasn't wrong about that.

"I'm not a fortune teller or clairvoyant," she said. "The cards offer guidance and food for thought. You can accept what they suggest, or not. I have a feeling the cards will help you, but only if you'd like to hear what they have to say." She smiled. "I won't insist if you'd rather not."

I'd been grateful for the cards' insight into how to help Malcolm, though they hadn't given us any leads on where he was or how to find him. For some reason, I feared what the cards would have to say about my situation. It would be foolish to refuse help, however, given the mess I was in, and as Carly had pointed out, the cards only offered advice.

"All right," I said. "How does this work? Same process as before?"

She unfolded the silk and spread it out on the table. "Basically, yes, but this time, as you breathe and shuffle the cards, think about the question you'd like to ask."

"Would you like me to go outside?" Sean asked.

I shook my head. "Thank you for asking, but no. Please stay." I closed my eyes and cleared away my worries about Malcolm and undead, soulless sorcerers. My life was mainly made up of questions at the moment—where Malcolm was, who this sorcerer was, why he stole my memories and magic, why he sent the spelled decanter to the gala—but those answers would reveal themselves in time, as Sean and I dug deeper into the mystery.

One question in particular kept bobbing to the surface. I had no idea how to answer it, and the more I thought about it, the less clear the answer seemed.

Without opening my eyes, I reached for the cards. I shuffled them, my fingers feeling their edges, weight, and texture. I placed the cards back on the silk and opened my eyes.

Carly met my gaze. "What's your question?"

"If I do find the sorcerer, should I try to get my memories back, or not?"

With my back to Sean, I couldn't see his reaction, but I sensed a sudden stillness that made me think I'd startled him with my question.

If Carly was surprised, she didn't let on. She picked up the cards, took the first one from the top of the deck, and placed it on the cloth closer to me and centered. She laid out the next eight cards to form a Celtic cross shape with a base or stand. She studied the cards, her manner unhurried. We waited.

"There's nothing simple about this question," she said finally, her eyes still on the cards. "What you are asking is whether you need those memories to have the life you want."

"Sean told me a lot about my past. It wasn't very good." I couldn't tell her the details, but the details weren't important. "I know just from being around Sean and the others for the past day that I'm different without those memories. I might be a better person without them."

"All that might be true. Your heart is lighter, despite all you've suffered in the past week. You no longer radiate anger and guilt and pain. The wall I always sensed between you and Sean is gone. Your level of intimacy is different, obviously, because you don't have the memory of your relationship, but your past made you too afraid for him and your pack, and sure you didn't deserve their love and acceptance. All that baggage is gone, and I can't say I'm not glad to see it gone."

"There's a *but* coming, isn't there?" I said, somewhat dryly.

She nailed me with a look. "*But...*I think the point you're missing is you aren't a better person because you've had your memories stolen. You're a better person because you're allowing Sean and your pack to fight for you. You finally believe you're worthy of Sean's love, and you're not allowing your past trauma to dictate your present actions. Believe it or not, all of those things could still happen if you had your memories. Your bad memories have defined you for way too long, but that doesn't mean you need them sponged from your head. That means it's time to put those burdens down and walk free."

She folded her hands on the table. "You have good memories too, and those you should want back. It's not the same to hear about how you and Sean first met, or how Malcolm came to be such an important part of your life, or how and why your pack accepted you as one of their own. You need those memories. And you need the bad ones too, not so they can hold you back, but so you can feel the peace and freedom of moving on. As the saying goes, let that shit go."

"Is that you or the cards talking?" I asked with a wan smile.

"It's one and the same." She didn't smile back. "You don't need those memories to be who you are, but you need them to know where you've been and how far you've come. Would you be happier without them? Maybe, especially short term. But long term, no, and you wouldn't be the person you can be—the person you *should* be."

"I still don't think it will be easy to know what's right if and when I find the sorcerer and my memories he stole," I confessed. "I think I was deeply unhappy with all those bad memories piled up in my head."

"We can't truly appreciate the light unless we have also known darkness." She covered my hand with hers. "Whatever choice you make, you'll have to live with the consequences of your decision. The choice will not be easy. No important choices in our lives ever are."

She tapped the Tower card, which was above the Magician—the card I assumed referred to me. "There is a great transformation coming. You will be remade."

I wasn't sure how to feel about that. "Because of my decision?"

She shook her head. "The forces of your transformation are already in motion. The decision you make will only affect the shape the transformation takes."

She glanced at Sean, still sitting behind me. "Whatever she chooses, she will need you more than ever." She tapped the seven of wands. "In ways you will expect, and in ways you won't." Her finger moved to point at the two of cups. "And you will need her, as well, because this unmaking will affect you both."

Her word choice puzzled me. "Unmaking?"

She frowned. "That's a strange word to use, isn't it? I'm not sure why I chose that word, but sometimes that's what happens during a reading. There will be an unmaking, a remaking, and a transformation." She indicated another card, the page of cups. "And a birth."

I stared at her. "As in a *child?*"

"Not in the literal sense, I think." She pondered the cards. "That's all I can see, for now."

"That's plenty." I was surprised to find I was trembling. "Thank you."

She smiled and gathered up her cards. "One last thing before you leave."

"Another reading?" I tried not to sound ungrateful, but her reading for me had been a doozy.

"No. I want to try another tracking spell on the cigarette lighter you had with you when Sean found you. I'm hoping your presence will help me see more than just a few glimpses of its owner." She wrapped the cards and put them in a small basket. She slid another basket over and set up what looked like the same small altar I'd seen at the motel.

When the altar was ready, she took the pink cigarette lighter from a linen wrapping and set it on the table. "Sean, can you sit next to Alice so I can close a circle around us?"

"Of course." He settled in beside me. I thought he looked relieved to be next to me. When he took my hand, I didn't pull away.

Carly took a small dagger from a basket and stood. Unlike the bone-handled and rather nasty-looking blade Bridget had used for her spells, Carly's was lovely. The double-edged blade was about six inches long and made of steel, with a groove in the middle lined with etched runes. The handle was made of what looked like red maple, with multicolored threads woven through tiny holes and a marble-sized piece of quartz embedded at the top of the handle.

She pointed the dagger at the floor and walked around us clockwise three times, reciting an incantation very different from Bridget's. "I cast this circle three times three to protect those in the circle that no harm may come to them or those outside the circle."

She finished walking and settled back in across from us. She closed her eyes and breathed deeply several times. Sean and I waited.

Carly opened her eyes and held out her hand to me. I took it and held on.

She picked up the lighter with her other hand. "Universe, hear me," she said. "Show me the owner of this object and the place she calls home so I may heal the wrongs that have been done to Alice Worth. As I will it, so mote it be."

I wondered if she was going to put the lighter in the cauldron. Instead, she did something entirely unexpected: she flicked it.

The lighter was almost empty, but a flame appeared. Carly focused on it. Not on the flame itself, I realized almost immediately, but at a point past it—somewhere far away, or in the past.

Finally, she spoke, her voice distant. "I smell earth and growing things. A sign sways in the wind." A long pause. "The sign is in shadow, but I see...

grapes." Carly opened her eyes and extinguished the flame on the lighter. "That's all I could see."

Sean's hand tightened on mine. "A vineyard?" he suggested. "Maybe that's what you saw in your dream, Alice. The labyrinth with the strange walls might have been grapevines on fences."

My shoulders drooped. There were thousands of vineyards in California alone. "Thank you," I said to Carly as she let go of my hand. "Was that all you saw of the sign? The grapes?"

She nodded. "And parts of a few letters. I'll look online at names of vineyards and see if anything jumps out at me."

She took a piece of paper from her basket and drew part of a rectangular sign with a small bunch of grapes in the lower-right corner. After a hesitation, she added a few lines—parts of letters. She folded the paper, slipped it inside a plastic bag, and handed it to me.

The reason for the bag became apparent a moment later, when thunder rumbled outside. "I hope that's not an omen," I said, half-jokingly.

"Not an ill omen, I would argue," Carly said as Sean and I rose from the floor. I had to use the couch to push myself to my feet, since my legs were sore and sitting had made my muscles stiff. "Rain cleanses and leads to growth."

"That's a good point." I noticed Carly moved slowly. "Are you all right?"

"I've done a lot of magic today. It really takes a lot out of a girl." She forced a smile and settled into her armchair. "Forgive me if I don't walk you to the door."

I gave her a hug. "Thank you for everything. I don't know how to repay you."

She squeezed me. "Next new moon, join me and my coven for a ritual."

Given everything she'd done to help me, it sounded more than fair. "It's a deal."

"Good." She picked up her mug of tea from the little table next to her chair. To my astonishment, steam rose from the liquid, well over an hour after the tea had been poured.

She winked at me. "A witch who owns a coffee and tea shop has spells useful for such things. Blessed be."

"Blessed be," I echoed.

We let ourselves out the front door and locked it behind us. Just as Sean and I stepped onto the porch, lightning flashed and the skies opened up. We stood for a moment in awe of the sheer force of the rain.

In their truck, Jack said something to Karen and she shook her head ruefully. Probably commenting on how unlucky we were to leave Carly's house right as the rain started.

"You told me I used to be able to command thunderstorms," I mused, staring out from our shelter. "That must have been pretty cool."

"It was the coolest damn thing I've ever seen." Sean took my hand. "I can't wait to see you do it again, someday soon. Smiting optional, of course."

I had to laugh at that.

"We're going to get soaked." He unlocked his truck with his key fob. "Want to make a run for it?"

"Nah. I feel like getting cleansed." I let go of his hand and stepped out from under the porch overhang. I was instantly drenched, but I didn't mind. The rain was lovely and cool.

When I was halfway down the front steps, Sean caught up with me and took my hand again. We sloshed across the yard as Jack and Karen watched, nonplussed.

"They think we're nuts," Sean said, bending his head so I could hear him over the rain.

"They might be right," I admitted. "Does that bother you?"

"No." He squeezed my hand. "You told me once we could be crazy together because it's more fun that way."

"I can imagine myself saying that."

He opened the passenger door of his truck for me. "My lady."

I grabbed the handle and climbed into the truck. "Thank you, sir."

He closed my door and walked around to the driver's side. When he was inside, I said, "I'm sorry we're getting the interior of your truck wet."

"Rain and mud is far from the worst thing these seats have seen," he said, turning the key in the ignition. He reached into the back seat and handed me a towel, then used one himself to dry his hair and face. He glanced at me. "You're so much like the way you were before you were taken, but then so different as well."

"Different for the better?"

"Yes...and no."

I hesitated in the middle of toweling myself off. "Do you think I should try to get my memories back?"

I expected him to say it was up to me, but he surprised me with a firm answer. "Yes."

"Really?" I asked, startled.

"I think Carly is right. You can be just as you are now, even with those memories, if you let the anger and guilt go. I think you need to do that, for the reasons she listed...plus a few others."

"Which are?"

He went quiet for a while as he drove. Finally, he said, "Because in my opinion the best version of yourself is the you that's *whole*. The day you agreed to buy a house and move in with me, I saw the woman Carly talked about: the person you should be. You were on the edge of a new chapter in your life—not because of me or anything I've done, but because you were ready to let the past go and move forward and be happy."

He reached over and covered my hand with his. "However this turns out, that's what I want for you, what I've always wanted. And I'm not going to let anyone—Moses, this sorcerer, or anyone else—take that away from you."

"Thanks," I said. "But I get the feeling if I was, or am, at a new chapter in my life, it has a lot to do with you, our pack, and Malcolm."

Something flashed across Sean's face. The truck slowed, then sped back up.

"What?" I asked.

"That's the first time you've referred to us as *our* pack. You struggled with that before, when you thought you were putting us at risk and weren't worthy of our acceptance." His hands flexed on the steering wheel. I wondered if he was rethinking his position on regaining my memories.

"I'm not rethinking anything," he said.

My mouth fell open. "Can you read my mind?"

He chuckled. "No, but I know how you think—even now, it seems. Just remember this when the time comes and you have your memories back and that little voice in your head tries to tell you something different."

"I'll try to remember. I'm going to be unmade, remade, and transformed. And something about a birth," I added wryly. "That's a lot."

"It *is* a lot, but I will be there all the way," he promised. He did something on his phone and turned up the radio.

"What's the name of this song?" I asked as he stopped at a red light.

"'Take Me Home Tonight' by Eddie Money and Ronnie Spector." He glanced at me. "You like it?"

I nodded. "I do like it. Did you play this song for a reason?"

"Yes." He smiled. "It's our song."

I wondered if he'd picked it as our song or if I had, and then decided it didn't matter. I liked this man—not because he'd come to my rescue or because he was protecting me when I was vulnerable, but because he loved me for me, and because he was happy to hold my hand and walk in the rain.

And then Sean freaked me out a little by reaching over the center console to take my hand. He said he couldn't read my mind, but I was starting to wonder if he was doing so without realizing it. Maybe I would have minded if I had all that baggage from my years as my grandfather's prisoner, but right now he seemed to know what I needed even before *I* did. That was comforting, and I needed some comfort after Carly's tarot reading and my guilt about almost stabbing him with a pen.

I squeezed his hand and listened to Eddie Money as we drove home through the rain.

21

SEAN

BEN AND NAN WERE ALREADY AT THE HOUSE WAITING WHEN SEAN AND Alice arrived. After greeting them with a sheepish smile and an apology for her bedraggled appearance, Alice excused herself to go upstairs and take a shower in the master bathroom.

Sean took a change of clothes to the guest bathroom. His wolf, already unsettled by Alice's long absence, the pain she'd suffered at the hands of the witches at Northbourne, and Carly's ominous tarot readings, was further agitated by Sean not joining Alice in the shower. The intimacy of showering together was time both Sean and his wolf cherished, and the wolf did not understand why they were showering separately.

The wolf paced in his head. *Play with mate*, he commanded.

Alice is not well, Sean explained, not for the first time. *No play until she's well again.*

The wolf sat on his haunches and stared at him. *Mate does not smell sick.*

Not all illnesses are easy to see or smell. We will not do anything that might hurt Alice. Sean shut off the water and stepped out of the shower to grab a towel.

Mate wants to play, the wolf argued, still far from convinced.

Sean had smelled it too during their drive home, even over the scent of mud and their rain-soaked clothes. Her reaction to his nearness was equal parts intoxicating and frustrating, but he hadn't asked her to stop thinking about him, even though not being able to act on their mutual desire was torture. For now, it was worth the frustration to have her at his side again.

Mate is frightened, the wolf told him, his voice thoughtful. *Frightened is not well.*

Yes, Sean agreed as he pulled on a polo shirt. *Frightened is not well.* He studied his face in the mirror.

The wolf stared back at him. *Kill witches, kill sorcerer, kill vampires, kill mate's grandsire. Then mate not frightened*, the wolf said.

Sean's arms prickled as fur pushed at his skin. *I intend to kill as many of those people as I can*, he told the wolf.

Mate's wolf is angry.

Sean stilled at his wolf's pronouncement. *What does that mean?*

Feel heat of anger. Mate's wolf may cause pain and sickness to mate.

Sean thought of Alice's fever. *What should I do?*

The wolf laid down with his head on his paws. *Speak comfort and patience to mate's wolf. Make mate well soon.*

Damn it, as if he needed another reason to find Alice's magic and memories and get them restored as soon as possible.

He opened the guest room door and headed for the stairs. The shower was still running in the master bathroom. He pictured Alice in the shower they'd shared many times. His wolf growled unhappily.

Sean hurried downstairs. Nan and Ben waited in the living room with Jack. "Cole came and picked Karen up," Jack told him. "She wasn't feeling well and needed to go home and rest."

"That's fine." Sean had made it clear to Karen she was free to take time whenever she needed to rest or if she felt ill.

"I hear you and Alice took a walk in the rain," Nan said with a smile. "How is she?"

Sean glanced up toward the sound of the shower. "She's doing well, given the circumstances." He ran his hands through his wet hair and exhaled. "Carly gave us some helpful advice. She suspects the person who dumped Alice on the side of the road was a witch. As for where Alice was held, we may be looking for a vineyard or winery."

"Good thing there aren't more than three thousand of those in the state," Ben said dryly. "Can Carly help us narrow down the search?"

"She got a glimpse of what she thinks is the winery's sign, so she's going to look online to see if she can find something that looks familiar. No telling how long that will take—or if she'll find anything." He took the plastic bag with Carly's drawing from his pocket and showed them the sketch.

Ben took the paper and studied it. "Doesn't look familiar, but I'll try to search for it." He took out his laptop and sat on the couch.

"Have you told the Court about the winery?" Nan asked.

Sean shook his head. "Not yet. I don't trust the vampires to have Alice's best interests at heart. I'd like to keep this in the pack if we can." After pausing to confirm Alice was still in the shower, he added, "Without her magic, Alice is vulnerable. Protecting her is our number-one priority. I'll authorize Karen, Jack, Patrick, and Phillip to provide security from my company. We'll just need others to take shifts as their work and family schedules allow."

"I'll coordinate the shifts," Jack said gruffly. "What else can we do in the meantime?"

"We need to find this winery," Nan said.

Ben looked up from his laptop. "What do we know that could narrow down the search?"

Sean crossed his arms. "We know where Alice was dropped off. You said the tire tracks of the vehicle that left her made a U-turn and headed north. Assuming they didn't make that turn deliberately to leave a false trail, for now, let's assume the winery is north of Landers."

"That still leaves a lot of area to cover," Jack pointed out.

"Carly said the spellwork that stole Alice's magic and memories was probably done around midnight, to use the power of the moon." Sean paced across the living room. "Then she was bathed, dressed, and driven to where she was dropped off and dumped around seven o'clock, after it had stopped raining."

"So that means the winery is probably within five hours of the drop-off point." Ben typed quickly and frowned at his laptop screen. "That doesn't help narrow it down much. We've still got dozens of possibilities."

"Dozens of possibilities are better than no leads at all, which was where we were only a few hours ago." Nan gestured at Carly's drawing. "Maybe Ben can find a sign or logo that matches what Carly saw within the radius we estimated."

Upstairs, the shower shut off. They listened to the familiar sound of Alice's light footsteps as she moved around in the bathroom and master bedroom.

"I'm glad to have her home," Nan said, touching Sean's arm. "Her resilience is really remarkable. Not much seems to faze her, even now. Most people I know would be a wreck after what she's been through."

Sean noticed Jack had gone quiet. "What's on your mind?" he asked.

His beta sighed. "Delia."

"I am not going to debate this with Delia, now or ever." Sean's words were clipped with anger. "I can well imagine what she thinks about this situation, and I want to be clear I will not put up with it anymore. No more complaints, no more arguments, no more attacks on Alice or our relationship. No more snide comments about children, no hostility, no hateful looks when she thinks I'm not looking. *No more,* Jack."

"What do you want me to say?" Jack laced his fingers behind his head, clearly frustrated. "I've tried reasoning with her and I get nowhere."

"There is a good chance Delia is alive today only because Alice granted her mercy after the hex," Sean reminded his beta. "I had every intention of dealing with Delia myself for what she did. You know if someone had done that to her, you would have killed them. And yet Delia continues to treat Alice with contempt and resentment and I have officially come to the end of my patience." His vision turned gold as his wolf growled low. "I am giving you and Delia a choice: accept Alice, or leave the pack."

"Is this what it's come to?" Jack asked, his eyes glowing amber. "An ultimatum?"

Sean stared at him until Jack dropped his gaze to the floor. "Delia has given me no choice."

Nan addressed Jack. "While the rest of us rally to protect Alice when she needs us, Delia suggests we turn our backs on her because Alice no longer has magic—which is the only value Delia will admit Alice has. I've always known Delia opposed taking my children and me into the pack when we had nowhere to turn. She said the same about Karen and Patrick when they came to us as refugees. Compassion is not weakness."

"Her pack wasn't like ours," Jack pointed out. "Her alpha was about strength and brute force, never about compassion or kindness."

"I know that," Nan replied. "But when she left them to marry you and join this pack, she didn't leave those attitudes behind, and I for one am weary of her selfishness and insecurity." Her voice hardened. "What she did to Alice and Sean with that hex was unforgivable. Asking Sean and the rest of us to reject Alice in her time of need is worse. That Sean is willing to offer her one last chance to make peace and stay is more than she deserves, and it's the last chance I think she should get."

The door to the master bedroom swung open upstairs. Sean glanced at Jack. The latter gave him a stiff nod.

"Does anyone want some coffee?" Nan asked.

Alice appeared on the stairs, Rogue at her side. She wore a tank top and jeans. Her feet were bare and her wet hair was braided. "I would love some." She glanced around at them, her brow furrowed. "Am I interrupting an argument?"

"Not an argument," Sean said, meeting her at the foot of the stairs. "Just clearing up some things with Jack."

She studied him, then looked at Jack. "About Delia?"

Jack nodded. "So you know about what's happened?"

"Yes. Sean filled me in." She joined them in the living room. "If Delia didn't like me with magic, she probably likes me even less without it. I've got bigger problems at the moment."

Ben chuckled. "Same old Alice."

"Did you just call me old?" She put her hands on her hips. "Because Sean told me you and I are the same age."

"Shifters age slower than humans, so I'm really closer to twenty-five." Ben grinned. "In dog years."

The tension broken, Nan headed to the kitchen to make coffee. "Where are we on looking for the winery?" Alice asked. "Anything I can do to help?"

"You just rest while I slave over this hot keyboard," Ben said from the couch. "We've got some digging to do and Nan can help me."

Alice frowned. "I feel bad doing nothing while you all work."

"You've been through more than enough," Ben said, growing serious. "If and when we need you to help us search, we'll let you know. For now, you and Sean need to take some time for yourselves."

"If you insist." Alice went to the patio door. "Still pouring out there," she said as Sean joined her. "But it looks like the patio's dry under the cover." She opened the patio door and a gust of rain-scented air swirled inside. "Join me outside?"

"I'll bring the coffee out when it's ready," Nan called from the kitchen.

"Thank you," Alice said. They went outside.

Alice lowered herself slowly into a chair as Sean settled into the one next to her. "Still sore?" he asked.

She made a face. "My calf muscles are killing me from all that walking. I thought it would get better, but I swear I'm more stiff now than this morning."

He patted his lap. "Put your feet up here and I'll see what I can do."

She scooted closer so she could put her feet on his thighs. He started with her right calf, digging his fingers into the tight muscles.

She groaned, her head falling back. "Oh, that feels *fantastic*."

He chuckled. "I'm not a trained massage therapist."

"Could have fooled me." She sighed deeply, then flinched.

"Did that hurt?" he asked, massaging more gently.

"Yeah, but it hurts so good. Keep going, please. I'll tell you if it's too much." She closed her eyes.

He watched her as he worked, enjoying the small movements she made as he tried to loosen her stiff leg muscles. Though she kept her eyes closed, he read her body language, watching for telltale tension or facial expressions that would tell him what she was thinking about. He saw a slight smile, a hint of a frown, a few flinches, and a flash of sadness. He imagined she was reliving the day's events, including the tarot reading and their walk in the rain.

"We'll find a way to get Malcolm back, even if we have to recruit an angel to do it," he told her.

She didn't open her eyes, but a ghost of a smile turned up the corners of her lips. "Reading my mind again?"

"Maybe I'm just very good at reading your body language." He slid his fingers down her calf, squeezing her muscles as he moved.

She moaned and went limp, her arms draped over the sides of the chair. "What's my body language telling you right now?"

"That you're enjoying this well-deserved massage." He repeated the sliding action and was rewarded with another moan.

"I *am* enjoying it, very much." She raised her head and peered at him through her lashes. "What if I never get my memories or my magic back?"

The abruptness of her question startled him. "We'll get them back," he said, resuming his work on her calf.

"Yes, but what if we don't?" She scooted up in her chair to see him better. "I'll no longer be a mage private investigator. I'll be of no use to the vamps or Moses anymore. The vamps won't care what happens to me, and Moses will just want me dead instead of a prisoner. I have to be able to protect myself and the people around me. You can't protect me every minute. And I wouldn't want you to, anyway," she added quietly, almost to herself.

Sean recalled his wolf's observation that Alice was frightened. "I don't accept that what the sorcerer did to you can't be undone," he told her, his fingers working methodically on her calf muscles. "All spells have counter-spells—that's a basic tenet of magic."

"Valas told me if the sorcerer took my memories and magic to use for power, he might use them up before we find him."

Suddenly angry and worried, he stilled. "When did you speak to Valas?"

"In the hallway, after we left the witches' room at Northbourne. She talked to me in my head." She looked at him, her eyes shadowed. "I don't know how she did it, but she made me feel like she'd taken me from the hallway and then brought me back when we were done talking. You said I was beside you the whole time, though, so I guess it was all in my head...literally."

Fighting his anger, he took a deep breath and focused on massaging her leg. "What else did she say?"

"She said the sorcerer didn't steal my life; he only stole my magic and my memories." Her mouth twisted. "It amounts to the same thing, I suppose, since without magic I've got a big target painted on my back."

He wrapped her in comforting magic. She sighed and leaned back into her chair again. "We'll come back to that," he said. "What else?"

"She said she might be able to restore my magic, if we find it in time. If not, she might be able to give me some power...for a price. Until then, she wanted me to stay at Northbourne, under their protection. She said I'm endangering you and everyone in the pack by staying here instead."

"Vaughan wanted you to stay at Northbourne too." He rubbed her leg and thought. "He'd given his word we wouldn't be held there against our will, but he wasn't happy you insisted on leaving. I thought it was part of his obsession with you, but to have Valas do the same makes me even more certain we need to deal with the sorcerer without the Court's involvement. I smell a rat—more so than usual."

He switched to her left calf. "As for giving you some other kind of magic at a price, that's your decision to make, but I don't like the idea of you making another deal with her, regardless of the terms. I trust the vamps less today than I did yesterday, and that was less than I'd trusted them the day before. At least with Moses, you know who your enemy is and what he's about. With the vamps, they're simultaneously an ally and an enemy. That makes them worse because you never truly know where you stand."

"I hear you, but I'd have to know Valas's terms before I decide. I don't think I'll live long without magic to protect myself, which she probably knows." She met his gaze, her expression grim. "That means I won't have much of a bargaining position, regardless of any prior deal we might have."

He slid his fingers along her calf, eliciting another groan. As her head fell back, he said, "If you were my mate, you'd have the full protection of the Were Ruling Council, and a much stronger bargaining position."

She said nothing for a long moment. Finally, she raised her head. "Was that a proposal?" He wasn't sure how to read her expression, other than a bit of shock.

He hadn't planned this—not by a long shot—but it seemed like the most natural thing he'd ever said. And once he'd broached the subject, he had no second thoughts. He searched his heart for any doubts and found none at all.

"A mate bond doesn't work like a marriage proposal," he explained. "It's not a matter of putting on a ring or just saying yes or no. It's metaphysical —a mutual connection between two people."

"A connection? Like a rope that ties you together?"

He shook his head. "Not a rope—like doors that open up. We'd share strength. Also emotions, like happiness, contentment, and hope."

Her face gave nothing away. "And fear? Anger?"

"Those too," he acknowledged. "Pain and joy, and everything in between. We had a mate bond for a few minutes, when we wore those shifter magic cuffs."

"I remember you telling me about it last night on the way to Northbourne. You said it was wonderful, and then I spoiled it by dying." Her mouth turned down. "You also said we'd discussed a mate bond before and decided there was no rush. You don't have to do this to protect me."

He rested his hands on her legs. "Do you think I'm bringing this up just because I want to protect you?"

She shook her head. "No. You wouldn't make a commitment unless you were ready for me to be your mate. If it just so happens it helps me stay alive, that's a bonus."

He exhaled, relieved she understood that about him. "This isn't how I'd imagined bringing it up, but if there's one thing I should have learned by now, it's that life seldom goes according to the plans you make." He rubbed her legs. "What do you think?"

She was quiet for a long time. "I think you're ready to be my mate, but I'm not ready. Even though my heart and all my instincts tell me I trust you and I'm happy with you, I barely know you. I don't even know your middle name—"

"Theodore."

"—What you wanted to be when you grew up—"

"Paleontologist."

"—Or what astrological sign you are."

"Aries."

Her mouth quirked. "Or why you're willing to put up with all of the chaos, stress, and worry I bring into your life."

"Because of all the happiness and strength that comes with the chaos. How do your legs feel?"

"Much, much better. Thank you." She moved her legs off his. He was disappointed until she got up and sat sideways on his lap, curling up against him and nestling her head against his chest. He rested his chin on top of her head.

They sat quietly, listening to the rain on the patio roof. Sean caught a glimpse of the others in the living room. Ben and Nan sat on the couch, their attention on their laptops, while Jack stood near the far windows, talking on the phone.

Nan glanced up and caught his eye. *Coffee?* she mouthed, pointing to the mugs on the table in front of her.

Later, he mouthed back.

She winked and returned her attention to Ben, leaning over to look at something on his laptop.

His wolf nudged him, reminding him about their earlier conversation. "Alice?" Sean asked.

"Mmm?"

"I think I know what's causing your fever—or at least, my wolf thinks he knows."

She raised her head to look at him. "Your wolf thinks...? What's wrong with me?"

This would be perhaps the greatest test of their relationship since Alice's return. He tipped her chin up with his fingers and drew on his shifter magic and alpha power. "Do you trust me?"

His heart leapt when she didn't hesitate in her reply. "Yes."

His vision turned golden as he stared into her eyes, searching for a hint of the wolf he'd glimpsed on the night she'd survived Caleb's attack and infection with the werewolf virus. Gently, he called to Alice's wolf, as he would call a skittish wolf within a member of his pack. Given everything Alice had been through and he'd never tried to do so before, he wasn't sure whether it would work.

It did.

Alice gasped, her back arching as her wolf rose in response to his call. Two beautiful golden eyes met his, peering out through Alice's dark brown eyes.

He sensed immediately that Alice's wolf was furious. No wonder Alice was running a fever. With the shifter magic torn out of both of them, the wolf was fighting for her life and angry to be powerless.

"Be calm," he told her wolf, his voice resonant with alpha power. "We will find this sorcerer and restore Alice's magic."

Out of the corner of his eye, he saw Nan draw the curtain across the patio door, blocking them from view. His pack mates must have sensed the rise of alpha magic and come over to investigate.

His vision went gold around the edges as his own wolf rose to look out through his human eyes at Alice's wolf. *Beautiful mate*, his wolf said, his voice gentle and comforting. *Have patience. Trust.*

Alice's wolf's fury abated. She settled down, resting her head on her paws, but her eyes remained fierce. She growled low. The message was clear: *hurry*.

What the effect would be on Alice if her wolf died, Sean had no idea. He had never heard of a human with a wolf within them, and he hadn't dared make inquiries in the wake of the attack. The ability to burn the shifter virus from the blood was unique to high-level blood mages, and no one could know Alice was one. He didn't know how the Were Ruling Council would react to the news of Alice's wolf either, and there were enough conservative voices on the Council to make him fear they would call for her death. Others might seek to capture her for study.

In short, no one could know about this wolf within Alice—not even the rest of his pack, for now.

One thing he knew for certain: he was not going to let Alice's wolf die, any more than he would accept Alice's memories and magic were lost permanently. That meant they had to find the sorcerer right the hell now and get back what he'd stolen, before Sean lost the woman who'd become his heart.

Alice's wolf faded from her eyes, relinquishing control over her body. Sean's vision cleared as his own wolf settled back down. His bones hummed, as they always did when he used alpha magic.

"Sean?" Alice whispered. Her eyes were her own again. "What the hell was that?"

He squeezed her hand. Her skin was already noticeably cooler. "Your

wolf needed some reassurance that we're going to get your magic back."
He rubbed his chin against the side of her head to comfort her. "She's
angry. Without the shifter magic, she's fading."

A pause. "You mean she's dying."

"Yes." He held her against his chest. "I don't know what her death
might do to you. It might not affect you at all."

"Or it might be one too many hits on this beat-up body of mine." She
exhaled. "So now we need to find that sorcerer and get my magic back
before Moses comes after me, the vamps either dump me like last week's
garbage or put me in chains, or my wolf dies." Her voice turned wry. "Well,
good. I was just thinking this all seemed too easy."

Behind them, Nan tapped on the patio door. At Sean's gesture, she slid
it open and stuck her head out. "We've got some possibilities," she said. "If
you're ready, Alice, you can come in and look at the pictures and see if
anything seems familiar."

"I don't think I'll recognize anything," Alice said, uncurling herself
from Sean's lap and rising. "I had a bag on my head when they took me
out."

Nan's eyes glowed in anger at the reminder of Alice's cruel treatment,
but she smiled. "Still, take a look. You never know what you might
remember."

Alice returned Nan's smile. "We'll be in momentarily."

Nan closed the patio door. Sean stood and kissed Alice's forehead. "So
your answer is no?" His heart hurt.

She smiled up at him and the ache faded. How he loved this woman.

"My answer is no *for now*, but I think yes might not be too far away."
She squeezed his hand. "No matter what happens, I won't ever forget this
perfect moment, when you proposed sharing the rest of your life with me
on this patio in the rain." She laced her fingers through his and tugged him
toward the door. "Now let's find this damn sorcerer."

"On the road again," Alice sang under her breath.

From the driver's seat, Sean chuckled. The wipers swished back and
forth across the windshield. "We have spent a lot of time in vehicles in the
past day. This is good, though. We're on the hunt." In his head, his wolf
showed his teeth, his eyes golden. The wolf was happy to hunt at last.

Alice propped her elbow on the door, her head resting on her fist.

With her fever gone, she'd complained of being cold. Despite the warm summer evening, she wore a hoodie sweatshirt, jeans, and tall boots. Sean had gone from worrying about her fever to concern that her hands felt too cold.

She glanced in the side view mirror. "I can't see Ben and Jack behind us anymore."

"They're still following us, just not too closely." He peered through the windshield. "The storm is letting up, finally." He turned down the wipers. "The next possible vineyard will be coming up on the left in about ten miles."

She made a face and turned back to the window. "Okay. I'll keep an eye out and see if anything seems familiar."

He rested his hand on Alice's leg and drove. Ben had found a few possible matches for the partial sign Carly had seen, but she hadn't been able to positively identify any of them as the sign she'd glimpsed. They'd put those at the top of the list of possibilities, added others that were in the radius they'd estimated, and headed out to get a look at the vineyards in person.

He'd borrowed Ben's SUV in case anyone was watching the roads for his vehicle, and Jack hung back in his truck so they didn't look like a caravan. Alice had seen nothing familiar near the vineyards they'd driven past already, but Sean refused to give up hope she'd recognize something.

"Stop the car," Alice said suddenly.

He immediately swerved to the shoulder. "What is it?"

She frowned. Ahead, on their right, he saw a large, old oak tree near a fence, and beyond it, an empty field. It looked much like every other tree and fence they'd passed in the last few hours, but something had caught her eye.

"I don't know," she said finally. "I just...give me a minute." She opened her door and hopped out, nearly losing her footing in the wet grass on the edge of the ditch. She shut her door, pulled her hood up over her head, and headed in the direction of the tree.

He put the SUV in park and turned off the headlights. In the rearview mirror, he saw Jack's truck approaching. Sean gestured for them to continue. This might turn out to be nothing. Ben gave him a little wave as they passed.

He got out, putting on a light jacket but leaving it unzipped in case he needed quick access to his gun. His sharp eyesight let him see well even in the dark, but he wasn't sure there was enough moonlight for Alice to make her way safely through the tall grass.

Ahead of him, she tripped and fell. He hurried to catch up, but she was already on her feet before he reached her.

"You all right?" he asked.

"Yeah." She grimaced at her muddy jeans. "I slipped."

They made their way through the ditch to the fence. Across the field, he saw rows of grapevines. Beyond the vines were several large and well-lit buildings. It was a small vineyard, and not one that had made their list of possible locations.

As Alice squinted into the darkness, straining to see the buildings in the distance, he took out his phone and pulled up a map. "It's called Broken Ridge Winery," he told Alice in an undertone, though he could not see or sense anyone nearby. "It's a small vineyard. Their logo looks nothing like what Carly described, so Ben didn't put it on the list, but it's obviously within the radius we're looking at."

She didn't answer. Her eyes swept the large, empty field in front of them and the faraway grapevines in neat rows. "I've been here," she said. "This field...this fence, this tree. This is where I tried to get away, but he caught me."

"Are you sure? We've passed a lot of trees and fences and fields."

"I'm sure. That's the tree I tried to reach, but I didn't make it." She stared at her wrists. "He dragged me back, all the way across that field and through the vines. He took me to one of those buildings and threw me down some stairs."

Her matter-of-fact tone stabbed right through him as much as her recollection of the sorcerer's mistreatment. Even without her memories, Alice had the affect of someone who'd suffered many years of torment. Pain like that was remembered all the way down to the bones.

All her life, Alice had endured unimaginable cruelties at the hands of her grandfather. He'd sworn she'd never suffer like that again—and yet she had, while he'd been unable to do a damn thing to stop it. Alice had worried he'd explode like a volcano with all his rage, but instead it had become a gnawing, living thing in his belly, hungry for the blood and bones of the sorcerer.

He ran his nose along her hairline, desperate for her comforting scent. She shivered and made a tiny sound that carried all the way through to his soul.

After several days and heavy rain, Sean knew there was no point climbing over the fence to see if he could catch Alice's scent. She seemed sure, and that was enough for him. "I believe you," he told her.

His wolf bared his teeth, his ears back against his head. *Kill sorcerer.*

We will, Sean told the wolf. He wrapped Alice in his arms and held her. "Let's go before anyone notices we're here and we lose the element of surprise."

She blinked at him. "Aren't we going in there to get the sorcerer?"

He growled. "We are, but we're not going right now, and we sure as hell are not going in alone."

22

ALICE

FOUR DAYS EARLIER

I FELL THROUGH THE VOID FOR A VERY LONG TIME. I COULD SEE nothing at all, not even the tiniest bit of light, but I still felt the rug-woman's coarse arms wrapped around me.

My fall ended as abruptly as it began. One second I was falling, and the next I found myself standing in blindingly bright light, still face-to-face with the rug-woman and unable to move. There was no sensation of stopping or landing anywhere—just of no longer falling. My stomach lurched and my ears rang.

Again, I fought to free myself from the rug-woman and reach for my magic, or even the magic in my tattoos, but something was suppressing everything. Even my shifter magic, as weak and unpredictable as it was, was dampened.

As my eyes adjusted, I realized the light wasn't as bright as it had originally seemed; it had only blinded me because my eyes had grown accustomed to the dark. The room was actually dimly lit. Not that I could *see* the room, with my nose pressed against the rough fabric of the rug, but I could turn my head just enough to see stone wall on the sides of the rug. I wasn't in the museum anymore—that much was clear.

The back of my neck prickled. I tried to crane my neck, but couldn't see behind me. "Who's there?" I demanded.

"Hello, Alice."

The voice was male and accented. I didn't recognize it. Something about the accent sounded familiar, though I couldn't quite place it.

"Who the hell are you?" I asked. "Come over where I can see you."

He chuckled. "I think not—not until you're secured. I'm told you're dangerous, especially when cornered."

I didn't like any of the words in those two sentences, especially not *secured* or *cornered*. "Face me, you coward."

"Prudence is not cowardice." His voice had a distinct edge. I'd hoped to provoke him into coming into my line of sight, but I heard no movement. "One does not get to be my age by being careless or impulsive."

The only people I'd heard talk that way were vampires, but I didn't think my captor was a vamp. Given the circumstances of my kidnapping—the rug-woman and the apparent magical transportation—there really was only one possibility, and it was a bad one.

"You're the sorcerer who tried to kill everyone at the Vampire Court gala," I said.

"Well deduced." I heard the smile in his voice. "I see your reputation as a capable detective is deserved. We must table this conversation until I am certain you are no longer a threat. Kathleen, if you please?"

Someone came up behind me. I looked down to see a pair of women's hands reaching for my right leg. She held a wide metal shackle.

My upper body was pinned, but I could still move my legs. I kicked backward as hard as I could. My boot made contact with something soft. The woman fell back with a cry of pain and surprise. I raised my leg to kick again, determined to fight back as best I could.

"*Be still*, my sweet," the sorcerer said, his voice resonant with magic.

I froze in place. I couldn't move a single muscle, not even to talk or scream. Or breathe. My lungs wouldn't draw in air. I was completely paralyzed.

The woman quickly removed my boot and sock and fastened the shackle onto my right ankle. A bolt slid into place. I felt a flash of heat and smelled hot metal. The sensation of my magic being suppressed increased sharply. The shackle wasn't just a restraint; it was a heavy-duty spell cuff.

Just as I thought my lungs would burst, the sorcerer spoke a command. "*Be free.*"

The paralysis spell vanished. I sucked in air and sagged in the rug-woman's grip, my lungs burning.

"*Release*," the sorcerer said.

The rug-woman let go of me and faded back into the rug, her smile still fixed and arms outstretched, just as I'd seen her the first time. Then the rug dissipated like smoke, leaving a bare stone wall and no hint of how I'd been brought here.

I stumbled against the wall, pretending to be nearly unconscious. My hand closed around my amulet. *Sean,* I thought desperately, but nothing happened. The room must have wards that dampened Carly's witch magic too.

Hoping to catch him off guard, I turned and launched myself at the man near the door. He didn't even blink at my sudden movement. I found out why a half-second later, when the chain connected to my shackle went taut, sending me sprawling on the stone floor. The metal of the cuff cut into my ankle and foot. I bit back a cry of pain and looked up to get my first good look at my captor.

He was dark-haired, slim, and tall, with an olive Mediterranean complexion, a well-trimmed beard, and piercing dark eyes. He wore a fitted long-sleeved black shirt, black trousers, and a gold earring in one ear. At first glance, I thought he was in his mid-twenties, but his eyes were much, much older. I might have called him strikingly attractive if he hadn't kidnapped me and chained me to the floor.

The woman who'd put me in the shackle was short and blonde, wearing a long black skirt and gray blouse. I wondered if she was a prisoner here too, but then she smiled at me in a way that indicated she liked the sight of me in chains. The side of her face and her right eye were swelling from the kick I'd given her.

We were in a stone room about twelve feet by twelve feet, with a heavy oak door that was currently closed. The room contained a bed pallet on the floor, a toilet and sink, and one single overhead light. It looked very much like a cell. I sensed we were underground—how far, I wasn't sure, but the sensation of being trapped increased. Despite my anger and intent to show no fear, my breathing became ragged.

I thought of Malcolm, still stashed in his crystal on my bracelet. Should I let him out so he could try to help me get out of here, or so he could try to jump to Sean and alert him that I'd been kidnapped? If I released him, would the sorcerer try to discorporate him—or, worse, try to capture him? The wards on the room might trap him here, and he was vulnerable outside his crystal.

The sorcerer studied me while I took in my surroundings and thought feverishly about how I might try to escape. He crouched, still well out of reach. His eyes were lifeless—completely devoid of emotion or even a hint of humanity. Valas's impassive, ancient gaze seemed positively merry by comparison.

"I am Miraç," he said. "You are my guest for a few days while I get all I need from you." His eyes went to my neckline. I was about to snap at him to get his eyes off my chest, but he smiled. "Ah, you will not need this. Kathleen, take the necklace."

My fingers wrapped around my amulet. Even with its magic dampened, it smelled of Carly's parchment-scented spells and Sean's hot golden shifter trace. "You're not taking this from me," I snarled at the blonde woman.

Miraç made a gesture with his hand. A bolt of red lightning blazed from his fingertips and zipped straight at my eyes. I flinched. The lightning stopped an inch from my face, sizzling with heat.

"You don't need your eyes to fulfill my purpose for bringing you here," Miraç said, his voice flat. "So if you wish to lose them, by all means, fight to keep your jewelry."

I was so angry I could barely talk. "I'm going to kill you," I ground out as Kathleen slid the chain off over my head.

Miraç didn't respond to my threat. He looked at my bracelet. "And I see you have brought me a friend. Get that as well."

Malcolm. Fear and fury washed over me. "*No!*"

The red lightning flared, searing my eyes. I screamed, sure he'd blinded me. I barely felt the tug on my wrist as she took my bracelet.

When my vision cleared, I blinked away tears of pain and saw Kathleen handing my wolf amulet and bracelet to Miraç. He rose, studying the items he'd taken from me. "Very interesting. The amulet is simplistic, but the spellwork on the bracelet is complex. You've protected your companion well. I enjoy a challenge. You've already proven quite diverting, and our time together has only just begun."

"What do you want from me?" I demanded. "Are you working for Moses Murphy?"

He shook his head. "I have no interest in cabals, or in humans, if truth be told, other than what powers they have. You are a means to an end, nothing more—but I think I shall have some fun with you first. I'm told you are tough and brave, Alice. You will be a delightful amusement."

"I work for the Vampire Court," I told him, my voice trembling with the force of my anger. "And I'm the consort of the alpha of the Tomb

Mountain Pack. You'll have the vampires *and* the shifters coming after you. And when I get out of this cuff—"

"I look forward to seeing your attempt to escape. Many have tried. None succeeded, but perhaps you will surprise me." He tucked the amulet and my bracelet into his pocket. "Farewell for now, Alice. Be good."

My breath caught. My grandfather had said that to me many times. Moses's cold voice echoed in my head: *Be good, stupid girl.*

Miraç chuckled. "You have so many terrible memories. How... delicious." He gave me a mocking half-bow. "I'll leave you to your escape planning."

Kathleen went to the door and knocked. Someone opened four sturdy-sounding locks.

"I'll strip your skin from your bones," I promised them as Kathleen opened the door. "Both of you. *Slowly.*"

Kathleen didn't react, but Miraç smiled. "Enjoy your defiance while you still have it, Alice. I'll be back." The door closed behind them. All four separate locks engaged.

Silence.

I examined the iron spell cuff on my ankle. "Shit," I muttered.

It wasn't the kind that could be unlocked with a key—instead, it had been locked onto my ankle with a steel bolt threaded through a set of interlocked loops. The odor of hot metal I'd smelled was the bolt being melted into the loops. Kathleen had done that, somehow. Clearly, she had powers, which probably made her useful to Miraç. She probably wasn't a sorcerer, since I couldn't imagine two of them working together, so she was probably a black witch—maybe the witch who'd twisted the magic on the decanter. That meant there was probably a black witch coven on the premises. Fantastic.

There was literally no way of removing the cuff without cutting through the iron. The heavy iron chain was bolted to a steel plate in the floor. And since I doubted I'd find either a diamond-bladed saw or similar cutting tool anywhere in this cell, I wasn't going to be freeing myself from the shackle anytime soon unless I took a page from a horror movie and cut off my own foot. My best bet was to try and escape when they took me somewhere outside my cell.

If they took me outside my cell.

I banished those thoughts and got stiffly to my feet. Escaping from Moses had seemed impossible until I'd done it, and I'd done it by myself. Now I had allies who would be looking for me—allies who weren't likely to be very forgiving or merciful. And if Miraç thought suppressing my magic rendered me helpless, he'd find out he was dead wrong.

I explored my cell thoroughly, as far as the chain would allow. It gave me free access to the bed pallet, the sink, and toilet, and most of the room, but I couldn't get within five feet of the door. The cuff's sharp edges cut into my flesh as I strained to look closely at the door. I could see nothing I thought would help me escape, even if I managed to get out of the cuff and reach the door. The walls sounded very solid. The thick timbers of the ceiling were well out of my reach, even if I stood on the top of the toilet—which I did. The sink and toilet were solid metal and could not be damaged or destroyed to yield any weapons.

The bed pallet was also not going to help me escape, as far as I could tell. It was a foam pad wrapped in a sheet, with a folded sheet and thin quilt on top. The room was cold. I wouldn't be warm under the bedding, that was certain. The bedding didn't look especially clean, either, and the foam pad did little to soften the floor or insulate against the cold seeping up from the stone.

I sat cross-legged on the bed and surveyed the room. I touched my chest where the amulet usually hung. I missed the reassuring warmth of Carly's magic and Sean's shifter trace immensely.

Belatedly, I noticed I could no longer sense the cold magic splinter in my chest. I wondered if it was suppressed by the cuff, or if it had dissipated, and what that might mean.

"I am not trapped," I said softly to myself. "I am *not* helpless." My voice sounded loud in the nearly empty room.

I thought about what Miraç had said, searching for a clue as to where I was or why he'd kidnapped me. He'd said he'd *been told* I was dangerous, so he'd been talking to someone who knew me. Hanson had sent me to the museum to see Blackstone, so maybe Hanson was his source. He might have others, though—others who had the rune cut into their flesh, or were his willing accomplices.

He'd said I was his guest for a few days until he got what he wanted from me, and that I was a means to an end. I supposed that meant he wanted me for my magic. That might be good news, because I couldn't use my magic unless he let me out of the cuff. Once that cuff was off, I promised myself I would do anything and everything in my power to escape.

I thought of Malcolm and took a shaky breath. Could I escape and leave Malcolm behind? If I got out, I'd come back with an army of vampires and werewolves, and I'd get Malcolm back. But what if Miraç destroyed Malcolm in retaliation for my escape? Or what if he threatened to discorporate him if I tried to escape? Could I sacrifice Malcolm if it meant getting away? I didn't think so, but if I got desperate enough...I swallowed hard. No, I couldn't leave Malcolm behind. I *wouldn't*, not even if it meant being trapped here. If our situation were reversed, Malcolm would never leave me behind either. We *both* had to get away, or neither of us would.

I leaned against the wall and shivered. My ankle bled where the cuff had cut me. I picked up my discarded sock and put it on so my foot wasn't so cold. The boot wouldn't go on over the cuff, so I set it beside me, taking a tiny bit of comfort from its presence. It was tangible proof of my life back home, outside of this cell and Miraç's lair.

I had the sudden thought that I had no idea where I was or how far I'd traveled. Miraç was powerful; his bizarre rug could have taken me a hundred or a thousand miles from home, or to the other side of the world, for all I knew. With the wards around me, how would Sean or the vamps find me?

They'll find me, I told myself firmly. They'd figure out I'd gone to the museum and discover Blackstone and the rug, even if Sean hadn't gotten the images I'd tried to send. They wouldn't rest until they figured out who took me and how.

I wondered if Miraç had a surveillance camera in the cell. I didn't see one, but it seemed unlikely he'd leave me in here without a guard unless he could watch me. Probably audio as well.

I draped my arms over my knees and leaned against the wall. "Screw you, Miraç," I said aloud, giving my middle finger to whoever might be watching. "You've messed with the wrong woman today."

Seemingly in answer, thick, oily, black smoke poured in through the tiny gap at the bottom of the door. I scrambled to my feet as it filled the room, all but blotting out the light from the overhead bulb. It smelled like a pit full of rotting dead things.

Mouths full of teeth snapped at me from the darkness, driving me back against the wall. I swiped at the black smoke. Razor-sharp teeth tore at my arm and something snarled.

I cradled my bloody arm and stared defiantly into the smoke. "You can't scare me with your little smoke monster. Go ahead and chew me up. See how far that gets you."

Something lashed out at me. On instinct, I turned toward the wall to protect my face. Whips slashed across my back, leaving three agonizing streaks of fire. I screamed and turned back to face the smoke. "Coward, come in here and face me yourself," I said through gritted teeth.

An eyeless, nightmarish face with just a mouth emerged from the oily darkness. "In due time, my sweet," the mouth said with Miraç's voice. A long, forked tongue slid out and flicked at me. Drops of saliva landed on my face and neck and burned my skin like acid. "When I tire of amusing myself, I shall visit you in my own form. Until then..."

The face turned into Sean's. I kept my face expressionless, but my gut wrenched with anger and hurt.

"My Alice," Sean/Miraç said, his voice a perfect imitation of Sean's. "I'm not going to look for you. My pack is better off with you gone."

"Screw you, Miraç," I repeated. "Sean *will* find me, and werewolves love the taste of sorcerer." I didn't know that for certain, obviously, but something told me Sean wouldn't let Miraç's taste stop him from avenging my kidnapping.

Sean/Miraç laughed. The sound was a horrible, atonal mix of both Sean and Miraç's voices. "You're far, far from home, my Alice," Sean/Miraç said, his tone mocking. "No one will come for you. Even if they do, they won't want what's left by then. You'll be nothing but scraps. But perhaps the pack will want the scraps. Wolves don't mind a bit of carrion from time to time."

"Screw—"

"Yes, screw me," Sean/Miraç said, smiling. "Now *there* is a thought. You're a lovely woman, my Alice. Oh yes, we're going to have *such* fun."

"Don't you touch me, you piece of shit," I raged.

The forked tongue flicked at me again. "Ah, such anger. It's like a symphony for my ears and taste buds. You'll be a full meal, for certain."

Before I could retort, Sean/Miraç's face vanished. The black smoke withdrew, disappearing back through the gap under the door. I stood with my torn back against the wall, cradling my arm and breathing hard.

The light went out, plunging the room into total darkness. I made my way to the sink, feeling my way along the wall with shaking hands. I found a small towel on the top of the toilet and tried to tend to my injuries without being able to see, or reach the wounds on my back very well. The pain was white-hot.

I followed the wall back to the little bed and sat down, setting my jaw to keep from making any sound.

I put the towel down on the bed to try and keep my blood from soaking into the bedding and lay on my side. The slashes on my back were deep. The blood was warm, but the room was cold. I thought it might have gotten colder since I'd been here, but that might have been my imagination.

I wrapped my arms around myself and waited.

* * *

Time passed slowly. I tried to stay mindful of the minutes and hours, but my mind wandered and eventually I lost track of how long I'd been lying bleeding and cold in my cell. I estimated it had been at least five or six hours, but already my perception of time was distorted by the darkness and silence. I'd finally given in and wrapped myself in the comforter and sheet, but neither did much to hold the chill at bay. I shivered and tried not to be miserable. Misery led to hopelessness, hopelessness to defeat— and I was *not* going to be defeated by Miraç.

To distract myself, I thought about Sean, imagining what he and the rest of the pack were doing to look for me. Maybe they'd already gone to the museum and found the rug. Maybe they'd spoken to Blackstone, figured out he'd helped kidnap me, and were in the process of interrogating him to find out who was behind my disappearance. Maybe they were on their way here now.

Sean would have probably also enlisted Carly's help. The Court would be looking for me too. If I was right about how many hours had passed, the vampires wouldn't be awake yet, but Bryan would know I was missing, Matthias too. Maybe Arkady was looking for me. I was sure she would want to, if she knew I'd vanished. When she woke—if she hadn't already— Valas would surely be involved in searching for me, since she needed me to run her little errand through the mirror-door.

It was reassuring to think about how many people cared enough to look for me. Just a few months ago, I'd been so alone. If I'd vanished then, I wasn't sure who would have even noticed, except maybe the Court—and they wouldn't have probably noticed right away, either.

Those thoughts led me to recall Carly's advice from yesterday about the house Sean and I wanted to buy. At this moment, I couldn't think of why I'd asked Sean for more time to decide whether to sign on the dotted line. I did want to live in that house with him and Malcolm and Rogue and welcome his pack—*our* pack—whenever they wanted to be near us...and whenever I wanted to be near them. Despite my conflicts with a few members of the pack, I felt safer and like I belonged when I was with them. In fact, right now, I missed them terribly, almost as much as I missed Sean and Malcolm.

Yesterday, in the wake of Rob Hamlin's surprise visit, I'd pushed back against Sean's request that we move forward on the house. Now I wasn't sure where my hesitation had come from. I'd told him I felt overwhelmed by everything we'd gone through in the past week since we toured the house, but right now, that made me *more* in favor of moving in together, not less. In fact, I couldn't find an ounce of hesitation in myself anywhere.

The difference between how I felt now and how I'd felt yesterday was noticeable—and in the wake of the hex that had almost destroyed my relationship with Sean, all too familiar.

With that realization, the pieces clicked into place in my head. There could only be one explanation for my seemingly sudden and complete change of heart. A wave of cold washed over me that had nothing to do with the chill of my cell.

"Charles, you son of a bitch," I breathed. My heart thundered in my ears and my breathing sped up as shock gave way to fury.

My murderous thoughts were interrupted by the sound of the locks turning on the door. I gritted my teeth and stood, using the wall for support. I vowed not to show any pain or weakness to Miraç.

When the door opened, however, it wasn't the sorcerer who entered my cell—it was Kathleen. The light in my cell turned on just enough to illuminate part of the room. I squinted at my visitor. She wore the same long black skirt and blouse she'd had on when I first arrived, but she'd put on a long hooded cloak. Her face was swollen and bruised.

I got a glimpse of the dimly lit stone hallway before she closed the door. Someone locked it behind her—all four locks.

"What do you want?" I asked.

"I'm bringing you supper," Kathleen said shortly. She placed two items on the floor just beyond the reach of my chain: a paper bowl of soup and a paper plate with a sandwich. "Eat. Drink water from the sink."

I shook my head. "Not hungry."

Her smile was cold. "It's not poisoned. There's not much point, since Miraç prefers you to be healthy and alive—at least for now. There's nothing a drug could do that he can't, so it would be a waste of time to drug you. I can take a bite from the food and a drink from the sink, if that would convince you."

She could be spelled or otherwise prevented from being affected by whatever had been done to the food or water. "There's nothing you could do that would convince me drinking that water or eating that food wouldn't harm me," I told her.

"Suit yourself." She went to the door. "Starving yourself won't make you less useful. You won't be here long enough to make a hunger strike effective. You'll only weaken yourself, which helps him, not you. Or maybe by tomorrow you'll be hungry enough to give in."

"If you serve Miraç, why didn't he heal your face where I kicked you?" I asked. "Is it punishment for letting me get the drop on you?"

She knocked on the door and glared at me. "I can't wait to watch you die."

I gave her my toothiest smile. "Back at you."

"Mage freak," she hissed.

"That's interesting coming from a black witch. Not to mention, sticks and stones, Kathleen."

"He won't be the one to kill you, you know," she said as the locks turned and the door opened on soundless hinges. I couldn't see who was opening it, but I caught a glimpse of black through the gap near the frame. Another member of her coven, probably. "You'll do it yourself. When he's done with you, you'll be happy to die. And I'll be there to watch."

With that parting shot, she left. The door shut firmly behind her and locked. The light in my cell went out.

I was hungry and thirsty, but nothing could compel me to eat or drink anything here—not even the water from the sink. Water could be spelled or drugged just as easily as anything else, even running water.

My bladder had been complaining for a while, so I said to hell with the surveillance in the room and used the toilet in the dark. At least Miraç was civilized enough to give me a roll of toilet paper. Small favors.

Wincing, I settled back onto my bed. My thoughts went back to Malcolm. I wished with all my heart I hadn't had him stashed in my bracelet when I went to the museum. I blamed myself for him falling into Miraç's hands. The spellwork on his crystal was a Fort Knox of protection spells. I knew of nothing that could get him out but me, but sorcery was a type of magic I had little experience with. I couldn't feel anything close to certain my ghost was safe.

Even if he remained unharmed in the crystal, one of Malcolm's greatest fears was becoming trapped in one. We'd both seen what happened to ghosts kept in crystals. They lingered in a state of being half-awake and went slowly mad over time, disintegrating from ghost to wraith until they were little more than a shadow.

That thought led me to close my eyes and think of the archangel who'd helped Carly counsel the ghost of murder victim Ashley Brown to move on to the afterlife. Other than what I'd seen on television, I didn't know how anyone got through to an archangel, or if anyone but someone like Carly could, but I had no better ideas at the moment than a prayer.

Hey, Suriel, I thought. *You told Malcolm he was sent here to be my companion and protector, and he's in real trouble. I don't know if archangels get involved in daily stuff, but if you can, could you help him get away from here? A sorcerer has him and I'm afraid for him. Thank you.* After a moment, I added, *Amen.* Couldn't hurt to be extra respectful.

No answer—not that I'd expected one. Either Suriel would hear me and be able and willing to help, or not. In any case, it was worth a shot.

My shirt was stuck to my back. I thought the cuts might still be bleeding. My arm stung. I wrapped the towel around it and pulled the sheet and comforter back over me. I used my towel-wrapped arm as a pillow and closed my eyes. *I'll just rest for a few minutes,* I thought.

My stomach hurt and my mouth was dry as dust. I coughed and entertained myself imagining the ways I'd pay Miraç back for kidnapping me.

Some time later, despite how hard I tried not to, I fell asleep.

23

"ALICE. ALICE, WAKE UP." MALCOLM'S URGENT VOICE WOKE ME FROM A restless sleep.

I didn't bother to open my eyes. "Go away, Miraç. You've tried this already. First Sean, then Carly, then Sean again. Now you're impersonating my ghost. You've been at this for the better part of a day. Give up, will you? I'm not that stupid."

"No, Alice, it's really me." Malcolm/Miraç insisted. "I got out of the crystal. Who's Miraç? Where are we?"

"Fuck all the way off," I muttered, wondering if he was as tired of hearing me say that as I was of saying it. "If you read my mind enough to know what my ghost sounds like, then surely you know he can't get out of that crystal unless *I* let him out."

"Maybe you did let me out," Malcolm/Miraç argued. "Maybe he compelled you to do it in your sleep. I don't know how I got out—I just found myself here, and then I found you. Will you please get up and talk to me?"

"I couldn't have let him out with this cuff on. And you don't have the voice right anyway. Go away."

A warm hand caressed my face. "My Alice," Sean/Miraç murmured.

I recoiled instinctively, my eyes snapping open.

I lay on Sean's bed in his house, wearing my sheep pajamas. Sean/Miraç sat on the edge of the bed, smiling down at me. "I miss you," he told me, his eyes glowing softly. "I love you, Alice. If anything happens to you, I won't be able to go on."

The bed, the sunlight coming through the window, and the smell of forest all seemed completely real, down to the softness of the quilt beneath me and the scent of fabric softener on my pajamas. This was by far Miraç's most detailed and painfully accurate illusion yet.

"He won't have to go on without me," I told Sean/Miraç, as he continued to smile at me. "I'll get out of here. If this is all an attempt to soften me up, it's having the opposite effect."

"Oh, I'm not trying to soften you up." It was Sean's mouth moving, but Miraç's voice. That was even worse, somehow. "Your anger and pain is what I want. You have so much already, but you were almost ready to give it up for the sake of this werewolf and the happy life you want with him. That's why I had to take you when I did. If I'd waited much longer, you would have let go of your past enough to be really happy, and then what use would you have been to me?"

When I said nothing, his smile widened. "He wants to have children with you, you know. Such a shame that won't happen. That will break his heart too."

I took a deep breath and fought my anger because I refused to give him what he wanted. "You have no idea what Sean does or doesn't want."

"I do, in fact." Suddenly, Miraç became a familiar blond man in his mid-forties, wearing a Maclin Security polo shirt. "He talks about you with his business partner, Ron Dormer," Miraç said in Ron's deep voice. "Except it's not always Ron he's talking to—at least, not for the past few weeks. He's not as guarded around Ron. I hear his thoughts. Ron's just recently had a child. Your werewolf looks at pictures of Ron and his wife and baby and thinks someday that will be you and him, holding a little wolf cub."

So Miraç had been fixated on taking me for at least several weeks, long before the decanter incident at the gala. How and why had I come on his radar? Hanson?

Ron/Miraç leaned down, his face inches from mine—close enough for me to smell coffee and cigarettes on his breath. "Little wolf, the big bad wolf wants to make little wolf cubs with you. He hopes you won't kill them like you killed Rob Hamlin's baby with that overdose."

I launched myself at him with a speed I didn't know I was capable of. I got my hands around his throat and rode him down as I tumbled off the bed—

—And hit the stone floor of my pitch-black cell, my fingers grasping at empty air. I screamed in rage. "Miraç, you cowardly, sneaking son of a bitch, come in here and face me yourself!"

"No, no, little wolf," Miraç's voice purred in my ear.

I spun and threw a punch in the direction of the voice, but my fist encountered nothing. I took deep breaths and forced myself to calm down, to rein in my hurt and fury. Damn it, I was cold and hungry and it was so hard not to be angry.

He chuckled. "No, this is so much more fun. You have so many triggers." The voice was my grandfather's. "Moses Murphy, Rob Hamlin, Sean, your ghost, even dastardly Charles Vaughan." Something sharp like a fang scraped against my throat. "Vampires and werewolves and ghosts, oh my," he added in Charles's voice. The sound made me sick to my stomach.

"What do you want from me?" I asked him. I hated myself for how ragged my voice sounded.

"Everything." It was Miraç's own voice this time, speaking softly in my ear. "There will be nothing left. As Kathleen told you, you'll take your own life with a smile when I've finished." A pause. "Of course, if you release your ghost from the crystal, I might be persuaded to make a trade."

I didn't believe him for one second, and I'd never even consider it anyway. "Do whatever you're going to do," I told him, my voice flat. "I don't trade in lives—mine, or anyone else's. Death doesn't scare me. Been there, done that, didn't bother to get the T-shirt."

"I do believe you're telling the truth," he mused. "How delightful. I must rethink my approach. In the meantime, I encourage you not to eat the food I sent yesterday. I suspect it's gone bad."

I cursed him again, but the sensation of something beside me had already faded. He really liked getting the last word.

I found my little bed and crawled under the covers. They smelled foul, like dried blood. My hands and knees hurt from falling on the floor. Those pains were minor compared to my back and arm.

I was so hungry and thirsty that I thought about drinking some water from the sink, but decided against it. I still suspected it might be spelled or drugged. With my magic suppressed and my body injured, the only thing I had left was my mind. I knew I wasn't thinking as clearly anymore because of the long, lonely hours in my cell and lack of food, but I could still tell reality from illusion and control my actions. I clung to those small comforts and wrapped the covers tighter, shivering in the dark.

Hours passed, then days—how many, I wasn't sure. At least two days, maybe three.

No one came into my cell, not even to bring food. Miraç had apparently abandoned his illusions in favor of solitary confinement and starvation. I forced myself to stay awake for long periods, sleeping only in what I hoped was something close to reasonable amounts. Part of me wanted to stay asleep as much as possible. I couldn't feel my hunger or thirst while sleeping, but too much sleep would only weaken me more. I had to be ready if an opportunity for escape presented itself.

When I did sleep, my dreams alternated between fantasies of being home with Sean and Malcolm and nightmares filled with tables laden with food. Sometimes I woke certain I'd been talking in my sleep or in a delirium, maybe to Sean, maybe to someone else. If someone entered my cell while I slept, I wasn't aware of it. The cell was always still and dark when I woke, the air stale.

I bathed at the sink a few times, at first self-conscious because I was sure someone was watching, but then I stopped caring about modesty. It seemed like a frivolous thing to try to hang onto, given my circumstances.

My arm and back were mercilessly sore and white-hot. The cuts were infected, either from something on the thing that lashed me, or from my cell, or both. I was no longer cold, but I suspected it was because of fever, not because the temperature in my cell had been adjusted. I still shivered, though, and sickness, hunger, and dehydration made it increasingly difficult to leave my bed.

On the third day, as I lay semi-conscious on top of the dirty bedding, covered in a cold sweat, I thought of the "divine wind" spell carved into my left femur. I wasn't sure what made me suddenly think of it, but my hand went to my left thigh. I was startled when I sensed the spell was not only still active but accessible. I could invoke the spell. I had only to cut into the flesh above it and speak the word that would trigger it, and I would be dead before I had a chance to feel any pain. My suffering would be over—and Miraç would be cheated out of whatever plans he had for me.

I lay still, my heart thundering in my ears. I wasn't actually contemplating killing myself, was I?

When I had that spell carved into my femur, I intended it as a last resort, my escape if ever my grandfather captured me or I fell into the hands of either a federal agency or another cabal, when suicide would be far preferable to that kind of captivity. I knew what torments I would suffer in the custody of the feds or a cabal, but I didn't know what Miraç planned to do with me. Would it be worse than death? It was definitely possible. Sorcery and black magic were frightening, even to me—and I was sure the vomiting of serpents Carly had mentioned was only the tip of the iceberg. If I didn't invoke the divine wind spell, I might end up wishing I had, especially if Miraç used me for some sorcerer's curse that hurt people.

Both Miraç and Kathleen had said I would be glad for death in the end, even willing to kill myself. My natural contrariness, a result of my years of captivity by my grandfather, reared up at that. If they wanted me to be suicidal, then I wouldn't be—not now, and not at the end. Besides, if I was dead, I couldn't escape, kill Miraç, rescue Malcolm, and buy a house with Sean. I didn't want to die. I'd find a way to get out of here...somehow.

I fell asleep composing my apology to Sean for asking for more time on the house, and woke with a start what felt like a long time later, certain I was not alone in my cell. I lay still and strained to see into the darkness.

Miraç's voice startled me. It had been days since I'd heard any voice but my own. "A very long time ago, in a great empire, twins were born to a rug-maker and his mistress."

The words came from the direction of the door, though I could still see nothing but darkness. At first I thought it was another of Miraç's illusions, but somehow I knew it wasn't. I sensed Miraç's presence in a way I hadn't during any of his illusions.

I wanted to tell him to go away, but I didn't. Something told me I needed to listen to this story—and anyway, it was better than just lying here alone in the dark.

"The twins' mother died in childbirth," Miraç continued. "The rug-maker couldn't raise them as his own, as his wife would not permit it, but he couldn't bring himself to end their lives. The twins were raised by the dead woman's mother, who hated the rug-maker but had loved her daughter dearly. She named them Kassia and Sala. She kept them clothed and fed as best she could. Perhaps she saw in their faces something of her daughter. If she did, she never said."

A small fire appeared. The sudden light, as dim as it was, hurt my eyes. I squinted and made out the figure of Miraç sitting cross-legged by the door. The fire was contained in an iron bowl in front of him. I didn't smell any smoke, so this was no real or natural fire. Possibly an illusion. As my eyes adjusted, I drank in the sight of the flames, happy to see light after so long alone in the dark.

Miraç gazed into the fire. "Their grandmother passed away when the twins were children, forcing them to survive on the street. They were quite adept at stealing food and moving unseen in the alleys of Constantinople, and learned to be nimble fighters. As such, they were in comparatively good health for street orphans. That is why the vampire Julius chose them as his servants."

That was an unexpected twist, but I'd already guessed this tale wouldn't be the sort typically found in a history book.

Miraç reached into the fire. The flames danced around his fingers as if playing with him. "Julius used the twins to help him lure his meals, to spy on those he thought suspected his true nature, and for his own pleasures." His voice betrayed no emotion at that statement. "More than a decade passed in this way. The twins grew into young women. Sala enjoyed the lavish life Julius provided and welcomed his attentions. Kassia did not, however, and searched for a way to free herself and Sala. Finally, in an unholy place in the very oldest part of the city, she discovered what she believed to be her only salvation. The price was steep, but one Kassia was willing to pay. She died in an occult ritual and was reborn as a sorcerer, with her soul in the keeping of the demon lord Malphas."

I was too hungry and enervated to react much, but I thought we might be getting closer to the reason for my presence here.

"Kassia promised Lord Malphas she would persuade her sister to join her and returned to Julius's home. Pretending she had not yet made the deal, she told Sala she had secured a way for them to escape Julius's control and called upon her sister's love to come away with her. Instead, Sala betrayed Kassia to Julius."

Miraç raised his hand and watched the flames dance on his fingers. "To punish Kassia, Julius forced her to watch him turn Sala, then locked the sisters together in a room. He intended for the newly risen Sala to kill her sister in bloodlust. When he rose the following night, however, he found the door to the room destroyed and both sisters gone. Followers of Lord Malphas had taken them away during the day while Julius slept."

"Why did they leave Julius alive?" I croaked, curious despite my hatred of my captor.

He traced a pattern in fire on the floor. "Julius's maker was an ally of Lord Malphas, so neither Lord Malphas nor anyone loyal to him could harm Julius. Lord Malphas simply took Julius's beloved offspring Sala and her sister as punishment for spoiling his plan to make Sala his own. Though Sala was not a sorcerer like Kassia and could not become one, Lord Malphas gave them equal power and saw they were trained to use it. The sisters served him well for many years."

I wondered how Miraç knew all this. I rested my head on my sore arm and waited.

"Both sisters were now nearly immortal, though in very different ways —Sala a vampire and Kassia a sorcerer. Their shared longevity did not bind them together, however. Sala believed Kassia to be bound for Hell because she had bartered her soul, and Kassia felt Sala should suffer for betraying her to Julius. Lord Malphas forbade either sister from harming the other, but soon his attention was drawn by war in the demon realm. Lord Malphas fell in battle, and his servants and followers on Earth were left to their own infernal devices. No longer united by their service to their lord, Kassia and Sala went their separate ways. Some four centuries passed before the sisters saw each other again."

For all his inhumanity, Miraç was a captivating storyteller. Also, the longer he talked, the more insight I gained into his history and motivations.

"In the year 1204, soldiers of the Fourth Crusade sacked Constantinople. As the city burned, greedy foot soldiers murdered civilians and pillaged everything of value they could find. Meanwhile, a small contingent of highly trained soldiers searched the city. Among their targets were vampires, sorcerers, or any other practitioners of the so-called dark arts, who were to be executed on sight. When a group of soldiers cornered Kassia in a wine cellar, she unleashed a great firestorm, killing the soldiers—and many others who had the great misfortune of being nearby. Kassia did not intend to kill them, but to protect herself, she did what was needed."

Despite Miraç's almost-mechanical tone, I detected a hint of emotion when he spoke of Kassia, and his accent became more pronounced. Somehow, he had crossed paths with her, but how? And what did this have to do with me?

"I see you grow impatient with my tale." Miraç smiled briefly. "Perhaps I should finish it another day."

"Finish the story," I rasped. "Don't be a dick. No one likes a cliffhanger."

He chuckled, though the sound lacked humor. "In the chaos of the city's sacking, Kassia's firestorm went largely unnoticed by the Crusaders, thought of as merely the result of overzealous soldiers. For the surviving members of the city's Vampire Court, however, its cause was obvious: Kassia the sorcerer, who had long been a thorn in their side for refusing to bow to their authority. Though they cared little for the humans who had died, the vampires dispatched their most powerful operative to bring Kassia to the Court for trial."

"Sala," I guessed.

"Indeed." The lines of fire on the floor flared, and for the first time, I saw real anger in Miraç's dark eyes. "Sala came to Kassia as her sister, claiming to have a way to escape the city undetected. In a moment of weakness, Kassia let down her guard. Sala took her prisoner. Rather than bring her to the Court, Sala imprisoned Kassia in a curse box and buried the box beneath a church. There Kassia stayed, languishing and suffering in a state of wakefulness for seven hundred years. In the meantime, Sala gained power and influence in Europe and then in the New World, her sister all but forgotten in her prison. And perhaps Kassia might have been lost forever, if not for a great war that consumed all of Europe and razed much of Constantinople. A bomb destroyed the church in the latter days of the first world war, damaging the box and freeing her."

"And so a thousand-year-old sorcerer appeared out of thin air in war-torn Constantinople." I blinked at Miraç, trying to process everything he had told me. "That's where you met her?"

"Saved her, though perhaps it was she who saved me." Miraç let the flames on the floor die, though the fire in the bowl still burned. "I was a boy of fifteen, badly injured by a bomb that killed the rest of my family. Bleeding, broken, and wanting to die, I came upon a beautiful woman wandering through the rubble, wearing clothing I had seen only in history books. Her language was strange to me and mine to her, but I understood she needed help and a guide to a city she didn't know. We found refuge. She healed my injuries. That was the first I knew of true magic, the first I knew of true power."

He pondered the fire in the bowl. "She offered to help me become a sorcerer like herself. All I had to do was gift my soul to the keeping of a demon lord, as she had done. With my family gone, I had no reason to decline. She insisted I wait until I became a man, so I didn't spend my many centuries in the body of an adolescent. It was wisdom, I knew later, but in those early days, I was impatient. She taught me patience, among... other things."

He went silent. There was no mistaking his tone. *Wow...talk about robbing the cradle*, I thought.

"My Kassia was terribly diminished by her entrapment," Miraç continued finally. "If not for her imprisonment, she might have lived for millennia, but the curse box's spellwork had fractured over the centuries. Whether that was Sala's intent or she simply didn't care, it's difficult to know. We had only ten years together. As she lay dying, my Kassia helped me summon a demon lord, as she had done so long before, and I made my pact. She asked my lord to gift me with her memories and what remained of her power, so I might fulfill an important task. He agreed, and it was done."

His eyes finally met mine. They reflected the flames in the bowl. "When I woke, reborn in this body, I knew all she had known, and received both her power and my own. I served my lord for many decades. When time permitted, I turned my thoughts to fulfilling my Kassia's dying wish."

"Revenge." I closed my eyes to rest them after looking at the fire for so long. "To find Sala and get back at her for imprisoning her sister."

"Yes."

I forced my heavy eyelids open again. "Okay, I can appreciate a good revenge tale, but what does all this family dysfunction have to do with..." My voice trailed off. Damn it, I was so hungry and thirsty and tired, or I'd have put it together ages ago. The accent alone should have been enough, if I'd thought about it more. "It's Valas, isn't it." I struggled to sit up. "Valas is Sala."

"Sala Veli was her name, a thousand years ago." Miraç rose smoothly, leaving the fire on the floor at his feet. "After she left the Vampire Court of Constantinople, she was known as simply Valas. A vampire with the power of a sorcerer, who has redefined herself as head of the Vampire Court of the Western United States. A heartless woman who imprisoned her sister for seven hundred years for the crime of defending her life against the bloodthirsty Crusaders who hunted her."

I was in no way surprised to hear Valas had the powers of a sorcerer. The woman had turned into smoke before my eyes and her power had always felt very different from any other vamp I'd ever known. I couldn't very well defend her against the charges Miraç made about her treatment of Kassia, because it also would not surprise me to find out the entire story was true.

I got to my feet, swaying unsteadily, and leaned against the wall. "Okay, now I know part of the reason for all this, but I still don't understand why you sent that decanter to the gala or the bowl and statue to the other Courts, or what I have to do with your vendetta."

"The decanter and the other items were partly tests."

"To see how well your magic could control your puppets from a distance, with the help of that little rune you cut into their skin?"

He smiled, though the expression didn't reach his eyes. "Indeed."

"And the other reason you did it?"

"The other items were misdirection, to disguise the fact my primary target was Valas's Court. The decanter's purpose was twofold: to undermine her authority and to ascertain you are as powerful as I believed."

My thoughts were entirely too sluggish. "The magic splinter that hit me was no accident."

"It was a spell that permitted me to measure your magic and track you, and grant you passage through the rug—a rug made by my Kassia's own father, many centuries ago."

I rubbed the spot on my breastbone where the splinter had lodged. "How did you know it would be me who would examine the decanter?"

"Who else would Valas ask but her pet mage?" His tone was mocking.

"I'm no one's pet," I snapped, my anger giving me a little energy.

"Aren't you? Do you fancy yourself her friend? Her confidant?" he scoffed.

I shook my head. "I'm not naive. Vampires don't have friends, and they certainly don't make humans their confidants. I'm an independent private investigator who works for the Court on a contract basis, nothing more."

"You are Valas's personal favorite; she has said so herself. As such, the fact I stole you from under her nose makes this all the sweeter."

I read his expression. "But that's not why you kidnapped me."

"No." At last, Miraç approached. He wore black, as always, but I could make out his form silhouetted against the dim light of the fire as he stood on the other side of my bed. "I am powerful—more powerful than any sorcerer I know—but Valas is more powerful than I. To avenge my Kassia, I must have more than my own magic. I must have hidden allies, greater cunning, and a plan devised over many years."

He leaned toward me, close enough for me to smell a hint of incense on his clothing. "I must have *your* power, Alice. Your power, and your life."

"You won't get either," I stated, straightening with difficulty. "And even if you do, you won't get to her. Valas isn't just powerful—she's been outsmarting people like you for what, well over a millennium? She outsmarted Kassia big time. She'll outfox you and drop your ass in a curse box too."

His eyes flared red. As his fingers closed on my neck, I raised my fist from where it had been hidden at my side and shoved a handful of rags into his mouth. The rags were torn from my bedsheets and soaked in the water from the sink—the sink Kathleen had insisted I could drink safely from.

Miraç staggered and made a garbled noise, maybe an attempt to shout a spell or call for help. The rags muffled the sound.

I jumped onto him, holding his mouth closed with one hand as my other scrabbled in his pockets, searching for any kind of weapon or something I could use against him. My fingers were clumsy and I was weak from lack of food and water.

To my disappointment, his pockets were nearly empty. My hand closed on something just as he punched me in the stomach, knocking me back. He stumbled away, pulling the rags from his mouth and cursing in what I assumed was his native Turkish. The words sounded a little slurred and he swayed, almost falling to one knee. Safe water, my ass.

I glanced at the item I'd found in Miraç's pocket. It was the photo of Rob Hamlin and the real Alice I'd found in Rob's wallet. I sagged against the wall.

Then Miraç slammed me against the ceiling in a flare of fiery magic, and it was lights out.

2 4

I WOKE TIED TO A CHAIR.

My arms and legs were leaden. I had a foul taste in my mouth, as if someone had poured something down my throat while I was unconscious. The back of my head hurt where I'd hit the ceiling, and my neck was sore because my head had been hanging down toward my chest for a while. At the moment, I didn't have enough strength to raise it.

"It was a good effort, my sweet." Miraç was behind me, arranging glass bottles and heavy objects on a wooden table or altar. "I commend you for ingenuity, if nothing else. You are the first to lay a hand on me in anger in a very long time."

"You should have just done what you needed to do and killed her before she woke up," Kathleen said waspishly from somewhere to my right. "She's dangerous."

"Now, now, Kathleen, I do believe you're holding a grudge." Miraç's bare feet and legs appeared in my line of sight. His fingers ran over my cheek. I tried to raise my head, but my muscles wouldn't obey. "See, she's quite tame now."

"What did you do to me?" I meant it to be a demand, but my throat was too dry and my voice rough. I coughed.

"Just a draught to help keep you comfortable."

"Since when does my comfort matter to you?" I rasped. "You left me to bleed and starve in a dark room for days."

"You earned a bit of comfort with your resourceful attempt to attack me. The least I can offer you is some peace, here in your final moments."

I finally managed to raise my head. I was in an iron cage, inside a large stone room much like my cell. The chain on my right ankle was bolted to a steel plate under the chair. Ancient glyphs and runes filled the circle around my chair. My bare feet rested in smaller circles drawn on the floor. Whatever old magic Miraç planned, it was big-time powerful.

Kathleen waited outside the cage, next to a black magic altar with a goat skull in the center of the inverted pentagram. Two other women wearing black hooded cloaks stood beside her. One was much older and gray-haired, the other young, with dark brown hair. Two's company and three's a coven. *The crone, the mother, and the maiden,* I thought. Not good.

Miraç stood in front of me in black shorts, his body covered with glyphs painted in blood. The dagger in his hand was bloody.

"Any last words before we begin?" he asked.

I was so dehydrated that it hurt to swallow. "Do you know why I'm Valas's personal favorite?"

He tilted his head. "Interesting. I expected a plea for your life. You continue to surprise me. Tell me why Valas is so fond of you."

"She isn't fond of me. She labeled me her personal favorite because I owe her a debt. Moses Murphy wants to kill me for smiting his daughter with lightning. He can't touch me as long as Valas and the Court are protecting me. The moment I fulfill my part of the bargain, she'll drop that *favorite* designation and then I'm fair game for anyone who wants to come after me, including Murphy." I shook my head. "You called me her pet, but I'm not. You care for a pet. I'm just one more thing she'll toss aside when I'm no longer of any use."

"What is this debt you must pay?"

"She's got a magic mirror that's a portal. She wants me to use it to travel to the fae realm to steal something. I don't want to do it, but I owe her for saving Sean's life. If I fail, she'll turn me and I'll be a vampire of her line for eternity."

Miraç studied me. "This is truth you speak."

It was part truth and part lies—a tactic I had used before to fool those who could perceive deception. Miraç hadn't been able to tell the difference, apparently. That gave me a little hope.

My shoulders twitched, the closest I could get to a shrug with my muscles still weakened by whatever potion he or the witches had poured down my throat. "No reason to lie about it. I hate the vamps." Heat rose in my chest. Had my magic not been suppressed, my eyes would have glowed with blood magic. "They're all the same. Not a conscience or heart among them."

"Who else among the undead has earned your ire?"

I shook my head. "It doesn't matter."

His expressed hardened. "I can compel you to answer."

"Of course you can," I said bitterly. "Just one more undead person stealing my free will. I've been compelled without my knowledge for weeks, maybe months...maybe longer. I don't know when it started, to be honest."

"I am not undead." Miraç scowled. "I live. My heart beats. My blood is warm." For some reason, me accusing him of being undead miffed him.

"Sire, the rituals must be completed within the hour if we want to harness the full power of tonight's moon," Kathleen said, her voice impatient. "She's stalling."

"Quiet," Miraç commanded without looking at her. "Who is this vampire who has forced you to act against your will?" he asked me.

"Charles Vaughan of the Court." I spat out the words like poison. "The bastard has been compelling me for years, probably, and I didn't realize it until I was here. Your suppression spells didn't just suppress my magic—they suppressed his compulsions too, which is how I figured it out."

His expression grew thoughtful. "Why do you tell me this?"

"Because I might be worth more to you alive than dead, and I have no loyalty to the damn Court—Valas, Vaughan, or anyone else."

He smiled. "An admirable try, but—"

"Hear me out. It's the least you can do, all things considered."

He raised an eyebrow. "Present your case."

"You want Valas. I can get her for you."

He chuckled, again with that eerie lack of emotion. "I will kill Valas myself. I need only your power to do so."

"Maybe, but you'll have to get through everyone else at Northbourne to get to her," I pointed out. "You've probably already considered that, since you've planned this for a while. You've got magic and power and people on the inside, but Valas isn't stupid—far from it. What you need is someone like me, someone whose power and ruthlessness are always underestimated because I pretend to be weaker and softer than I really am. I can be your Trojan Horse."

"Sire, this is ridiculous," Kathleen protested. "Your plan is already in motion, and it's a good one. She's just trying to save her own skin."

"Of course she is. Would you not do the same? That does not mean her words are untrue." Miraç spun the dagger in his hand. "She speaks the truth about her hatred for the vampires, and about Valas." He walked around me, thinking. "What guarantee do I have you will not betray me?"

"I fear you more than I fear Valas."

He laughed. "That is a lie."

"Yes," I admitted. "Fine, you want the truth? I want out from under Valas's thumb. I don't want to travel through the mirror, and I don't want to be turned into a vampire. I want Vaughan dead for manipulating me all these years and for biting me twice—once while I was in a coma, and once through blackmail. You kill them both, and I'm free to live happily ever after with Sean."

Again, he failed to notice the lies within the truths. "What of Moses Murphy's threats?" he wanted to know. "With Valas dead, you will no longer be a favorite of the Court."

"I'll figure out a way to deal with him. If being Valas's pet, or whatever I am, is the price of being safe from Murphy, I'd rather take on Murphy and be off her leash."

"Surely you can't be considering this." Kathleen approached the cage, her expression incredulous. "She's a liar."

"With that one exception, she has spoken nothing but truth." Miraç shook his head. "Still, you are correct—Alice cannot be trusted to keep her word. We will proceed as planned."

"Bastard," I ground out. "Without me you'll fail, and I'll have died for nothing. At least if I died helping you take out Valas and Charles Vaughan, I'd go down swinging. Why should you be the only one who gets that privilege? Do you think you're the only one who deserves revenge?"

He hesitated.

"I've met with Valas alone four times," I added, sensing my words had registered with him on some level. "I stood within a foot of her the last three times. Tell me you could get that close anywhere near that easily and I'll stop arguing with you."

He didn't respond. Expressionless, he walked behind me and returned carrying a freshly harvested human heart, dripping blood and branded with three runes. I couldn't suppress a choked sound.

He crouched and placed the heart in the center of one of the glyphs on the floor. "As I told you when you first arrived, suffering and pain—both physical and emotional—are potent sources of power for sorcery and black magic," he said, his gaze on me. "You have many such memories, and you have used your magic to cause suffering and death. That's the most significant reason I chose you to help fulfill my mission. It's interesting and useful that so many people you know have also experienced great suffering." He glanced down at the heart. "And many of those have suffered because of you. That personal connection makes my spellwork even more powerful."

I let out a strangled sound. I didn't want to ask, but I had to. "Whose heart is that?"

Miraç ignored me. He cut the heart with his dagger and dipped his fingertip in the dark blood that oozed out. He used the blood to paint two glyphs next to the heart, then stood. "Kathleen, are you and the others ready?"

"We are," she said, giving me a look of triumph. "We await your word."

My breathing was shallow. "Miraç, whose heart is that?"

"It belonged to a man whose heart was broken by your disappearance." He smiled. "A broken heart is so full of anger and pain—especially a strong man's heart. He fought hard, but in the end, even a shifter can't survive having his heart ripped out."

I was shaking with anger. "You're a liar."

"How do you suppose I got this, then?" He reached into his pocket and took out an amulet in the shape of a wolf's head. The stone was smeared with dried blood.

He held it close so I could see the inscription on the back: *Alice*. Carly had etched my name onto Sean's half of the amulet, and his onto mine. The wolves' heads on our amulets faced opposite directions. Mine faced my right. This amulet faced left.

Still, I shook my head. "No. It's an illusion."

He held the stone to my nose. "No illusion, my sweet. Do you smell his blood?" He put the chain over my head and let it drop. The chain was longer than mine, and the amulet hit my stomach instead of my sternum.

I tried to pull free of the ropes that bound me to the chair, but my arms and legs were still leaden. "I'll kill you for even lying about this to me, Miraç. Do you hear me? I'll kill you. That is not Sean's heart. *That is not Sean's heart*."

"What use is a broken heart to anyone? You should thank me for ending his suffering." He walked around me again. Bottles clinked on the table behind me.

I didn't believe it was Sean's heart, not for a second. Miraç said pain and anger were powerful ingredients for spells, so he was trying to make me hurt. There was no way Sean was dead.

The amulet was heavy around my neck. The coppery scent of blood made my stomach churn.

Miraç reappeared, carrying an iron bowl. He set it on the floor about ten feet in front of me. In it was another amulet—this one round and made of silver, with a green crystal in the center. He ran his fingertip around the edge of the bowl and it glowed bright red. He said a word that sounded Turkish. I didn't know the word, but his tone was unmistakable. It was a command.

Malcolm appeared, floating above the bowl. A chain made of glyphs tethered him by the ankle to the amulet. Our eyes met, and somehow I knew this was no illusion. Miraç had found a way to pull Malcolm from his crystal and chain him.

"Alice? My God, what has he done to you?" Malcolm tried to flit to me, but the chain held him in place. "Let me go, you bastard," he yelled.

Miraç smiled. "He isn't the angriest ghost I've ever encountered, but he's definitely the most powerful. Thank you for bringing him to me."

"Let him go," I demanded.

"I think not," Miraç countered. "But I *am* letting you see each other one last time, so you might say thank you."

"Go to hell," Malcolm and I said at the same time. He looked down at the floor and recoiled. "What the...is that a *human heart?* You sick bastard."

Miraç ignored him and glanced at the three witches by their altar. "The moon is at its most powerful. Begin the ritual."

The women began to chant. Kathleen picked up a black athame and cut the palm of her hand, dripping blood into a small cauldron. Smoke rose, filling the air with the scent of rotting things.

Malcolm stared at me, wide-eyed. "What's going on?"

"Get out of here any way you can," I told him. "Tell Sean what happened and make sure he burns this place to the ground."

He flitted in place, yanking on the magical chain. "Don't talk to me like you're going to die. Don't you *dare*."

Miraç met Kathleen at the door of the cage. She used her thumb to paint runes on his forehead with the substance in her cauldron.

"I asked Suriel to help you," I told Malcolm. "I hope he steps up. If he does, just be ready when he shows. If he doesn't, I'm sorry. I tried."

"Damn it, Alice, this is not happening," Malcolm said.

"It's happening." I raised my chin defiantly as Miraç headed for me, blade in hand. "Screw you, Miraç. I hope Valas sticks you in a curse box and throws it in a septic tank."

Miraç positioned his feet on two glyphs on the floor in front of my chair. "Very creative. I will, however, give Valas your best when I see her." He used the tip of his dagger to cut three runes into the inside of his forearm. He set the dagger on the floor and picked up another round amulet. This one had a red crystal in its center.

He closed his eyes and held out his arms. The spellwork on the floor ignited in a roar of power and black magic, pulsing out from the heart in the center. The magic traveled along the glyphs and up Miraç's legs. He opened his eyes. They glowed bright red.

Behind him, Kathleen and the other witches resumed chanting, their voices rising. Malcolm flitted frantically, but the chain binding him to the amulet held.

Miraç spoke a word in some long-dead language and plunged his hand into my chest. The glyphs and runes on the floor blazed. I screamed and tried to pull away, but the ropes held me fast to the chair and the chair wouldn't budge. The agony was indescribable.

"*Alice!*" Malcolm's shout was anguished. "Miraç, you bastard, leave her alone!"

The sensation of Miraç's hand moving inside my ribs was worse than the sight of his forearm disappearing into my chest. I didn't understand how I was even still alive until I realized his hand and arm shimmered with magic. He hadn't actually physically punched through my sternum, but it hurt as if he had.

Miraç's fist closed on something in my chest. He studied me, his gaze thoughtful. "How unexpected," he murmured, his voice strangely calm in the midst of the witches' chants and my hoarse screams. "The natural magic and shifter magic, I expected to find. But this...this is quite unique."

He pulled his arm out of my chest, a ball of white, green, red, black, gold, and purple magic clenched in his fist. The sensation was like when Malcolm had pulled the void-black magic from me in Northbourne's basement, but infinitely worse. My back arched and I screamed in a long, agonized sound.

When it was over, I hunched in my chair, gasping for air. My chest felt like all of my internal organs had been ripped out through my sternum, leaving me entirely hollow. I no longer sensed my magic suppressed by the cuff on my ankle. I no longer sensed any magic in me at all, because Miraç had ripped it out of me. I had never felt so empty—or so incredibly angry.

Miraç pondered the ball of magic in his hand. "Like holding a star," he mused. He raised his other hand and brought the amulet to the ball of magic. "*Mine*," he commanded. My magic went into the crystal in the amulet.

"You bastard," I said, my voice ragged. "You soulless, thieving, cowardly *bastard*."

He hung the amulet around his neck. "You're still alive." He sounded surprised. "Most mages I've encountered died having their magic torn out, or were nothing more than empty shells after."

"I'm not most mages," I told him, my chest heaving.

"No, you are not. I was right when I said you would be a good diversion, but now you're no longer of any use to me." He picked up his bloody dagger. "I'll be merciful and cut your throat. Perhaps your lifeblood will be of use to the witches." The last blood drained from a dying victim was a powerful ingredient for magic.

Kathleen smiled at me. "Thank you, sire," she said sweetly. "I'll bring you a vessel to gather her blood."

The crystal in Miraç's amulet glowed. I sensed its warmth. I missed my magic more than I could have imagined, and it was torture to see it just out of reach. Damn Miraç to the bottom of hell.

"What did you mean about my magic being unexpected?" I asked.

"Is it possible you didn't know?" He raised his eyebrows. "Perhaps not, if it were far enough back in your lineage, or it was magic done without your knowledge. It matters little now, however."

I wasn't going to beg him to tell me, any more than I intended to beg for my life. But as he went to the door of the cage to get the spelled vessel from Kathleen, I asked another question. "How did you get the picture of Robert Hamlin and me? The one you had when you came to see me, pretending to be Robert, like you pretended to be Sean's partner Ron?"

Malcolm looked shocked. I'd asked the question partly so I could let him know Miraç had been disguising himself. I still hoped my ghost could escape somehow, and I wanted him to be able to tell Sean as much as possible.

Miraç smiled that eerie, soulless smile. "Did I come to you as poor, broken-hearted Robert Hamlin? Or did I encounter him at the bus station after he'd left your home, and after his interrogation by the Vampire Court?" His gaze flicked to the heart in the middle of the circle.

It belonged to a man whose heart was broken by your disappearance.

"That's not Sean's heart," I said, my voice ragged. "It's Robert Hamlin's."

"It is a sad story. They will say he broke his parole and vanished, never to be seen again." Miraç stood in front of me, holding the vessel Kathleen had given him. "Just another casualty among your acquaintances, like your uncooperative, soon-to-be discorporated ghost."

He put the dagger to my throat. I stared up at him, unwilling to give him the satisfaction of seeing me flinch or hearing me beg.

"Wait," Malcolm said.

Miraç didn't turn, but the blade stilled. "You have something to say, ghost?"

"Spare her life," Malcolm said, his voice devoid of emotion. "Free her, and I will serve you."

My stomach heaved. "No, don't you dare. Not for me." I tilted my head back, stretching my throat against the edge of the dagger, and glared up at Miraç. "Do it. Get it over with."

"Miraç, my full name is Malcolm Earl Flynn," Malcolm said tonelessly. "I will willingly serve you in whatever manner you want, but *only* if you don't harm Alice any further and set her free."

"Malcolm, no," I pleaded. My eyes burned with angry tears. "Don't do this. Sean will find this place and kill Miraç. He'll avenge us both."

Miraç turned. "Declare yourself my servant first, and then I will release her."

Malcolm shook his head. "No. You release her first, and swear a blood oath that neither you, or anyone associated with you will harm her in any way, by action or inaction, and then I'll take your oath. You have my full name, so you can summon me if I try to renege."

Miraç was silent.

"You know how powerful I am," Malcolm floated back and forth. His expression was harder than I had ever seen it. "You want my power, these are my terms. Let Alice go."

"No," I repeated.

"It's not up to you," Malcolm told me.

"I'm giving you an order. Do not do this."

He ignored me and turned to Miraç. "Do we have an agreement?"

"Sire, don't free her," Kathleen protested. "The first thing she'll do is warn Valas and tell them where we are. With her lifeblood, I can make spells that will help your attack."

Miraç nodded slowly. "Kathleen makes a fair point. How can I ensure your silence?" He paused and added thoughtfully, "Better yet, how can I use your freedom to my advantage?"

"Sire—" Kathleen began.

"Miraç," Malcolm said, sounding impatient.

"*Silence.*" Miraç's voice reverberated through the room.

I found myself mute. Judging by the looks of shock on both Kathleen and Malcolm's faces, they had been rendered speechless too.

Miraç bent to look me in the eye. "You suggested earlier you might make a splendid Trojan Horse. Indeed, I think the idea has merit, but you cannot be allowed to reveal our location or our plans." He straightened and turned to Malcolm. "I accept your proposal, with a minor alteration. I must have one more thing from Alice before I free her. You may speak."

Malcolm shook his head. "You can't harm her, or the deal's off."

Miraç smiled, and I felt a distinct chill of fear. "Don't worry, Malcolm Earl Flynn. What I must take from Alice, she will hardly miss. Do we have a deal?"

Still mute, I shook my head furiously at Malcolm.

He didn't look at me. "We have a deal."

My heart broke.

"Good. I will summon my lord to hear your oath." Miraç turned to me. "I will see you very soon, little wolf," he told me, his voice mocking. When Malcolm started to object, he added, "Don't worry, ghost—I keep my bargains. When Alice and I cross paths again, it will not be in anger, and my Trojan Horse will suffer no harm at my hands."

Outside the cage, Kathleen glared at me. The other witches stood silently beside her.

I didn't know how Miraç planned to use me as a Trojan Horse, but I promised myself he wouldn't win. I'd find a way to kill him, no matter what it took.

He leaned close, his eyes glowing red. He put his palm against my forehead. "Say goodbye to Malcolm, Alice."

The spell that kept me silent broke. I didn't waste my breath cursing Miraç again. "I'll come back for you," I promised Malcolm.

"No, you won't." Miraç's palm grew hot against my forehead and dark magic rose. "*Sleep,*" he commanded.

The last thing I saw before unconsciousness swept me away was Malcolm, his face a mask of despair, floating at the end of his chain.

25

I DRIFTED IN AND OUT OF CONSCIOUSNESS IN A HAZE OF PAIN AND confusion. My dreams were strange and jumbled, full of faces and voices I didn't recognize.

The strangest dream involved fleeing from a dark underground prison while naked. My desperate attempt at escape failed when a figure in black captured me, cursed me in a language I didn't know, and dragged me back across a field. The dream ended when I tumbled down a long set of stone steps and a heavy door slammed closed behind me.

In another strange dream, voices rose and fell on the edge of my awareness—female voices, three of them. They spoke in unison, chanting in another unfamiliar language.

I realized it was not a dream when I became aware, in a vague way, that I was awake and being bathed. I sat in chest-deep water that smelled foul, though I had no memory of getting in the tub. In fact, I had no memory of where I was, or *who* I was.

My head hurt so badly I felt like I might vomit, and my body ached all over, especially my chest. My arm, back, and feet sizzled with pain, too. I thought I might have been hurt while trying to run away, but I couldn't remember why I'd been running.

Before I could think more about it, someone pushed me under the surface of the water and held me down until I lost consciousness again.

My next moment of awareness came some time later, when various sensations told me someone was dressing me, and none too gently. I moaned.

"She's coming around." A woman's harsh voice spoke near my ear as she yanked something on over my head. "I don't want her fighting us and trying to get away again. Let's get this done. We need to leave soon or he'll be angry."

"She'll be easier to move if she's asleep," another woman said. "Give her this."

A sweet liquid filled my mouth. Reflexively, I tried to spit it out, but someone held my mouth closed until I swallowed. I passed out again.

The third time I woke, it was to the sensation of being in a vehicle traveling at high speed down a rough paved road. Something covered my entire head—a black cloth bag, cinched loosely around my neck. My wrists were still bound with rope, but my legs were free. I was too disoriented and weakened to move, however.

"This is ridiculous." It was the harsh female voice I'd heard earlier. "He should have killed her, especially after she tried to run."

"Stop complaining," an older woman said. "The sire has his reasons. It's not for us to question him."

"Her lifeblood would have been useful," the woman beside me argued. "Even without magic, her life force is powerful. Imagine what we could have done with that blood."

"I'm sure he considered that," a younger woman said, her tone mollifying. "We might get to use it anyway, once he's done with her."

"I hope so. How much farther?"

"Another hour. Stop talking," the older woman snapped.

Some hazy time later, the vehicle pulled over and stopped. "Get up. Move," the woman beside me said crossly, shaking my shoulder. "Get out and help me," she ordered the others.

Doors opened. Someone grabbed my feet and pulled. I tried to kick, but my muscles didn't want to obey. I ended up rolling off the seat onto the floor. Pain lanced through my back and I whimpered.

The woman beside me cursed. "Get her out before she starts bleeding everywhere."

Afraid they intended to pull me out of the vehicle to kill me, I scrabbled to find something to grab, but with my hands bound, I couldn't get a grip on anything. My fingers closed on something under the seat—something small and plastic. I held onto it as they pulled me from the back seat.

I tumbled out of the vehicle onto gravel-covered asphalt that cut into my palms and knees. I fell over onto my side, hitting my head hard on the pavement. Dazed, I lay still and kept my little prize hidden in my hand while someone cut the rope on my wrists.

If they killed me on the side of the road, maybe someone would find the little object I'd grabbed. I didn't know where that thought came from, but somehow, I knew it was important to leave a clue for whoever found me.

A hand touched my forehead through the bag on my head. "You will hide in the ditch until you can no longer hear our vehicle before removing this hood," the woman who'd sat beside me commanded.

I nodded, though I didn't know why. My forehead burned at her touch, even through the hood.

"Bury the hood in the ground so no one can find it. Then you will walk along this road toward the mountains, and you will not stop until you get there." She shook me, her fingers digging into my shoulder. "Do you hear me? *Keep walking and don't look back.*"

Her words ignited something deep inside my head. The leaden feeling in my limbs faded, replaced by a strong compulsion to follow her commands.

"Yes," I whispered.

"Good." She stood and delivered a kick to my side. "Hide in the ditch. Don't let anyone see you."

Obediently, I crawled down the embankment. I curled up in the ditch with my arms around my aching ribs.

The women returned to their vehicle. Doors slammed and tires crunched in the gravel as they pulled away, making a wide turn and accelerating away from me.

When I could no longer hear the engine, I reached up and found the drawstring of the hood. I loosened it and pulled it off my head, squinting in the sudden light. The early-morning sun was barely above the horizon.

I dug a hole with my bare hands in the soft, wet earth and buried the hood. That chore done, I got to my feet and clambered out of the ditch to the road. All around me, I saw nothing but farmland. No cars, no houses—just large, empty fields marked with fences along the road.

My body hurt and my chest felt hollow. I ached like I'd left something important behind, but I didn't remember what it was. I didn't know anything except what the woman had told me to do.

I looked down at the item I'd stolen from the car. It was a pink cigarette lighter. I couldn't remember now why I'd grabbed it, but I thought it was important. I closed my fist around it and told myself not to drop it.

Keep walking and don't look back.

I turned my steps in the direction of the mountains and started walking.

2 6

ALICE

Our tour guide's name was Nicole.

"Welcome to Broken Ridge Winery," the young brunette said with a smile, addressing our little group. "Thank you for joining me on this last tour of the day. We're a small, family-owned operation. We'd like to get to know you before we go exploring. Why don't you all introduce yourselves with your first names and where you're from?" She turned to Sean and me. "How about you two first?"

"I'm Theodore," Sean said with an easygoing smile that didn't match the tension in his shoulders.

"I'm Evelyn," I added, adjusting my wide-brimmed hat and tucking my blonde hair behind my ears. "We're from Pleasanton."

"Welcome, Theodore and Evelyn!" Nicole said warmly.

As the others in the rather boisterous group introduced themselves, Sean and I looked around. The tour began in front of the event building where they hosted receptions and wine tastings. From our vantage point, we could see the six main buildings, the owners' residence, the visitor lot where we'd parked our rented convertible, and about a quarter of the vines. The vines and field I thought I'd run through during my abbreviated escape attempt were on the other side of the event building and out of my line of sight.

Other than the tree and the field, nothing seemed familiar. Last night, I'd been certain we were in the right place, but now I wasn't so sure.

Nicole took a few steps back from our little group and raised her voice. "We're going to start with a short walk through some of the vines," she said cheerfully. "It won't be far, I promise. Next, we'll see the vats, the casks where our wine is aged, and how we bottle our wine. Finally, we'll come back here for the best part of the tour: the tasting! Everyone stay together."

We followed Nicole down the wide sidewalk toward the vineyard. As she chatted with the others, Sean and I ended up at the back of the group. He wore a polo shirt and jeans, with a baseball cap and sunglasses. Though I would have been more comfortable in jeans and boots, I'd opted for slip-on walking shoes, calf-length yoga pants, and a long-sleeved shirt. I also wore a blonde wig, hat, and sunglasses. In case we were in the right place, I wanted to look nothing like Alice Worth.

"You okay?" Sean asked as we walked.

"Fine." I made a face. "A little tired." We hadn't gotten much sleep, and it had been a very busy day getting ready for this reconnaissance mission.

He tucked my hand into the crook of his elbow. "I like those pants. Why don't you wear yoga pants more often?"

"Down, boy," I said with a smile. "Because they don't go with my boots."

He laughed.

Nicole led us on a fifteen-minute walk through the grapevines. We got an entertaining lecture on the growing of grapes, soil types, and the benefits of California sunshine. Though it was late afternoon, quite a few workers were busy tending the vines. The first harvest was several weeks away.

We toured one building where the grapes were processed, then another filled with casks where the wine aged. Nothing looked familiar or resembled the sign Carly had glimpsed. How could a sorcerer live and do magic here without being noticed? I felt foolish for thinking this was the right place. If the sorcerer *did* live at a vineyard, it must be a less-busy one —or maybe even one that had closed.

As Nicole led us back toward the event building for the tasting, I hurried to catch up to her. "Quick question, Nicole. You mentioned Broken Ridge is family-owned. Who are the owners?"

She smiled. "A lovely family, the Talmadges. We don't see much of Mr.

Talmadge, since he travels a great deal. His wife Kathleen runs most of the day-to-day operations with her niece Julianne."

That matched what we'd found online about the owners of Broken Ridge. "And they live here?" I gestured at the enormous house in the center of the winery.

"Yes. Kathleen's mother Olivia Olsen lives there as well. She's older, but still very spry. They're quite a family." Nicole turned to the others. "Is everyone ready to sample some wine?"

The others cheered and two women clapped. As they filed into the event building, I hesitated outside the door, looking up at the owners' house. At the top of a hill, separated from the rest of the buildings by an enormous sloping lawn, it gave the owners a splendid view of the entire vineyard. Impossible to get up there without someone seeing me, but I wanted a closer look. If there was a sorcerer's lair somewhere on the property, the house was the most likely location.

"Coming inside?" Nicole asked us, holding the door of the event building open for us.

"We'll be right behind you," Sean said, giving her a smile that would have made me a little jealous if I hadn't known he was deliberately trying to charm her. He pinned me between his body and the building and slid his hand around my waist. "We need a minute to ourselves."

Nicole's smile turned a little frosty. "Visitors aren't allowed to go anywhere other than with a tour guide."

I grabbed Sean's butt and pulled him closer. "I promise we'll be right here for the next five minutes, and then we'll come in and buy some wine."

"All right. Five minutes." With obvious reluctance, she went inside and closed the heavy wooden door.

I dropped my hand to my side. Sean ran his nose along my hairline. "You don't have to move your hand," he murmured. "I liked it where it was."

I smiled. "Aren't we going to sneak off to snoop around?"

"We promised Nicole we'd stay here." He moved his mouth along my jaw and kissed me lightly on the lips. It was our first real kiss—well, the first I remembered—and it was wonderful. He tasted just as I'd imagined, like coffee and something wild. It was a heady and delicious combination I doubted any wine could rival.

I wrapped my arms around his neck and kissed him back. His hand slid down my side to my hip, then under my shirt to curve around my waist, holding me against his body.

"This is a crazy time and place to make out," I said when we broke the kiss. "And odds are someone is watching us."

He moved his mouth close to my ear, making me shiver. "This is probably going to sound weird to you, but shifters like to see their alpha and his consort being happy with each other."

I glanced down between us, where his level of happiness was rather obvious. "'Being happy,' huh? Is that what they're calling it these days?"

He nuzzled my neck. "I think they've been calling it something along those lines for a long time."

I met his eyes. "So if this doesn't pan out and we end up going home after the wine tasting, can we tell the others to go outside and keep an eye on the house while we have some happy time, or are you still not wanting to do that?"

He kissed the tip of my nose, which tickled, and smiled. "If this doesn't pan out and we have no other leads to follow, we might..." His smile faded as he stared at something over my head.

"What?" I turned to see an old, battered sign hanging on the side of the event building. It read *Chateau Nuit Winery* in curlicue lettering. Bunches of grapes framed the words on both sides.

He leaned down to murmur, "You see what I see?"

"I see it." My heart pounded in my ears. "It's the sign Carly saw in her vision. The style of the letters and the grapes match her drawing exactly."

The door opened behind us. Nicole stepped out onto the sidewalk. "You two ready to come in?"

"Just about." Sean gestured at the sign. "What is Chateau Nuit?"

"That was the name of this winery before the Talmadges bought it. They kept the sign, for nostalgia, I think." She gestured at the door. "We're about to taste a shiraz, if you'll go on in."

I took a step toward the door, but Sean's hand on my arm stopped me. "I think we might stay out here a few more minutes." Something about his tone made me instantly wary. What had he seen or heard that I hadn't?

Her smile vanished. "I think you should come inside with the rest of the group."

"What group?" Sean's voice was growly. "I don't hear anyone inside."

I realized I didn't either. Instead of the loud, boisterous voices of the others in our tour group, I heard absolute silence inside the building. "What happened to the others?" I demanded.

She frowned. "What do you mean? They're inside, at the—"

A large black panther appeared in the doorway behind her. It peered around Nicole's hip and stared at us, its eyes golden. Sean snarled.

Nicole looked down at the panther and screamed. She stumbled back to plaster herself against the wall of the building. "*What the hell is that?*" she screeched.

The panther emerged from the building and faced us, its ears back and teeth visible.

"Panther shifter," Sean murmured, moving in front of me. "They're solitary."

A second panther emerged from the building. Sean glanced over his shoulder and went still. I stole a glance and spotted five more panthers behind us.

"So much for solitary," I muttered.

"It's a whole clan." Sean growled. "They must all be loyal to the sorcerer. Panthers never stay in groups."

Her face pale and breathing ragged with terror, Nicole inched her way along the wall toward the open door of the event building. The largest of the panthers opened his mouth and showed her his fangs. She froze.

I wondered if we'd been spotted last night driving near the winery, or been recognized once we arrived despite our disguises. I supposed it didn't matter. They were ready for us.

I took off the hat, wig, and sunglasses and tossed them aside. I reached into my left sleeve and pulled an eight-inch knife from its sheath. Sean discarded his sunglasses and cap.

"Where is the sorcerer?" I asked Nicole.

"The w-what?" Her eyes were like saucers. "You're joking."

I gestured at the panthers surrounding us. "Does this look like a joke to you?"

"No," she wailed. Either she was an innocent bystander or a hell of an actress. I couldn't turn my back on her in case she was working for the sorcerer, but we had to keep her alive either way.

My stomach knotted. "What if the sorcerer is controlling the panthers somehow? Are they pawns, or willing attackers?"

"I don't know, but if they try to kill us, we'll have no choice but to defend ourselves." Sean's hand found mine and squeezed. "Stay next to me. Don't get killed."

I showed him my knife. It buzzed in my hand and the runes etched along the center of the blade shimmered with Carly's magic. "I might not remember much, but I know the pointy end goes into the bad guy. And you better not get killed either," I added. "You promised me a good time tonight."

The largest of the panthers moved forward with a low snarl. The others did the same, closing in around us.

Sean dropped to his knees. A fiery burst of golden magic almost knocked me over as he shifted. His wolf was enormous, his head well above my waist. Around his neck, he wore a chain with his wolf amulet and two other amulets etched with runes. He bared his teeth and growled at the panthers, his ears flat against his head.

The panthers hissed and growled. They weren't much smaller than most of the wolves in Sean's pack. Seven of them versus one extra-large alpha werewolf and his knife-wielding consort. It must have seemed like a total mismatch.

The alpha panther growled and crouched, preparing to leap. I raised my knife. Sean snarled. Nicole sobbed and tried to flatten herself against the wall.

And that's when ten werewolves tore around both sides of the building, moving at full speed.

The wolves of the Tomb Mountain Pack, wearing collars and amulets provided by Carly, hit the panthers in a blur of teeth and claws.

A big-cat scream split the air as a huge brown wolf tore the throat from the panther who'd stood beside the alpha. Blood sprayed across the wall, splattering Nicole and me. She whimpered and squeezed her eyes shut. I recognized Jack by the color of his amulet and his size.

Sean pushed me back against the wall with his body and guarded me, facing the bloodbath in front of us. The wolves were bigger and outnumbered the panthers, but I soon realized the cats were quicker and more agile. Blood flew everywhere, splashing the pavement, the building wall, me, and Nicole—who was frozen in terror.

Two panthers teamed up against Ben, a tawny-brown wolf with dark ears and a white chest. As one attacked Ben head-on, the other jumped onto his back and sank his teeth into the wolf's neck. Ben yelped and whined, trying to throw the panther off his back while the other slashed its claws across his face.

"No," I breathed. I started forward, gripping my knife, but Sean growled and pushed me back. "Damn it, let me help!" I shouted. He snarled at me.

Jack, his coat dark with blood, took two long strides and leaped, hitting the panther on Ben's back hard enough to send the big cat flying. It landed on its feet, but Jack dropped right on top of it. He sank his teeth into the cat's neck and shook violently, nearly tearing its head off. More blood sprayed, and the panther screamed. When the panther was motionless beneath him, Jack raised his bloody muzzle and howled in triumph and rage. Sean responded with a howl of his own and several other wolves chimed in.

The entire pack was here, except for Karen, who was pregnant, and Delia, who waited nearby with Karen, awaiting either an all-clear or a signal that our attack had gone south and we needed backup.

The alpha panther tore free of the large gray wolf he was fighting, who I believed was Nan, and leaped at Sean with a vicious-sounding snarl. Sean met the alpha in midair with a snarl of his own that made the hair stand up on the back of my neck. The big cat was larger than any of the others. When Jack started to join the fight, Sean growled warningly, as if to say *This one's mine.* Jack backed away.

Sean and the alpha panther tore into each other with a level of viciousness that stunned even me. Jack noticed one of the panthers running away. He took off after it with a snarl, following it around the corner of the event building and out of sight.

With several of the panthers dead, Nan and her children, Felicia and David, came over to stand guard over me as Sean fought the alpha. Felicia was gray and white and David was black with gray on his chest. All three had bloody wounds, but nothing very serious.

Ben, John—a black wolf—and Thea, who was almost completely white, had what looked like the most severe injuries. They moved back and let Thea's mate Eddie, Nan's son David, and Karen's brother Patrick, who were all dark gray and black wolves, take the lead in fighting the remaining two panthers as Jack chased down the one who'd run.

The alpha panther screamed in anger and pain as Sean twisted around and sank his teeth into the cat's shoulder, tearing one of its front legs almost completely off. Now badly injured, the alpha was no match for Sean, who'd suffered several wounds but didn't seem to notice. Moments later, the alpha panther was dead. Sean stood over the corpse, raised his head, and howled. The pack responded in a chorus. He returned to my side, bloody and breathing hard, his eyes glowing bright gold.

I caught movement out of the corner of my eye and turned to see three figures wearing black hooded robes approaching from the direction of the warehouse that stored the winery's casks. For a moment, I thought it was Morgan and Bridget Clark and another of their coven. We hadn't told anyone outside the pack we were attacking the winery, however, so the Clarks wouldn't be here. These were different witches—maybe the ones who'd dumped me on the side of the highway.

With the last two panthers now dead, the wolves lined up between me and the witches. I didn't like that I had to stay back, but with no magic to defend myself and only an eight-inch blade as a weapon, I had to let the wolves do the heavy lifting.

As the witches approached, they flipped their hoods back. One was about sixty and gray-haired. The middle one, a blonde who looked to be about forty, had a large dark bruise on the right side of her face and a black eye. She glared at me. On her right stood a brown-haired girl of about twenty.

I didn't recognize any of them, but Nicole did. "Mrs. Talmadge?" she squeaked. I'd almost forgotten she was still behind me, cowering against the blood-splattered wall. "Mrs. Olsen? Why—"

She didn't get to finish her sentence. The older woman and the girl shouted something in Latin and threw small cloth bags at the line of wolves in front of me. I didn't think they had aimed at anyone in particular—perhaps the curses were meant for all of them, or as many as they could take out at once.

The little bags landed on the pavement in front of our wolves. The amulets hanging on their collars flared as Carly's magic sent the curses back to the witches who'd thrown them. It was Carly's strongest defensive spell, one she'd called *Return to Sender,* and its effect was instantaneous and devastating.

The oldest witch shrieked and doubled over, retching violently. The girl on the right let out an agonized scream. She collapsed, her arms and legs crumpling with the nauseating sound of bones shattering. The curse she'd thrown had apparently been meant to shatter the legs of the wolves, and Carly's protection amulets had cast it back on her.

As the blonde witch in the middle stepped back, the older woman gagged. Black snakes with strange red markings slithered out of her mouth, one after the other, then two at a time. She fell to her knees, choking and gagging, as the snakes poured out and writhed on the pavement around her. I retched. Nicole bent over and vomited.

The blonde witch started chanting in what sounded like Latin, but the snakes didn't stop pouring out until the gray-haired woman lay still. Meanwhile, the girl, who must have been Julianne, had lost consciousness. She and Mrs. Olsen had tried to inflict those horrible curses on Sean and his pack, so I didn't feel much sympathy for either of them.

Carly had warned the amulets we wore might not protect against more than one or two strong curses, but Kathleen Talmadge—if that was her real name—didn't know that. She ran for the large cask warehouse, leaving the others bloody and unmoving on the pavement.

Rather than chase her in wolf form, Sean startled me by shifting back to human. Ben, Nan, and Patrick followed suit, as if by some prearranged plan or a signal from Sean I didn't see.

To my surprise, Kathleen ran toward the side of the warehouse where there was no door. She threw open a door that appeared before our eyes and disappeared inside the building.

"What the hell?" Ben asked, staring. "You all saw that door appear out of nowhere, right?"

"I saw it," Sean said grimly.

"I recognized her voice," I told him, handing him the pair of drawstring pants I'd brought for him in my shoulder bag. "The witch who ran was the one who cursed me to walk."

He pulled the pants on and headed for the warehouse, barefoot. "Ben, Nan, come with Alice and me. Patrick, stay with Nicole and see if you can find out what happened to our tour group. The rest of you, keep watch for any more trouble."

The pack scattered to follow Sean's orders. Jack appeared from around the corner of the event building. Like Ben, Nan, and Patrick, he was nude and in human form. "I took care of that last panther," he told Sean, falling into step next to us as we ran for the door Kathleen had used. "I don't know where he was going, but I made sure he didn't get away."

"We're following the witch who cursed Alice to walk," Sean said as we reached the doorway. Beyond was a steep set of stone steps leading down into near darkness. "Nan and Ben, stay up here and watch our backs. Jack, you're with me and Alice."

He started down the stairs with me behind him and Jack at our rear. I could tell Nan and Ben didn't like staying behind but they did as Sean asked.

Jumbled fragments of memory surfaced as we slipped quietly and cautiously down the steps. The echoes of our footsteps on the stone stairs elicited a sick feeling in my stomach. I knew this place.

Halfway down, Sean growled. His eyes shone like golden lanterns in the near darkness. "I smell your blood," he told me. "On the stairs, and more up ahead. You said you remembered trying to escape and being thrown down some stairs. I think we've found where it happened."

I was breathing hard, and not as a result of running. "I remember these stairs. I remember landing at the bottom, and Kathleen laughing at me."

Sean snarled. Jack touched my shoulder, probably in an attempt to reassure me.

We reached the bottom of the steps and a wide stone hallway lined with heavy wooden doors. Kathleen was nowhere in sight.

"Watch out for bad magic," I said. "We don't know what kind of traps the witches or the sorcerer have waiting for us."

"Which is where this comes into play." Sean unhooked one of the amulets from the chain around his neck. "*Reveal*," he commanded, and tossed it ahead of us into the hall.

Carly's spell flared to life. The walls, floor, and ceiling shimmered, revealing bright red and black symbols and glyphs. The entire hallway was webbed with spells. Another growl came from Sean, this one frustrated.

"Shit," Jack said gruffly from behind us. "We don't want to walk into that."

I raised my knife. The runes along the blade glowed in the presence of the spells around us. "I've got this."

Sean held out his hand. "Let me."

"I had to watch you and everyone else fight the panthers," I reminded him. "Let me do *something*."

"I'll do it," Jack said, surprising me. "Sean needs to keep you safe and you're without magic."

If one more person reminded me I didn't have magic... I ground my teeth.

"I'm less vulnerable to attacks that might injure you," he added. "It's no reflection on you. You'll have your power back soon, and then you can go back to taking risks."

I sighed. Damn it, Jack was right. As a shifter, he was less likely than me to succumb to whatever magic was down here. I supposed just like

Sean, Jack's instincts told him I needed protection while I was vulnerable.

Reluctantly, I handed him the knife Carly had given me. She'd charged it with power with the help of her entire coven on the full moon, and she thought it would be able to cut through almost any black magic spellwork we encountered—at least, until its power ran out.

Jack pointed the tip of the athame at the ceiling, keeping it about an inch from the stone, and started walking. The spellwork in the hallway tore as the athame cut through it. The hair prickled on my arms. The red and black threads of magic disintegrated with pops and sizzles I could hear as well as see. We owed Carly big time for this.

Kathleen peered out of a doorway halfway down the hall and spotted Jack cutting the spellwork with the knife. Her eyes widened.

"I came back," I said. "And I brought friends."

She stared at Jack, then at me. "You killed my coven," she screamed. She brandished a spell bag.

"Don't throw that, unless you want to die here and now," Jack snarled, advancing on her with Sean and me in his wake. The knife slashed effortlessly through the spellwork, clearing a path for us. "Where is the sorcerer, witch?"

Kathleen paled. "I...I don't know," she stammered. "He's gone. He knew you were coming." She backed away from Jack, her face a mask of terror.

"How did he know?" I asked.

"He saw you last night," she said, her eyes still on Jack. "He knew you'd found the winery. He gave everyone the day off. That's why no one was here but the panther clan."

"Posing as the workers," I said, exchanging a glance with Sean. "Were they controlled by him?"

She raised her chin defiantly. "We serve him by choice."

"What about Nicole?"

She sneered. "She's an employee, nothing more. We had to stay open for tours. Someone had to lead the damn things."

As the rest of the spellwork in the hallway disintegrated, Jack pointed the knife at her chest. "Where are Alice's magic and memories?"

She cowered. "He has her memories in an amulet he's wearing." She pointed with a shaking finger at the double doors at the end of the hall. "Her magic is in there, in the sacred room. Spare my life and I'll tell you how to return it to her."

Sean moved fast. In a blink, he had Kathleen by the throat and pinned against the wall. "You laughed at Alice's suffering and cursed her to walk until she dropped dead," he snarled, his eyes glowing like golden suns. "You get no mercy from Alice, me, or anyone in my pack. Show us how to return Alice's magic and I'll make your death quick."

Her eyes went to Jack, as if hoping he'd intercede on her behalf, but he snarled at her. "Please," she rasped. "I had no choice. He would have killed me if I'd disobeyed."

Jack growled. "The *sorcerer* ordered you to curse Alice to walk until she died? Or did you decide to do that on your own?"

She whimpered and didn't answer.

Sean's hand tightened on her throat. "What is the sorcerer's name?"

"Miraç," Kathleen gasped. She dropped her little spell bag and pulled at Sean's arm with both hands, but his grip didn't loosen.

"Last name?" he demanded.

"I don't know, I swear." Her face turned red. "Full names have power. He never told us his." It sounded like truth.

Sean's eyes blazed. "Show us how to get Alice's magic out of here safely and return it to her, and I'll consider sparing you. If any of us so much as get a hair singed down here, your head comes off your shoulders. Do you understand?"

She nodded rapidly. "I swear, nothing will harm you here."

Sean released her, leaving red marks on her skin where he'd gripped her. I flinched, remembering the bruises I'd had on my wrists after the sorcerer dragged me across the field and through the vineyard back to this building.

"Show us where Alice's magic is," Sean ordered Kathleen.

She walked ahead of us. Jack stayed at her side, keeping the blade an inch from her ribs in case she tried to run or spell us.

All of the doors in the hallway were closed. We were halfway to the double doors at the end when Sean halted outside a door on the right. He ripped it off its hinges and tossed it aside before going into the room beyond.

"Wait," Jack ordered Kathleen. She backed against the wall, flattening her palms against the stone.

Leaving Jack to watch her, I followed Sean into the room. It was about twelve feet square, with stone floor and walls and a high ceiling made of heavy timbers. It contained a metal toilet and sink—the kind used in a jail cell—and a bed pallet on the floor. The bedclothes were dark with what I realized was dried blood. More stains darkened the wall near the bed and around a steel plate with a ring embedded in the floor.

Sean's snarl made the hair stand up on my neck. "This is your blood. This was your bed. Your *cell*. You were chained here. I smell your sickness and suffering." He ripped the bed pallet in half, throwing the pieces aside. "I smell Miraç here, and the witch too."

I picked up the torn sheets. They were stiff with dried blood. The smell made me sick.

Sean had been halfway to the door, but he came back and crouched beside me as I studied the blood-soaked sheets. "I have no memory of this," I told him. "Whatever happened in here, I don't remember it."

"I don't want you to," he said roughly, taking the sheets from me and crumpling them in his fist. "Damn it, I want you to get your memories back, but I don't want you to remember this. *Your blood is on the ceiling.*" It was almost a roar.

I touched his face, feeling his rage in the heat of his skin. "I survived it. I didn't break here. I don't know how I know that, but I do."

"I know." He touched his forehead to mine. "Once we have something of Miraç's—something he used in a ritual, or a personal item—someone will be able to track him. We'll find him, Alice. I swear it."

We rejoined Jack and Kathleen in the hall. Whatever Jack had said to her while we were in my cell, she was shaking in terror. I thought of my blood splattered on the ceiling in that cell and wondered what part she'd played in my torment beyond cursing me to walk until I died.

We passed another room that contained a large clawfoot tub in a circle inlaid in the floor. The tub sat in the center of an inverted pentagram. Tall black iron candleholders stood at each point of the pentagram.

I paused in the doorway. "I know this room. This is where they bathed me before they let me go."

"What was the purpose of that bath of blood and ashes?" Sean asked Kathleen. "To wash away the scent of this place and the traces of the magic used on her?"

Despite her fear, she glared at him. "Obviously."

Jack gave her a shove. "Keep walking."

When we reached the double doors at the end of the hall, Kathleen pushed them open, revealing a large room that must have stored casks of wine before Miraç turned it into a place to practice black magic and sorcery.

On one side of the room I saw a black magic witches' altar similar to the one Bridget and Morgan had used in Northbourne. This one had a goat skull and various bones, jars, and athames on it. Most of the room was taken up by an enormous iron cage. Inside the cage, the floor was scrubbed clean, but it was easy to guess it had once been covered with spellwork.

The cage contained another, much larger altar I assumed belonged to Miraç. The altar included, among other things, two human skulls, wooden boxes carved with glyphs, several daggers, animal teeth and claws, a half-dozen amulets, glass jars in various sizes—

—And a very fresh-looking human heart in a cast-iron bowl.

The sight of the heart froze me in my tracks. Nothing in this room seemed familiar, but that bloody organ and its container elicited a surge of something beyond natural revulsion. Something told me Miraç had left this heart for us to find.

"Whose heart is that?" I asked. I didn't recognize my own voice.

Kathleen's harsh laugh startled me. "You asked the same question of Miraç when he showed it to you. What difference does it make? The man is dead. He's dead because of you."

"That heart wasn't cut out two days ago," Sean snarled. "It's fresh."

"It's preserved with a spell, you dumb wolf," Kathleen snapped. "The sire kept it as a trophy, and because the heart of a broken man is powerful for magic. Now it's a gift for *her*." She jerked her chin at me.

Sean reached for her, but I blocked his arm. "Show us you have some trace of humanity, if for no other reason than to give us a reason to spare your life," I said.

She scoffed. "You won't let them kill me. You talk tough, but your heart's soft. I watched you beg Miraç to kill you to spare your ghost an eternity of servitude."

I went cold. Beside me, Sean growled low. I wondered if she was deliberately trying to bait us into killing her.

I stepped forward until we were nose-to-nose. "I have killed more people than you and Miraç combined," I said, my voice flat. "I commanded a storm and struck Moses Murphy's daughter with lightning because she threatened people who were strangers to me. Imagine what I would be willing to do to someone who tortured me, hurt people I care about, and cursed me to walk until I dropped dead. My love for my friends is not my weakness. It's what gets people like you and Miraç dead, and not in any particularly quick or merciful way. Murphy's daughter has been suffering for months, and I hope she lives that way *for years*."

She stared at me with wide eyes.

"Now," I said icily. "Tell me whose heart is in that bowl."

"His name was Rob," she said, lifting her shoulder in a half shrug. She was feigning indifference, but I'd rattled her. "I don't know his last name or where he was from."

Sean snarled. "Rob Hamlin."

The man from Chicago who'd been the real Alice Worth's boyfriend, who'd witnessed her death and showed up on my doorstep five years later looking for answers and an end to his grief. Sean had told me about him, and about my guilt over how I'd stolen Alice's identity. I couldn't grieve for Rob in the way I would have if I'd remembered him and what I'd done, but as I looked at the heart, my throat felt tight.

Kathleen continued talking, either oblivious to my reaction or enjoying it. "The sire used his lifeblood for spells and his heart in the rituals that took your magic and memories. We've been using his bones for our own magic." She gestured at a small bowl on the witch altar, containing what looked like finger bones. "Waste not, want not," she added, her voice dripping with sarcasm.

"Where is Alice's magic?" Sean demanded.

She smiled. "In an amulet. In the bowl, under the heart."

Jack snarled and jerked her by the arm. "Where's the trap? What's going to happen when someone picks up that heart?"

"No trap." She cowered away from Jack. "The spell on the heart will break when you pick it up and that's all."

"Why the hell did Miraç leave it behind?" Sean's eyes glowed. "If he wanted Alice's magic for power, why is it here? Why take her memories instead?"

"Because he couldn't use it. There was something strange about the magic, he said. He didn't tell me what. He couldn't take it into himself as he did with others he'd taken magic from. He tried to figure out how to use it, but then you found us and he had to leave it behind."

"But why leave it out for us?" I asked.

She shrugged. "He said you wouldn't be able to put it back, so it would be worse for you to see it."

"I don't buy it," Sean snapped. "It's a trap of some kind."

"It's not," she said harshly. "It's my only bargaining chip to stay alive. You need me to restore Alice's magic. If it's not what I say it is, I'm dead."

"Let's take the magic and her to the vamps," Jack told Sean. "They'll be able to tell if she's telling the truth."

Kathleen recoiled. "No, not vampires. They like drinking witch blood."

At this moment, I would have happily served Kathleen to the vampires myself. Sean was silent. I knew he didn't want to involve the Court, but if my magic was in an amulet like Kathleen claimed, I needed to know if it could be restored, and if she could be trusted to restore it. On the other hand...

"We don't need her," I said to Sean. "We can have the other witches restore my magic if what she says is true."

"They don't know the spellwork," Kathleen protested. "*I* do."

"They'll figure it out," Jack said. He hefted the dagger in his hand and eyed her like he was deciding where to stab.

She shrank back. "It might take them years. Do you have years to wait, or do you want her magic restored tonight?"

Sean turned to me, his expression grim. "Alice?"

"Let's go have a look at the bowl," I told him.

"Here—you may need this." Jack handed me the dagger and picked up one of the athames from the witch altar. "This one looks like it would work." He stared at Kathleen until she stepped back against the wall.

Dagger in hand, I headed for the open door of the cage. Sean told Jack to watch Kathleen and joined me as I entered the cage and headed for Miraç's altar.

As I got closer, I smelled the blood from the heart and saw several runes branded into it. I wanted to turn away from the altar and its gruesome contents, but I didn't. Not because of the amulet, but because I was the reason Rob Hamlin was dead. If I couldn't face that truth, I had no right to ever forgive myself for it.

"I'm sorry, Rob," I said softly. When the dagger's point got near the heart, spellwork shimmered and broke. The heart, no longer unnaturally preserved by the spell, turned black. The strong iron smell made me gag.

Sean touched my hand. "I'll pick it up."

"No, this one's my responsibility." I steeled myself and picked up the heart. It felt surprisingly heavy and rubbery, and a nauseating combination of sticky and slick with old blood.

Underneath, in the blood that had pooled and separated, were two items: my half of the wolf amulet and a round gold amulet with a glowing red crystal in the center.

Sean picked up the amulets. I worried they would be booby-trapped, despite Kathleen's assurances, but nothing happened. He set the bloody wolf amulet on the altar and held up the round one. The crystal pulsed with power even I could sense, despite the fact I had no magic.

"It feels like your magic, for whatever that's worth," Sean told me. "I recognize it."

Despite my skepticism, hope stirred. "Just a trace of my magic?"

He shook his head. "There is a *lot* of power in here. I suppose it could be a trick, though. This has all been much too easy."

I'd been thinking the same thing. I turned my back to Kathleen and lowered my voice. "It's rather convenient, isn't it, that Kathleen survived and offered to lead us to my magic in return for sparing her life? And that Miraç had to leave my magic behind when he took off?"

Sean spoke into my ear. "Very convenient. He left the witches and the panthers here to defend his lair, but his spellwork broke easily. I was under the impression a sorcerer's magic was extremely powerful."

"That probably means all of this is part of some kind of plan, or an elaborate trap." I gestured around us. "I don't—"

Magic burst from the crystal in a flare of purple lightning. Sean flinched but didn't drop the amulet. The power arced like electricity from frayed wires.

I turned toward Kathleen. "What the hell is going on?" I demanded.

She gave me a nasty smile. "I told you your freak magic was strange. It won't stay contained in the crystal. That stasis spell wasn't just protecting the heart—it was keeping the magic contained. Now it's fracturing the crystal and escaping. Once it's gone, it'll be gone for good and there'll be no putting it back."

And she hadn't told us that until after the stasis spell was broken. My grip tightened on the handle of the dagger.

Sean closed his fist around the amulet. If the leaking power hurt, he didn't show it. "What do you want to do?"

I put the heart back in the bowl and stared at the blood on my hand. I didn't want to rely on the Vampire Court's help to restore my magic and indebt myself further to them, but I needed my magic—needed it more with each passing hour. My power to defend myself and the people I cared about was inches away, in Sean's hand, and even if it meant owing the vamps, I was going to get it back.

"Call whoever we need to call to take care of the mess outside," I said. "Let's get some medical help for Julianne if she's still alive and send the others home, except for Jack and Nan. We'll go to Northbourne with Kathleen. I want my magic back. Then, when we've gotten what we've needed from her, maybe we can get her to tell us what Miraç's plan is and where we can find him."

He growled. "I'm looking forward to asking her." He wrapped both amulets in a cloth from the table beside the altar and handed them to me. "Let's go."

WITH MY MAGIC LEAKING OUT OF THE CRYSTAL AT AN ALARMING RATE, Sean ignored all speed limits on the way to Northbourne with Jack, Kathleen, and Nan in the back seat of his truck.

Unsurprisingly, Kathleen hadn't told us the whole truth about what it would take to restore my magic. On the way, she admitted she couldn't do the ritual by herself. We'd need two more black witches and a long list of ingredients—some of which were downright nasty. After we debated what to do, Sean sent the information ahead to Charles Vaughan and asked him to make the necessary arrangements with Bridget and Morgan Clark.

Sean left Ben in charge of the mess at Broken Ridge. Ben made a joke about being "middle management" and started making phone calls. Patrick had found the rest of our tour group in the event building, all unconscious. Ben said their wine had probably been drugged. They were all on their way to a local hospital in ambulances. Julianne was miraculously still alive. At Sean's request, Ben called the Supernatural and Paranormal Entity Management Agency, or SPEMA, to take custody of her, as well as Olivia Olsen's body and the contents of Miraç's lair. I wasn't sure what Nicole would do after the feds debriefed her, but I figured her days leading tours at Broken Ridge were over.

According to Ben, the Were Ruling Council was sending people to find out where the panther shifters had come from and why they'd served

Miraç. Once the Council representatives finished talking to the members of our pack, they would all be headed home.

Sean had collected several items from Miraç's altar and brought them with us, stuffed in a bag and stowed in the truck's tool box. Kathleen swore she had no idea where Miraç had gone, claiming he'd simply left her and the others there and vanished, along with my memories and Malcolm, stashed in amulets he wore.

We'd found Miraç's living quarters adjacent to the sacred room, but he'd burned its contents to ash before he left, leaving nothing we could use to find him. We hoped the items from his altar could be used to trace his whereabouts.

Using Sean's phone, I texted Carly on the way to Northbourne to let her know we were all right and to thank her again for both the dagger and the amulets that had protected our pack. I would have preferred to call, but with Kathleen in the vehicle listening, I didn't want her to know who'd provided those items.

Carly was relieved by how well her gifts had worked for us. She was surprised to hear the dagger had cut through all of the spellwork in Miraç's lair and the amulets had been able to repel both witches' powerful curses completely.

When I told her we were on our way to Northbourne to have my magic restored, there was a long pause before she responded.

Carly: Let me come to Northbourne. You need a witch at the ritual you can trust.

Me: I'll be all right. No need to get you more mixed up in this. The vampires will keep the witches in line. That was the theory, anyway.

Carly: Please, Alice. If one of these women harms you, I will never forgive myself. I can be there in about ninety minutes.

I showed Carly's text to Sean. "It's your decision," he murmured. "I vote yes."

I was reluctant to put Carly in any kind of danger, but Morgan and Bridget already knew she was involved. Carly had said she didn't fear them, and I knew she wouldn't walk into Northbourne without being able to defend herself. Those *Return to Sender* amulets had proven more than just how much power her magic had; they'd also demonstrated that though Carly wouldn't throw any curses, she had no trouble sending them back on those who cast them.

Finally, I replied to her text. *Me: We're about an hour from Northbourne. We'll meet you there. Thank you.*

Carly: I'll see you soon. Keep that dagger I gave you handy, just in case.

I touched the dagger. I'd returned it to the sheath on my forearm, hidden under my long-sleeved shirt. Its warmth was reassuring, as was its pointy end. I hoped I'd get a chance to use it on Miraç—wherever he was, the soulless bastard.

Most of our drive to Northbourne was silent. Jack exchanged a number of texts with someone I assumed was Delia. Meanwhile, Nan watched Kathleen like a hawk. Since Sean was driving—and at speeds that made me not want to look at the speedometer—I fielded texts from Ben and others on his behalf, updating us on the situation at the winery.

"How did you, Olivia, and Julianne end up serving Miraç?" I asked, turning in my seat to look at Kathleen.

She glared at me and didn't answer.

"Was it his power? Or did the three of you just get off on hurting people, same as him?"

She gave me a big smile. "Both."

There was clearly no point trying to find anything redeeming about her. I didn't know why I kept trying.

Sean's phone buzzed with an incoming message from Delia. *Is Jack all right?* she asked.

Puzzled, I held up the phone so Sean could see the message. He studied Jack in the rearview mirror, then gave me a nod. I texted back. *This is Alice, responding for Sean because he's driving. Sean says Jack seems fine.*

A long pause, then a reply from Delia: *Thank you.*

I took the amulets from my pocket and unwrapped them. Rob's blood stained the cloth and had dried on the amulets. I used the cloth to clean them, returned the wolf amulet to my pocket, and held the round one in my hand. The red crystal in the center pulsed against my palm, almost like a heart. It *was* my heart, in a way, if this truly was my magic stored inside. The purple magic flared occasionally, reminding me we were racing to get my magic restored before it broke free of the crystal and was lost. I held the amulet tightly in my fist, as if I could hold my magic in the crystal by sheer force of will.

The leaking power sizzled against my palm in little painful bursts. I'd hoped the tendrils of magic would return to me once they escaped the amulet, but they dissipated instead. Something about the spell Miraç had used must be preventing my magic from coming back to me on its own.

I tried not to get my hopes up too much that Kathleen, Bridget, and Morgan would be able to restore my magic. Kathleen might be lying about what was in the amulet, or about knowing the ritual needed. I didn't trust Bridget and Morgan at all, and I trusted Kathleen even less.

And then there was the very strong possibility—no, the certainty—this was part of Miraç's plan. Not our trip to Northbourne, but the rest of tonight's events felt orchestrated in a way that made me itch between my shoulder blades. I couldn't figure out what Miraç's endgame was, or why he'd want me to have my magic back after he'd stolen it in the first place. If I could indeed get my magic back, I figured I could deal with him when the time came, with help from my friends.

For now, we were headed for a vampire stronghold. I had three powerful werewolves with me and a witch on her way to back me up. Whatever Miraç's plan was, I doubted he'd try to attack us there.

Of course, that didn't mean he wouldn't try to attack us before we arrived.

Thirty minutes from Northbourne, Sean glanced at the rearview mirror and growled, his eyes bright gold. "Six motorcycles coming up behind us fast."

The others turned in their seats to look as I checked my side mirror. I caught the faint glint of moonlight reflecting off chrome. The riders weren't using headlights. Sean's vision was much better than mine.

Nan grabbed Kathleen by the throat. "What do you know about this?"

"Nothing!" she protested. "I don't know who's chasing us or why."

"I can guess why," Sean said, his voice harsh. He stepped on the gas and glanced at me. "This could get bad."

"I've got my seatbelt on," I told him. "Everyone else buckled in?"

Seatbelts clicked in the back seat. "Here they come," Jack warned. "Two on each side and two on our six."

Gunshots rang out and bullets thumped into the sides of the truck. Nan yelped.

Sean wrenched the steering wheel to the right. Something heavy hit on the passenger side near the truck bed. Sean had struck one of the bikes. He straightened the wheel and accelerated sharply as a series of light thumps from the bed of the truck indicated we'd been shot at several more times.

"One down," Jack reported. "The other five are still on us."

"Nan!" Sean's eyes flicked to the rearview mirror, then back to the side to watch for the motorcycles. "Are you hit?"

I twisted in my seat to look behind me. Nan held her right thigh. A dark stain was spreading on her jeans. "It's not silver," she said through clenched teeth. "It didn't hit anything important. I'll live." She picked up a towel from the floor, tore it into strips, and tied them tightly around her thigh.

More gunshots. My side mirror exploded as a bullet went through it. I bit back a yelp and ducked.

Sean swerved again, this time to our left, and hit another of the riders. As we accelerated away, a fireball erupted behind us. Two down.

Three heavy thumps in the bed of the truck. The vehicle jolted. "They jumped into the back!" Jack shouted.

Sean braked so hard my seatbelt bit into my shoulder and chest. Kathleen let out an abbreviated shriek as two huge black panthers tumbled over the roof and onto the hood of the truck. Sean swerved sharply. My head hit my window hard as the big cats fought to hang on, their claws scrabbling across the metal hood. He yanked the wheel back the other way and they flew off into the darkness.

The back window shattered. Screaming, Kathleen ducked and covered her head as pellets of glass rained into the back seat. Out of the corner of my eye, I caught sight of a large figure wearing a black helmet and riding leathers in the bed of the truck. Sean stomped on the gas pedal and sent the unwanted passenger tumbling.

Gun in hand, Jack stuck his arm out the back window. I clapped my hands over my ears, but that did little to muffle the deafening noise as he fired five shots at the figure in the truck bed. Sean shook his head rapidly, his face a mask of pain. Given I could hear almost nothing over the ringing in my ears, I could only imagine how much those shots had hurt the shifters' sensitive ears.

A motorcycle engine roared behind us. Jack unfastened his seatbelt and disappeared out the back window. Sean kept his speed and direction steady as Jack fired three more times.

I felt rather than heard multiple thumps from the truck bed, but I couldn't tell what happened to the one remaining attacker since I was mostly deaf. Jack climbed into the back seat and Sean sped up again, flooring it in the direction of Vamp HQ.

"The last one's down," Jack said, his voice barely audible over the ringing in my ears. "I tossed the dead one out."

"Good work, Jack." Sean looked over at me. "Are you all right? You hit your head on the window."

I gingerly touched the side of my head. "Just a bump." My voice sounded tinny. "Good driving."

A large dark shape hit my window with a muffled thump, then disappeared into the night. I jumped. "What the hell was that?"

Sean stared disbelievingly out the windshield. "You've *got* to be kidding me."

Dozens of huge black birds descended from the darkness to batter the truck on all sides. Screeching, they slammed into the windows and doors, flapped their wings in front of the windshield, and stared at us through the glass with glowing red eyes. The noise of their bodies hitting the truck became deafening.

Jack and Nan fought to keep birds from getting in through the broken back window, but it was a losing battle against so many attackers. As Sean tried to keep us on the road, Jack resorted to killing the birds that got in and throwing them back out the window.

One got past him and attacked Sean, causing the truck to swerve violently. I grabbed it and yelped as its beak gouged my arms. I turned and shoved it into Jack's hands so he could get rid of it. Black feathers, stabbing beaks, and glowing red eyes covered the entire windshield. It would only be a matter of time before the triple-damned things cracked it.

The truck swerved again violently. "Damn it, I can't see!" Sean attempted to use the windshield wipers to frighten the birds away, but they redoubled their attack on both the wipers and the glass.

Out of the corner of my eye, I saw Kathleen cut her hand with a tiny broken bone she must have taken from one of the dead birds. "What are you doing?" Nan demanded.

"Saving us," Kathleen snapped. She smeared bird blood across her palms, mixing it with her own, then drew a circle and a rune in the blood.

She clapped her hands together. "*Avis Fractus!*"

With a sickening crunch, the bird in Jack's hands went still, its neck twisted. Dead birds fell on and around the truck in a macabre hailstorm of avian corpses, all with their necks broken. The blood-smeared windshield cleared as our attackers died and rolled off the hood. Sean accelerated sharply, and within moments we saw no more birds.

With a grunt of disgust, Jack threw the dead bird out the back window. "I suppose we should thank you."

Kathleen took a wet wipe from a package in the pocket on the back of my seat and cleaned her hands. "I didn't want your alpha to kill us by crashing into a tree." Her shaky tone didn't quite match the defiance of her words. She must have been as rattled by the attacks as we were.

Sean checked the rear view mirror. "Nan?"

"Still alive and kicking." Her voice was strained. "I'll need this bullet taken out soon."

"We'll get it taken care of." He glanced back at me. "Ask Ben to let the Council know about the panthers and birds that attacked us. Tell Vaughan we need an ambulance to meet us at—"

"I'm not leaving when Alice needs me," Nan cut in. "You can give me a painkiller and cut the bullet out at Northbourne."

"I'm fine, in case anyone was wondering," Kathleen said, crossing her arms over her chest.

"I'd be more comfortable if you went to the hospital," Jack said, ignoring Kathleen.

Sean met Nan's eyes in the mirror. "I agree with Jack, but it's your call," he said. "You know it's going to hurt if we do it ourselves."

"I know." Her tone made it clear the discussion was over. "How much farther?"

Sean checked his GPS. "About fifteen minutes."

I found bloody feathers in my hair. Ick. "Why attack us?" I asked. "Why leave us the amulet, then sic the panthers on us again? And then the birds? I don't understand."

"Because we have *her*," Jack said, meaning Kathleen. "She wasn't supposed to survive our attack. You were never supposed to be able to get your magic back, Alice, but now you might because of her. He clearly doesn't want us to get to Northbourne."

Sean touched my leg. "How's the amulet doing?"

I opened my hand. A tiny crack, no bigger than a hair, had appeared on the face of the crystal, emitting little puffs of energy. Purple magic pulsed in the fissure.

My stomach knotted. I looked up at Sean. "We're running out of time."

THE MOMENT WE ARRIVED AT NORTHBOURNE, THE VAMPS HUSTLED US downstairs. They took Kathleen to the black witch room while Sean, Jack, Nan, and I stayed next door in an unused mage workshop. Adri Smith stayed in the room with the witches while they discussed the ritual and hashed out their respective roles.

Getting Bridget and Morgan to agree to work with Kathleen had apparently taken some persuading. I didn't know what the vamps had to promise them, but given the parties involved, I was sure it had to be something substantial.

Nan had lost a lot of blood by the time we arrived. Bryan Smith, Charles Vaughan's head of security, offered to get the bullet out and patch her up, but she declined. Jack brought in the first aid kit from Sean's bullet-riddled truck and disappeared into the little bathroom with Nan.

My ears were still ringing, but not nearly as badly now. "You can go in there with them," I told Sean as we stood in the workshop area of the suite. "She could probably use some of your comfort right about now. I'll be fine in here."

Sean shook his head. "She said I shouldn't leave you alone under any circumstances. We don't know who else Miraç might be controlling." He closed his hand around mine, with the amulet held tight inside both our hands. "It's going to be difficult for me to let these witches perform a black magic ritual on you, even if it's to restore your magic." His eyes glowed.

"I know. If the situation were reversed, I'd feel the same way."

He kissed my temple. "You would?"

"I would." I smiled. "Funny how—"

I didn't get to finish my sentence. Magic surged inside my chest, like when Sean spoke to my wolf on the patio yesterday evening. This time I hurt like claws were digging into my guts and pulling. The pain made my knees buckle.

Sean caught me. "Alice!"

I dropped the amulet with a hoarse cry. Something shoved me aside inside my own head. My vision went gold around the edges and my eyes felt hot. "*Dying*," I heard myself say. The word was a growl, and the voice was not mine.

"Damn it," Sean ground out. His eyes turned bright, pure gold. A powerful wave of comfort wrapped around me.

My wolf slashed at it with her claws. "*No time*," she snarled.

"If you die, will Alice die?" Sean asked.

"*May die. Need magic now*," my wolf growled. She was fading fast. This last burst of anger had taken all she had.

"We have to save her," I whispered to Sean. "Please, don't let her die."

The door of the workshop swung open, revealing Charles Vaughan and Bryan Smith. Vaughan's expression was unreadable. If he understood what had just happened and what it meant, I couldn't tell.

Sean picked up my amulet and pressed it into my hand. He looked at Vaughan. "We can't wait any longer. The witches have got to be ready."

"Carly Reese has arrived," Vaughan told us. "She is on her way down. Come with us."

Sean set me on my feet and steadied me with a hand on the small of my back. Jack emerged from the bathroom. "Nan needs to rest for a few minutes," he told Sean. "What do you want us to do?"

Nan appeared in the doorway, pale and unsteady. She had apparently already shifted and re-dressed. "I'm good. Just give me a chair to sit in." She took a step and stumbled. "And maybe someone to lean on."

Jack offered her his arm. We followed Vaughan and Bryan down the hall.

The door of the black witch room opened as we approached, revealing Adri. "They're about ready," she told Vaughan. "They say it's all right to come in."

We filed in. Apparently just because Bridget and Morgan had agreed to do the ritual with Kathleen didn't mean they weren't salty about it. The level of hostility in the room was rivaled only by the smell of the ingredients they'd collected for the ritual.

Bridget and Morgan, wearing their long, hooded cloaks, prepared something at the altar. Crouched in the circle, Kathleen drew glyphs and runes with chalk on the floor around a heavy wooden chair someone had placed in the center of the inverted pentagram. I took a deep breath and gripped my amulet.

Jack helped Nan to a chair by the work table on the other side of the room. Bryan closed the door to the hall and stood in front of it. Adri and Vaughan waited beside Sean and me.

Kathleen rose. "Take off your shoes and come sit. Bring the amulet."

"Would it kill you to say 'please'?" I muttered, toeing off my shoes.

Sean squeezed my hand. I squeezed back, then padded barefoot to the circle, stepping carefully over and around the symbols on the floor. I sat in the chair, placing my feet in the small circles in front of the chair legs.

Just as I got settled in, someone knocked on the door. Bryan opened it. He bowed and stepped aside.

Kathleen dropped her chalk. Bridget and Morgan turned and stared.

Three women strode into the room, wearing emerald green hooded cloaks. It took me a full two seconds to realize the woman in front was Carly. I'd only seen her twice since my return from Miraç's lair, and both times she'd been in her home, dressed for comfort.

Tonight, she was someone completely different, and for the first time I truly realized who Carly was: not just my friend and ally, but the High Priestess of her coven. She dressed to impress in a white, off-the-shoulder blouse with a silver bustier over it, a long, gauzy, white skirt with silver threads, and silver-accented sandals. A silver diam with a moonstone held her hair away from her face. Around her neck, she wore a silver chain that held a vial of what appeared to be ash and a pentagram with a compass rose in the center. Runes drawn with henna covered her hands and arms.

Her companions wore similar clothing and jewelry. When they all flipped their hoods back, the pink hair of the young woman on Carly's left drew my gaze. She held her chin high and stared straight ahead. The woman on Carly's right was older, her hair graying and expression cold. Carly and her coven sisters represented a triple threat, in more ways than one.

"Welcome to Northbourne, Ms. Reese," Vaughan said, echoing Bryan's bow. He inclined his head toward the other two women. "Ms. Clark, Ms. Long. We are honored by your presence."

Carly gave him a regal nod. "Mr. Vaughan. Thank you for your hospitality."

Bridget glared daggers at Carly, who seemed unruffled by her hostility. "Why are you here?"

"I'm here on behalf of my friend, Alice." Carly gave me a smile, which disappeared when she turned back to Bridget. "I am balance. You bring darkness; we bring light. You bring blood; we bring air. You bring suffering and death." She gestured at her companions. "We bring healing and life."

"Still sanctimonious, I see," Morgan said snidely. "And vindictive. You dragged my daughter Katrina here."

At Carly's nod, the girl with pink hair responded. "It's Katy now, and I volunteered." She met her mother's angry glare with a flat stare. "Alice needs protection from black magic curses. Who better to help her than Carly, Ellen, and me?"

"You don't belong with *them*," Bridget told her granddaughter, her voice icy. "You belong with your family."

"My family turned their back on me a long time ago. Carly and my new coven are my family now."

Morgan flinched, but Bridget's eyes narrowed. "You're an ungrateful little girl."

If Bridget's words hurt her, Katy didn't let on. She glanced at Carly. "Do you want me to look over the spellwork?"

"Yes, please," Carly told her. "Thank you."

As Katy came over to examine the runes and glyphs Kathleen had drawn, Carly and Ellen went to the altar, where Bridget and Morgan were preparing the ingredients for the ritual.

Kathleen had recovered from her surprise at Carly's arrival and reclaimed her chalk. "Who are you?" she demanded as Katy studied the spellwork around my chair.

"Katy of the Emerald Star Coven." She frowned and bent to get a closer look at a glyph. "Is this the sigil *gedur*? In this combination, with *medon*, it will chain any energy released into the circle."

Kathleen made the mistake of trying to look down her nose at Katy. "That's the point, child—to keep the magic from escaping before we can return it to its owner."

Katy straightened. I caught a flash of bright white around her hands and smelled something like burned paper. "Call me *child* again," she said softly.

You can take the girl out of the black magic coven, but can you take the black magic coven out of the girl? I wondered.

Carly said nothing. She was studying the items on the altar, but she was listening to Katy's conversation with Kathleen. She let Katy fight her own battle, but was ready to intervene if it became necessary.

"If you chain the energy, that chain stays even when the energy transfers to its host," Katy said while Kathleen glared at her. "Which would mean your spells here would be chained to Alice."

"Only until we knew for certain she could contain that much power," Kathleen argued. "It's a safeguard."

Katy pointed at the circle around my chair. "That will contain her magic and protect us until she gains control. You don't need the chain."

Sean snarled. Talk of chains had apparently made him angry. "Get rid of that chain spell, *right now*."

Katy removed the offending spell with a wet cloth, then checked the rest of Kathleen's work as Carly supervised what Morgan and Bridget did with the ingredients at the altar.

Finally, when the preparations were complete, Carly came to stand outside the circle. "I'm here to help protect you," she told me. "As far as we can tell, they've prepared a spell that will return your magic to you. I can't give you any charms to protect against black magic or even against harm, because this ritual is black magic and will cause you harm, but if anyone deviates from the ritual in any way or does anything suspicious, we're ready to intervene."

"What do you mean, this ritual will harm her?" Charles Vaughan demanded.

"It's a ritual based on the practice of sorcery and diablerie—magic based on demonic or infernal power. There should be little physical harm done, but it will hurt." She turned back to me, her expression sympathetic. "You might not remember the agony of having your magic torn out of you, but it will hurt just as much to have it put back."

"If I survived having it taken out, I can survive this too," I said, echoing my words to Sean in my cell at the winery.

"I can take her pain." Sean joined Carly at the edge of the circle. "I've done it before."

"Not this time," Carly said gently. "Not with this kind of magic. Just be here for her when it's finished."

"We can use him for more than just emotional support," Kathleen said. "We need a heart to anchor the spellwork."

Jack was at Sean's side in a blink, Nan right behind him. I was on my feet before I realized I had moved. "The hell you will," I said.

"We don't have to cut out his heart," Bridget snapped, as though we were all insufferably stupid.

"Though I'd prefer that," Kathleen added. "But no, for the purposes of this ritual, we don't need a freshly harvested heart. We do, however, need to know...does this woman have your heart?"

Sean locked his eyes on mine. "Yes, she does." He said it without hesitation, in front of a dozen witnesses. I promised myself that regardless of what happened here tonight, I would never forget it.

Kathleen indicated the bottom point of the inverted pentagram. "Then come stand here."

Sean went to the point and stood straight, his eyes on me.

"If you hurt him, I'll kill you," I promised the witches.

"It won't be anywhere near as bad as what you're going to go through," Kathleen said. She sounded much too pleased by that.

Claws ripped at my insides again, reminding me my wolf was dying while we stood here talking. I dropped back into the chair and took a ragged breath.

Everyone stared at me with varying levels of alarm. "Got some wicked heartburn," I said, my voice shaky. "Nothing to worry about."

"What's wrong with you?" Bridget demanded. "If there's a problem, we have to know. It might affect the ritual."

"There's nothing wrong." If I was going to tell a complete lie, I might as well do it sitting in the middle of an inverted pentagram. "Let's get this show on the road."

Morgan picked up the silver tray and followed Bridget into the circle. "Take off your shirt," Bridget told me. "We need to paint runes on your chest."

I took off my long-sleeved shirt and handed it to Bridget, who passed it to Nan. I took off my knife sheath and my tank top, wrapped the top around the knife, and handed them over. Sean clearly didn't like how vulnerable I looked without a shirt on. I gave him what I hoped was a reassuring smile, but his frown only deepened.

Kathleen brought over some strips of black cloth. "We have to tie you to the chair."

"No, you don't." I gripped the arms of the chair. "I stayed standing while Bridget stabbed me in the chest with a foot-long silver needle. I can take whatever you're going to do if I'm sitting down."

"You may try to run from the pain," she argued. "You did last time."

Sean growled. I stared up at her. "Did I try to run from the pain, or from what Miraç was doing to me?" I looked over at Bridget. "Just do it."

Bridget closed the circle around us with an invocation similar to the one she'd used the last time I was here, closing me inside with Sean, Morgan, Kathleen, and herself.

Carly, Katy, and Ellen took up positions around the circle, watching every move the three black witches made. Each of them had something concealed in their hand. I couldn't see what they held—maybe spell bags. I assumed the spells were in case one of the black witches tried something. Carly's lips moved, as though invoking her own goddess to protect us.

Bridget picked up a small iron bowl from the tray. From where I sat, I couldn't see what it contained—which was just as well, I supposed, because the smell made my eyes water and my stomach churn.

Kathleen took a dagger from the tray and cut her hand over the bowl, squeezing her fist to make the blood run more freely. As it ran into the bowl, she chanted in a language I didn't recognize.

I focused on breathing deeply and evenly and didn't look at Sean. I didn't have to see his face to know he and his wolf hated every moment of this. I was more or less at the mercy of black witches who'd made it very clear my value began and ended with the money they were getting from the Court for helping me.

Kathleen said something in that same strange language and spat into the bowl. Bridget and Morgan followed suit. Kathleen stirred the contents of the bowl three times counter-clockwise with her index finger, then took it from Bridget and brought it over to me.

She used her finger to paint a rune on the center of my chest, over my sternum. It was a circle ringed with V-shaped runes, each with one straight leg and one curved. In the center, she drew three additional runes. The sight and smell of the gray-green sludge she used to paint made me acutely nauseated. I thought I'd be grossed out by the spit, but as it turned out, saliva was least-worst ingredient in the bowl.

When she finished, all six witches in the room studied the spellwork on my skin—though for very different reasons. Carly and her coven sisters were checking to make sure Kathleen hadn't added any spells they didn't recognize, and Bridget and Morgan were no doubt learning the spellwork for their own purposes.

When no one voiced either a question or an objection, Kathleen crouched and pressed her bloody hand on a glyph in front of me—the one connected with a thick chalk line to the point of the inverted pentagram where Sean stood.

She glanced up at him. "Speak your heart."

He met my eyes with his own glowing ones. "I love you," he said.

The spellwork in the circle ignited, pulsing red. Sean jerked but didn't stagger or fall. Bright golden shifter magic ran down his legs to the point of the pentagram. The line connecting the point where he stood to the glyph in front of me shone gold.

Kathleen rose and held out her hand to me. "The amulet."

To say I didn't want to hand it over would have been an understatement. I opened my hand and stared at it, watching the purple magic pulsing in the crack in the crystal—the crack that had only minutes before been the width of a hair, but was now several times larger. This magic was *mine*, and it meant more to me than anything else except the man standing at the point of the pentagram who'd unconditionally given me his heart. If I didn't hand it over, however, I would end up losing Sean, or he would lose me. I didn't know how I knew that, but I did. I needed my magic.

So I put the amulet in Kathleen's outstretched hand, gripped the arms of my chair, and raised my chin.

She took a dagger from Morgan's tray. The blade was black, about eight inches long and jagged on one edge. The other edge was lined with runes. Unlike the ceremonial athame she'd used to invoke the circle around us, it looked sharp enough to cut anything it came into contact with.

Kathleen contemplated the blade. "I served Miraç for nearly twenty years. In that time, I watched him kill dozens of strong mages for their magic. Yours is the only magic he couldn't bend to his will. Despite how you attacked him and how you almost escaped, you are the only mage he let live. I think he even feels something for you, and he's felt nothing for anyone in a century."

I started to get a bad feeling about the way she studied the dagger.

"Why are you so special, Alice Worth?" she demanded. "Why you and not me?"

Everyone but Bryan, who was guarding the door to the hallway, converged on the circle. Charles Vaughan's eyes were solid black. Carly,

Katy, and Ellen readied themselves. Sean growled. Jack leveled a cold stare at Kathleen, his anger nearly palpable.

Bridget took a step closer to Kathleen, her own dagger in her hand. "Finish the ritual," she said. "The power we've invoked won't last more than a few more minutes."

"Finish what we came here to do," Jack ordered her. "No more stalling. No games."

Kathleen drove the point of the knife into the tiny crack in the crystal. "*Exsolvo ex capio.*"

The crystal ruptured in a flare so bright it hurt my eyes. My magic erupted from the crystal and flowed directly into the dagger until it glowed. The sheer power of the magic prickled on my skin in a sensation that was strangely familiar.

When the crystal went dark, Kathleen discarded the amulet onto Morgan's tray. She moved in front of me, the tip of the knife pointed at my sternum. The air was so heavy with tension from the witches, werewolves, and Vaughan that I almost couldn't breathe.

Kathleen smiled at me. "*Mea.*" Mine.

She reversed her grip on the dagger and aimed it at her own chest. She was trying to steal my magic. I didn't see how she could if the sorcerer couldn't, but clearly she was willing to try—and if she failed, my magic was likely to be released from the dagger and be gone forever.

Sean couldn't move—he was anchoring the power in the circle. Maybe that was why Kathleen had chosen him for that role. The others were outside the circle, unwilling to break it and risk releasing the power it contained.

Bridget stabbed Kathleen in her shoulder and twisted the magic-infused dagger away from her. As Kathleen screamed in pain and rage, Bridget handed me the dagger hilt first. "The word is *remigro*," she said.

Before I had a chance to be afraid, I wrapped both hands around the handle and plunged the knife into the center of the circle on my chest. "*Remigro!*" I shouted.

The blade's heat was like being stabbed with a fragment of the sun. I screamed. My head fell back against the high back of the chair and my vision went dark.

The room erupted in shouts, growls, and cursing. All that noise vanished, swept away by the roar of my magic pouring out of the dagger into that cavernous empty space in my chest. It filled almost instantly.

The magic then filled the rest of my body, spreading from my center out to my fingertips and toes. My world turned green and white, with pulsing swirls of black, red, and purple, and traces of gold and blue. The pressure built until my skin felt stretched to the point of bursting.

I felt every inch of the dagger buried in my chest. It hurt worse than I could have imagined. It seemed impossible that I wasn't dead. *Possible and impossible are not useful concepts when magic is involved*, Valas had said.

Gradually, the deafening roar in my ears and the agony of the dagger and my magic returning became the kind of discomfort that accompanied an early morning stretch: pain mixed by a sense of deep contentment and pleasure. My magic was *home*. I was whole again, or nearly so. In the past few days, I'd almost become accustomed to the emptiness and broken feeling left behind by having my magic stolen, but now I had it back. It was *mine*, and so help me, no one would ever take it from me again.

I became aware some of my magic had escaped my body and was thundering within the circle Kathleen had inscribed around my chair. I thought perhaps the floor beneath me might be shaking as well, but I couldn't see or hear anything beyond my own head. I drew my magic into my body as if taking a deep breath. It took a great deal of effort, but finally the power settled into my cells. My entire body hummed. The roar in my ears faded and my vision slowly cleared.

Deep inside my head, two golden eyes stared back at me. My wolf rose and stretched, her body strong and full of magic again. My back arched as she moved. When she settled down and slipped back into the shadows in my mind, I slumped in the chair and took a deep breath that turned into a sigh.

"Alice." Sean's voice called me back to reality.

I opened my eyes and found myself looking into Sean's bright golden gaze. The magic in the circle was gone, either burned up or released by Bridget. All the books from the shelves on the other side of the room lay strewn across the floor and furniture was overturned. I wondered if my magic had shaken the entire building, or just this room. Everyone was staring at me, but the person I cared most about was inches away, his hands on the arms of my chair as he gazed into my eyes.

The dagger was still buried in my chest. I pulled it out. It slid out with only a tiny sizzle of pain. Blood stained the blade and my chest, but not much. The wound closed before my eyes, leaving a white line on my breastbone. I knew I would carry that scar for the rest of my life.

The dagger was inert in my hand. None of my magic remained in its blade or handle.

"Alice?" Sean asked again, more forcefully this time.

"I'm good," I told him. And for the first time since my return from captivity, it was true.

That's when I noticed what lay on the floor beside us. At first I couldn't tell what it was. I looked closer and saw bones, organs, and bloody flesh, tangled in a black hooded robe. A silver dagger glinted somewhere in the pile. There was so much blood, it covered the floor around us. Over the stench of death, I smelled the same musty odor I'd smelled in Miraç's lair. Bile rose in my throat.

Bridget's hands were bloody. "What did you do?" I asked. My voice was hoarse. Had I been screaming, or was it only a reaction to the nightmarish sight in front of me?

"I didn't do this." Bridget looked pale. Whatever had happened to Kathleen while I was consumed by my magic's return to my body, it had rattled them all. "I stabbed her to prevent her from stealing your magic, but I most certainly did not...did not..." She seemed at a loss for words.

"Turn her inside out?" I suggested. "Then who the hell did?"

"She betrayed the sorcerer," Morgan suggested. She'd put the tray on the altar and stood off to the side, her arms wrapped around herself. "She tried to steal your power. He punished her."

"But how did he know?" Carly demanded. She leaned on Ellen Long, who supported her with an arm around her waist. Belatedly, I noticed the warm parchment scent of Carly's magic. She must have done something to protect the rest of us when the sorcerer killed Kathleen, and it had left her weakened. "How did he know what took place in this room? Our wards should have prevented it."

No one had an answer to that question.

My feet were in Kathleen's blood. I didn't know what she'd done before tonight, but it was hard to believe she'd deserved this ending. Punishment, certainly. Death, maybe. But this...this was inhuman. Then again, sorcerers were not human.

While we reeled in shock, Miraç was out there somewhere, planning and plotting and killing his way toward his goal. Kathleen might have known Miraç's plans, but she was dead. We'd have to figure out what was going on ourselves. I had my magic back. That was a good start.

"Now what?" Sean asked me.

"I'd like to see Valas." I glanced down at myself. "Right after I take a very hot shower."

29

BY THE TIME I EMERGED FROM THE BATHROOM, CLEAN AND WEARING Court enforcer black, employees of the Court were busy cleaning up in the main room. I thanked Carly and promised to come see her soon, and she departed with Katy and Ellen. Katy left without looking back at Morgan or Bridget. If Morgan was upset about that, she didn't let on. She and Bridget focused on packing up their altar, once Bridget had reclaimed her dagger from the mess that had once been Kathleen Talmadge.

I'd thought Valas would want to speak to me privately, but Vaughan informed us the head of the Court wished to speak to Sean, Jack, and Nan as well. I certainly didn't want to discuss certain things, especially our agreement, in front of the others, but maybe she wanted to hear from each of us what had taken place tonight at the winery. Once that was done, I'd try to get a private audience, and then I'd see if with my magic I could somehow figure out where Malcolm was.

We followed Vaughan, Bryan, and Adri down the hall and up several flights of stairs. Even with the knife wound healed, my chest ached like someone had stomped on it. The sensation of magic sizzling on my skin and throughout my body made the pain seem distant.

Back on the main level, they led us down several wide hallways to a long gallery that ran along the back of the building. I thought we would be taken to a meeting room, but to my surprise Vaughan led us through a set of French doors to an enormous terrace.

Beyond the terrace were Northbourne's spectacular gardens. The centerpiece was a long rectangular reflecting pool with fountains and a sculpture of a huge dragon in the middle. Exquisitely maintained flowerbeds, low walls, grassy areas, and a dozen statues of various mythical beasts ran the length of the pool on either side. On the far end of the pool, I saw the entrance to a vast maze. The view from the terrace took my breath away. I could well imagine vampires hosting elegant parties out here in the moonlight.

At the moment, however, only two people waited at the foot of the steps leading to the garden: Valas, in a black pantsuit, and the guard Vaughan had called Hanson.

Valas watched us cross the terrace and descend the steps. Her gaze moved from one face to the next, studying each of us.

When we reached the lawn, Vaughan bowed. "Madame Valas, may I present Ms. Alice Worth, Mr. Sean Maclin, Mr. Jack Hastings, and Ms. Nanette Lowell?"

"Thank you, Charles." Valas inclined her head toward me. "It would seem the ritual was successful, after a fashion. You look more like yourself, Miss Worth." I couldn't decide if she was pleased or disappointed by that.

"I'm happy to have my magic back," I told her. "Thank you for the Court's assistance in restoring it."

"We are pleased to offer assistance. I hope to see your memory restored as well." Her eyes went to Sean. "Mr. Maclin, you are to be commended for your pack's success during the raid on the vineyard, though I feel you might have included the Court in your plans." Displeasure darkened her tone.

Sean gave her a formal bow, though his eyes glowed with anger. "This was a matter for the pack, Madame Valas, not for the Court. We needed to find answers about Alice's disappearance. And we did, though not everything is sorted out quite yet."

"Apparently not, but soon, perhaps." With that cryptic comment, she turned to Jack. "Mr. Hastings, welcome to Northbourne. It is your first visit, is it not?"

"It is," Jack said. "I'm here to help ensure Alice's safety."

"Very admirable." Finally, she greeted Nan. "And Ms. Lowell. Thank you for accepting my invitation to meet. Your wound has healed?"

"Yes, it has, thank you." Nan still wore her bloody jeans, but if the sight and smell of the blood affected either Vaughan or Valas in any way, I couldn't see it.

Valas turned back to me. "Now your magic is restored, I am sure you are anxious to continue your search for your missing memories."

"Very much so," I told her.

"And you have no inkling of where this Miraç has gone?"

"None at the moment, unfortunately."

She studied me. "I believe you speak the truth," she said finally. "Interesting."

I blinked, confused. Sean's brow furrowed. "Was there some reason you suspected Alice of lying?" Anger made his voice sharp.

Valas glanced at Vaughan. "Would you excuse us?"

He gave her a deep bow. "As you wish, Madame Valas. Call on us if we are needed." He gave me a half-bow. "Alice."

"Mr. Vaughan," I said.

A slight frown creased his forehead, as though my refusal to use his first name angered and puzzled him. After a last glance at me, he and his security escorts climbed the steps and disappeared back inside Northbourne.

When the doors closed behind them, I said, "Madame Valas, I wondered if I might have a word with you in private."

"We shall certainly speak, but other matters must be resolved first." Valas clasped her hands in front of herself.

Something prickled on the back of my neck. I spun around and caught sight of a strange shimmer in the air, as if an invisible wall or veil had formed between us and the building. The veil grew to encircle the entire garden around us.

Sean put himself between Valas and me. His eyes glowed. "What the hell is this?"

"It is a reckoning, though not the one I had expected." Silver rings appeared in her eyes. "I must face my past, Mr. Maclin, as we all must do, and I do not wish us to be disturbed."

Sean snarled. "Get rid of that barrier *right now*, Valas."

Jack touched my shoulder. Something warm passed from his fingertips into me and settled over me like a heavy blanket. I found myself rooted in place, my hands at my sides. I tried to move, to speak, to warn Sean, but my muscles and my mouth wouldn't obey.

Jack leaned close, his lips a millimeter from my ear. "*Little wolf*," he murmured. His voice was a strange blend of two voices: Jack's, and another I recognized from my nightmare of running through the vines.

A wave of darkness rose inside me. I fought back, pushing against it with all my might, but it was too deeply rooted within me and too powerful.

At the last moment, I gave up fighting the dark magic and focused everything I had on one word. I grabbed onto the faint, comforting warmth of Sean's golden magic and screamed in my head. *SEAN!*

That was the last coherent thought I had for a very long time.

30

SEAN

A CRY OF ALARM FROM ALICE MADE SEAN TURN TOWARD HER BEFORE HE realized he had heard her not with his ears but with his mind. She stood behind him, frozen, her eyes wide.

Jack touched Sean's shoulder and Nan's. "*Stay,*" his beta commanded, his voice a strange blend of two distinct voices and resonant with dark magic.

An invisible force slammed into Sean and drove him to his knees. Nan went down at the same time, landing in the grass on his right. Foul-smelling black magic crushed them both to the ground.

His ribs cracked as he fought to rise. Beside him, Nan growled and let out a short whine as her own ribs and one of her arms broke under the crushing weight. Sean's wolf snarled and added his own strength, but the power holding him down felt as heavy as a building.

He managed to turn his head, expecting to find Alice on the ground on his other side. Instead, she was still standing, frozen in place. Her eyes were fixed on Valas, her expression vacant. Something or some*one* had taken control of her.

Sean's vision went gold. His wolf shoved forward, attempting to force him to shift. The same crushing weight stifled the attempt to shift. The wolf pushed repeatedly, but the spell clamped down harder. The agony barely registered over the force of his rage.

Jack moved into Sean's line of sight. He faced Valas, his hands at his sides, his expression calculating. As his wolf paced in anger, Sean sensed something through his pack bond with Jack that had not been there only minutes before: a dark, almost nauseating wrongness that made him think of death and decay. Beside him, Nan gasped. She'd felt it too.

The clues fell into place at lightning speed: Jack disappearing for a few minutes when he chased the panther at the winery; Miraç's spellwork disintegrating easily as Jack walked down the hallway; Kathleen's fear of Jack and her obedience when he gave her orders; Delia's concern for Jack during their drive to Northbourne; how Miraç had known Kathleen had attempted to steal Alice's magic and killed her for her betrayal.

There was only one explanation, and it chilled Sean to the bone.

"Miraç," Sean growled. "Where's Jack?"

Jack didn't turn around. "His body stands here before you." The voice was Miraç's now, with no trace of Jack's familiar deep voice. "As for where *he* is, I cannot say. My faith says if he was a good and just man, he's gone to his reward. If not..." He lifted one shoulder in a shrug. "Perhaps he burns."

Nan's grief and anger left a bitter taste in Sean's mouth. He snarled. "Jack is not dead. We would have felt him die."

"You feel and see nothing unless I allow it," Miraç said, his voice cold.

Nan let out a barely audible whine of pain.

"Spirits can't possess dead flesh, not even sorcerers. Jack is still alive," Sean murmured to her. He turned back to Miraç. "You possessed him at the winery, when he chased the panther."

"Perhaps I possessed him several days ago, once I released Alice. I had to keep watch on you, after all." Miraç smiled. He seemed to be deliberately trying to cause Sean and Nan pain with his answers.

Miraç returned his attention to Valas. "You anticipated my arrival." It was a statement rather than a question.

She gave him a slight nod. "I recognized a trace in the magic you used on the decanter. At first, I believed it was *her*, but soon I came to understand she is gone." Sean saw a flash of something in Valas's expression—something that might have been grief and regret. It vanished as quickly as it had appeared. "So her lover comes to me instead to seek revenge, with hostages and in a stolen body." Her tone turned derisive. "You are a cowardly man."

If she'd hoped to anger him into acting recklessly, Miraç didn't oblige. "So says the heartless creature who imprisoned her own sister in a curse box for seven hundred years."

Sean continued to fight the magic pinning him to the ground, but

Miraç's words startled him. Miraç's quarrel was with Valas over her mistreatment of her own sister. That explained the attacks on the Court, but not why Miraç had targeted Alice.

He closed his eyes and focused on the golden threads of the pack bonds. He sensed alarm spreading through the rest of the pack as Jack's possession was no longer hidden by Miraç's sorcery. He gave a hard tug on the bonds—an alpha's all-hands-on-deck signal to the rest of the pack. They knew he had gone to Northbourne. They would be on their way immediately.

Valas's head tilted slightly. "I did not imprison Kassia."

Miraç made a low, guttural sound. "Don't speak lies, corpse."

She ignored his insult. "Perhaps I should say, I did not imprison her against her will. My sister was ill. She could no longer control her rages and her power. She feared the Vampire Court of Constantinople would capture and torment her for the remainder of her long life—or she might fall into the hands of the fanatical Crusaders, some of whom had devoted their lives to inventing new and brutal tortures. She was safe in the curse box...safe from herself, and from those who hunted her."

"You lie," Miraç spat. "My Kassia told me what you did to her—how you tricked her into that box and left her to languish for seven hundred years."

Valas gestured toward the reflecting pool. "Come to the water and I will show you what transpired, Miraç. I will share my memory with you, and you will know I do not lie. Kassia stepped into that box of her own accord. Perhaps she came to hate me while there and told you something quite different when you found her, but that does not change the truth."

"I would never trust anything you would show me." Miraç's fists clenched. "Do you also deny that before you imprisoned her, you betrayed her to your vampire master Julius?"

"That I cannot deny, but it is ancient history."

"Not to Kassia. Not to me." Miraç turned and gestured at Alice. "Little wolf, come," he commanded.

"Don't call her that," Sean snarled.

Alice walked forward, her steps robotic. Sean managed to reach out and brush her ankle with his fingers. She didn't react or look down as she passed. Sean's wolf howled.

"What have you done to her?" he demanded.

"What she wished me to do: turn her into my Trojan Horse." Miraç smiled as Alice stopped at his side. "I wanted her power, but I could not wield it, so I opted to find another use for her. She told me of her hatred of the vampires—particularly Valas, to whom she owes a debt, and Charles Vaughan. She wished to be rid of you all and offered to join me. She is not the only one whose loyalty you have misjudged."

Sean's rage went ice-cold. While he was certain Miraç had lied about Jack being dead, his instincts told him Miraç spoke the truth about what Alice had said regarding Valas and Vaughan. It was possible Alice had told Miraç those things in an attempt to trick him into thinking she would be his ally. He had no difficulty imagining her doing so, but that didn't mean they weren't true.

If Valas was angered by what Miraç claimed Alice had said, or his insinuation the Court had traitors in their midst, her expression gave nothing away. "I misjudge very little, as you will see. Hanson?"

The blond Court enforcer moved to her side. "Yes, Madame Valas?"

Her eyes stayed locked on Miraç. "How long have you served this sorcerer?"

Hanson took a step back.

"Did you think your betrayal was unknown to me?" she asked, her voice soft. "I assure you I was aware you served another. I am many things, but a fool, I am not."

Hanson turned to run. Valas moved faster than any human could have seen, and much faster than any human—even one with enforcer reflexes— could react. She lifted him off his feet, broke his neck, and tore out his throat in less than a second.

With a hiss, she dropped him at her feet. He gurgled helplessly. She didn't look down or react as his blood spurted across the grass.

Valas took a black handkerchief from her pocket and wiped blood from her mouth. "It was Hanson who helped smuggle the decanter into the gala," she told Sean, returning the cloth to her pocket. "He sent Alice to be taken at the museum."

How long have you known and kept it to yourself? Sean wanted to demand. But this was not the time for such questions. Instead, he said, "Then I would have preferred to kill him myself." The weight on his chest made speaking difficult.

"He was mine to punish," Valas said.

At her feet, Hanson took one last gurgling breath and went still, his eyes wide and staring up at her in shock.

Miraç had watched Hanson's death throes without expression. "A swift kill. More merciful than he deserved for his betrayal."

"What do you know of mercy?" Valas asked. "You slaughtered dozens of people to reach this moment."

"Hundreds," Miraç corrected her. "I spilled the blood of witches, mages, vampires, shifters, and humans."

"Had you presented yourself at my gate, I would have granted you entry." Valas's eyes were deep black and ringed with silver. "I do not run from any enemy, nor any battle. If Kassia told you any truth of me, you would have known this."

The sorcerer arched an imperious eyebrow. "I *did* know."

"Then why the slaughter?" Sean ground out, his bones creaking under the weight of the curse that pinned him to the ground. "Why possess Jack? Why kidnap Alice and torture her?"

Miraç smiled. "For the power, and for fun." The smile vanished. "I am your reckoning, Sala Veli. You will die."

"Perhaps someday, but not by your hand, and not on this day." Valas extended her arms. Power prickled on Sean's skin.

CRACK. CRACK. CRACKCRACKCRACK. The air filled with the sound of stone breaking. Ten feet to Sean's left, a marble centaur sculpture reared up on its hind legs and brandished its bow and arrow as bits of stone rained to the ground. On the opposite side of the terrace, the other centaur did the same.

With roars, shrieks, screeches, and growls, the rest of the statues came to life. They broke free of their pedestals and trotted, ran, flew, and galloped to form two lines on either side of Valas. The centaurs took the positions on her left and right, their glowing arrows aimed at the center of Miraç's chest.

Miraç raised his hands. The ground trembled.

Nan's hand found Sean's and held on tightly as hundreds of ghosts erupted from the earth behind the sorcerer. Not ghosts, Sean realized almost instantly—some other form of spirit. Black and ragged in appearance, they weren't shaped like humans, as Malcolm was. Like the birds that had attacked them on the way to Northbourne, their eyes glowed bright red.

The spirits opened their mouths and screamed. The air turned cold.

Alice waited at Miraç's side, her eyes still fixed on Valas.

"Alice," Sean called. "*Alice,* fight him. You can do it. Listen to me."

Miraç waved his hand. The curse bore down on Sean, crushing the air from his lungs and silencing him. If Alice had heard him, he saw no sign.

At Miraç's gesture, the spirits dove toward Valas, shrieking. As the ancient vampire and her strange companions readied for the assault, Miraç turned to Alice. "Destroy the stone army," he ordered. "I will guide you."

Without a word, she obeyed.

Bright green earth magic coiled up her arms as she crossed the grass behind the attacking spirits. Some of the spirits formed a protective perimeter around her as two enormous stone trolls lumbered forward.

Meanwhile, Valas's magic was shredding the first wave of spirits who'd attacked. They disintegrated with ear-splitting shrieks. A second wave reached her, while a third focused on the stone army, breaking stone limbs with sounds like gunshots.

Valas vanished and reappeared on the far side of the long reflecting pool. As the spirits screamed and swooped toward her above the pool, the water seemed to boil. A swarm of human-shaped spirits no bigger than birds burst through the surface of the water and tore into Miraç's spirits with swords. Miraç's spirits were nearly wiped out in less than a minute by the fierce army of tiny female water spirits.

"Crinaeae," Miraç spat. He gestured at one of the broken stone bases that had once held a centaur statue. It tore out of the ground and flew toward Valas. A second enormous stone base followed it.

Valas saw the stone and moved aside so quickly that she seemed to blur. The stone landed where she had been standing only a moment before. The second stone pedestal she swatted from the air and sent it careening off course to smash into the wide stone steps leading to the terrace.

Sean watched with growing apprehension as Alice confronted the stone trolls. Moving jerkily, like a marionette on strings, she lashed at the trolls with earth magic, coiling it around them. The green magic flared and the trolls exploded, sending chunks of stone flying. She spun and wrapped her coils of earth magic around the stone sphinx that had been approaching on her right. As it burst, Valas's centaur guards launched their arrows at Alice.

"Alice!" Sean shouted.

She reacted to the centaurs' attack, raising a shimmering white air-magic shield that deflected the arrows, which stuck into the ground about ten feet to Nan's right. Undeterred, the centaurs fired again and again. New arrows appeared in their hands as soon as the previous ones took flight.

With her now engaged in fighting the stone army, Miraç paid no attention to Alice. His focus was entirely on Valas. To Sean, it appeared

Alice's function was to take on Valas's army, and he doubted very much if Miraç cared whether Alice survived this battle.

As they destroyed the last of Miraç's spirits, the Crinaeae turned their attention to the sorcerer himself. They converged, swords in hand, and tore at him, opening dozens of small gashes on his arms, chest, and back.

Sean snarled. "Valas, call them off. That's Jack Hastings they're attacking. Miraç is possessing his body."

Her response was cold. "That is your beta's misfortune."

Only Miraç's magic prevented him from shifting in rage at Valas's callousness. He forced himself to focus on Alice and freeing himself from the curse.

Alice's air magic shield was still fending off the centaurs' arrows, but two more of the stone creatures broke away from the attack on Valas and headed toward her: the other sphinx and a winged gargoyle. Both took to the air and circled overhead, out of reach of Alice's magic.

"Alice," Sean said, hoping she could hear him. "Alice, fight him. You don't belong to him. You don't belong to anyone but yourself. *Alice.*" He repeated her name and tried to sink as much of his alpha magic into his voice as possible, doing everything he could to help her break Miraç's hold over her.

He focused on the familiar sensation of Alice's magic, as faint as it was, and tried to push a thought through to her. *ALICE!* he shouted in his head.

She gave no indication she'd heard him. Alice had told him repeatedly her freedom and autonomy were more precious to her than anything else. Miraç had stolen both twice.

Sean thought he could not have been more furious than he was the day Alice disappeared, but he'd been wrong. Miraç had bound her and turned her into little more than a puppet. As Sean watched her methodically and robotically destroying every stone attacker that came within reach, his rage grew until it seemed to burn clear through his bones.

He wrenched harder against the curse, dislocating his shoulder. He snarled and slammed it against the ground. The joint popped back into place with a stab of pain that barely registered.

That was when Sean noticed the growing discolorations on Jack's skin. At first, he thought they were bruises, but the blackened areas were spreading fast. Beneath his skin, magic glowed. A sorcerer's power was like a nuclear reactor. It was never meant to be housed in another body for long—not even a shifter's.

Miraç was burning through Jack's body faster than even his shifter healing abilities could keep pace with the damage. If Miraç didn't leave Jack's body soon, Jack might not survive.

A tornado of black magic formed around Miraç, smashing the tiny armed water spirits into each other. Their blood splattered him. Shrieking, the surviving Crinaeae flew away and disappeared into the reflecting pool. Valas screamed in fury.

Miraç threw two enormous fireballs at Valas—one right after the other. She reacted with magic of her own and intercepted the first, but the second slammed into her and sent her stumbling back with a cry of pain.

Miraç let out a shout of triumph and strode over to where Alice had just disintegrated the stone gargoyle as the sphinx and other gargoyle continued to circle overhead.

He shoved Alice ahead of him as he headed for Valas. "Kill her, little wolf. Kill the vampire and earn your freedom."

Sean redoubled his efforts to free himself. The curse holding him in place might have been weakened by all the other magic the sorcerer had used, but he couldn't seem to break it.

CRACKCRACKCRACK.

He watched in disbelief as the enormous dragon statue in the center of the reflecting pool stirred. The dragon's nostrils glowed red. It opened its mouth and flames emerged.

The dragon's wings spread as bits of stone rained into the water. It flapped its wings and took off into the air. The massive creature dipped a wing and banked, headed straight for Alice.

"ALICE!" SEAN SHOUTED. "*DRAGON!*"

To his surprise, Miraç raised his arms and released a bolt of energy that knocked the dragon off-course. It tumbled through the air, heading directly for Nan and Sean. It would crush them. Nan's hand tightened on his.

At the last moment, the dragon righted itself in the air. It dove at Alice and Miraç again, its mouth open wide. Flames licked at its stone teeth.

Miraç reached up toward the dragon, his hands curving as if he was grabbing its sides. The dragon sent a blast of fire directly at them just as Miraç used his telekinetic abilities to throw the enormous stone beast directly at Valas.

Miraç flung Alice out of the dragon's path. She landed hard and rolled across the grass, coming to rest against the wide stone steps leading to the terrace. The dragon's fire missed her by inches. It swept over Miraç, burning away parts of his clothes and the skin on his upper body. Nan let out a whine.

Valas vanished. The dragon hit the ground where she'd been standing and lay half-buried in the earth, unmoving.

Miraç staggered. It had apparently taken an enormous amount of power to throw the dragon, and Jack's body had withstood almost as much abuse as it could. The curse crushing Sean and Nan to the ground wavered.

Over by the steps, Alice got to her feet, clearly favoring her left side. The fall might have broken or cracked some of her ribs. Still under Miraç's control, she showed no sign of pain. For Sean, her indifference to her own injuries was as infuriating and heart-rending as the injuries themselves.

"Miraç, let Jack go," Sean said. "His body won't last much longer."

Valas reappeared, standing in front of Hanson's body. "Enough fighting through proxies, Miraç. Release the werewolf and face me yourself. I will send you to meet your demon lord master."

The sorcerer shrugged out of what remained of his T-shirt. His chest was dark and discolored. "Who will you meet when you die for the final time, Sala? Who waits for the undead?"

To Sean's horror, Hanson's eyes suddenly glowed red. The corpse, animated by Miraç's sorcery, reached out and grabbed Valas's ankle. She looked down, her expression bemused.

Alice's blood magic formed a blade. Without hesitating, she sliced through Valas's abdomen, nearly cutting the vampire in half.

With a burst of power, Valas struck Alice and sent her flying, then staggered and nearly fell. Blood poured through her hands, pressed to the gaping wound in her stomach.

Alice landed next to Miraç and hit the side of the reflecting pool. Sean flinched at the telltale sound of a bone breaking, but she didn't react. She got to her feet, her left arm bent oddly at the elbow, and stood in front of Miraç, blocking him from an attack by Valas. Sean's rage made it difficult for him to breathe.

Hoping to goad Miraç into leaving Jack's body before it was too late, Sean said, "You're hiding behind Alice and Jack both." His voice dripped with contempt. "You're a coward, Miraç. Face Valas yourself and stop cowering."

Miraç turned, his eyes glowing. "Do you not wonder why you and Nan are here, Alpha? It is because once Valas kills your consort and I kill Valas, I will take your hearts, so full of pain and anger, and bathe in your blood. I will use the great power you will give me to destroy this Court and all who belong to it, and I will salt the earth where this building stood so nothing of the monster Sala Veli remains."

"Miraç."

A woman in a black robe appeared a few feet from Miraç. Her dark hair was long and loose, her eyes a startling shade of emerald green. Except for the eyes, she was identical to Valas.

"Miraç, stop," she pleaded, her voice heavily accented. "This was not what I wished for you, my love. Come away with me."

Miraç's face reddened. "This is not my Kassia!" he screamed at Valas. "This is an illusion!"

He threw a ball of fire at the woman. To Sean's surprise, the illusion appeared to catch fire. She screamed, fighting the flames with her hands, her skin turning black. Miraç flinched and started toward the burning woman.

In a blink, Valas picked up one of the centaurs' arrows, murmured something, and threw it directly at Miraç. Its shaft glowed with red magic.

Miraç reacted instantly, swinging Alice in front of himself as a human shield. Sean wrenched against the curse holding him and felt something break—maybe his shoulder, maybe something in his back. The pain was distant and meant nothing to him. The curse held fast.

Sean's eyes met Jack's at the moment they turned bright amber.

Jack seized control of his body for a split second—just long enough to spin Alice back around and put his own body between her and the magic-enhanced arrow. Through their pack bond, Sean sensed Jack's fury at being possessed and a fierce determination. Jack believed the arrow could kill Miraç, and by his death, he could save Sean, Nan, and Alice.

The arrow went through Jack's back and came out through the center of his chest, through his heart.

Jack fell. His anger faded, became sadness. Turned peaceful. And vanished.

His death was a physical blow. Sean let out an agonized sound as his wolf threw back his head and howled. Jack had been a constant, fiery presence from the moment he and Delia had joined the pack. That fire was gone, leaving a horrible, almost unbearable emptiness.

Nan let out a strangled sob. She howled, the sound full of sorrow and anger. Through the pack bonds, Sean felt the others' pain and grief. They knew Jack was dead. They had all felt him die.

Pain, sharp as a knife, seared him through the pack bonds. *Delia.* Her husband and mate was dead. Sean hoped she was with others from the pack, on their way to Northbourne. They would need to care for her. She would be nearly mad with shock and grief.

The pain of Jack's death was so great, it was a full five seconds before Sean realized the curse holding him to the earth hadn't broken.

Miraç was not dead.

A shadow of a man formed beside Jack's body. Miraç appeared in the grass between Alice and Valas. He was dark-haired and tall, with a closely trimmed beard, dark eyes, and an olive complexion. He wore a black shirt and black pants. His feet were bare. Around his neck, he wore two large amulets—one with a black crystal in the center, one with a green crystal. Both pulsed with power. Sean was certain one contained Alice's memories, the other Malcolm. The bastard was using them for power.

Valas launched several blasts of magic at Miraç, but he swatted them away. She stumbled. When she didn't attack again and the two stone centaurs froze in place, Sean figured she was too low on magic and power to animate them any longer.

Miraç reached out and took Alice's broken arm in his hands. As Sean fought to free himself, the sorcerer stroked her skin, his fingers glowing. He murmured in a language Sean didn't recognize—possibly Turkish.

"You boasted you misjudge very little," Miraç said, looking up at Valas. His fingers continued their ministrations on Alice's broken arm. "Yet you did not suspect Alice was bound to me and I had sent her back as my spy. You welcomed her return to your Court."

"I did indeed welcome her return." Valas's voice was hoarse. Sean had expected her stomach wound to heal fairly quickly, given her age and power, but it hadn't. Perhaps she'd used too much of her magic animating the statues and fighting Miraç. "But much as I knew you had turned Hanson against me, I recognized Alice had been bound to you."

Sean's rage made fur prickle under his skin. "You knew this would happen." His voice was guttural. "You knew he planned to use Alice as his puppet."

"I wished to meet the sorcerer who attacked my Court and my most valued mage," Valas said. "Clearly he desired a duel, but he would not come here unless he believed I had been fooled." Her smile was more like a grimace. "You proved to be a more worthy opponent than I thought, but that is the only surprise you brought me tonight, Miraç."

Sean's vision sharpened and turned gold as his wolf stared out through his human eyes. "You let Alice be taken and tortured. When this is over, you and I will settle that account."

She flashed her fangs. "You are most welcome to try, Alpha, but perhaps you will find it is not so easy a task."

Miraç released Alice's arm. "There—you are mended, little wolf." He leaned down and kissed her temple. She didn't react, but the intimate touch enraged Sean's wolf further. "Now, kill Sala," Miraç told Alice.

Obediently, she started across the grass toward Valas.

Calculation flashed in Valas's eyes. She was not nearly as badly wounded and drained as she let on.

Once Valas kills your consort, I will take your hearts, so full of pain and anger, and bathe in your blood, Miraç had said. The sorcerer fed on pain and anger. There was no greater suffering within reach than that of the pack.

Sean shut his link to the rest of his pack, cutting himself off from their grief and fury. He closed his eyes and breathed deeply to rid himself of his own pain and anger.

A wave of warm comfort washed over him as Nan squeezed his hand. He squeezed back and opened his eyes. His wolf waited, watchful and calm.

The curse crushing him wavered. He pulled himself forward, his fingers digging into the ground. Every inch was a battle.

His wolf changed shape, his legs elongating and sliding through Sean's arms and legs. His strength added to Sean's as he dragged himself toward Valas.

Miraç turned and laughed. "You're resourceful, wolf. Perhaps you will have more luck swimming to Alice's side."

The ground in front of Sean fell away, forming a shallow moat separating him from Miraç, Alice, and Valas. The ground bubbled and filled the channel not with water, but with molten rock. The heat blistered Sean's face. This was no illusion. Miraç had transformed the earth into a moat filled with lava and Sean couldn't cross it.

Triple-damned sorcerers, Alice would have said.

Separated from the rest of the pack, Sean's mind was silent. He couldn't feel anything but the warm trace of Alice's magic. She'd found a way to contact him when she was being taken from the museum. He'd be damned if he wouldn't find a way to reach her now.

He grabbed that trace of magic and poured his alpha power into it, not caring about anything but reaching her. He sensed Miraç's dark, chilling magic mixed with hers, hard and cold as iron, but she was still there, if he could only get through to her.

He might have imagined it, but he thought he saw her hesitate for just a fraction of a second before taking another step toward Valas. Dark magic swirled around Valas's hands. Miraç smiled.

Alice, Sean said, pushing his thoughts at her as hard as he could. *You've never given up, baby—not once in your life. You don't even know how.*

Alice stopped a few feet from Valas. Blood magic blades emerged from both of her hands. Valas straightened, her eyes going bright red.

ALICE, he shouted in his head. *Baby, no.*

A whisper in his mind, softer than the tiniest breeze: *Don't call me baby.* Alice. His heart soared.

The iron grip of Miraç's magic wavered. The sorcerer's roar rolled across the garden like thunder.

Moving jerkily, as if fighting Miraç for control of her own body, Alice tilted her head, exposing her neck to Valas. "Do it," she ground out.

In a blink, Valas crossed the distance between them. She gripped Alice's upper arms and sank her fangs into her throat.

Later, Nan would tell Sean he'd reacted instantly, tearing himself free of the curse though it broke most of the bones in his arms and legs to do so. He'd pulled magic and energy from his pack through the bonds to shift faster than he ever had before. As Miraç flew across the grass toward Valas and Alice, Sean's wolf, berserk with a week's worth of pent-up rage, circled back, ran, and leaped over the moat.

He remembered none of it. From the moment he saw Valas's fangs puncture Alice's throat until his wolf landed on Miraç's back, there was nothing but a blank. One moment he was on the ground, and the next his wolf's mouth was full of foul-tasting blood and splintered bone as he tore into Miraç's neck.

Kill sorcerer, kill vampire, the wolf snarled.

Lethal black magic tore at him, but neither Sean nor his wolf noticed. Nothing mattered but killing these creatures and freeing Alice.

Her mouth bloody, Valas released Alice and stepped back. The bites on Alice's neck were large and ragged. There had been no time for finesse. The sight and smell of Alice's blood filled the wolf's nose and sharpened his focus.

Eyes glowing with blood magic, Alice faced Miraç.

"Kill Sala," he commanded.

Blades emerged from her hands, but she didn't turn on Valas. Instead, she drove the blades into Miraç's chest and twisted.

Choking on his own blood, Miraç fell at Alice's feet. The wolf rode him down, savoring the sorcerer's blood and bones, though they tasted of death and rotting things.

Valas traced a glyph in the air in blood. It fell onto Miraç's chest and burned deep into his flesh. The sorcerer screamed. The magic that had been spiraling from his hands vanished.

"Move back, Sean," Alice said, her voice reaching him through the haze of rage.

My kill, the wolf snarled. He locked his jaws on Miraç's throat.

Crouching beside Miraç, Alice ripped the amulets from around his neck and put them in her pocket. Without hesitation, she pulled Carly's knife from its sheath on her forearm and sliced into his chest. She tore out his heart and raised it, her hand covered in gore.

"If you kill me, you will die," Miraç rasped. Blood bubbled on his lips. "Your ghost will never be free."

Bright golden rings appeared in Alice's eyes. "I won't die," she told him. "I will be remade. A witch told me so." She set the heart on the ground and picked up Carly's dagger.

Valas caught the wolf's eye and smiled. There was nothing about the smile the wolf or Sean liked at all.

A spike of fear went through Sean's heart. *Valas is always three steps ahead of everyone else,* he'd told Alice once. She'd *wanted* this to happen.

The wolf snarled a warning, but he was too late.

Alice raised her arm and drove Carly's blade through Miraç's heart with all her might. It crumbled into ash.

The blast was a supernova of power and magic. The earth thundered. The shockwave sent them flying as it rolled across the ground, flattening and blackening everything it touched. The veil Valas had drawn around the garden shimmered, blazed, and died.

Power and pain seared every nerve in the wolf's body. His howl was lost in the roar of the magic released by Miraç's death. The agony blinded him.

Alice screamed his name.

Suddenly, his own pain didn't matter. He needed to be human, right the hell *now.*

Drawing on the pack bonds once more, Sean shifted fast. His body was in agony from two fast shifts, but it registered only in a very distant way. His magic sizzled on his skin, as Alice's often did when she was angry. Power pulsed through him, searing his bones. He'd absorbed some of Miraç's power. What the effects would be, he wasn't sure, but for the moment his only thoughts were of Alice and Nan.

A quick look confirmed Nan still lay on the ground where she'd been held by Miraç's curse. She'd been far enough away from the blast to avoid its effects.

He staggered to his feet. The lava moat had turned to stone. Most of the garden was leveled. Miraç's body was nothing but ash. His stomach contracted. *Alice.*

He spotted her about thirty feet away, near what remained of the terrace steps. She wasn't moving. "Alice," he said, starting forward.

A cold hand touched his arm. "Stay back," Valas said.

His hand raised to grip the vampire's throat, but she was suddenly on the terrace and no longer beside him. A dozen Court enforcers had emerged from the building, their faces a mixture of shock and confusion at the sight of the garden. Charles Vaughan, Bryan, and Adri headed for Valas. Vaughan demanded an explanation for what had occurred and why Valas had hidden the battle from them.

Alice stirred. She sat up and raised her hands. Magic arced between them, blazing not white or green, or even red or gold, but with every color of the rainbow.

As she stood, power and magic arced to the ground and crackled around her, like electricity from a Tesla coil. The air smelled of ozone.

Many of the enforcers on the terrace took a step back. Vaughan stared at Alice, horrified. Valas's expression was calculating.

"Alice," Sean said, approaching her despite Valas's hiss of displeasure. "Are you all right?"

"I don't know," she said, staring at the magic and power arcing between her hands and the ground. "I feel like I'm made of lightning." Her eyes glowed. "It hurts."

The ground rumbled. He spun as a tear formed in the air behind him. A massive figure with red skin and eyes stepped through the rift.

The odor of sulfur burned Sean's nose. A demon. No, Sean realized—a demon *lord*. He towered over them, nearly twenty feet tall and wearing battle armor covered with glowing sigils.

"I am Lord Orias." The demon's voice rolled across the ground. "My servant Miraç is dead. I come to punish the ones who killed him." His glowing eyes fixed on Sean. "Was it you, werewolf?"

Before Sean could respond, Alice spoke. "I killed him."

The demon lord slammed his staff on the ground. The resulting earthquake cracked the terrace and knocked several enforcers off their feet. "You did not kill my sorcerer, little one."

Alice's expression went blank. She walked past Sean to stand fifteen feet from Orias. She gestured for him to stay back, but he joined her anyway. As far as he was concerned, Alice would never stand alone ever again.

"I am done being called little," Alice said softly. "By you, by your sorcerer, by anyone else." She lifted her hand. Fine ash swirled, stirred by her magic. "If you doubt me, here's what remains of Miraç's heart, Lord Orias."

Orias roared. It was a sound meant to terrify demons. Most of the enforcers on the terrace fled. Vaughan and Valas took a step back. Nan, who had made her way to the terrace steps, sat down hard.

Sean didn't back away. Neither did Alice.

The demon lord raised his staff and pointed it at Alice. It glowed with dark red demon magic. "Kneel, slayer," he thundered.

She smiled, her eyes going bright gold. "You first."

Shifter magic rose. The surge was sudden and more powerful than any shifter magic Sean had ever felt.

In his mind, his wolf showed his teeth. *Mate's wolf rises.*

Alice's back arched and her arms extended. Sean thought she was going to shift. On instinct, his alpha magic surged, preparing to call her wolf and take as much of the pain of the shift as he could.

He'd been preparing for this moment ever since Alice had survived Caleb's attack, in case burning the virus from her blood hadn't worked after all. For a moment, he was deeply sorry, because he knew she hadn't wanted to become a werewolf. Hard on the heels of that sorrow was joy at the thought they would be able to run together now as wolves.

But she didn't shift.

The shifter magic he sensed from Alice changed from pure gold to every color of the rainbow. Something else was rising in Alice, and it was not a wolf—at least, not any kind of wolf he'd encountered. His joy vanished, replaced with a mixture of awe and fear.

With a howl of fury, a golden wolf made of pure magic leaped from Alice's body and landed on the blackened earth in front of her. In a swirl of magic and power, the wolf grew to gargantuan size—large enough to nearly look Orias in the eye.

"Holy fuck," someone on the terrace gasped. It sounded like Adri Smith.

The wolf collided with Orias, who roared again and tried to strike out with his staff, but the wolf was too fast. Dark, foul-smelling demon blood spurted across the ruin of the reflecting pool. The demon lord staggered, his neck and shoulder torn down to the bone. The massive golden wolf snarled and snapped her teeth, her mouth dark with demon blood.

"Go back to your domain, Lord Orias," Alice said, stepping forward. "Or die here and now. Your choice."

Sean had never heard that tone in Alice's voice, but he sure as hell liked it. A *lot*.

"Your mercy makes you weak," Orias snarled. He spat black blood onto the ground.

"Mercy is not weakness." Alice's eyes blazed and her golden wolf growled. "And this is not mercy—it's a warning. If I see you again, you'll find out how merciless I can be. Or stay and find out right now."

Without a word, Orias tore a rift in the air and disappeared through it.

With a pulse of magic, the golden wolf returned to normal size and trotted to Alice's side. She rested her hand on its head.

Dead silence fell in the garden.

Sean had feared revealing the truth about Alice's wolf. Now the situation was far more complex...and dangerous. For whom, however, he wasn't sure.

He went to Alice. Her golden wolf met his eyes with her own bright white ones. His wolf padded to the front of his brain and looked out through his human eyes. *Mate*, his wolf said.

The golden wolf showed her teeth. *You are worthy*, she replied.

Before Sean or his wolf could respond, the rest of the Tomb Mountain Pack ran through the doors onto the broken terrace. The enforcers moved to intercept them.

"Let them pass," Valas said.

The pack crossed the terrace to the steps with Delia in the lead. Her red-rimmed eyes were fixed on Jack's body. Sean wondered if she saw anything else.

Nan went to speak to the others as he approached Delia. She sat on the ground beside Jack, her hands on his face. Her grief was an anvil crushing his chest.

Knowing she liked physical touch less than most shifters, Sean crouched beside her and wrapped her in comfort. "I'm sorry, Delia."

"What happened?" Her voice was raw.

His voice pitched so only she could hear, he told her. Nan told essentially the same story to the others, while Alice waited with her golden wolf, her eyes shining with unshed tears. When he finished his account of Miraç's attempt to kill Valas, Nan, Alice, and himself, and Jack's death, Delia bowed her head and wept.

Sean's heart ached. The reality of Jack's loss had barely begun to sink in. The others were weeping or struggling not to. Most of the enforcers had retreated inside Northbourne. Only Vaughan, Valas, and Vaughan's guards remained on the terrace. Sean wanted to snarl at them to go inside and leave his pack to grieve.

When Delia looked up, her eyes were bright gold. She looked past him, at Alice. "This is your fault," she said, her voice a low growl.

"It wasn't," Sean said firmly. "It was Miraç's doing, all of it." And Valas's, though that was a matter he would settle later, in private. "Jack fought hard, Delia. He fought Miraç every inch of the way. He died trying to kill Miraç, and Alice finished the job."

"She sure did." Delia rose. "She finished the job she started the day she first tried to attack our pack through her connection to you, when she slashed Jack's face. She wants to destroy us. She's a *mage*. They're all killers. They're all monsters. How can you not see that?" Her voice rose. "*Look at her!*" she screamed. "She has a demon!"

The golden wolf growled.

"She's no demon," Alice said, her hand on the wolf's head. "I've had a wolf within me since the night Caleb attacked me and infected me. I never imagined she would manifest like this, but absorbing Miraç's power and magic has had some...unexpected consequences."

Mouth agape, Delia turned to Sean. "You knew about this?"

He nodded grimly. "We told no one. We had to protect her."

"You had to protect *her*." Delia's voice dripped venom. "Not Jack, not the rest of us."

Growling in warning, Ben stepped forward. "Stop, Delia. Sean would die for any of us."

"He would have saved Jack if he could have," Nan said. "You know that."

"How hard did you try?" Delia demanded.

"God damn it, Delia, I tried with everything I had," Sean snarled.

Delia looked at her husband's body. "Jack," she said, her voice breaking. She faced Alice and hissed, "He was my world. You took everything from me, you bitch." Shifter magic surged.

Magic spiraled out of Alice's hand. Sean moved between them. "Don't do it, Delia. Don't make me kill you."

"You killed Jack the minute you brought Alice to us," Delia said harshly. "You might as well kill me too."

She shifted and launched herself at Alice. With a snarl, Sean shifted and met Delia's wolf in mid-leap. Despite his exhaustion, she was no match for his size and strength. It was over in seconds.

Near the terrace steps, Felicia went to her knees, sobbing in Karen's arms. The others gathered around them, except for Ben and Nan, who joined Sean as he shifted back to human.

The golden wolf changed shape, coiling around Alice's arm and spiraling into her chest. Her eyes returned to their normal dark brown, but with golden flecks that hadn't been there before.

Heart heavy, Sean crouched beside Delia's wolf. There was little blood. He'd made it as quick and merciful as he could. He touched the wolf's shoulder and hung his head. "Damn it all."

There would be a time for grief. For now, there was business to attend to. He looked up. "Ben?"

Ben shook his head. "We all know who the new beta should be."

Sean and the others looked at Nan. She said nothing.

"Nan, this is where you belong," Ben told her. "You know it, and I know it. We've sensed it since the day you, Felicia, and David joined our pack. Jack knew it too, and so did Delia, though they'd have rather eaten roofing nails than admit it."

"We need you now, more than ever, to take your rightful place in this pack," Sean said. "Given your past, I understand why you're reluctant. There will be challengers from other packs and objections from members of the Council. It's not going to be easy, but this is who you are, Nan. You can't hide from that forever, as much as you might want to."

"I know." Nan rubbed her face. "I've been in hiding for a long time, and it's helped no one, not even me."

"Same here," Alice said quietly, coming to stand at Nan's side. "But maybe realizing that, and choosing to stand up and fight when it's time, is what's important."

With a deep breath, Nan squeezed Alice's hand. "Unless anyone wishes to challenge me, I accept the position of beta."

The faces of Sean's pack mates showed pain, grief, and anger, but no dissent. "Thank you, Nan," he said.

"I'll look after the others," she said. "You take care of our new wolf."

Sean looked at Alice. Valas's bite stood out against the pallor of her skin. "The amulets?" he asked quietly.

She reached into her pocket and held them out. "I feel the magic in them. Miraç's magic is in me now. I think I can use it to get my memories back."

"And Malcolm?"

"Carly said she knew someone who could help us with that, remember?" She took a shaky breath. "A remaking and a birth. She was right. I'm so full of this magic and power, and I don't know how to use it... or what the consequences will be." She looked up at him. "It burns."

He kissed her forehead. "I know. I feel it too." He took her hand and placed it on the center of his chest. "We will face this the same way we've faced everything else: together."

Soft footsteps descended the broken terrace steps as Valas returned to the ruin of the garden. Sean released Alice's hand and turned with a growl. "We have an account to settle, Valas."

"I am aware." She studied Alice. "I am also aware Alice is now bound to me. As such, we should table our discussion of accounts until she and I have sorted out the details of her formal relationship to my Court."

Alice took Sean's hand and squeezed. "It was the only way to break Miraç's binding," she told him. "It was my choice—the best I could make of a bad situation."

She smiled at Valas, and to Sean there was something distinctly predatory about the smile. "And as for *you* and my relationship to your Court, here's something to think about." Her eyes glowed. Magic, in a dozen different colors, swirled around her hands.

Staggering slightly, Valas flinched. "Do not do that again," the vampire hissed.

Alice's smile vanished. "Don't force me to."

The head of the Court turned on her heel and marched up the steps.

Charles Vaughan started toward them. "Stay away from us, Mr. Vaughan," Alice said, her eyes blazing gold. "Whatever you have to say, this is not the time."

Valas gestured. "Come, Charles. We must speak in private."

Vaughan hesitated. For a moment, Sean thought he would defy Valas and head their way. Instead, he gave Alice a grave nod and followed Valas inside Northbourne, leaving Bryan Smith alone on the terrace.

Sean leaned down and murmured into Alice's ear. "What did you do to Valas?"

"She drank my blood thinking it would give her power over me." Alice kissed his jaw. "I sense my magic in her, and I used it against her. She miscalculated if she expected me to roll over for her." She squeezed his hand. "I heard you in my head. You said I belong to no one. Now she knows what that means."

His heart was raw, but her words and the reassuring sizzle of her magic were a balm for his pain. He would wait until they were alone to talk more about this binding.

They had to deliver Jack and Delia's remains to the Were Ruling Council, record official statements regarding their deaths, and formally recognize Nan as the pack's new beta. It would take the rest of the night to clear all the red tape. He could only imagine what the Council's reaction would be to the news—and to the revelation of Alice's wolf. The ramifications of tonight's events would take months or even years to sort out.

For now, he and Alice joined the rest of the pack, who had gathered around Jack and Delia's bodies. He and Nan offered what comfort they could.

Bryan came down the terrace steps. "Respectfully, we offer our assistance to move your dead to your vehicles."

"We've got it." Ben crouched and picked up Delia, still in wolf form.

Sean picked up Jack and put him on his shoulder. The weight of his former beta's body was nothing compared to the heaviness in his heart.

"I'll take you to the side gate," Bryan said. "This way."

Silently, they followed.

3 2

ALICE

"A GIANT GOLDEN WOLF JUMPED OUT OF ME," I SAID.

Sean leaned against the counter, watching me draw runes on his kitchen floor. "To be fair, she wasn't giant at first."

I finished one set of runes and started on the next. "She got real big real fast."

"Yes, she did." He sipped his coffee. "Can you sense her? Talk to her?"

"Sense her, yes." My chalk scratched across the tile. "Talk to her, no. It feels like she's sleeping. I think she's waiting for something scary to show up so she can jump out again and kill it."

Before she went to sleep, my wolf had told me she was hungry. Her hunger was a nagging sensation in my belly. It wasn't hunger for food, but for blood, and Orias's flesh hadn't sated her. I'd tell Sean about the hunger soon. It scared me.

"I wish to hell I knew if the power and magic we absorbed will fade or stay, and what we can do with it," I said to distract myself. "And what its effect on our pack will be."

"For me, it created more power and strength in the pack bonds. I sense the others more clearly." He paused. "My bones are buzzing. Is that how magic feels to you?"

"Yes. It feels good. Comforting. I don't remember how it felt before, obviously, but I like it. I'm powerful now instead of vulnerable."

He looked over the runes I'd drawn and the books he'd fetched from my basement. "You feel comfortable trying this?"

I sighed. "Honestly? Not really. Using the raw power of my magic felt instinctual, but I don't remember how to do spellwork." I tapped one of the books. "Luckily, I know how to read and follow directions."

"How does this spell work, then?"

"There are two steps involved: releasing my memories from the crystal and returning them to where they belong." I finished drawing the last rune and rose. "If I can release them but not put them back, they'll dissipate and be lost forever. If I get them put back, it might scramble things up in my head for a while. I might lose parts of what's happened since they were stolen." I took a deep breath and exhaled. "Or everything might go just fine. But let's be honest: what are the odds of that happening?"

He set his coffee mug on the counter. "Miraç might have used them as a power source."

"If he did, that means I may not get everything back, even if this works like it should." I went to the counter, carrying the book with the spellwork I was using. I took off my shirt and stood in front of the mirror he'd propped against the cabinets. The scar from the knife wound was plainly visible on my sternum, as was Valas's ragged bite on my throat.

Sean wrapped his arms around me. He met my eyes in the mirror. "I hate seeing that bite mark." He pressed a kiss into my hair.

"I know. I'll heal it as soon as I remember how to do that." I pierced the tip of my finger with the point of a dagger. With my blood, I drew three runes on my chest as Sean's arms stayed wrapped around my abdomen.

When I finished, I turned to face him. "You're a good man, Sean Maclin."

He cupped my face with his hands. "Not that I don't appreciate hearing that, but why are you telling me this now?"

"In case my egg gets scrambled." I raised up on my toes, careful not to let the runes on my chest brush against his shirt, and kissed him lightly. "I just wanted it on the record."

He kissed me back and rested his forehead on mine. "I love you, Alice Worth. I want that on the record too." His worry prickled on my skin.

Reluctantly, I let go and went to the small circle I'd drawn on his kitchen floor. I sat in the middle of the runes and picked up a small dagger and the amulet I believed held my memories.

I took a deep breath, smeared my blood across the crystal in the amulet, and looked up at Sean one last time. His expression was grave.

"I like the way the corners of your eyes crinkle when you smile," I said. He smiled.

With that image in my mind, I closed my eyes, gripped the amulet tightly, and spoke the words I hoped would release my memories and return them to my brain.

SEAN

"*Exsolvo et revorsio,*" Alice said.

The crystal in the amulet shattered, the sound as loud as a gunshot. Magic erupted from Alice's clenched fist. Sean smelled Miraç's magic, but that scent burned away quickly.

Alice's memories—if indeed that was what he saw—burst from the crystal in a cloud of tangled multicolored threads held together by blindingly white magic that hurt his eyes. Alice had said memory spells were a form of air magic.

Instead of heading directly for Alice, the magic hung in midair. "*Revorsio,*" Alice repeated, her voice a command. She opened her eyes and stared into the cloud of magic. "*Veni ad me.*"

The runes on Alice's chest flared brightly. The cloud pulsed, zipped toward her face, and flowed into her eyes.

She screamed. Her eyes were wide open but he didn't think she saw him. The flood of memories—most of them horrible, he was sure—were all she could see. Her magic burst through her skin and swirled around her —black, red, green, white, blue, and gold—and seared him with its unchecked power.

She flung her head back and screamed again. Blood gushed from her nose. She'd told him never to touch her when she was doing anything magic-related, but no way in hell was he going to let her suffer alone.

He went to his knees beside her and wrapped her in his arms. She tried to push him away. He held on and buried his face in the side of her neck, at her shoulder, and breathed in her scent. The roiling magic tore at him, opening wounds on his arms and back, but he barely noticed them. When she started to fall over, he held her tighter.

Do you trust me? He didn't say the question aloud because he didn't think she would hear him, but with every cell in his body he willed her to understand him anyway, somehow, through the haze of magic, memories, and pain.

For a moment, she didn't react. Then, in his mind, he heard her voice. It was faint and full of agony, but it was unmistakably her. *Yes.*

As an alpha, it was his role and his privilege to take the pain of a member of his pack who was injured or grieving. Unwilling to allow anyone to suffer on her behalf, Alice had always been reluctant to accept his help, but this time, she did.

So he took it all—all of her pain, grief, and terrible loneliness. The weight of her suffering nearly crushed him as flat as Miraç's curse.

With the pain and misery came the memories, vivid and bloody. They tumbled over each other in his head like an avalanche, flashes of faces and dark rooms and people. He saw Moses Murphy. He witnessed the torments Alice suffered at the hands of blood mages. He glimpsed the lieutenant they'd encountered at Moses's haunted mansion—the one named Kade. He saw Kade's pleasure and arousal at Alice's suffering and Moses's cruel indifference, and howled in rage. How could she have borne it all? He couldn't begin to understand.

In the midst of the terrible memories, he caught rare moments of happiness: Alice with her parents; Alice in her room, playing with her toys secretly after bedtime; Alice lying in the grass outside the compound, gazing up at the clouds. His eyes burned with unshed tears.

He witnessed her escape from the compound, the massive explosion she'd engineered in order to breach the wall and get away. He saw her weeks on the run, her time in Chicago, the moment she'd found the real Alice Worth's body and hatched the plan to take her identity. Then her arrival in California and how she'd slowly built a life for herself. He saw her job interview with her late mentor Mark Dunlap, her first meeting with Charles Vaughan, and a smattering of her cases. A handful of brief relationships, all of them pleasurable, none of them love.

And then there was Vaughan, over and over and over again. Her intimate memories of him—their late-night talks over whisky at Hawthorne's, the times she'd drunk his blood for healing, Vaughan biting her on a bed in his home, their dance at the Vampire gala—made his wolf howl in fury.

Then came Malcolm and himself, and Alice's life changed. Her loneliness became happiness. And then...love.

The pain diminished. The magic that had slashed at his skin faded.

Alice's cries became whimpers. Finally, she went quiet except for ragged breathing.

He held her, his eyes closed and heart pounding. For a long time, neither of them moved or spoke. Had it worked? Did she have her memories back, in part or in full? Would she know him when she opened her eyes? He waited for an eternity for her to speak.

Part of him thought he should let her go. The transfer of memories was over. He didn't know if she wanted him to hold her, but he couldn't make himself release her. She felt so good, so *right*, in his arms.

"Sean?" It was a hoarse whisper.

"Yes?" If she asked him to let go, he'd obey, but it might be the hardest thing he'd ever had to do.

"I remember everything," she rasped. "From before, and after. My grandfather, my parents, Chicago, my life here, you and Malcolm... everything. And my brain doesn't feel scrambled. I think...I think it worked." Her voice was full of wonder. "It *worked*."

He buried his nose and mouth in her hair and breathed in her wonderful scent. "Why did you choose 'Take Me Home Tonight' as our song?" he asked, when he found his voice.

She let out a little half-laugh, half-sob. "It was playing the night we met in Hawthorne's."

In his mind, his wolf curled up, content and happy. He held her tightly, his taut muscles relaxing. She was finally, *finally* home. "My Alice," he said.

"Your Alice," she agreed. She moved so she could see him. "I remember how much I love you." Her face was wet with tears.

He kissed them away. "I love you too, Girl with the Golden Wolf."

"I like Miss Magic better as a nickname. Girl with the Golden Wolf is too wordy." She wiped her nose and blinked at the blood on the back of her hand. "My head hurts."

His stomach lurched, remembering the time she'd suffered hemorrhages in her brain after a psychic accidentally shared his visions with her. "How badly?"

She kissed his jaw. "Not like that other time. The pain's fading already." Her smile disappeared. "I remember what Miraç did to me, and what he did to Malcolm." Magic sizzled on her skin—a hot, painful sensation he'd missed more than he'd realized. "And what Malcolm did for me."

He nuzzled her neck, taking comfort in her scent. "Tell me."

She didn't tell him what she'd gone through in her cell at Broken Ridge, either to spare him the details or because she wasn't ready to talk about it. She described only how Miraç had ripped her magic out and how Malcolm had ended up as Miraç's prisoner.

"He traded himself for my life and freedom," she said, her head on his chest. "Being enslaved again was his greatest fear, but he did it for me."

He rested his chin on her head. "I have no trouble believing he did that for you."

"I want to get him out of that damned amulet right the hell now."

"I know." He kissed her hair. "But we need Carly's help for that, and she had to get some rest after last night. She said to call her around noon, so that's what we'll do. Are you ready to go upstairs?"

She nodded. "I'll clean all this up later, if that's all right."

"It's perfectly all right." He helped her to her feet. She made her way slowly to the steps leading to the second floor. She started up the stairs, dragging herself up using the handrail.

Less than a third of the way up, she sat on a step and looked at him. "I don't like asking for help."

He sat down next to her. "I know you don't."

"I needed a lot of help when Miraç got through with me." She stared straight ahead. "I wasn't comfortable letting you all help me, but I appreciated it. It made me feel safe and loved. And now I've got my memory back and I remember why I didn't ask anyone for help for most of my life. Part of me wants to force myself to get to the top of these damn stairs by myself." She rested her head on his shoulder. "And the other part wants you to carry me, because I'm hurting all over and you'd be happy to carry me if I asked."

"I *would* be happy to do it." He rubbed his chin on top of her head. "Even happier if you knew it doesn't make you weak if you ask for help when you need it."

She turned to face him. "From now on, I will ask for help when I need it. And whenever I get hurt, I will heal myself at the first opportunity, because I don't want you to worry about me and because I don't believe I need to punish myself for my past anymore."

He scooped her up and headed upstairs. "Are you *sure* your head didn't get scrambled?"

She laughed, sounding tired but contented.

He took her to his bedroom and set her on her feet near the bed. "Let's shower and get some sleep."

"Shower and sleep sound phenomenal." She went to the dresser for a pair of pajamas as he went into the bathroom and stripped off his shirt.

At the sight and sound of the shower coming on, the wolf showed his teeth. *Time for play*, he said, sounding pleased.

Sean chuckled to himself. The wolf was more than ready to welcome Alice home properly, but he'd take his cue from her. They'd both been beat to hell, emotionally and physically. She might just want to rest.

His mood was short-lived. "Sean?" Alice called from the bedroom.

Her tone sent chills through him. He was out of the bathroom and at her side in a blink. "What's wrong?" he asked.

Alice stood in front of her nightstand, staring at the framed picture of them lying in a hammock. Her shoulders were rigid. "When was this picture taken?"

His stomach filled with dread. "Last month, during our trip to the Bahamas."

She took a step back. "I don't remember this." Her voice was edged with fear. "I don't remember this at all."

He opened the small jewelry box on the nightstand and took out a bracelet made of tiny seashells. She took it from him. "Is this mine?"

"I got it for you in the Bahamas." He wanted to howl in rage and grief. "It was the first gift you ever accepted from me."

She slid it onto her wrist. Without a word, she went into the bathroom, took off her tattered clothes, and put them in the trash. She got into the shower and shut the door.

He took off the rest of his clothes and joined her. She stood under the spray, her eyes squeezed shut.

"We'll make new memories," he promised her.

She didn't reply. Her pain was a knife twisting in his heart.

When he took her in his arms, she didn't resist. And when she started to shake, he held her and wished he could resurrect Miraç so he could help her kill the son of a bitch one more time, and far more slowly.

33

ALICE

WE FELL INTO BED WELL AFTER DAWN AND SLEPT FOR A FEW HOURS. Sean curled around me and held me, but even his warmth and comfort wasn't enough to bring me anything but fitful dozing. My worry about Malcolm and fear over the blanks in my memory drove me from our bed long before noon.

Sean got up before me to field calls from the Were Ruling Council. He was downstairs, so I couldn't hear every word, but it sounded like the Council wasn't happy about our account of what happened at Broken Ridge and Northbourne, and even less happy about Nan becoming our pack's new beta. My indignation about their resistance to the idea of a female beta was a welcome distraction from more personal worries.

We hadn't told them about my wolf manifesting in our official statements about last night's events. Sean said it was only a matter of time until they heard, since there had been a half-dozen witnesses. I could tell he was worried about how the Council would react.

While Sean argued with various members of the Council, I called Carly. She confirmed she was recovered enough to help us contact an archangel about releasing Malcolm. I told her I'd gotten my memory back, but admitted some pieces seemed to be missing. Saying it out loud made it more real.

When our call ended, I had to spend a few minutes hugging Rogue, my face buried in his fur. So far, the trip Sean and I had taken to the Bahamas was the only major memory I knew I'd lost, but there were sure to be more. I was angry and grieving for those losses, in addition to those of Jack and Delia. It hadn't sunk in yet—any of it. Jack and Delia gone. Chunks of my memory gone. I couldn't wrap my brain around it.

Sean was sitting on the couch when I came downstairs, his expression stony. His phone lay at the other end of the couch like he'd thrown it there.

"Is the Council still being ridiculous about Nan?" I asked, heading for the kitchen, following the scent of fresh-brewed coffee.

"Probably, but that's not their biggest concern at the moment."

His tone made me veer off-course and join him in the living room. "What's their concern?" I put my arms around him from behind and kissed the back of his neck.

He folded his arms over mine. He was so warm. "You."

I exhaled. "They heard about the wolf."

"Yes."

"And?"

He kissed my shoulder. "You are an abomination against nature and your wolf is a demonic familiar. I'm to cut all ties with you immediately."

"And what did you tell them?"

He pulled me over the back of the couch into his lap and kissed me hard. "I told them what Nan told me to tell them: to fuck off."

I gasped. "Nan said no such thing."

"You're right—it was Ben who said that. Nan's phrasing was a bit more polite, but it amounted to the same thing."

I rested my head on his chest. "What are we going to do?"

"Two things. First, take a page from the Alice Worth book of *screw you* and do what we know is right—namely, make Nan our beta and bring you and your beautiful golden wolf into our pack, if you'll have us."

That little voice piped up in my head and tried to tell me I didn't deserve to be a part of Sean's pack. I told the voice to shut up and laced my fingers through his. "And second?"

"The Council has a four-three conservative majority. I want to swing the pendulum the other way. There's an election coming. I want to run for a seat on the Council."

I blinked. "Wow."

He cupped my face with his warm hand. "It's not enough to buck the system; we have to change it. But I won't run unless you want me to."

"That's a lot for me to take in before I have any coffee," I told him.

He kissed me. "No decisions have to be made right now. Did you call Carly?"

"Yes. She'll be ready for us when we get to her house."

"Good." He stood and put me on my feet. "Then let's pour that coffee into travel cups and hit the road. We'll grab some breakfast on the way to Carly's. We need our Malcolm back."

"Yes, we do," I said fervently. I missed my ghost so much. "Yes, we damn well do."

<hr />

On the way to Carly's house, between bites of two big breakfast burritos and gulps of coffee, I explained how I'd been taken from the museum via the rug. I also told him Miraç's story about Valas and Kassia and how and why Miraç had taken it upon himself to avenge his long-dead lover.

I wasn't ready to talk about my three days of captivity yet. He didn't push me—just held my hand and told me he'd be ready to hear about it whenever I wanted to talk.

When Carly opened her door, her mouth fell open.

I raised my hands palm up. "Is it my new power, my weird rainbow aura, or my golden wolf? Or do I have something stuck in my teeth?"

"You look like a prism." She hugged me, then hugged Sean. "Your aura is beautiful and your wolf is content. There's nothing in your teeth as far as I can see. Come in."

We followed her inside. As always, Carly's house smelled of herbs, plants, incense, and something baking. I hoped that meant fresh-baked scones.

Bless her, it did.

A few minutes later, we sat in her living room, eating blueberry scones and drinking our coffee while Carly put the finishing touches on the altar she'd set up on the coffee table. In addition to the usual items on the altar, she'd placed two tall candles in the center: one black and one white. She'd scattered large white feathers on top of the pentagram. A rose incense cone burned in a holder in front of the ceramic angel at the top of the pentagram.

When she was ready, Sean and I settled in on one side of the table while she invoked the circle around us. She sat down across from us and held out her hand. I took a small velvet bag from my pocket and slid the amulet out onto my palm.

Carly sucked in a breath. "Brigid, protect us," she murmured. "What a horrible thing this is."

I knew what she was reacting to: the amulet's nasty, black, oily aura, and the ancient spellwork carved into its face. I hated to look at it too. "Malcolm willingly took an oath to serve Miraç in exchange for my release. He accepted this as his prison to save my life." My eyes grew warm and glowed as my magic and anger rose. "I'm sorry to ask you to touch this, but we need your help to get him out. I don't want him in there one more minute."

"I don't fear this magic, any more than I feared Miraç's curses or Bridget and Morgan's threats." She placed the amulet on the altar in front of the incense, so the smoke would drift over it. "We are here to right this wrong and free a trapped soul, and we have a mighty ally to help us."

From a lined basket, she took a crystal goblet and matching plate with a small scone and placed them on the altar on either side of the candles. Into the cup, she poured an amber liquid from a decanter. I scowled. I might never look at a decanter the same way again, and that went double for antique rugs.

Then I caught a whiff of the liquid. My eyes widened. "No way."

She smiled as she stoppered the decanter. "Normally I use wine or water, but given it's you who is asking this favor, I thought a good single-malt would be more appropriate."

"Let's hope whoever we call upon for this appreciates good Scotch."

"Offerings are made from the heart, and that's what's generally appreciated." Carly rested her hands on the table. "Ready?"

"Super ready," I said, impatient for the ritual to begin.

She smiled. "That sounds like something Malcolm would say. Let's see what we can do to bring him back to us. First, meditation." She closed her eyes and breathed deeply, in through her nose and out through her mouth.

Sean and I followed her lead. It was difficult to clear my head and let go of my anger, fear, and guilt. The harder I tried, the more those emotions dug in their heels. Warm comfort washed over me as Sean tried to help, but it wasn't working.

"Alice," Carly said softly. "Look at me, sweetie."

I opened my eyes. Sean started to take my hand, but Carly shook her head. "No, she needs to do this on her own." Her eyes locked on mine. "Do you love Malcolm? As a friend and a brother?"

"Yes."

"And you believe he loves you as a friend and a sister?"

I swallowed hard. "Yes."

"Then why are you angry at him?"

"I'm not!"

She nailed me with a hard stare. "No lies in this house, Alice Worth."

Beside me, Sean stiffened. She pointed at him. "Don't. If you love her, let her deal with this."

Though I sensed his displeasure buzzing on my skin, Sean stayed silent.

Carly turned back to me. "Now, tell me why you're angry with Malcolm."

I started to argue, then closed my mouth. Damn it, I *was* angry with Malcolm. It was buried under a mountain of fury at Miraç, as well as all my worry, grief, frustration, and fear, but I'd already processed those emotions. I hadn't confronted this anger at all—partly because I'd only remembered what happened to Malcolm seven hours ago, and because I didn't know how to deal with it.

"I am so mad at him." My hands balled into fists. "I told him not to make that deal with Miraç. I begged him not to do it. *I gave him an order not to do it.* He did it anyway." My nails cut into my palms. "I swore I would never give Malcolm an order, but I gave him one, because I didn't want him to enslave himself. It was what he feared most, and he did it."

"Why did he do it?" Carly asked.

"So Miraç would spare my life and let me go."

"No, why did he do it?"

"I just told you—" I began.

She frowned at me.

I thought about what she wanted me to realize. She waited.

"He did it because he loves me and he's a good and unselfish person," I said. "And because he believed I would find a way to free him."

"He gave you an enormous gift, despite the fact you tried to give him an order as if you had the right to do that." Carly's words felt like a slap, but one I deserved.

"I shouldn't have given him that order," I sighed.

She gestured. "Keep talking."

"I'm angry because he made the deal against my wishes, and because I didn't think I deserved that kind of sacrifice." I took a deep breath and let it out. The anger began to fade. "I'm not sorry I tried to talk him out of doing it, but I don't get to give Malcolm, or anyone else, orders. And if he believes I am worth that kind of sacrifice, I don't get to tell him otherwise."

Warm comfort washed over me as Sean laced his fingers through mine.

Carly smiled. "Bingo." Her smile faded. "Much like Lily's hex, which brought us together, Miraç's actions have had some unintended consequences. Your relationship with Sean is stronger. *You* are stronger and more powerful. Your beautiful golden wolf will be your companion, and now you know in your heart you deserve to love and be loved—even if it means someone is willing to face their greatest fear for your sake." She offered me a small piece of paper and a pen. "Write it down."

I took the paper and wrote, *Thank you, Malcolm.* Below that, I added, *I deserve to be loved.* When I finished, I felt noticeably lighter. Sometimes I forgot anger and guilt were physical burdens.

Carly picked up the paper and set it on the altar. "Well done. Now, let's try meditation."

This time, my mind cleared quickly. I might have been imagining it, but Sean seemed more at ease as well. Maybe he'd let go of some anger and guilt too.

Carly spoke. "Our Guardian Angels, sacred forces of light, I call upon your might. Protect us from this evil magic and energy." I heard a match being struck. I opened my eyes to see her light the black candle. She blew out the match and dropped it into a small bowl. She struck a second match. "I call upon Archangel Suriel for his help to free a trapped spirit." She lit the white candle, blew out the match, and added it to the bowl.

When Carly had summoned Suriel to help guide a lost soul to the spirit plane, only she and Malcolm had seen and heard him. I'd sensed a presence so powerful and full of grace that it both awed and terrified me. I wasn't sure what to expect this time.

A breeze swirled around me, like someone had opened a window. Strangely, it smelled like the sea.

"Did you guys—" I started to say, before I realized I was alone, and no longer in Carly's living room.

I sat on a grassy hill overlooking a creek. The breeze wafted through my hair, bringing with it the scent of country air. Birds flew overhead in a clear blue sky. In the distance, I saw a familiar enormous house, surrounded by a wide lawn, several smaller buildings, and a tall wall. My grandfather's compound.

For some reason, I was entirely calm, despite the fact I'd apparently been snatched from Carly's house and dropped on a hill in Maryland.

"Hello, Alice."

I turned to find a blonde woman in a white suit sitting in the grass beside me. She hadn't been there a heartbeat ago, as far as I knew. She wasn't beautiful, but her features were striking. Her eyes were very light blue, almost the color of glacier ice. Like the breeze in Carly's living room, she smelled like the sea.

"Hi," I said. "Are you Suriel?"

"I am Tura." Her voice reminded me of church bells, or distant chimes.

I glanced at her back. "I know this is a terribly cliché thing to ask, but don't you have wings?"

"I do. However, in this form, and on this plane, I choose not to manifest them. They are quite cumbersome." She looked around, taking in the view. "You came here once or twice, I believe, on the rare occasions when you were permitted to leave the compound?"

I didn't bother asking how she knew. "Yes. This is a park about five miles from my grandfather's compound. Moses would sometimes arrange an outing here for my mother and me when I was little. He'd bribe someone to close the park to other visitors for a few hours. Why am I here?"

"This is where your mother met your father."

I blinked. "Where my mom met my dad?" When she said nothing, I added, "Or where my mom met Daniel?"

"The latter."

"Okay, but that still doesn't answer my question about why we're here."

"You wish Suriel to free Malcolm from his prison. I have come in Suriel's stead to do as you request, and to ask a favor."

My eyebrows shot up. "You want to make a deal to help us?"

The ground shook beneath us. "Angels are not demons, who make deals and peddle lives." Her voice could have cut through diamond.

"I apologize. No offense was meant."

She inclined her head, apparently accepting my apology. "I will free Malcolm from his infernal prison and restore his power, much diminished by his abuse at the hands of the foul creature who called himself Miraç."

She paused, so I said, "Thank you. And the favor?"

"You will soon make a journey, through a door we cannot use, to a place we cannot go."

Valas's damned errand through the mirror-door. "Yes?"

"On the other side of the door, you will encounter a man who calls himself a knight of no court or kingdom. I request you give him a message."

I blinked. "That's it? Just deliver a message?" Sounded more than reasonable. "What's the message?"

"Do you agree to deliver the message?"

"Not until I know what the message is, and how I'm going to be expected to deliver it."

"The message is in the language of angels, and you will deliver it like so." She leaned in and pressed her lips to mine.

My mouth filled with a sound unlike any I had ever heard. It was like a choir, a symphony, a roll of thunder, the roar of a waterfall, and the ringing of a bell, and as sweet as honey on my tongue.

She drew back. The sound faded, though its echo stayed in my ears.

"You're not going to give me the translation of that?" I asked, a little breathlessly. Not from the kiss, which had all the passion of a wet paper towel, but because I felt like I'd just swallowed an ocean of sound.

"It is not necessary that you understand the message, only that you deliver it."

"So I'm expected to find this knight with no court and give him a big ol' smooch. Okay. I need to know: when I deliver the message, what's likely to be his reaction? Will this knight be happy to hear the news, or will he be angry and try to kill the messenger?"

She tilted her head, as if my question had startled her. "I am not certain," she said. A tiny frown creased the perfectly smooth skin between her eyebrows. "His current disposition is not known. Either is possible."

"Fantastic." I sighed. "Anything else I need to know?"

"There is much, but all will unfold as it is meant to."

Damned cryptic angels. Suriel had given Malcolm the same answer when he'd asked about the mysterious condition that would break our binding.

I twitched, suddenly remembering something. "Hey, you never explained why you brought me here."

"This is the place where your life began."

"You said this is where my mom met Daniel." I stared at the ground. "Wait...are you saying...my mom and Daniel...*right here?*" *Dang, Mom,* I thought. On top of a hill overlooking her father's compound. I couldn't decide whether to be freaked out or impressed.

Tura made a sweeping gesture. "And this is where it will end."

I went ice-cold. "What?"

We were sitting in a field. I scrambled to my feet and spotted a familiar two-story farmhouse behind us. There was a FOR SALE sign in the yard. It was the house Sean and I had offered to buy.

Tura stood beside me, though I hadn't seen her rise. "Explain what you just said," I demanded. "And if you tell me everything will unfold as it's meant to, you can deliver your damn kissing telegram yourself."

"Suriel is an archangel who protects, counsels, and guides lost spirits. I am an angel of prophecy. I do not always know every bend in a path, but very often, I see where the path begins, and where it ends."

"Just where, though? Not why, or how, or when?"

She gave me that eerie smile again. "No one can know all, Alice, or control where journeys begin or end, not even angels."

"I feel like Ebenezer Scrooge being shown his gravestone." My throat was dry. "So, Ghost of Christmases Yet to Come, how long do I have?"

"I do not perceive time as you do, but I believe your time grows short." Her eyes shone from within, like moonlight behind a cloud. I wondered if she was seeing my death. "Your new power comes at a great cost. No human is meant to contain the power of a sorcerer—even a mage with shifter blood, who counts among her ancestors a member of the fae."

I stared at her, dumbfounded. "You're joking."

"One's lineage is never a matter for jest." Her brow furrowed again. "Surely you knew your magic was unique. The sorcerer could not wield it. Your grandfather could not command it. Neither was for lack of trying. Had you never wondered why your magic contained purple trace?"

"I thought that had to do with my blood magic." I wanted to sit down, but there was nowhere to sit but in the tall grass. "Fae magic is violet," I added, almost to myself.

"Indeed it is, and ancient fae magic is a darker shade. You have only a little, from many generations ago, but it has helped protect you."

It made a hell of a lot of sense, given the weird things I'd been able to do with my magic throughout my life. For now, I had some follow-up questions, most especially this one: "Why are you telling me all this?"

"Some of this knowledge you will need for your journey through the mirror. Some, you will need much sooner." She clasped her hands in front of her. "And the rest may change your fate."

"So there's a chance my life doesn't end here?" I gestured around us at the house and field.

She gave me a slight nod. "A slim chance, yes. Given your lineage and propensity to overcome great odds, you may make a different path than what I have seen."

"All I need is a chance." My life so far had been a series of slim chances; why should my future be any different? "Can you give me any insight into what I need to do to make it happen?"

"I am no angel of revelation, but I see one moment of decision that approaches soon. When you must choose between your life and that of your lover, you must choose your own."

Magic spiraled up my arms. "Screw that," I said automatically.

"Choose your own," she repeated. "By doing so, you will save him. You will save them all." She looked up. "I am called to return."

"Wait—" I began.

She became a pillar of blinding white light. I took an involuntary step back—

—tripped over a cushion, and sprawled on the floor next to the coffee table in Carly's living room.

Sean's face appeared above mine, his eyes golden. "Alice?"

I looked past him, to the figure floating beside Carly's altar. "Hi, Alice," Malcolm said. His aura was bright and pure and I saw no trace of Miraç's chain. He was grinning. "I was stuck in there for *ages*. What the hell took you so long?"

I found my voice. "It's been a crazy couple of days," I managed to say.

"You're telling me." He stared at me. "Wait, is that...what the...do you have an actual *wolf* inside you now?"

"That's Alice's golden wolf," Carly said, getting to her feet. "Isn't she gorgeous?"

Malcolm put his hands on his hips and glared. "I cannot leave you alone for *five minutes*."

I couldn't help it; I started to laugh.

And then I cried.

34

SEAN

ANOTHER UNSEASONABLY HEAVY RAINSTORM ROLLED IN, BUT SEAN didn't mind at all.

He and Alice sat on his back patio. She lay curled up on his lap, her head on his shoulder. Rogue snoozed by the glass door as Malcolm floated near the edge of the patio roof. Small gusts of wind blew raindrops through him to land on Sean's legs, propped on the seat of a chair.

Before they'd left Carly's house, Alice had revealed it was an angel named Tura, not the archangel Suriel, who'd spoken to her and freed Malcolm. Sean could tell there was more to the story than what Alice had revealed at the time, but hadn't pressed her on it.

Once they were home, Malcolm filled them in on what had happened to him after Miraç stole Alice's memories, and Alice and Sean described the events of the past several days. Malcolm was horrified by the condition in which Alice had been found and shocked and saddened by the deaths of Jack and Delia.

Malcolm had compared his time stuck in Miraç's amulet to "being trapped in a music festival Port-a-Potty"—an analogy that made Alice snort coffee out her nose. Despite the unpleasantness of being used as a power source for at least several rituals and during Miraç's fight with Valas, Malcolm assured them his captivity had been less of a torment than what Alice had gone through. Sean suspected Malcolm wasn't being entirely truthful about that. If Alice had the same suspicions, she kept them to herself.

Alice had enjoyed hearing about Miraç's frustration at not being able to wield her magic. He'd demanded Malcolm help him find a way to use it, threatening him with all manner of creative torments, but Malcolm hadn't been able to come up with a solution before Alice and Sean found the winery. Their arrival forced Miraç to change his plan and leave her magic for them to find, so she could have it restored and be used as his puppet during the attack on Valas.

When Alice told them the rest of what Tura had said, Sean understood why she'd been hesitant to discuss it in front of Carly. Alice's trace of fae heritage was a surprise, but that quickly became the least of Sean's worries. She revealed holding Miraç's power was killing her, and her death might be imminent unless she could find a way to forge a different path—news that made his wolf pace in agitation.

"I don't believe in destiny," Alice said bluntly when both Sean and Malcolm expressed concern about the news. "Obviously Tura does. I'm not in the habit of picking arguments with angels."

"Not a bad personal policy," Malcolm interjected. "Tura sounds like she might enjoy unloading a good smiting every now and then—just like you."

She smiled at him. "I missed you, bro."

Malcolm winked. "Missed you too, sis."

Her smile faded. "Miraç's power is burning through my cells faster than my little bit of shifter healing ability can repair them and it's going to kill me. My body is holding power it's not meant to hold. But as for following a predestined path, with a set beginning and end...I don't buy it. Maybe it's my natural contrariness, or maybe it's that I've found a way so many times when I wasn't supposed to. I *do* know prophecies are subject to interpretation. She says it's the end of my path; I say it's not."

"That's our Alice," Malcolm said approvingly. "Middle finger to fate and anyone who says something can't be done."

"With or without her memories, that's pure Alice." Sean nuzzled her hair. "Contrary and stubborn, down to her bones."

Malcolm grinned. "I wish I could have seen you before you got your memories back, just to see what *that* Alice was like, but I'm glad we got you back." He grew serious. "So, what are we going to do about the Were Ruling Council freaking out, Valas's binding, your fae heritage, Miraç's power, Tura's prophecies, and your missing memories? Oh, yeah—and your great big golden wolf?"

Sean kissed Alice's hair. "We're working on a plan for the Council and bringing Alice and her wolf into our pack." His wolf peered out through his human eyes, turning them gold. "As for the rest, we're going to do what Alice does best."

Malcolm perked up. "Smite people with lightning?"

"Race headlong into danger with little or no regard for my own personal safety?" Alice suggested.

Sean chuckled. "Probably yes on both counts, but I was thinking we'd pour some good Scotch and figure it out."

"You really get me," Alice said, kissing his jaw. His body responded instantly to her breath on his ear. She chuckled softly and wiggled on his lap.

"And *that's* my cue to leave," Malcolm said, floating back. "I'm sure you two would enjoy some long-overdue private time, and I've got to find Liam and tell him I'm still ghosting around."

Alice looked up. "I'd like help to fix my house wards. I still haven't been able to get in because my new magic is different and the house doesn't recognize it. We can do that tomorrow while Sean's at work. I'm staying here tonight, and I'm sure you and Liam have a lot of catching up to do."

"I'll see you tomorrow," Malcolm promised.

She winked. "Not too early. Hey, Malcolm?"

"Yeah?"

Sean sensed a surge of sadness and regret. He wrapped her in comfort and kissed the top of her head.

"Thank you," she said to Malcolm. "I'm sorry I tried to order you not to make that deal with Miraç. It will never happen again."

"Wow, thanking me and apologizing instead of yelling at me," Malcolm said with a grin. "That's more personal growth. Get your well-deserved werewolf TLC and I'll see you on the flip side." He vanished.

"It's good to have him back," Sean said, his lips against Alice's hair. "He seems fine."

"That's what worries me." She moved so she could see his face. "He's not fine, not after what he went through. He's putting up a front for us, so we don't worry."

"Sounds like someone else I know." He nuzzled her hair. "He'll talk to us when he's ready. In the meantime, can I interest you in some werewolf TLC before tonight's pack meeting? Or should we wait until after?"

Her eyebrows went up. "I don't see why this is an either-or situation."

"Good answer." He stood up with her in his arms. "You know, as long as it's been, it might take me a couple of times to remember exactly what you like."

"It's only been a week, Sean. I'm sure it'll come back to you." Her smile was playful. "If not, I have no trouble telling you what I want."

"What did you have in mind?"

She whispered in his ear.

His jeans were suddenly uncomfortably tight. "I think I can do that," he said.

ALICE

Malcolm and I spent the morning at my house. After we modified the wards and I finally got inside, I tidied the house, which had been left empty for nearly a week, while Malcolm spent some time in the basement. He needed to heal, and I knew from my own experience working on spellwork was soothing. I gave him space. Sean was right; Malcolm would talk when he was ready.

In the afternoon, I ran some errands, then went back to Sean's house. Malcolm said he wanted to stay at my house and work on the wards, then he'd go to see Liam. That worked out fine for my own plans for the evening, which required that Sean and I had the house to ourselves.

When Sean's car pulled into the drive just before six, I checked my reflection in the bathroom mirror and adjusted my new wolf amulet—a gift from Carly—so it rested just right in the center of my bosom. I turned off the light and went into the bedroom.

The kitchen door opened and closed downstairs. I heard several thumps as Sean dropped his work gear in the foyer. "Alice?" he called.

"Upstairs," I called back.

His footsteps climbed the stairs. "Sorry I'm late," he said, his voice drifting down the hall as he reached the top of the stairs. "Some equipment we needed for a project was backordered and I had to—"

He reached the bedroom doorway and stopped dead in his tracks. His mouth hung open.

I smiled and curtseyed. "Welcome home, sir."

He stared at me. After a beat, he remembered to close his mouth.

"Wow," he said finally, his voice sounding a little strangled. "Wow," he repeated.

I rotated slowly, the dress swishing on the floor. When I turned back around, he stood in front of me, his eyes bright gold. "My Lady Alice."

To my surprise, he bowed, then took my hand in his and slid his other hand around my waist. I wasn't sure what he was doing until he placed my hand on his shoulder, returned his hand to my waist, and nudged me backward, then to the left.

Sean Maclin, alpha werewolf, knew how to waltz.

"I never did get a dance at the gala," he told me as we waltzed in a slow semi-circle around the bed. My dress swirled around our legs and rustled against the furniture. "I was ready to spin you around the dance floor, but Vaughan monopolized you. Then Elizabeth arrived and stole my chance."

"I still saved my next dance for you." I smiled up at him. "You like the dress?"

"I like it very much," he assured me. "The red one was beautiful, but this green one suits you better, I think."

"I have it on good authority that this dress's bodice is very rip-able."

He raised an eyebrow. "Do you, now? That's very interesting."

I mimicked his expression, raising an eyebrow of my own. "I'm interested to know what you plan to do about it."

His eyes glinted. "If we're going to do this, let's do it right."

Before I could ask what he meant, he untucked his Maclin Security polo shirt and undershirt and pulled them off over his head. He tossed them aside, making sure to flex a bit, then dipped me backward for a sizzling kiss.

"Oh," I said breathlessly when he set me back on my feet. "Pardon me, sir, but what do you mean by disrobing like this in front of me?"

He took my face in his hands, his skin so wonderfully warm. My new wolf amulet hummed when his brushed against it. "My lady, your comments about your bodice led me to believe disrobing was expected." He kissed me, gently at first, then with more hunger as my hands slid down his back to grab his butt. He smiled against my lips. "How brazen, Lady Alice."

"I'm hardly a lady," I told him. "And this corset is not comfortable."

"I believe I can help you with that problem." His hands moved from my face to the front of my dress. Anticipation sent a wave of heat through me.

He smiled wickedly. "Fair warning, Lady Alice—I plan to plunder everything under this dress. And I do mean *everything*."

"I should bloody well hope so," I said.

He ripped the top of my dress open, baring my breasts. The rush of arousal was so powerful and sudden my knees nearly gave out. His mouth moved from my lips down to my collarbone and the delicate skin of my breast.

He growled low. "Alice."

"Yes?" I panted, fumbling with his belt.

"I'm trying to go slowly, because I want to savor this," he said, his voice rough. "But damn it, I don't *want* to go slowly."

I kissed him. "Then don't, because I don't want to go slowly either."

He swung me up into his arms and brought me to the bed, laying me on top of the quilt and crawling up my body. He gripped the dress with both hands and ripped it down the front, leaving me in just the corset and matching lacy undies.

He closed his eyes. "Alice, are you trying to kill me?"

I reached up and cupped his face with my hand, enjoying the feeling of his bristly cheek against my palm. "You promised you wouldn't go slowly," I teased.

To my surprise, he started unfastening the hooks on the front of the corset. "I think we should keep this," he told me, kissing me as his fingers moved quickly. "We might want it again."

When the corset was off, I was able to get a full, deep breath. He slid the undies off instead of tearing them, then set both aside. Then he stripped off the rest of his clothes and lay down, pulling me on top of him.

Last night, we'd simply wanted to sate our hunger for each other's bodies. This was more about healing and rebuilding our nascent bond. I let a little bit of magic out as I moved, allowing it to swirl around and through us so it blended our power. I kept my eyes on his as I rode him, watching him as he watched me, and there was no place I would rather be.

At his urging, I moved faster and more deliberately. He left one hand on my hip and slipped the other between us, teasing and caressing just the way I liked—just the way I needed.

With a gasp and a cry, I threw my head back and let the wave break. Beneath me, Sean gripped my hips tighter and moved beneath me, drawing out the pleasure until I couldn't take it anymore.

He rolled us over and took control—slowly at first to make me shudder and beg for more, and then faster to hear me call out his name. He moved my calves onto his shoulders and leaned forward, driving me back toward pure bliss. Despite our shared impatience, he held back, making sure he took me to the edge and over it again before lifting me to my knees in front of him and turning up the heat.

Several minutes, and several well-timed and welcome swats on my backside later, I came one final time. This orgasm was softer than the others, but our most intimate moment as my rainbow-colored magic tore free and swirled around us.

Sean's golden shifter magic blended with mine. "Alice," he groaned, his arms wrapped around me. He shuddered and held me tighter, pulsing hot inside me with his own release. Our magic thundered around the bed. It brought a second wave of pleasure as it settled back into our bodies.

Finally, he rolled us to our sides, his leg around mine. I drifted hazily in his embrace and forest scent, lost in the sensation of his warm body fitted against my curves.

He nuzzled my neck. "Alice?"

"Mmm?"

I sensed him smiling. "Thank you for the dress. Even if you never get me anything else ever again, I will still die a happy man."

Good grief—my legs were still shaking. "It was entirely my pleasure, I promise you."

"If I'd known you were planning this, I would have gotten another pirate outfit."

I turned in his arms so I faced him. "You can still do that anytime you like. I don't see myself getting tired of this little fantasy anytime soon."

He kissed the tip of my nose and tucked me against his chest. "Me either. In fact, I'd like us to keep this up for a long time, if that's okay with you."

"That's fine with me."

"Would you be willing to make that official?"

I raised my head to look at him. "What are you asking me?" I asked suspiciously.

"We have two days to give the realtor an answer on the farmhouse." He locked gazes with me. "I know this isn't the best time to press you for an answer. We're grieving for people we loved. You've lost some of your memories and Tura's prophecies are grim. We just got Malcolm back. And Vaughan..." His eyes glowed with anger. "I know your feelings for him are complicated."

"They *were* complicated," I admitted. "But not anymore. One silver lining of what Miraç did is I'm thinking more clearly about Charles and the other vamps than I have in a long time. In any case, my feelings for you aren't complicated at all. The answer is yes."

A pause. "Yes, what?"

"Yes, let's buy the farmhouse. I want to live with you."

He stared at me like he wasn't sure he'd heard right.

I took his face in my hands. "I want to live with you," I repeated. "I want us to live together in that farmhouse and play pirate or whatever other fantasy we'd like whenever we want. Give me the papers to sign. I'll call a realtor about my house on Monday."

He kissed me hard, then rested his forehead on mine. "I love you."

"I love you too," I told him. "I'm going to say something ridiculously sappy and if you make fun of me, I will zap you into next week."

Sean blinked. "Okay, I'm listening."

I kissed him on the jaw. "Another silver lining to all this mess is I got to fall in love with you all over again."

His mouth twitched.

I glared at him and raised my hand. Magic sparked on my fingers. "I warned you—"

He laughed and rolled us over so he was on top of me, his weight on his forearms. He kissed me until I forgot I was mad.

When we came up for air, I said, "You know, you promised to plunder everything under that dress."

"I did promise that, didn't I?" he said, his lips on my throat.

"But you didn't. I feel quite...unplundered."

He bit my earlobe and murmured, "I guess I'd better get to work."

"I guess you should."

And he did.

EPILOGUE

Sean had to work all day Sunday and well into the night on an installation job that had fallen behind schedule. In the meantime, I took Malcolm out to the new house to show him around and start building the house wards.

The FOR SALE sign in the front yard had a big red SOLD sticker across it. Except for what I considered normal mixed feelings about selling my house, I was excited about the prospect of moving in with Sean. The crippling doubt that held me back before I was kidnapped was gone. Whatever Charles had done to muddle my feelings, my head was clear now. What I could—or *should*—do about Charles messing with my head was less clear.

Around sunset, Malcolm left to go visit Liam. I promised to summon him if I needed him. I didn't intend to stay much longer, but I wanted to finish weaving one complete set of door wards before I left. The foundation wards would have to wait until another day. The night before a new moon wasn't a good time to set blood wards.

Once I finished the first set of wards around the doorways, I turned off all the house lights and sat on the steps of the deck to look at the stars before heading home. Sean would join me in bed when he got off work. I looked forward to sleeping in his arms.

The back of my neck prickled. I was not alone.

"Come out, Charles." My tone was frosty. I rose and turned toward where I'd seen movement in the shadows along the house. I hadn't planned to confront him tonight about his manipulations, but I would if he'd decided to force the issue. "No need to lurk. How did you get here? I didn't hear a vehicle."

The silence stretched out. No answer from the shadows. Someone was there, and it wasn't Charles. I found Malcolm's trace in my mind and gave it two quick tugs.

"I am not Charles Vaughan." The heavily accented voice came from the darkest part of the shadows.

I knew that voice. The first and only time I'd heard it, it had hissed a threat in my head—a threat in Romanian. *Teme-te de mine*, he'd said. *Fear me.*

I spooled blood magic. Golden shifter magic rose in my chest as my wolf raised her head and growled. Her snarl vibrated through my bones just as the crystal pendant around my neck buzzed with Malcolm's reassuring arrival.

I hesitated, unsure whether I should let him out. If my visitor was who I thought he was, I might be facing the most terrifying foe I'd ever encountered. If I didn't let Malcolm out and something happened to me, however, he'd find me somewhere in the afterlife and I'd never hear the end of it.

I focused on the sensation of Malcolm's magic. "*Release.*"

Malcolm appeared next to me. "What's wrong?" He followed the direction of my gaze and froze. "Oh, shit," he said involuntarily. He spooled magic. Our combined power seared the air.

The shadow moved, sliding along the side of the house in a way that reminded me of Miraç's oily smoke monsters. "You are like the chimera—a bit of this, a bit of that, a bit of something else," the voice mused.

"So I've been told," I said.

Vlad hissed. The sound was a vampire's, but more sibilant, like a snake. "You smell of angel and white witch."

"I have an eclectic circle of friends." I sniffed. "You smell like a vamp sorcerer. Like *Valas*."

His dry chuckle made the hairs stand up on my arms. "As well I should, for she is my maker."

My world tilted ninety degrees. Valas had made...*no way*. My brain wouldn't accept it.

"I am what results when a vampire who is a sorcerer turns a warlock." The shadow detached from the house wall and glided over the deck toward us. The boards turned black and rotted beneath him. I still couldn't see any of his features. The shadows shrouded him and no light would touch him—not even the moonlight.

"You look very different in your profile pic," I said, because what else could I say to Vlad Tepes, Wallachian warlord?

He stopped about ten feet away, his feet—or maybe *hooves* might be a more accurate word—not quite touching the deck. "I can take human form, obviously, as I have lived many lifetimes among humans, but this form is my own."

The smell of him turned my stomach. My skin crawled. Beside me, Malcolm shimmered, clearly unsettled. "Why are you here?" I asked.

Suddenly Vlad was right in front of me, in the shape of a dark-haired man with void-black eyes completely devoid of life. "You destroyed an item that belonged to me."

Power thrummed under my skin, ready to be unleashed. Beside me, Malcolm's magic surged. "*Belonged* being the operative word," I said. "The stone was in someone else's possession. If the magic inside had gotten loose, it might have wiped out a lot of vampires. It was a vamp WMD and it shouldn't have been floating around."

His black-nothingness eyes bored into me. "It was not yours to destroy."

"Agreed. It belonged to Charles, who gave me permission to destroy it to save him and all the vampires of his line."

"I came to spill your blood for your insult." He flashed his fangs. They stood out against the shadows that shrouded him.

I slashed with a blood magic blade, opening a gaping wound across his chest that gushed thick, dark, putrid blood. The cut almost went deep enough to reach his spine. It was the fastest I had ever moved.

Vlad laughed. Magic that smelled like rotting things swirled, healing the wound before my eyes. "Is it true you offered to ally yourself with the sorcerer Miraç against my maker?"

Maybe Valas had told him that. Miraç had revealed that information during the fight in the garden. "That's what I told Miraç, yes. I tried to make him think I was on his side, hoping he'd free me. I lied to him, though. I wouldn't ally with someone like him. He was a monster."

"Some say vampires are monsters." He hissed again, as if to emphasize the point.

"Some of them are," I agreed. "So are some humans, some shifters, and some mages, but Miraç was a whole new level of evil." Though by Vlad the Impaler's standards, Miraç might have been amateur hour.

"And Valas? What do you think of her?" His voice whispered in my mind: *I will know if you lie.*

"Stay out of my head," I snapped. "I think she used me to bring Miraç to her. She was willing to let me and others suffer as long as she got what she wanted. She needs me to do something for her, but the moment she decides I'm not useful enough, or something better comes along, she'll probably remove her binding and my status as a favorite of the Court and let me fend for myself."

"What do you think you owe her?" he asked.

"Other than what I owe her for helping me save my partner's life, nothing at all."

"You feel no loyalty to her?"

"She has no loyalty to me."

He studied me. "You healed the bite mark on your throat."

"I won't be branded. I won't be owned."

He floated around me, his form slithering over my skin like a snake. I stood still and ignored the nauseating sensation. "You are dying," he murmured. "I can smell it."

"I'm working on that."

He flashed his fangs again. "I could turn you. You could live forever, have more power than you could imagine."

"No."

His magic coiled around me. "I could insist."

My magic erupted, tearing through his like a machete through tissue paper. He recoiled.

"Don't try it," I said softly. "I'm a blood mage. That means any vamp who bites me against my will gets to watch himself boil alive from the inside out, or lose his head."

"You are devious." He didn't say it like he meant it as an insult. "Devious and powerful. I can see why she finds you appealing."

"Birds of a feather," I agreed. "Are we done?"

He hissed. "I am owed a debt for the theft and destruction of my stone of power."

"Maybe you are, but not by me. Whoever stole it is your enemy. I just contained the fallout and saved as many lives as I could, which is something I seem to end up doing on a regular basis."

He drifted back, his form turning to an oily black shadow again. He opened his mouth impossibly wide and showed me different, more terrifying fangs: one set upper, and one lower. What the hell *was* he?

"Do not betray Valas, Alice Worth. I am not the only creature she commands. We are the shadows you will not see until it is too late." With that, he vanished.

Sorcerers. They really liked getting the last word.

I sat on the steps, my back against the railing. Malcolm floated down to eye level. "So that was really him?" he asked.

"Yeah, I guess so."

"Wow."

"Yep."

We stared at each other.

"That's twice you've been threatened by Dracula," he said. "I wonder what the record is."

"Probably not too much higher than that, if I had to guess." I rubbed my face.

On the other side of the house, heavy tires crunched in the driveway as someone parked out front. "I'll go see who that is," Malcolm said, and zipped away.

I'd just gotten to my feet and started toward the front of the house when Sean, still wearing his Maclin Security polo shirt and work jeans, appeared around the corner with Malcolm trailing behind him.

I met him halfway across the backyard. "Surprise," he said. He wrapped his arms around me and kissed me hard, then drew back, his brow furrowed. "You're trembling."

"No, I'm not." I rested my forehead against his chest.

"What happened? When I got out of the SUV, Malcolm said I should have been here five minutes ago. Was someone else here?" His frown deepened. "Was Vaughan here?"

"Not Charles, no."

He inhaled, and his eyes turned golden. "I smell something foul. Alice, who came here?"

"Come look at the deck."

He followed me up the back steps. "What the hell?" He crouched to get a closer look at the damage. The blackened wood crumbled at his touch. "What the hell?" he repeated. "This isn't burned—it's rotted. What did this?"

"So, funny story...you remember that incident with the stone at Charles's house?"

He rose, his expression somewhere between disbelief and fury. "Yes, I do. Are you all right?"

I let out a little laugh. "Not a hair out of place. He just wanted to let me know he's mad about the stone and ask whether I feel any loyalty to Valas. Who is his maker, by the way."

Sean used a couple of words he usually saved for special occasions.

"He didn't come to harm me—just to see who I am, and to warn me not to cross Valas," I added as he tried to wrap his brain around what I was telling him. "I think he was more curious than anything."

"Vlad Tepes was here." His tone was deceptively neutral. My skin tingled as his incredulity gave way to anger.

"Right where you're standing," I confirmed. "Well, more or less. You can see where he was standing, because that's where the wood rotted away."

"You gonna tell Ben?" Malcolm wanted to know when Sean said nothing. "He's a Dracula fanboy. He'll lose his freaking mind."

"Maybe later, once I've processed it myself," I told him.

Sean growled. "Why didn't you call me?" He was angry, but not at me.

"We had it handled." I touched his hand. "No sweat."

"Dude, you should have *seen* her," Malcolm said with a grin. "He got in her face and she sliced him like a Christmas ham. He tried to use his magic on her, and she barely had to lift a finger to shred it. He was impressed by her." He floated back and forth. "Your girlfriend impressed *Dracula*."

"Stop calling him that," Sean and I said at the same time.

Malcolm crossed his arms. "Don't act like it wasn't bad-ass."

Sean pinched the bridge of his nose.

"I guess it *was* pretty bad-ass," I said. Thinking about it in those terms banished the last of my shaky feeling—which was probably why Malcolm had said it.

Sean kissed the top of my head. "I'm sorry I didn't get to see it. I'll just have to imagine how bad-ass you looked staring Vlad Tepes down." He shook his head. "He ruined our deck before we even got to use it."

"Warlocks-turned-vampire-sorcerers have zero respect for personal property," Malcolm quipped. "Can't wait to see the look on the insurance agent's face when you file this claim."

We walked around to the front of the house, where Sean's Maclin Security SUV was parked next to mine. With both our vehicles totaled—

his by panther shifters and mine by fire—we were both driving company cars for the time being.

Sean laced his fingers through mine. "Come home with me instead of driving separately. We'll come back for your car tomorrow."

I smiled and tugged playfully on his hand. "Can't stand to be separated from me for even thirty minutes?"

"No, I can't." He crushed me against his body and gave me a sizzling kiss.

Malcolm cleared his throat loudly. "Since Alice is in good hands, I'm going back to the mansion to hang out with Liam. You crazy kids have a fun night. I'll see you tomorrow." He vanished.

Sean leaned his forehead against mine. "We don't have to wait until we get home, you know. No one's around, and there's plenty of room in the back of my SUV if we get creative—which I'd be very happy to do."

"I'm barely recovered from yesterday," I teased.

"I want to make the most of every second we have." He kissed the tip of my nose. "What do you think?"

I pretended to mull it over.

He gave me a toothy grin that made me warm all the way down to my toes. "I promise to make it worth your while."

"You better," I warned. He chuckled and smacked my rump. Mmm.

While he rummaged around in the cargo area, making room for us, I put my phone in the passenger seat and pulled my T-shirt off. I spotted a small, flat shipping box on the floor with my name on the label. "What's this package?"

"That came for you today. I swung by my house and found it on the porch. I brought it with me in case we went back to your place. Looks like something from a pet supply store."

Curious, I tore the strip off the box. The return address was an online retailer I'd ordered dog treats from before. I hadn't bought anything recently, but it might be free items, or something Ben had sent. He'd gotten Rogue a collar that said BAD TO THE BONE and a matching leash.

When I opened the box, I found a second package inside: a thick manila envelope full of papers and sealed with tape. I dumped it out onto the passenger seat. My name was written neatly on the envelope in black marker. I recognized the precise feminine handwriting immediately.

Heart pounding, I shook the box. A small folded note fell out. Its outside had a familiar drawing of a bottle of poison and a rose. Cyro. I hadn't heard from her since I'd asked her to track down my biological father Daniel.

Sean came around the side of the SUV, his eyes shining gold. He'd probably sensed my reaction to the box's contents. "Alice? What is it?"

"Cyro sent me something." With a shaking hand, I picked up the note and opened it.

Inside was a short, three-word message: *I found him.*

THE END

Thank you for reading! Did you enjoy?

Please Add Your Review! And look forward to HEART OF VENGEANCE, book 6 coming this Fall! Turn the page for a sneak peek.

Want even more urban fantasy?

Try BLOOD AND MAGIC, book 1 in the Blood & Darkness trilogy by City Owl Author, Melissa Sercia!

HEART OF VENGEANCE SNEAK PEEK

"You should go in. The owner doesn't bite."

Startled, I turned. The speaker was a lanky college kid with long blond hair, a Love and Rockets T-shirt, and ripped jeans sitting at the other end of the bench.

"Excuse me?" I asked.

He gestured with his half-eaten sandwich at the record store across the little outdoor pavilion from where we sat. "I'm just saying, go in and check it out. You've been staring at the place for like twenty minutes. Daniel doesn't bite."

"Thanks. Maybe I will." I crossed my arms and resumed watching the store.

My body language was lost on him. "We're the last real record store anywhere around," he said with obvious pride. "New and used, all genres. We'll order anything you want if we don't have it."

I didn't reply. My attention was on the figure of a tall, well-muscled older man inside the store. In the past half-hour, he'd helped customers, sorted through bins of new inventory, and cleaned the glass in the door. At the moment, he was ringing up a couple of guys and talking with them, maybe about their purchases. I hadn't seen him smile...or sit down for one moment. Shifters tended to have a lot of energy, but he seemed more restless than most.

Mr. Love and Rockets was talking again. "What are you into? I bet classic rock." He finished off the last of his sandwich in one big bite and gulped water from a reusable bottle.

He seemed friendly, I supposed, and might be a good source of information about his boss. "I am, actually," I said, turning toward him. "How could you tell?"

He grinned. "I've been working in this store since I was sixteen. I get a vibe about people, you know? And I'm almost always right. So who are your favorites?"

"Pink Floyd, The Eagles, Led Zeppelin, AC/DC, The Who, Queen, Fleetwood Mac."

"On vinyl?"

I feigned confusion. "Are there any other options?"

He grinned. "Rock on. I'm Detroit." At my expression, he laughed. "It's really Henry, but Daniel's been calling me Detroit since forever."

"Are you from there?"

He shook his head. "Nah, I'm from here. I'm super into KISS, though, so I guess that's where it came from. Daniel claims he doesn't remember how he thought of it—just says Henry doesn't suit me."

"Daniel sounds interesting. He owns the store?"

Detroit nodded. "He's been running it for something like thirty years. It's his life."

That's what the file I'd received from the hacker Cyro had reported. Daniel had a simple life: the record store, a house on the outskirts of town, and a truck. No wife, no kids, no living family.

Except me.

"Daniel loves classic rock too," Detroit said, folding his insulated lunch bag. "He'd probably love to talk about it with you. Pink Floyd is his favorite band of all time. If you think *Dark Side of the Moon* is one of the best things ever made by a human, you and he will get along just fine."

My throat was dry. "The first vinyl album I ever bought was *Dark Side of the Moon*."

"Then come on inside and see what we've got. Bet we've got albums you need to own. I'll even slide you a first-time customer discount." He got to his feet. "You from around here?"

I shook my head. "A couple hours away."

"What brings you to town?"

I had an answer prepared for that question. "I planned to go on the ghost tour tonight."

"Mary Ann's tour? You'll like her. She knows all the local lore—and what she doesn't know, she makes up." He winked. "Coming in? I'll introduce you to Daniel."

I rose, but I made no move to follow him toward the store. I'd faced demons, ghosts, vampires, sorcerers, witches, poltergeists, angry werewolves, blood mages, panther shifters, an angel, a demon lord, and Vlad the Impaler, but the prospect of being introduced to Daniel Holiday made me want to run.

Running was not an option, however, because someone else might be coming after Daniel. That someone was my grandfather, crime lord Moses Murphy. For some reason he wanted Daniel dead for knocking up my mom with a half-mage, half-shifter baby. Why that would make Moses want to kill Daniel, I wasn't sure. I'd recently unearthed a forgotten memory from my childhood that indicated Moses would have killed all three of us back then if he'd known my real father wasn't John Briggs, the man who'd raised me as his own daughter.

Both my mom and my dad were long dead, murdered by Moses when I was eight. Now Moses knew I was part shifter, and he might be hunting for the man who'd fathered me. Luckily, ace hacker Cyro had found Daniel first. I had a chance to warn him that Moses or his goons might be headed this way.

As far as I knew, Daniel had no idea I existed, and I had absolutely no clue how to break the news. Since the day I learned about him, I'd rehearsed it a hundred times saying it a hundred different ways, but none of them seemed right. My alpha werewolf partner, Sean Maclin, had kissed me goodbye this morning and assured me the right words would come to me when it was time. As I stared through the front windows at my probable biological father, however, my brain was totally blank.

"For Pete's sake, Alice, show some fortitude." Malcolm crossed his arms and glared at me from where he floated a few feet to my right. "You heard Detroit Rock City over there—Daniel doesn't bite and he's got a sense of humor and he likes Pink Floyd. What else do you want?"

"A less judgmental ghost sidekick," I muttered.

Detroit turned around, his brow furrowed. "What was that?"

"Nothing." I ignored Malcolm's exaggerated eye roll and took a deep breath. "Sure, I'd love to check out your store."

"Awesome." Detroit headed for the front door of Blue Moon Records, whistling. "Oh, hey, what's your name?"

"Alice," I told him. "Alice Worth."

He opened the door and held it open for me. The familiar sound of Aerosmith's "Dream On" washed over me through the doorway. I smiled.

Was it possible to inherit a love of classic rock through genetics? I certainly hadn't gotten that from my parents, and I sure as hell didn't get it from Moses.

Detroit made a gallant sweeping gesture. "After you, Alice."

"Thanks, Detroit." I let Steven Tyler's vocals carry me inside.

The moment we walked in, Daniel sent Detroit to the post office to ship some online orders. As nice as the shop assistant was, I was relieved to not have to make conversation right now.

Daniel was still engaged in conversation with his customers, who were regulars judging by the way they chatted. I busied myself bin-diving in the classic rock section of the shop's used records inventory and listened to their discussion about the highlights of Black Sabbath's lesser-known tracks. Unsurprisingly, Daniel was highly knowledgeable on the topic. Though he didn't laugh or smile and seemed generally very solemn, he was friendly. We were the only customers in the shop at the moment—not entirely unexpected for a weekday morning.

I hadn't necessarily planned to buy anything, but darned if they didn't have several albums I really wanted, all in excellent condition. I made a stack and continued browsing.

Malcolm floated around the store, "checking the perimeter," as he called it, and reported nothing strange and no wards. He floated beside me, arms crossed again. "Alice, you're stalling."

"Hush," I muttered. "He's busy with customers."

"They're just yakking. I'm sure if you went up there, he'd send them on their way and talk to you."

"What part of this seems like it would be easy?" I asked testily, still in an undertone, as I flipped through records. "I'm working up the nerve to go up there, okay? And I've still got six more bins to go through. They've got a huge inventory."

Malcolm sighed. "I know this isn't easy, but I think you're getting *more* nervous the longer you stand here and think about it. Just go up there and ask him about some random album and chat for a bit. Break the ice and go from there." He glanced behind me. "Scratch that. He's coming to you."

I spun and locked eyes with Daniel, who was striding down the aisle toward me. The other customers were on their way out the front door, purchases in hand.

Besides his physique, the only indication he was a shifter was the way light reflected in his eyes. I was sure he'd already caught Sean's scent on me, but he didn't comment on it.

"Can I help you find something?" he asked.

I picked up my little stack of albums and showed him what I'd chosen. "Just adding to my collection. Your store is amazing."

"Thank you. I'm very proud of it." He looked over my albums. "Some excellent choices. Are you new to collecting vinyl?"

"I only started buying albums about five years ago. I didn't really have the means before that." I'd had no way to buy records while a prisoner of my grandfather, but I'd started building my collection as soon as I had my own place.

He nodded gravely. "I understand." He probably assumed I meant I hadn't had the money. "What other albums are missing from your collection?"

I smiled. "So many, it would take all day to list them. I can tell you a couple that are at the top of the list, though."

He didn't return my smile. Given what I'd read in the file Cyro sent me, his solemnity wasn't unexpected. Even thirty years later, the memory of seeing most of his pack slaughtered would be raw. He'd lost everyone because of Moses.

Other than some DNA, we had that in common too.

Think of it like this, Sean had told me last night as we lay in bed. *You are a gift to him. He believes he's alone in this world. He has no pack and no family, as far as he's aware. Not all lone wolves are lonely, but my gut tells me this is a lonely man. I don't see a scenario where your news isn't welcome, once the shock wears off.*

Sean had offered to come with me, but the presence of an alpha would complicate things considerably. I'd decided to just bring Malcolm—who had drifted over to a different area of the store to give us the illusion of privacy.

"What's on your list?" Daniel asked.

I named a few albums. We found two in the used section and one more in the back, in a crate of new inventory he hadn't had a chance to go through yet. I ended up with a healthy pile of seven albums, all in great condition.

Detroit wasn't back yet, so when another customer came in, Daniel went to help them for while I looked over the flyers plastered on the front counter. Most of them advertised local bands, record swap meets, and other locally owned shops. A couple of bands were holding auditions. One specified they needed a drummer with a working vehicle capable of transporting the band to gigs. I chuckled.

Daniel's voice startled me. "Do you play an instrument?" He went around the counter to ring up my purchases. The new customer left empty-handed, apparently unable to find what he was looking for.

I shook my head. "No. I sing a little."

"Ever sing with a band?"

"Never got the chance to try. I think it would have been fun."

He gave me the total. "I assume Detroit offered you a first-time customer discount."

I nodded. "He did, but I know a small business counts pennies, so I won't hold you to it."

"I count happy customers." He hit a few buttons on the register and told me the revised total. "Cash or credit?"

I handed over my card and he ran it. As the slip printed out, he studied me. "Did you find out what he sent you to find out?"

I blinked. "Who?"

"The alpha of whatever pack you're associated with." His expression hardened. "I assume he sent you to do a little snooping on the local loner. You didn't make much of an effort to clean off his scent, so he must have wanted me to know. Tell him I'm not interested in joining his pack and not to bother sending any more cute girls to entice me."

"It's not what you think." I signed my name on the receipt and handed it back. "That's my partner you smell, and he didn't send me."

His expression didn't change. "Your partner? Not your mate?"

"Not yet. Maybe someday. We just bought a house together." I wasn't sure why I told him that, but it just came out.

"The Council's letting him have a human mate?" Daniel sounded skeptical.

"They don't exactly approve," I said, which might be the understatement of the century. "And I'm not exactly human."

For the first time, his dark brown eyes glowed golden. "What are you, then, besides a mage?"

I took a deep breath. "That's why I'm here, actually."

Before I could say more, three SUVs pulled up in front of the shop. Warning bells went off in my head. Daniel turned to see what had caught my attention and snarled.

Men and women emerged from the SUVs. I didn't recognize any of them, but I recognized a team of cabal soldiers when I saw one.

Shit.

The passenger door of the middle SUV opened. Nora Keegan, my grandfather's newest lieutenant, stepped out.

Double shit.

Nora was a high-level blood and air mage. She'd been one of local boss Darius Bell's top lieutenants, but had switched allegiances and killed Bell on Moses's order as part of his takeover of the city. She'd also been present when Malcolm was tortured to death on Bell's orders and kidnapped ones of my clients right from under my nose. We had a *lot* of unfinished business.

Our eyes met through the window. She looked very surprised to see me, which told me they hadn't followed me here. Moses had tracked Daniel down and sent Nora to bring him in.

Nora smiled at me and raised her phone to her ear. I knew who she was calling: Moses.

Triple shit.

Daniel turned to me, his eyes bright gold.

"You've got to get out of here," we said at the same time.

"They're here for me," Daniel said. He must have recognized someone in Nora's goon squad, or he knew Nora worked for Moses now. He might have been keeping tabs on Moses's organization.

I shook my head and spooled magic. "They're here for *us* now. Go. I'll hold them off."

"The hell you will," he snarled. "That's Moses Murphy's top lieutenant out there." So he *did* know who Nora was.

"I know. The first time we met, I cut off her left hand and she blasted me through two walls." In the interim, I'd absorbed the magic and power of a sorcerer I'd killed and developed some new abilities. I looked forward to evening the score between us.

Malcolm floated over next to me, his magic prickling on my arms. "I can take out the humans with sleep spells," he told me. "Then we unleash hell on Nora and the other mages."

Daniel looked right at where Malcolm was. He couldn't hear or see my ghost, but shifters were sensitive to the presence of spirits.

"I've got a mage ghost here backing me up too," I said to Daniel. "We can handle them. Do you have another way out of here besides the front and back doors?"

Outside, Nora finished her brief call and stuck her phone back in her pocket. She waggled her fingers at me. Air magic coiled around her arms and her eyes turned white.

With a snarl, Daniel vaulted over the counter, picked me up with one arm, and ran toward the back of the store, moving so fast I didn't have time to protest. Malcolm was right behind us. Thank goodness Detroit wasn't back from the post office yet.

The front windows exploded in a massive burst of air magic that swept through the store, destroying everything in its path. Shards of glass flew toward us in a blizzard of potentially lethal edges. Daniel swung me in front of him and grunted as glass embedded itself in his back.

He kicked the door to the office open and shoved me inside just as gunshots rang out. He staggered inside, slammed the door, and locked it with several solid-looking deadbolts. Belatedly, I noticed the door and the frame were reinforced steel. The office was a panic room, apparently.

"If they've got a high-level earth mage with them, they'll be able to get in here," I told him. He probably knew that, but I wanted to make sure.

Inside the room, I couldn't hear anything from the store, but I assumed Nora and her crew were destroying everything and surrounding the panic room.

Daniel pulled a pocketknife from his jeans pocket. He tossed it to me and turned his back. "Cut them out," he ordered, his voice hoarse.

His shirt was soaked with blood. His back had several large shards of glass embedded in it, but the two bullet holes were the immediate problem. I pulled out the glass so he could start healing and ripped his shirt open. The skin around the holes was black.

"Silver bullets," Malcolm said grimly. "Son of a bitch."

"I guess their orders were to bring you in dead or alive. Brace yourself." I sliced across one of the entrance wounds, stuck my fingers into the opening, and used my earth magic to sense the silver. How he'd known I'd be capable of rendering this kind of first aid I had no idea, but shifters usually had good instincts about people. Or maybe it was some kind of test.

Daniel snarled. "Hurry."

"I *am* hurrying." I pulled the first bullet to my fingers using my earth magic. Daniel grunted.

Thankfully, the bullet was intact and easy to remove. I pulled it from the wound and tossed it on the desk. "One down."

I tried to repeat the process with the second bullet, which was also still in one piece, but it had shattered his right shoulder blade and gotten lodged in something—probably his collarbone. "It'll be easier from the front," I told him.

He turned to face me. "We need to go before they figure out how to get in here." He wiped his mouth, leaving a streak of blood on the back of his hand. One or both of the bullets had punctured something important.

"I know." I cut into his upper chest and stuck my fingers inside his flesh. One quick pull with my earth magic and the bullet came loose. I dropped it onto the table beside the first one. "Done."

Daniel balled up his bloody shirt and pressed it to the wound on his chest. "Thanks."

"You're welcome. Nora is a monster. You should've let me kill her."

"I want answers about why you're here. You can kill her some other time."

He grabbed a tall metal cabinet and swung it away from the wall, revealing a ladder. He climbed up a few rungs, pushed a ceiling tile aside, and punched in a code. A door swung up, revealing a tunnel leading up.

Daniel jumped down off the ladder. "You go first. I'll follow."

I turned to Malcolm. "Go up and make sure it's clear."

"You got it." The ghost zipped away up the tunnel. A few moments later, he returned. "The tunnel leads to a hatch on the roof. It's clear for now. I'll go back and keep watch."

"Okay. Be careful."

He zipped away again. I started up the ladder. When I got to the tunnel, I glanced back to see Daniel pour liquid from a small container onto the bloodstain on the floor. I smelled gasoline. He tossed the container aside, left his bloody shirt on the floor, and started up the ladder behind me.

I climbed up the tunnel. When Daniel got to the tunnel, he took a metal lighter from his pocket. He flicked it, dropped it into the room below, and slammed the trapdoor on the flames. The panic room's air vents would supply oxygen, ensuring the fire consumed the contents of the office, including Daniel's blood and whatever else was in there he didn't want Nora to get her hands on.

He looked up at me, his golden eyes bright in the near pitch-darkness of the tunnel. "What are you waiting for?"

We climbed the ladder quickly. The record store was on the ground floor of a four-story building, so we only had to climb three stories to get to the roof.

When we reached the top, I found a glowing number pad on the wall. "Code is one three nine five," Daniel told me.

I punched in the number and the hatch unlocked. I turned a handle and pushed it open. The daylight was blinding.

Malcolm was waiting. "All clear. Hurry."

I clambered out to the roof. Daniel emerged right behind me and shut the hatch. Shouts drifted up from street level. Sirens blared in the distance.

"Follow me." Daniel headed for the far end of the roof. Clearly, he had an escape route already planned in case something like this ever happened.

I scurried after him with Malcolm at my side. "What's the plan?"

Daniel didn't look back. "Get off this roof and get the hell out of here."

"They'll be watching your vehicle," I reminded him.

"I know. I have a backup plan."

I glanced at Malcolm. "Go check and see if there's anyone lurking around my car. If there is, come back. If not, stay and keep an eye on it until we get there unless I summon you."

"Will do." He vanished.

We reached the edge of the roof. I didn't see any way of getting down to street level. There was another building across the alley, but it was a good twelve feet to that roof and a forty-foot drop.

Daniel turned to me, his expression cold. He'd lost everything again. His beloved record store was gone. Even if we evaded Nora, he couldn't go home—they'd be waiting for him there. For thirty years, he'd made the best life a man could after watching everyone he'd ever loved die, and in a matter of a few minutes, it was all gone.

"Why did you come here?" he asked. He didn't sound angry, just resigned, as if he'd known this day would eventually come.

None of the imaginary scenarios I'd rehearsed included standing on the edge of a roof while Moses's goon squad destroyed Daniel's record store. Soon Nora would realize we weren't in the burned-out panic room and start looking for possible escape routes, if they hadn't already.

I reached into my back pocket and pulled out a four-by-six photograph of two adults and an eight-year-old girl. It was a duplicate of the original, which had been damaged in my escape from Moses's compound five years ago. I held it up so he could see it.

"My mother's name was Moira Murphy," I told Daniel. "That's her husband John Briggs with us in the photo. He raised me as his child, but I wasn't."

I reached for the golden shifter magic in my chest. My eyes grew warm, and I knew they had telltale golden rings. "I'm your daughter," I said.

The hard mask vanished. A parade of emotions crossed his face: shock, disbelief, grief, anger. A flash of fear. Not for himself—for me.

"Where is your car?" he asked finally, his voice tight.

I pointed. "A couple of blocks that way. I wanted to walk."

"All right." He gestured at the other roof. "We have to get moving."

I spooled air magic. "You go first."

He growled. "No way in hell I'm leaving you behind." *Again*, his expression said.

"I'll be right behind you. I think I can jump it with my air magic. If you're there waiting, you can catch me if I put a little too much oomph into the jump." Which sometimes happened when adrenaline got into the mix. Unfortunately, I knew that from painful experience.

Daniel held out his hand. "If you trust me, I'll get us both across."

Though the injuries had begun to heal, he'd been shot twice with silver bullets and had his back sliced to ribbons by shards of glass. When I looked into his eyes, however, I knew he wouldn't have suggested it if he didn't know he could get us across safely.

I'd known him thirty minutes and he was asking me to put my life in his hands. Then again, I'd hired a black-hat hacker to track down my biological father and then driven three hours to meet him. What was one more leap of faith?

I took his hand. "Okay."

He didn't give me time to think about it too much and swung me onto his back. I locked my arms around his shoulders and my legs around his waist. I'd done this with Sean a few times, but for fun and certainly never to jump between buildings. Like most shifters, Daniel's body was solid muscle, and though he was quite a bit older than Sean, he was powerful and strong.

He circled back to pick up momentum, adjusted his pace to account for my weight, and ran full speed toward the edge of the roof. He launched off the low parapet wall, flew over the gap between the buildings, and landed with plenty of room to spare on the other roof.

I let go of him and slid to the roof. His blood stained the front of my shirt, but that was low on my list of problems at the moment. "Thanks for the lift. What now?"

He gestured at a rooftop door. "Down those stairs and out to the alley. My buddy Sal who owns the deli won't mind if we borrow his truck to get out of here."

Before we went to the door, we peered over the edge of the roof to check the alley. It was empty.

"Hey, what happened to the sirens?" I asked.

Daniel growled. "Murphy probably made some phone calls. The cops aren't coming. Let's go before they figure out where we've gone."

He opened the door, revealing a dimly lit stairway. I followed him down. We moved silently and quickly.

At the bottom of the stairs, Daniel paused with his hand on the doorknob, listening for any sounds in the alley. Hearing nothing, he unlocked the door and opened it.

Two of Moses's goons stood on the other side of the door. They looked as surprised to see us as we were to see them.

I unleashed a blast of air magic that sent them both flying back to smash into the wall on the other side of the alley. They hit the ground and lay still, either dead or out cold.

I heard slow clapping and turned. Nora stood in the mouth of the alley, flanked by four more goons with guns raised. "Alice, it's lovely to see you again. It feels like fate keeps bringing us together."

I rolled my eyes. "It's not fate; it's that your dick bosses keep sending you on little errands."

Her smile vanished. "My orders are to bring him in. You can come too, if you like." She pulled a pair of spell cuffs from her belt and twirled them around her finger. "Just slip these on like a good girl and I'll make sure you get there without so much as a scratch."

"I think we'll take door number two," I said, inching in front of Daniel. He growled.

"There is no door number two, sunshine." She dangled the cuffs. "It's my way...or the dead way."

"Moses needs me alive," I murmured to Daniel. "She can't kill me, but she can kill you. I'll buy you some time to get out of here. When you can, get to Sean Maclin, my partner. Our pack will protect you."

He snarled. "I'm not leaving, and I'm not bringing danger to any pack, especially not yours."

"Come on, Alice," Nora called. "Don't make me insist. I don't know why you're here, but it's time for you to either run along home or decide to come with Mr. Holiday and visit my boss. I know he'd love to see you."

She had no idea how badly Moses wanted me, or why. Moses had to make sure no one knew I was really his granddaughter, who had apparently died five years ago in an accident at his compound in Baltimore. If that news got out, everyone would be after me, from the feds to every cabal in the country and every Vampire Court too.

"Do you have somewhere safe to go?" I asked Daniel.

He growled and didn't answer, but I saw from his expression that he did have a place to go.

"Do this for me," I said. I knew it wasn't fair of me, and the last thing I wanted to do was to send him away when we'd only just found each other, but I wanted him far away from Nora. "Come find me soon. We have a lot to talk about."

He planted his feet shoulder width apart. "You can't fight them all by yourself."

I smiled. "I'm not by myself. Trust me, Daniel." I paused. "The first album I ever bought was *Dark Side of the Moon*. When you come find me again, we'll listen to it together."

He stilled, his face a mask of both pain and wonder.

"Go." I repeated. Out of the corner of my eye, I saw two mages and two goons at the opposite end of the alley. Malcolm floated behind them, unseen and waiting for my signal. He gave me a thumbs-up.

I turned back to Nora. "A while back, I told you we'd have to take a rain check and finish that conversation another day."

Magic spooled around my arms in every color of the rainbow. My cells buzzed with the magic I'd absorbed from the sorcerer I'd killed. The power was enormous and strange and I was only just beginning to learn how to use it.

It was also slowly killing me, but that was a problem I'd have to solve another day.

My wolf raised her head and growled. My eyes grew warm and my vision went gold around the edges. "How about today?" I asked Nora.

She stared. The goons with her exchanged glances.

Beside me, Daniel smiled at her. It was a purely predatory smile—one I used myself from time to time. I guessed I knew now where I'd gotten it from. If he was weirded out by my magic or my wolf, he didn't let on.

"You want to play?" I asked Nora. "Then let's play."

Instead of leaving, Daniel dropped to his knees and shifted in a surge of golden shifter magic. His wolf was enormous, dark gray with a band of black fur across his shoulders. He flattened his ears back against his head and showed Nora all of his teeth. It occurred to me Daniel had just as much reason to hate Nora and anyone else from Moses's cabal as I did. Fair enough—we could do this together.

My wolf raised her head. My skin prickled like fur was pushing at it from the inside. She wanted out.

Go play, I told her.

With a growl, my wolf leaped out of my chest in a brilliant surge of magic. She was the same size as Daniel's wolf, but made of pure golden magic. She landed on the pavement, raised her head, and howled. I might be biased, but I thought her howl was the most beautiful and terrifying howl I'd ever heard.

Two of the people with Nora turned to run. She formed a blood magic blade and cut them in half before they had a chance to take two steps.

The humans at the other end of the alley dropped, thanks to Malcolm and his sleep spells. The two mages, who couldn't be spelled because of their natural shields, headed in our direction.

"Sic 'em," I told Daniel's wolf. "I'll deal with Nora and the others."

He snarled, turned, and headed for the mages.

Judging by Nora's expression, she was trying to think of a way to take out my golden wolf. My wolf, on the other hand, eyeballed Nora like she thought she looked tasty.

"What *are* you?" Nora asked me, her eyes on the golden wolf. "And what the hell is that thing?"

My wolf showed her teeth.

"I'm a mage with some special skills, and this is my wolf. And *that*—" I hooked my thumb over my shoulder toward where Daniel's wolf was snarling at the mages "—is someone you aren't taking back to Moses, so maybe *you* should just run along and tell him if he wants Daniel, he can come get him himself instead of sending his lackeys to do it."

Needling Nora about being an underling was one of the few ways I'd found to get a reaction from her. People like her didn't let others get under their skin very easily, but she had an ego. Poking it was one of my favorite pastimes.

Nora's eyes turned white. I didn't know how much power she'd expended earlier blowing out the front windows of Daniel's store, but she could pack quite a wallop. Then again, so could I. Thanks to the sorcerer magic I'd absorbed, I had some new tricks up my sleeve.

I spun my blood magic into round blades on my fingertips. Nora smiled. As far as she knew, from this distance and without a focus, the blades couldn't harm her or her companions.

Surprise, bitch.

Dark magic flared on my hands, igniting glyphs on the blades. With twin quick movements and a burst of air magic, I threw them at Nora, and two more right after.

She reacted fast, her reflexes enhanced—I suspected—by drinking vampire blood. Her air magic sent the first two blades into the walls on either side of the alley, where they gouged chunks out of the bricks. The second set of blades ended up in the chests of the man and woman on either side of Nora. They went down, gurgling.

Behind me, Daniel's wolf tore into someone. I glanced over my shoulder. One mage was on the pavement, unconscious. The other stopped screaming abruptly. Daniel's wolf raised his bloody muzzle and howled. Malcolm appeared at my side, looking quite pleased with himself.

"You are just *the most* stubborn person," Nora said, shaking her head. She was spooling air magic again. "Why do you insist on doing everything the hard way? Don't you know you'll only end up suffering more in the end?"

"Why? Are you planning to talk me to death?" I jerked my head in Nora's direction. "Kill her," I told my wolf.

She headed for Nora, growling low.

Nora unleashed a blast of air magic. I formed an air magic shield in front of me, but I wasn't her target. Instead, the magic hit the corner of the building whose roof we'd jumped onto.

The impact was like a bomb going off. The entire corner of the building crumbled. I had no time—and no*where*—to run.

I hit the ground, grabbed a ley line, channeled its power into my air magic shield, and curved it over my head. Falling bricks couldn't hurt Malcolm or my wolf, but they could hurt me.

Debris piled on top of my shield. It wavered, threatening to give way and drop a ton of rubble right on top of me. I curled into a ball and made the shield as small as I could to focus my power.

I gritted my teeth and channeled more ley line power. The pain was intense, but it was better than being squashed flat. Had the building stopped falling, or was the pile on top of me getting heavier? I couldn't tell.

My wolf came back. She spiraled up my arm and disappeared into my chest. The sensation was of a puzzle piece finding its home. Her power combined with mine and the shield held steady.

I could use air magic to try to blast away the debris on top of me, but I worried I would lose the shield if I did that. I couldn't tell how deep I was buried. If I lost the shield without clearing an opening big enough to get out, the results would not be good. On the other hand, I had to get myself out soon, before I ran out of air or my shield gave out.

Just as I was about to try an air magic blast, Malcolm's head and shoulders appeared in the tiny space occupied by my body and the air I had to breathe. I could barely see him through the dust.

"I knew it! You're alive," he crowed.

I coughed. "For the moment."

"Daniel's digging you out. Hang on—let me go tell him where you are." He disappeared.

I heard the faint sounds of pieces of debris moving. The sounds got louder and closer. The pile on top of me lightened, and chunks of rubble crashed as Daniel picked them up and threw them aside. Holding the shield became far easier as he cleared the wreckage.

Suddenly, sunlight and relatively fresh air streamed through an opening above my head. "Alice!" It was Daniel's voice, growly and worried.

I coughed again. "I'm here. I'm okay."

The opening got bigger until there was nothing left above me. I let go of the ley line and let my shield dissipate.

Daniel appeared, covered with sweat and dust, his eyes golden. "Can you get out?"

I got to my feet, a little woozy from channeling the ley line and holding the shield for so long. The entire corner of the building lay in a pile around me. Sirens wailed in the distance again, and I had a feeling they would be responding to this scene.

"Nora's gone?" I rasped, doubling over to cough out dust.

"Yeah, she gave up and hightailed it out of here," Malcolm said. "I think we should do the same before the cops and feds arrive."

Daniel helped me climb out of the rubble. Bystanders and employees of the businesses housed in the building picked their way through the debris, looking for anyone else trapped in the wreckage.

He'd had found some basketball shorts to wear. They weren't his size—maybe he'd found them in his friend's truck. When he'd shifted, his wounds had healed, though the silver bullets had left scars.

I followed Daniel to his friend's truck, parked at the other end of the alley in a small lot. "Come back with me," I urged. "Moses won't stop hunting you. For some reason, he's angry I'm part shifter, and he wants to take it out on you."

Daniel leaned against the truck. "I can't believe I have a daughter. All these years...you're sure?"

"I'm sure. I have it on the highest authority." That highest authority happened to be an angel named Tura, but I didn't think now was the time to tell him that. He'd had enough revelations for one day.

"Why the hell didn't Moira tell me?" he demanded, his eyes blazing gold. He was angry now that the shock had worn off. I couldn't blame him. "I never would have left. I never would have abandoned her, or you. *Why?*" He snarled.

"She wanted you to live—to get away from Moses and have a life. I don't know why, but she believed Moses would have killed all three of us if he'd known you were my father. She and my dad kept it a secret until the day they died. I only found out because of a spelled mirror that showed me a forgotten memory of overhearing them talking."

"She had no right to keep this from me." He scrubbed his face with his hands. "You look nothing like the picture you showed me." It wasn't an accusation, just a question.

"When I escaped from Moses, I had to steal someone's identity to hide from him. I had plastic surgery and became Alice Worth, who died in Chicago five years ago. My real name is Ava." I swallowed hard. "Come home with me."

He shook his head, his expression grim. "I'm better off on my own. I don't want to bring more danger to your door."

"I used to think that way too, but I was wrong. Out there, you're alone. If you come home with me—"

"Alice, stop," he said quietly. "I will find you again soon, I promise. I have to sort some things out."

The sirens were loud now, and there were a lot of them. "We've got to go," Malcolm urged.

Apparently Malcolm had taken some energy from Daniel, because Daniel heard him. He turned toward Malcolm and pointed at him. "You keep her safe, and tell Sean Maclin he'd better do the same."

"Yes, sir," Malcolm said. "Come on, Alice."

Daniel cupped my cheek with his hand. "You may not look like her, but I hear Moira when you talk," he said, his voice rough. "Go home. I'll see you when I can."

"Let me know you're safe, at least," I said. "Get me a message when you're somewhere safe."

"I will." He released me and got in the truck. He turned the key in the ignition, gave me a nod, and floored it in the direction of the lot's exit. In seconds, he'd turned the corner and disappeared.

I wanted to punch something. "Damn it."

"Yeah." Malcolm touched my shoulder. "You okay?"

"Not even remotely." I headed for my car with Malcolm trailing along behind me.

Thank you for reading! Don't miss HEART OF VENGEANCE, book 6, in the Alice Worth series, coming this Fall!

Want even more urban fantasy? Try the Blood & Darkness trilogy by City Owl Author, Melissa Sercia, and discover more from Lisa Edmonds at www.lisaedmonds.com

---

With supernatural powers and an insatiable need for blood, her existence is cursed.

When Gray awakens from a three-year spell induced coma, she not only discovers her lover as the one responsible, but that he has joined with a dangerous organization, the Consilium, to help them create a new breed of hybrid demons.

Humans and Witches are being taken against their will, and fear is growing throughout the covens.

Gray never had a choice—forced to become a monster, the Dhampir. Yet after four hundred years, she still yearns for her humanity, like a long-lost echo from another life.
She cannot allow the Consilium to do this to anyone else.

With a renewed lust for vengeance, and a target on her back, Gray must use the one thing she swore never to in order to stop them—blood magic.

Armed with a magical pirate ship, an immortal monk, and a flower plucked from the Underworld, Gray will stop at nothing to start a war.

Yet in her quest to track down her enemies, she uncovers a dark family secret that threatens to destroy the last shred of humanity she has left.

All reviews are **welcome** and **appreciated**. Please consider leaving one on your favorite social media and book buying sites.

For books in the world of romance and speculative fiction that embody Innovation, Creativity, and Affordability, check out City Owl Press at www.cityowlpress.com.

ACKNOWLEDGMENTS

Author acknowledgements are a special opportunity to thank the many people who provided support, expertise, constructive criticism, coffee, wifi, and tacos during the long process of turning ideas hastily scratched in a notebook into a published novel. I try to shout out to these wonderful people in other ways, but here's a formal list of those to whom *Heart of Shadows* is dedicated.

I owe an enormous debt of gratitude to my editor, Heather McCorkle at City Owl Press, for guiding me from that first query e-mail proposing the series to this milestone of the fifth full-length book in the Alice Worth series. Thank you also to Tina Moss and Yelena Casale at COP for their tireless work, wonderful humor, and amazing talent. Ladies, you are the best. Publishing with a woman-owned press is a gift and a privilege, one I never take for granted.

I am lucky to have a squad of fantastic beta readers—most especially Dr. Marie Guthrie, who, as alpha reader, has the (mis)fortune of seeing how the sausage is made. You're the best. I'm not sure I tell you that enough. A huge thank you to Luna Joya, Shannon Butler, Dr. Kimberly Dodson, Amy Hopper, Carla Schultz-Ruehl, and Dr. Robert James, for their thoughtful feedback on the various drafts of this book (as well as many others).

Once again, I am grateful for the expertise of Lady Beltane, High Priestess of Coven Life Coven. Lady Beltane continues to breathe life and magic into the character of Carly, as well as provide insight and guidance in the development and practices of the black witches in this book. I look forward to having Carly along for more of Alice's adventures! For more information about the Craft, visit covenlife.co.

My extended family and cherished friends continue to be wonderful and supportive. All my love to my mother, my brilliant sister Susan, my brother-in-law Josh, and their great kiddos. Hugs and love to Antoinette and Felicia, Tom and Pam Snowe, and Mike and Teri Belanger, as well as JC Krueger, Jen Bauer-Krueger, and Neda Benitez. A very special thanks to Bridget Talmadge and Jennifer DeWitt at The Full Cup Books & Coffee, for all the coffee, lunches, laughs, and friendship. You guys rock. To anyone I accidentally left off the list: I love you, I'm sorry, and I'll get you next time!

And finally, because he's my bedrock, thank you to my husband Bill for...well, literally everything. The love, the laughs, the *Family Guy* quotes, for never fussing when I want to binge-watch *Forensic Files* AGAIN, and a million other things. It ain't easy to love a Gemini. You get me, and I love you.

ABOUT THE AUTHOR

LISA EDMONDS was born and raised in Kansas, and studied English and forensic criminology at Wichita State University. After acquiring her Bachelor's and Master's degrees, she considered a career in law enforcement as a behavioral analyst before earning a Ph.D. in English from Texas A&M University. She is currently an associate professor of English at a college in Texas and teaches both writing and literature courses. When not in the classroom, she shares a quiet country home with her husband Bill D'Amico and their cats, and enjoys writing,

reading, traveling, spoiling her nephew, and singing karaoke.

Want an exclusive look at the playlists for the Alice Worth novels? Check out her website: www.lisaedmonds.com

And be sure to find Lisa Edmonds across social media.

facebook.com/Edmonds411
twitter.com/Edmonds411
instagram.com/edmonds411

ABOUT THE PUBLISHER

City Owl Press is a cutting edge indie publishing company, bringing the world of romance and speculative fiction to discerning readers.

www.cityowlpress.com

Manufactured by Amazon.ca
Bolton, ON

11425140R00229